Voices of the Dead

Battling the Yellow Fever Epidemic of 1878

A Novel

John Babb

δ
Dingbat Publishing
Humble, Texas

VOICES OF THE DEAD

ISBN 978-1-096831266

Published by Dingbat Publishing
Humble, Texas

Reviewer Comments

Brother Joel William McGraw, Catholic historian, author, and educator: As a native Memphian whose great-grandfather survived two epidemics of yellow fever in Memphis, I had immediate interest in Babb's *Voices of the Dead.* As a member of the DeLaSalle Christian Brothers, whose Memphis community survived those two epidemics in 1873 and 1878, I had even more interest in this story of Memphis. This work of historical fiction is an important chronicle and human face of those times which brought Memphis to its knees and altered its history forever. This important era is vividly captured in Memphis and other Southern cities affected by the yellow fever.

Reverend Milton Winter, Presbyterian minister, historian, and author: A remarkable job of transforming brittle historical documents into a faithful and interesting account of those fateful days—days marked by sadness and terror, but also by faithfulness and courage. Lest we think something of the sort could never happen again, Babb helps us think about how we might respond. May God grant us strength and hope when called to face trouble, sorrow, sickness, or adversity in our own lives!

Eugene McKenzie, M.D., longtime Memphis internal medicine physician: An excellent read. The statistics are appalling but accurate. The fictional characters make this a very human story—a human tragedy.

Retired Rear Admiral and Assistant Surgeon General Robert Williams, Diplomate of Environmental Engineering: Drawing quotes from newspaper archives blended with his own vivid descriptions, the author accurately portrays the unsanitary conditions and public health crisis of a troubled time in America. The reader can almost touch, smell, and feel the misery of the deplorable conditions endured by those along the Mississippi. From the beginning, you are immersed in the story, inspired by the courage of the public health heroes and heroines, and continually reminded that these events truly did happen.

Contents

Cover art by
Victoria Babb (www.vickibabb.com)

For Victoria:
Upon reflection, everything I do is because of Victoria.

Author's Note

All text in italics represents actual communications of the time period: *newspaper articles, letters, telegrams, diary entries, public documents, and speeches*. Many of the people in this story were heroic figures during the epidemic, and great effort has been taken to accurately portray them. A number of others are figments of the author's imagination, used to relate anecdotes discovered in my research.

Chapter 1
Where Did You Say You Were From?

Memphis, Tennessee

Why do some people not understand that the very act of doing nothing is sometimes every bit as important as actually taking an action? Thus, when Fannie Lester decided to ignore the two men in a rowboat on the night of August 1, 1878, who's to say how many thousands of lives might have been saved, fortunes retained, millions of dollars in commerce not lost, and orphans not created, if only she had acted to sound the alarm? Then again, the tragedy might well have happened no matter what Fannie did.

All of Memphis was on edge, what with yellow fever being reported in July, first in New Orleans, then in Vicksburg. The city had prohibited the docking of any steamboats traveling up the Mississippi River from the south, hoping and praying they could avoid the disease spreading to Memphis this year. They certainly had previous experience, as the city had endured recent epidemics of yellow-jack in 1867 and 1873.

Many old-timers were talking about how the wet weather of a mild spring, and the hellishly hot, humid summer they were enduring, were strong predictors of yet another fever year. For the last month, the newspapers had been full of stories about the latest outbreak of the fever in the Caribbean, as well as downriver, and every Memphis citizen was fully aware that the big island immediately below their city had already been designated as a quarantine stop for steamboats traveling upstream. Other quarantine stations were established fifteen miles east of the city on the Memphis and Charleston Rail Line at Germantown, as well as six miles to the south on the Mississippi and Tennessee Railroad at White Haven.

Some of the more sanctimonious citizens blamed the earlier epidemic of 1873 on God's wrath, due to the shameful local celebration of Mardi-Gras. But that pagan custom had been abolished in Memphis well before the summer of 1878, so those who were quick to blame idolatrous and evil living for bringing forth the bacterial and viral vengeance of the Almighty were at a loss to find someone or something to blame.

However, on this night, Fannie was preoccupied with her own troubles. She was worried she might be pregnant—let alone suspicious that her man-friend, Willis Abbott, had taken off back to Mississippi when she'd told him why she was upset. Apparently his devotion was short-lived when he discovered there might be dues to be paid.

Fannie had visualized Abbott as her knight in shining armor, come to rescue her from life as a chambermaid at the Peabody Hotel. He was armed with a believable story that he was in town to see a couple of cotton merchants in order to pre-sell his cotton, which he predicted to be "the biggest crop in Tunica County." In Fannie's mind, he not only had money to spend, but a future to offer.

When she thought about improving her poor prospects, it wasn't in terms of wearing beautiful dresses and living in a fine house. She just wanted to have enough money to stop walking everywhere she went. She coveted nothing so much as riding in a buggy wherever she needed to go. The daily trek from her rooming house on Chickasaw Street to the Peabody on Union Street, some fourteen blocks distant, involved wading through muddy and manure-filled streets, which often remained that way for a good week after a significant rain. Her shoes, battered and bedraggled as they always were, had been pulled off her feet by the mud on more than one occasion.

Worse, there was the aspect of dealing with all the vulgar comments and catcalls from the lowlife miscreants who seemed to inhabit half the street corners along those many blocks. An attractive female who had to walk during the early evening was apparently assumed to be a woman of the town, no matter how much she tried to carry herself like a lady. When the weather was extremely bad, she had spent her hard-earned cash a few times to ride the horse trolley, but that indulgent expense consumed a fourth of her daily income.

Now with Abbott's cowardly retreat, her dream of escaping her job and her poverty, let alone all the walking, was not going to happen. So she stood at the foot of Union Street, contemplating for at least the tenth time whether or not she should commit the most grievous of sins, thus making it impossible to even be buried in the Catholic cemetery. However, depression blinded her to the future, and she continued to gaze out at the roiling current of the Mississippi, considering if she should just simply wade out into the river and allow herself to be swept away.

Perhaps it was understandable that she did not raise the cry for a constable when the small boat appeared out of the fog and gloom. The only light was but a glow from the sparse street lamps up on the bluff. The black man rowing the boat was wearing bib overalls without a shirt. His arms and torso were covered with a sheen of beef tallow mixed with ground-up marigold petals, presumably in an effort to repel the clouds of mosquitoes hovering in the quiet water near the shoreline. The rippling muscles in the boatman's arms and shoulders were testimony that he was well practiced in maneuvering his small craft through the whirlpools and unexpected surges of current, which were everywhere in the powerful river; but the object of suspicion for even a casual observer was the young white man slumped in the front seat, his head held tightly in both hands.

When the boat ground to a halt on the rounded stones of the landing, the boatman hurried forward to assist his passenger as the man struggled to climb over the side and gain his footing. Despite the temperature being close to ninety degrees just after nine o'clock in the evening, the man gathered his jacket tightly around his hunched shoulders and slowly began to make his way up the riverbank to the town.

With his back turned to her, Fannie found herself staring at the black man's right shoulder blade. Although she couldn't be certain, it appeared that the raised scar on his back was actually in the form of letters. What in the world could have caused such an injury?

Oblivious to her attention, and assured that his two-legged cargo was headed to his destination, the man rowing the boat, John Johnson, quickly shoved his craft back into the river and hopped aboard. He shot Fannie something more than a curious glance, hoping she would stay silent long enough for him to disappear into the gloom of the river as he headed back downstream. The last thing he needed was for some skinny white woman to holler for a constable. He knew without a doubt he wouldn't fare well if a policeman answered her call. However, the prospect of earning three dollars simply to row a man four miles had been too tempting to worry about the law and their quarantine.

Fannie watched the boat's arrival and departure, but was so caught up in the drama of her own life that she probably couldn't have given anyone an accurate description of the man—except for the hellish scar—ten minutes after the rowboat had headed back to the south. Finally making her decision, she made her way across the cobblestones to the river, hitched her hem-frayed dress up to her calves, and stepped to the edge of the water. She paused briefly, considering whether or not to leave her hat on the riverbank. However, it possessed a considerable droop, having lost its shape as well as two of its three feathers, so she decided it was no particular loss for the hat to remain on her head.

She couldn't help but reflect on her pap, who was rumored to have fallen in the river somewhere along the Memphis riverbank, and how his loss had been so devastating to her, as it had occurred on the same day as her mam's burial. As a result, in Fannie's case, there was no one left now to mourn her passing.

For the first time that evening, she became conscious of the overwhelming putrid smell of the river, as it was the depository of well over a million privies all the way from Minnesota to where she stood, some thousand miles downstream. Additionally, Memphis' own vile sewer ditch discharged into the river only three hundred yards upstream of where she stood. Fannie was repulsed by the slimy foulness floating on the surface and changed her mind, suddenly and irrevocably deciding she had no desire to meet her Maker at the pearly gates while covered with a sheen of all that nastiness.

Perhaps it was her condition which made her squeamish, or maybe the realization of what she had almost done, but nevertheless her stomach heaved and she lost what little supper she had eaten. Finally raising her head, she turned her back on the river and began the long walk to her rooming house in the Pinch District. For the first time that evening, she was conscious of the irritating mosquitoes which were engulfing her ankles, and swished her dress at the pesky creatures as she retreated back to her life.

William Warren continued his shuffling journey up the embankment, finally reaching Front Street at the top of the river bluff. His headache at this point was almost unbearable, and despite the fierce August humidity, he was shaking with a chill. He had left his ship, which was tied up to the south on President's Island, just after sundown, after finally convincing the fisherman, John Johnson, to row him ashore for an exorbitant price so he might find a doctor.

Warren was quickly coming to the realization that he was not able to wander around seeking medical help much longer, so he began looking for a business that might still be open. Maybe they could direct him to a physician. Besides, his dizziness was only getting worse, and he had to find a place to sit down.

Thankfully, he spied a couple of gas lanterns which illuminated the ground floor of a building across the street, and weakly found his way to the door. The place appeared to be empty, save the proprietor. The woman who greeted him had a big smile on her face, which almost immediately disappeared as she assessed her new customer.

Kate Bionda was a full-figured Italian woman of some thirty-five years of age who, along with her husband, ran the fruit stand and snack-house. Mr. Bionda had manned the store all day long, but once Kate was able to get her daughters in bed, he went upstairs to the living quarters and Kate took his place downstairs in case they had any more customers. They were hard-working, but business had not been good at all since the city had imposed its quarantine.

Their specialty was fried fish, along with whatever other meats might be available. As was the case with most businesses along the waterfront, the slops and refuse from the shop were sometimes thrown out in the street, but most often down the side of the bluff toward the river. In daytime or night, the rats and dogs usually took full advantage of the opportunity.

The Biondas' business location made it very understandable that dockworkers, as well as crewmen from steamboats and flatboats, visited the eating establishment at all hours, so it wasn't surprising her customer showed up well after the supper hour. She immediately noticed the shellback turtle tattoo on his right forearm (which indicated he had sailed across the equator at some point in his nautical career); but her attention was drawn to his pasty gray skin color, his blood-filled eyes, and the lank hair which was plastered against his forehead with sweat. "When's the last time you had a decent meal, mister?"

His response was slow, and so weak she had to strain to understand him. "I cain't hardly keep nothin' on my stomach, miss. I didn't hardly feel like eatin' a-tall the last few days."

She reached over and tentatively placed the palm of her hand on his forehead. "You're hot as the devil's outhouse! Have you seen a doctor?"

"No, miss. I need one bad. Where might I find one?"

"Old Doc Henderson stays just a couple blocks away at the Gayoso House Hotel. I'd imagine he'd see you tonight."

Warren pushed himself to his feet, but the dizziness grabbed hold of him and he collapsed back into the chair.

"Looks like you're in no shape to go anywhere. Why don't I send my cook up the street to fetch the doctor? You just stay put."

Dr. Thomas Henderson appeared in about fifteen minutes. He was completely bald, bigger about the waist than he was in the shoulders, and visibly in his cups, having already consumed a bit more than one dose of whiskey that evening. After taking his patient's temperature, as well as some rudimentary poking and prodding, the doc looked suspiciously at his new patient. "Just where did you say you came from, young man?"

"I come off the *Golden Crown* from downriver."

The physician cut his eyes sideways. "Whereabouts downriver?"

"New Orleans."

"Damn, son!" The doc backed up halfway across the room. "We've got to get you in the hospital!"

Noting the alarm in his voice, Kate grabbed the physician's arm. "Just what are you takin' on about, Doc?"

He turned his back on Warren and looked her in the eye. "Did you have the yellow fever back during any of the recent outbreaks?"

"The fever?" Kate looked as though she was about to run out of her own café. "No, sir. I was sure enough lucky not to catch it."

"Then you best pray I'm wrong."

"What difference does it make if I had it or not?"

"Most of us believe if you had the yellow-jack before, you've got a resistance to catching it again."

Kate pointed at Warren and said in a hushed voice, "Oh, my Lord—my family is just upstairs. I suppose I've got my own self in trouble. He's been in here a good half hour, and I been waitin' on him hand an' foot. But what about my family?"

"I'll get him out of here and in the city hospital. Probably get him started on Simmons Liver Regulator, but it looks like it might be too late for him. You'll have to air your place out, then scrub everything down with some lime or carbolic acid as an antiseptic and fumigator."

She began to cry. "But my girls upstairs—and my husband, too. What should they do?"

"Hard to say. But they need to stay completely away from anywhere this fellow has been."

"Shouldn't I start takin' that Liver Regulation myself?"

"Wouldn't hurt. It cleanses the stomach and the bowels, and gets rid of all the dangerous humors."

"Where can I get some?"

"Now, honey, you get on up to Robinson's Drug Store on Second Street. And don't you be telling anyone what I think we've got here. Sure don't want to start a panic."

Chapter 2
A Spell of Death

New Orleans

August 1, 1878—"The New Orleans Board of Health publishes the following information: The onset of yellow fever is apt to be more sudden and violent than that of other fevers which prevail here, and is more likely to occur at night. Those who have not had the fever previously should avoid localities known to be infected, and should stay in their houses as much as possible in the evening. Preventive medicines are useless, and alcoholic potions are the worst preparations for countering the fever. Regular habits, tranquility of mind, and moderation in all things should be observed."

"Mayor Pillsbury is exploring the purchase of a barge load of ice now lying at St. Louis for from 17 to 20 dollars per ton, delivered, and the city would furnish it to our citizens upon arrival at 1½ cents per pound." New Orleans Times-Picayune

Starched white cap and collar in hand, Emilie Christophe was halted at the door by the disdaining voice of her grandmother, Vivienne. "If you're so determined to go be a nurse, why in the world can't you work at the Touro Infirmary? At least you'll be around a better class of patients. You certainly won't find anything except beggars and street people if you insist on going to the Hotel Dieu."

"That's just the point, Grandmère. The poor people at Hotel Dieu need all the help they can get. You and most of the city would just as soon pretend they don't exist—even in the middle of another fever outbreak."

Her grandmother was on the wrong side of sixty years and finally beginning to look her age. Her skin was still almost without flaw—some had compared her complexion to porcelain in days gone by. Her gray eyes, though still striking, unfortunately only saw things through the cataract of calculation and commerce. Her hair, which had once been luxuriously black and wavy, was now maintained in that style only through the secrets of an apothecary.

Her grandmother's voice was tremulous. "The city officials say they've got everything under control this year, and they don't look for an epidemic. They're going to use a new sanitation method—sprinkling carbolic acid on all the streets. Anyway, you should stay at home where you belong. You ought not to run off and leave a poor old woman like me alone when the fever is about."

Emilie snorted at that—'poor old woman,' indeed—her grandmother only referred to herself in that way when it suited her needs. "I'll be back at the end of the day."

"You'll be there half the night. Besides, I'm always plagued by thoughts of you when you're not here."

Emilie wanted so badly to retort that the old woman certainly didn't waste any time thinking about her when she was sitting in the same room. But she let that pass as well, simply replying, "It's the least I can do for Mama's memory."

"I've told you not to speak about her in my presence."

It was a terrible thing, having nobody who she could talk to about her mother. Emilie started to tear up, but shook her head, refusing to let the old woman get to her today, of all days. "They need me at the hospital. It's the yellow fever, Grandmère."

"Ah, it's always the *fièvre jaune* with you! How do you expect to meet a man worth anything at all if you insist on working with the Daughters of Charity?"

"I'm not worried about finding a husband, and I won't just stand by and do nothing while our people are dying."

Emilie noticed the purple vein in the old woman's forehead begin to swell and pulsate before she made her feelings crystal clear. "Our people? Don't you dare include me in that descriptor."

Emilie silently gritted her teeth, exasperated yet again by the prejudice exhibited by her Haitian Creole grandmother. She opened the door, departing with a less than submissive "Yes, Grandmère."

Emilie possessed a skin tone similar to the city's famous pecan pralines. Her black hair was long and curly, and her lips were full (full of promise, most young male observers would say). Her eyes were framed with a pair of highly-arched eyebrows which seemed to ask a never-answered question. Most described her eyes as gray, but her grandmother would say they turned green when she was being stubborn, and secretly wondered if this change in eye color indicated her granddaughter possessed the ability to cast a spell. On closer inspection, one might remark that Emilie seldom smiled, and had an almost constant look of melancholy on her face, although contrasted with a kind and generous heart.

There were four entities in New Orleans which could loosely be described as hospitals. As the second-oldest hospital in the entire country, *Charity Hospital* was now run by the Orleans Parish Medical Society. The *Touro Infirmary* was owned by a group of Jewish physicians and businessmen, but served people of all religions. The *Hotel Dieu*, sometimes referred to as the Hostel of God, was administered by the Daughters of Charity and accepted any and all, but realistically only took care of the poor and destitute. And finally, there was the *City Insane Asylum*, which was a stretch to call a hospital, as it really only served to house people rather than provide any semblance of medical care.

Emilie's daily commute from the Marigny neighborhood, just east of the French Quarter, to the Hotel Dieu, consisted of some fifteen blocks, and took her to her destination directly north of the Quarter. She could see the Hotel Dieu from quite a distance—an imposing three-story brick structure which took up an entire block—with black iron-railed balconies running from one end to the other on the second and third floors. It was surrounded by a ten-foot iron fence, with an imposing entry gate to admit staff and patients. Some wondered if the fence was to keep patients in or the public out.

It was an everyday occurrence for Emilie to pass by a drunkard or two, still passed out on the street near the hospital from excessive libations of the night before, or perhaps be approached by a beggar or a band of street urchins. She was a bit surprised that morning to still see men sleeping on the streets, particularly since warnings had been widely circulated that yellow fever was back in the city. She assumed everybody understood the fever seemed to be afoot after dark.

In her journey to the hospital, she couldn't help but notice a sign affixed to a nearby gas-light post. There were several similar postings in the area, and, along with the drunks and beggars, sadly seemed to present an affirmation of her grandmother's sour opinion of the Hotel Dieu's clientele.

BEWARE
PICKPOCKETS
AND
LOOSE WOMEN
New Orleans Police Dept.

Perhaps it was also telling that a hopeful candidate for Mayor of New Orleans had posted handbills all around the French Quarter, hawking his most important political position: "*More Wine—Less Crime!*"

It was widely known that yellow fever had occurred earlier in the summer in Havana, and that the steamer *Emily B. Sudder* had departed Havana, bound for New Orleans. The *Sudder's* arrival on May 23rd at the quarantine station had been awaited with some amount of dread by the people of New Orleans, and the ship had been quickly inspected by a physician. While he'd noted the ship's purser, John Clark, was ill, he'd decided it was nothing more than neuralgia and a hangover, and so the doctor had allowed the ship to pass through the quarantine and into the port.

Clark died on May 25th, his death officially recorded as malaria. The day the purser was buried, the ship's engineer became ill and died five days later. Complicating the identification of the actual beginning of the outbreak was that the *Sudder's* mate eventually snuck ashore around July 1st, and cases similar to yellow fever occurred as early as July 13th in the neighborhood where he lived.

At the same time, the *Charles B. Woods* arrived and was placed under quarantine. But within a few weeks, all of the family members of the ship's captain and engineer had contracted a suspicious fever. Then finally, yesterday morning, a telegram from Dr. Chopin of the New Orleans Board of Health, addressed to Dr. John Woodworth, Supervising Surgeon General of the Marine Hospital Service in Washington, D.C., had been published in the *New Orleans Times-Picayune*, wherein the Surgeon General was advised New Orleans indeed had confirmed cases of yellow fever.

All hell had broken loose. As a major port, the city had a long and painful experience with yellow-jack, with 37 separate outbreaks since 1800. Just in recent memory, cases had been reported during six summers since the end of the Civil War, and large epidemics resulted from two of those outbreaks. So the population had good reason to be fearful, particularly since several new cases had been identified in the twenty-four hours since the publication of the telegram to the Surgeon General.

Underlying the reluctance of New Orleans officials to acknowledge the presence of yellow fever was the fact that nearby towns and cities, as well as plantation river landings which engaged in commerce with the city, would set up a quarantine or blockade against her. The city could ill afford this kind of publicity.

July 24—"It is well known that New Orleans has suffered greatly every year on account of exaggerated and false reports circulated in other places related to its sanitary condition and dangerous diseases. Such reports are either untrue, or have barely a coloring of the truth. Sensationalized fabrications are thus spread abroad. The result is that strangers have been educated to believe everything bad about this city, even though our general health is as good as any city of the same population in the Northern Hemisphere." New Orleans Picayune

July 26—"The City Council is requesting the Parish Prison utilize convict labor for assistance in cleansing streets and gutters with Mississippi River water whenever required." New Orleans Picayune

July 27—"As a yellow fever preventive, we should not indulge too much in cold bathing, as that is apt to check perspiration and drive in the heat. The sponge bath is sufficient. We must try to avoid being out in the rain and allowing our clothing to get wet for the same reason. We should live regularly, take reasonable exercise, not go too much in the sun, and do nothing to overheat the blood." New Orleans Picayune

Author's note: It should be acknowledged that the state of medical knowledge of practically all diseases in 1878 is hard for us to believe in light of modern medical advances. Physicians had no understanding of the cause of yellow fever, how it was transmitted, how to treat it, nor how to prevent it. They often disagreed on what should be diagnosed as a case of yellow fever, and what might instead be one of several other "malarial fevers."

Today we know that yellow fever is an acute viral hemorrhagic infection which is transmitted by the bite of the female *Aedes aegypti* mosquito. In order to be infectious, that mosquito would have previously bitten a person infected with yellow fever, then transmitted the virus through its bite to one or more other people. There is now a yellow fever vaccine, but still no "cure" exists, other than to aggressively treat the patient's symptoms. Prevention steps in areas where yellow fever is still prevalent include vaccination, attacking areas which harbor mosquitoes, wearing long sleeves and pants, using mosquito repellent, staying indoors during early morning and evening hours, and using bed nets while sleeping.

In 1878, the newspaper was full of supposed cures—all of which were quackery. Physicians usually began treatment of diseases of unknown origin by either cleaning out the intestinal tract or by bleeding the victim. Neither approach was beneficial, and often made the patient worse.

Emilie's commitment to help "her people" was no idle gesture. Depending on the year, yellow fever could be extremely deadly to patients and anyone who came into close contact with them. It was widely acknowledged that someone with a previous infection might well have developed immunity against the disease—but at that time, such immunity was not a proven scientific fact. Indeed, there were a few reports of people who were supposedly immune yet had become reinfected. There was also evidence that blacks had apparently inherited at least a degree of immunity from their African ancestors which reached across many generations, as their rate of infection, as well as the percentage of those dying, was much lower than that experienced by white people. Unfortunately, there had also been exceptions to that particular belief in past outbreaks of yellow fever.

Although Emilie had been infected with the fever some five years previously, there was no guarantee (per the state of science for the period) that walking into the Hotel Dieu would not have dire consequences for her. However, the passion she felt against the disease which had taken her mother exerted a powerful pull.

That fateful day in 1873, which had so much influence on her ensuing life...

She had been struggling herself with a case of yellow fever for almost a week, and finally felt as though the worst had passed. Emilie vaguely remembered being brought to her grandmother's house when she'd begun to get sick, and had spent the next few days in a small, airless room, tended only sporadically by the old woman. Yet soon after arriving, she'd heard the unmistakable sounds of sickness in the adjacent room, and so the fourteen-year-old girl wrapped a blanket around herself and, on wobbly legs, sought out her mother, Eugenie.

The curtains were drawn to keep out as much light as possible, and the room was hot, with the unmistakable stench of an advanced case of the fever. Emilie hesitated in the darkness before finally confirming it was her mother lying in the bed, the dreaded black vomit on the bedding and floor. On the other side of the room, in deep shadow, sat her grandmother, eyes focused on the ruins of her only daughter in the soiled bed. Eugenie lay there, fever raging, the yellow sign of jaundice in her eyes, undoubtedly beyond the possibility of sustaining her life.

A once beautiful, very light-skinned Creole, Eugenie rallied briefly after seeing her daughter leaning against the wall. Her eyes flicked back to her own mother before speaking with a whispering yet surprising clarity. "Give Emilie the locket. We both know it's mine, but now should be hers."

"I fear the child is not yet ready for that responsibility. In fact, neither of you understand how overwhelming a burden the locket can be. The constant demands are almost more than a person can tolerate." With the memory freshened, the old woman gave an involuntary shiver.

Eugenie tried to raise her head from the pillow, but failed. Her voice grew weaker still. "Maman—do the right thing for once." And as suddenly as Eugenie rallied, she almost immediately failed. Emilie cried out as she watched her mother's soul—a subdued, sad flow of fluorescence—depart what was left of her body.

No sooner had this final separation of body and spirit occurred than Vivienne spoke with coldness. "*Elle mourra depuis des années.*" (She has been dying for years.) "Dying since the day she ran off with your dark-skinned father. Now I am left with you—a child of that man who is of no worth to you or me." The old woman slowly rose from her vigil and left the young girl alone with Eugenie's corpse.

Emilie soon recovered from her own sickness, but was economically unable to return to the noisy, third-floor room above the Eagle Saloon on Rampart Street, where she and her mother had lived. Her new home with her grandmother was in a once substantial residence in the Faubourg Marigny neighborhood of New Orleans. But now the house was merely tired and sad. Like quite a few other homes in the area, it had been gifted to her grandmother as a reward for a *plaçage*, or "left-handed marriage" between the Haitian Creole and a wealthy, white Baton Rouge sugar cane planter.

As the offspring of the planter, Emilie's mother, Eugenie, had led a sheltered early life. She had received an education at the St. Louis Convent School from the Sisters of Charity with other girls of her kind, learning writing, literature, music, French, English, and Latin—all the while under the tight control of Vivienne. Eventually, Vivienne's wealthy planter had married a Mississippi debutante fifteen years his junior, and settled into a life more socially acceptable in the years immediately preceding the Civil War, as many no longer considered it appropriate for white Southerners to carry on relationships with women possessing even a trace of Negro blood.

So the privilege payments were discontinued, Vivienne was left behind, and she was forced to support her lifestyle by engaging in the timeless Creole skills of fortune-telling, séances, and even the black arts. Despite her diminished social status, Emilie's grandmother was happy to tell anyone who would listen that her ancestry went back to the first emperor of Haiti, Henri Christophe, her grandfather, and she spent a great deal of time trying to convince Emilie that they rightfully should be considered royalty, even referring to herself as "la Princesse Vivienne" in her business dealings

Meanwhile, her daughter Eugenie had ignored all entreaties to join in her business proceedings, preferring instead to support herself as a seamstress. Emilie had been born in November of 1859 as a result of the tumultuous relationship between Eugenie and a black man from Cuba—a gambler and card shark—who was shot and killed in the days immediately before Admiral David Farragut and the Yankee Navy captured New Orleans in April 1862. Emilie had no memory whatsoever of her father, and Eugenie only spoke of him when Vivienne was not around. Oddly, Emilie never heard her mother express any hint of real affection for the man, and she began to wonder if her mother had partially been motivated by the urge to prove to Vivienne that she did not share her prejudices when it came to skin color.

Eugenie was determined to pass on her skills to Emilie, and so she began to self-tutor the girl in the conventional studies of an educated young woman. However, she was also convinced these talents would not be enough to allow her darker-skinned daughter to succeed in the new, less genteel world of Reconstruction in which they found themselves. For at least two hours per day, the little girl was also taught the traditional skills of a seamstress.

After Eugenie's death during the epidemic of 1873, Emilie often spied on her grandmother when she had a customer. The two of them always retreated to a small room, which had probably once been the sleeping quarters for a maid or a cook. There was a tea table in the center of the room, with three chairs. The third chair was undoubtedly to accommodate the presence of any spirit to be summoned during a séance. The space was lit only by a small pewter candelabra.

Her grandmother always donned a specific outfit when she entered this room with a customer, all the while liberally sprinkling her conversation with French phrases. She wore a brilliant emerald-colored silk headdress, a sweeping black gown, and likewise never had business dealings without the gold locket around her neck, which she apparently believed came with special powers. Sometimes Vivienne used an odd set of playing cards, and other times she relied on a handful of chicken bones, which she claimed to "read" when she told fortunes or communicated with the dead.

Perhaps the occasion that Emilie would never forget was when her grandmother had an entirely different kind of discussion with a white woman who, given the quality of her clothing, was quite well-to-do. The lady wore a veil which thoroughly obscured her face, and never removed it during her entire time in the household. When the two women entered the special room, Emilie crept close enough to the door that she could hear every word.

"I have two serious problems, Princesse Vivienne, and I hope you can help me with them."

Vivienne smiled, pleased that she had been addressed appropriately. "Of course, madame."

"My husband has secreted quite a bit of money somewhere in our house, and try as I might, I've been unable to find it."

"Hmm ... that is a difficult question, madame. Can you tell me your husband's name?"

"Certainly, Princesse. But only if you can also help me with my second problem."

"And what might that be, madame?"

"Are you able to," she paused a moment to compose herself, "cast a spell? And by that, I don't mean some temporary pain or discomfort. I am referring to a permanent, perhaps catastrophic spell."

Vivienne sat back in her chair, appraising the woman. "May I assume you mean *sort de la mort*, madame?"

"Ah, yes. A spell of death. Exactly so. Is this something you can do?"

"Then I must have his name, madame. And the spell must be administered at a time when you have a perfect alibi."

"Agreed. His name is Chester Dupree, Princesse."

Vivienne tried not to react to this information, as Chester Dupree was none other than a successful lawyer and very prominent politician of the nearby Plaquemines Parish. "Madame, for such a man, that would be very expensive."

"That won't be a problem if you are able to help me with problem number one."

At that moment in the conversation, Emilie inadvertently bumped the door, and she quickly fled down the adjacent hallway lest she be discovered. Unfortunately, the remainder of the conversation she did not hear. However, she did observe her grandmother escorting Mrs. Dupree to the front door a bit later, and Vivienne was wearing a seldom seen brilliant smile. From that point forward, Emilie resolved not to listen to anything her grandmother said related to joining in her business dealings.

She was, however, very curious regarding the gold locket. Over a period of weeks, she thought about it every night, until finally Emilie resolved to uncover whatever secret it held. She knew her grandmother kept it in her chiffoniere, only wearing it while she had a customer.

One afternoon while the old woman was visiting a friend, Emilie snuck into her bedroom, opened the large piece of furniture which served as a closet, and found the locket hanging from a wooden peg. Its appearance did not give any indication of a particular power, and she placed it around her neck without much hesitation.

Suddenly a voice spoke to her, and Emilie jumped, thinking her grandmother had returned. However, the voice was not speaking harshly; rather, its words were directed specifically to her. She looked around the room, seeking the source of the voice. What in the world was going on? She found herself shaking.

When the voice spoke again, Emilie suddenly realized its source. Amazingly, she identified it as coming from her own mother, dead now these several years. "Emilie—you have a destiny. Do not let my mother prevent you from pursuing your dream."

"Mother—how is this happening?"

"It's the power of the locket. Remember always, I'm watching over you. I love you."

"Please—don't go. I need you."

"You must make your own decisions, Emilie. You know what is right for you. Don't use the locket to tell fortunes and relieve people of their money. Use it only to do good."

And then the voice was gone. Trembling, Emilie removed the locket and quickly returned it to its peg. What a wonderful privilege—to be able to talk with her mother! For the remainder of the day, and even in the ensuing weeks, she was overwhelmed with a single thought. What stirred in her breast was the feeling that she should do whatever was possible to do battle with the disease which had killed her own mother.

And so, by the age of sixteen, Emilie was spending hours each day at the Hotel Dieu, volunteering to assist in any way she could, all the while observing and learning the skills and duties of a nurse. Before long, the nuns began to entrust her with increasingly greater responsibilities.

Two of the sisters took her under their wings, making it their business to ensure that the bright young girl had a good understanding of not only biology, anatomy, and medicines, but also the nurse's responsibility for patients with a variety of issues. Under their tutelage, Emilie was exposed to people dealing with post-surgery, chronic diseases, tuberculosis, advanced syphilis, smallpox, malarial fevers, cholera, child-birth, mental afflictions of all descriptions, and even two cases of leprosy, with many of her patients at the doorstep of death.

Emilie thrived in this environment, and eventually was granted nurse status at the hospital. When she told her grandmother about her achievement, Vivienne had an unexpected gleam in her eye. "Don't you see, Emilie, all of this has prepared you to be a *traiteuse*."

"Isn't a *traiteuse* a Creole healer?"

Her grandmother was not to be sidetracked. "We'll need a healer's garden, of course."

"But Grandmère..."

Emilie was ignored as the old woman continued. "We'll have lizard's tail, jackberry, jimson weed, and coral bean—and hibiscus root for whooping cough, sassafras tea for measles, poultice of cocklebur leaves with salt for snake bite, and—" Vivienne paused. "But I'm sure you know all that. You can be a regular *médecine de feuille*."

"A leaf doctor?"

"Yes, of course. You will prepare medicines and potions of herbs and oils. Between the two of us, people will come from all over the city—perhaps all over Louisiana—to see us. Why, those fakers, Marie Laveau and her daughter, will be squashed under our feet. The very idea of the woman calling herself a voodoo priestess!"

Emilie could plainly see where the old lady was headed. "Isn't it true that a *traiteuse* does not accept payment when she treats someone?"

"Why, yes. But accepting a gift instead of money for your services is the general rule." Vivienne's eyebrows arched in anticipation of her impending good fortune. "And sometimes those gifts can be very grand indeed."

"Grandmère, you know how important it is to me to be able to help people who have yellow fever."

"Yes, of course. That's why you would give them elderberry tea—for their fever."

Emilie slowly shook her head. "Grandmère, I want to work in a hospital—with doctors. I don't want to hand out magic potions while you tell fortunes."

For once, Vivienne held her tongue at the slight, as she was determined to sway Emilie to her wishes. But try as she might, the old woman was unable to elicit a positive response from her granddaughter, and despite all her appeals to good sense, the stubborn girl would not be convinced. Vivienne could only conclude Emilie's impeccable Creole ancestry had been so diluted and be-fouled by her very black father that she did not inherit any of her family's business attributes.

As she entered the grounds of the Hotel Dieu early that humid July morning in 1878, Emilie took little notice of the twenty-foot-tall crepe myrtles, which were blooming in all their glory in various shades of pink, red, and white. Likewise, she failed to see the huge clay pots filled with bougainvillea on the second-story balconies just over her head, nor the beds of caladiums, hibiscus, and elephant ears which bordered the walkway from the gate to the entry. All her energy was focused on steeling herself for what she would find within.

People were standing in line, some lying on the floor, waiting to see one of the two physicians on staff. The smell of vomit, diarrhea, and the unwashed was overwhelming in the stuffy heat of the hallway. Even the normally nonchalant tuberculosis patients, carrying their sloshing spittoons wherever they went, had retreated to their own quarantine area.

Emilie was almost relieved to quickly be assigned to the yellow fever ward. But any feeling of appreciation was short-lived. The ward itself was a five-fold magnification of the visual and olfactory assault of the hallway.

Sister Catherine met her just inside the doorway with a cotton mask to cover her nose and mouth, then directed her to the female side of the ward. Sister indicated five patients for which she would be responsible, and gave her a bit of information about the current status of each of them, as well as what phase of treatment they were in. In less than ten minutes, Emilie was alone with her patients.

Three of them were new admittances, and were all dealing with a high fever, headache, and severe body aches. They all had been given laxatives to thoroughly evacuate their stomach and intestinal tract, which kept Emilie very busy trying to relieve their fever with towels soaked in cool water, as well as making sure they had a bedpan close at hand.

Her other two patients, Mrs. Lucienne St. Pierre and her daughter Grace, had made it through the fever phase for the most part. Currently, Emilie's primary activity for them was to give cool water or ice chips, and try to get them to take liquid nourishment like beef or chicken tea. If they were lucky, they might convalesce from this point forward, and simply be put on bed rest for another week or so. If unlucky, as at least a fourth of patients were, they might decline into a phase where their high fever reoccurred, followed by the failure of their kidneys and their liver—causing their skin and eyes to yellow and their urine to cease flowing. The next step was a hemorrhaging in the gut, followed by the almost unmistakable mark of impending death—the black vomit. Their next stop was almost invariably either the Girod Cemetery for the Protestants and non-believers, or St. Louis for the Catholics.

Unfortunately, neither St. Pierre was lucky. Just overnight, both had experienced a return of their fever, and this time it was unresponsive to sponging with an ice water and whiskey mixture, nor were they conscious enough to take liquid nourishment. Emilie began to despair of the survival of both mother and daughter.

At this point, they had an unexpected visitor. Jules St. Pierre, Lucienne's seventeen-year-old son, had received a letter from his mother in Mobile, where he had been working with his father. Her communication had been brief and to the point, telling him that she and Grace were ill with the fever and would have to enter the Hotel Dieu. Against his father's strong objection, Jules had traveled to New Orleans to see his mother and sibling.

When he realized just how tenuous their situation was, he of course was upset. But what caused the greatest distress was the last sentence in his mother's letter. 'I've sent

Emma (the St. Pierres' six-year-old daughter) to Texas with some friends in order to get her away from the city.'

Jules stared at his unresponsive mother and sister before turning to Emilie. "To Texas with some friends—did my mother say who these friends were?"

"She and your sister have been very sick since they've been here, and she never mentioned a word about even having another daughter."

He reached down and smoothed his mother's hair on her brow. "What are their chances of surviving this?"

"It's too early to tell. Perhaps, if we can get their fever down, they'll be able to answer your question."

"But if they can't, how can I ever find my sister Emma? I don't even know where they went in Texas!"

"It's not a good idea for you to be here in the hospital if you've never had the yellow fever." Emilie looked at him for assurance and he shook his head. "Then give me an address where you can be reached, and when one of them wakes up, I'll see if I can get the information you need."

In two days' time, Emilie sent a messenger to the hotel where Jules was staying, with an urgent request that he come at once to the hospital. He arrived within the hour, but not soon enough to tell his family goodbye. Neither Lucienne nor Grace had been lucid since his previous visit. Emilie asked one more question. "In case your sister returns to New Orleans, how can you be contacted in Mobile?"

The young man was just barely holding his emotions in check when he answered. "The Battle House Hotel, Royal Street, in Mobile." Then, with tears running down his face, he watched as his mother and sister were each placed in their coffins. He turned to Emilie. "I just realized I may never see my little sister again. It looks like the only way I can find her is to figure out a way to talk to the dead."

Within days of Emilie beginning work at the Hotel Dieu, some 40,000 people had fled New Orleans—a fifth of the population—in a panicked effort to escape the fever. The streets of the city were almost unoccupied. Even the drunks and beggars were out of sight. A weak attempt at humor in *The Picayune* pointed out that "*only our mosquitoes keep up the hum of industry.*"

In a reflection of the medical profession's lack of knowledge related to the disease, Dr. Holt, of the Louisiana Board of Health, observed, "*Yellow fever is a mystery in nature—one of the hidden ways of God.*"

Chapter 3
Jesus, Mary, and Joseph

Memphis, Tennessee

August 4, 1878—"New Orleans reports their total cases of yellow fever to date as 233, with 60 deaths. The fever has prevailed there for at least three weeks, but it cannot be said that a disease is in the least sense epidemic that numbers only twenty deaths per week out of a population of 192,000. When deaths are twenty per day, then there may be some grounds for the fear that currently prevails in every city and town from the Gulf Coast to the Ohio River."

"In spite of the safeguards with which the Board of Health has surrounded Memphis, a person by the name of William Warren, from New Orleans, found his way here, arriving in our city Thursday night, and becoming sick, and being poor, he was sent to the City Hospital, where his disease developed into a clear case of yellow fever. The Health Board was at once notified by his physician, and the man was removed to the Quarantine Hospital, where he expired last evening. This need not be a cause of alarm for our citizens. It was a clear case of development of disease contracted in New Orleans. We deem it our duty, however, to publish the facts, in order to keep the public fully informed. The Health Officer is vigilant, and people may rely upon him that everything is being done for their safety that mind can suggest." Memphis Daily Appeal

After reading the Sunday paper, Kate Bionda was terrified of what the immediate future might bring. Although exhibiting no symptoms yet, she knew enough about yellow

fever to realize that most people who were exposed to the disease became sick themselves from three to six days later. She didn't know whether to have faith in the liver medicine or not, but today was day number three for her. She still had not told her husband about her sick customer of three nights past. No point in getting into a fight if it wasn't necessary. But there was no way around it. She had to go to Mass.

She walked with purpose up Main Street to Adams and turned to the east. Although still two blocks distant, the tower of St. Peter's was easily visible, reaching high above the rooftops of the substantial homes along the street. The church had been built by the Dominican Friars in 1855, and the stones were beginning to show their age a bit, but it was still one of the most imposing buildings in the city.

Kate stepped into the narthex of the church just prior to the service, worked up her courage, and entered the nave. She remembered to take a bit of holy water from the font, crossed herself, and walked over to the back corner of the church. She placed a penny in the cup, lit her votive candle, and knelt on the kneeler. She couldn't remember saying a more sincere prayer in her life. She then stood, genuflected, and slid onto one of the bench seats. Of the hundred or so parishioners, she estimated less than a handful of the attendees were Italian.

Most of her nationality attended the new Catholic church of St. Joseph's, with Father Luiselli, as it was located closer to south Memphis, where the majority of poor Italians lived. But her family lived In St. Peter's parish, and even though they didn't fit in at all with the wealthier attendees, on the rare occasions when she went to Mass, she resolutely kept to her own parish.

Once upon a time, she had learned enough Latin to get by in school, but that was long ago, and she understood almost nothing the priest had to say. Besides, the entire congregation seemed to be preoccupied with fanning themselves in an attempt to alleviate the heat, as well as repel the gnats and mosquitoes. When the church members were invited forward to take communion, she kept her seat, acknowledging that as long as she had been absent from services, she would have to go to confession before she was welcome to participate in the most important of sacraments.

When the service was finally over, the priest and his assistants walked up the middle aisle of the church to the rear, where he stood to greet his flock. Kate hung back, waiting on the crowd to thin a bit, as she didn't want to be overheard. Finally only a small handful of people remained, but they seemed determined to stand around and gossip a bit before going outside to meet the full force of the August humidity and sunshine.

When Kate finally approached Father Kelly, she leaned toward him as close as she dared and whispered, "Father, will you hear my confession today?"

He was a bit shorter than she was, and on his way to a completely white head of hair. He didn't recognize her, but then he encountered new people all the time. He assumed that was why she was unfamiliar with his schedule. "I hear confessions on Tuesday, Thursday, and Saturday, my dear."

Kate twisted her handkerchief nervously. "Father, I don't know that this is what you would call an emergency, but I might not last that long."

He looked at her skeptically. "You look to be in fine fettle to me. What seems to be the problem?"

Kate looked behind her to be sure no one was within hearing. "I've been exposed to the yellow fever, Father."

Although it was said in a whisper, Kate unmistakably heard a woman fifteen feet away exclaim, "Jesus, Mary, and Joseph!" before she clamped her hand over her mouth, grabbed her husband, and scurried outside.

Kate took a deep breath and continued. "I have no symptoms yet, Father. Maybe I'll be all right. But I wanted to clear things—you know—with my soul and all, just in case."

He nodded his head. "You just sit here for a few minutes." He glanced at the small group remaining in the church. "I shouldn't be long."

August 6, 1878—From Brookhaven, Mississippi—"Strict quarantine here against persons and woolen goods from infected cities as of today."

From Ouachita Parish—"Our Parish has set up a quarantine here against New Orleans consisting of 35 militiamen armed with Remington rifles."

"Deaths in New Orleans in last twenty-four hours: 12. Total deaths to date: 83."

(Ad) "As a preventive of yellow fever, as well as a curative in all periods of the attack, use INDIAN CORDIAL, as a purely vegetable Mexican compound which has been used successfully in Puerto Rico, Havana, and Vera Cruz. PL Casachs, Druggist" New Orleans Picayune

On Monday morning, Fannie Lester peered through the filthy window overlooking the open, swampy sewage ditch known by most as Happy Hollow, but by the city's administration as the Gayoso Bayou. In the absence of a recent rain, the water in the bayou ceased to flow toward the Mississippi River, and simply sat stagnant, with nary a trickle of movement.

The foul ditch passed through the Pinch on the north side of her one-bedroom flat. On the other side of her block was the large building belonging to the Memphis Gas Light Company. She could never be sure if the green flies, the mosquitoes, or the rats were winning the battle of nastiness. Dead animals of various types were decaying in the deeper pools of the ditch, and served to further nauseate the senses. Not only was the bayou one of the main sources of the horrible stench which permeated much of the city of Memphis, but many of her people suspected it was primarily responsible for the high prevalence of diseases in the Irish section of town.

Fannie was also convinced the ditch deserved at least half the blame for the way she felt that morning. She knew that some of the Irish who lived near the ditch complained bitterly of the bayou's filthy water seeping into their cellars after a rain. Thank goodness she lived on the second floor of her rooming house. Of course, diarrhea was a fairly regular companion for almost everyone living in the immediate area of the sewer, but today her head hurt so badly it was difficult to look out upon the bright August sunshine without shielding her eyes and simultaneously holding her forehead in a death grip. A fever had hold of her—that was for sure—as a rigor had already struck her hard enough to make her shake for a good five minutes.

There was no way she could fathom going to work at the Peabody Hotel. She was too dizzy to even stand up. Under normal circumstances, Fannie would have looked for a doctor who might not expect her to pay very much, but she was so ashamed of her possible pregnancy that she didn't want anybody—particularly that young Dr. Josefson—to discover her female situation. She lay back on her pallet, cursing Willis Abbott for what he had done to her.

She was awakened while it was still dark with terrible cramping, and when she found the chamber pot, she realized something different was happening to her. When Fannie finally was able to light the coal oil lamp, she was aghast at all the blood. Although she had heard of miscarriages, she had no experience with such a thing. The only remedy she could think of was to use cotton and muslin wadding to try and staunch the bleeding.

Could it be she had lost the baby? She alternated between feelings of sorrow and loss, and those of relief and thanks. If that was true, at least she wouldn't lose her job, let alone be ostracized by her church, not to mention her family—that is, if her father was even still alive. But then, the baby—if there had been one—was the only thing she had which connected her to Willis Abbott. Damn him! She was dizzy again and lay back down, trying to put it out of her mind for a couple of hours and get some sleep.

Sometime after dawn the next morning, she gradually became aware of persistent knocking at her door. Although Fannie still felt terrible, she raised herself from her pallet and realized the dizziness and headache were much reduced from the day before. She examined her shift to be sure no blood was visible and then went to the door.

She was surprised to see one of her fellow chambermaids, the colored girl Leah Feathers. Come to think of it, she had never seen a Negro at all in her rooming house. The occupants all appeared to be either poor Irish or Jewish, but that wasn't stopping Leah. "Fannie—girl, you gonna lose yo job if you don't get yo'self to work today." Leah paused long enough to take a good look at her friend. "You lookin' awful! How long since you had somethin' to eat?"

Fannie ran her fingers through her hair in an attempt to improve her appearance. "I guess it was Saturday afternoon. I been too sick to put a meal together."

Leah rummaged around in her apron and produced a biscuit wrapped in a hanky. "Here—you need this worse'n I do."

Fannie thanked her and began to nibble, despite her protesting stomach. Leah looked around the Spartan one-room flat. "I thought you white folks was all s'posed to be in high cotton. I swear you ain't got no more than me and Mama." She hugged her friend to take any sting out of her words. "Looks like me and you got more in common than just that job."

"Leah, can I ask you a favor?"

"What's that, girl?"

"I still feel pretty peaked. Would you walk with me to Doctor Josefson's office over at the corner of Adams and Fourth?"

"Sure, girl. That be sorta on my way back to the hotel anyways."

Leah was thin as a rail, but looks were deceptive. There was no job too tough for her, and the drudgery of their work didn't seem to affect her in the least. In fact, she was just plain impervious to whatever came her way. Jobs for young black women were too precious a commodity for her to ever take employment for granted. And her mother's health was so precarious that both of them were totally dependent on Leah's earning ability. She and Fannie had become fast friends almost immediately when they each found themselves employed at the Peabody. But Fannie had not told even Leah about her suspected pregnancy.

Saul Josefson had graduated from Georgetown Medical School in 1875, and immediately moved to Memphis to be close to his parents. His father, Samuel, had come to Tennessee soon after the war to establish a garment factory, taking full advantage of the city as a transportation hub, not to mention the availability of cheap labor, as well as all the cotton one could ever need in the clothing business. After all, sixty percent of the nation's cotton was grown within two hundred miles of Memphis.

Dr. Josefson set up his medical practice in his parents' large home on Adams Street, and quickly became known to the poorer population of the city as a man who understood their economic difficulties. It was for this reason, as well as the acknowledged fact that he was young, handsome, and unmarried, that some mornings his patients—mostly female—had to stand out on the lawn for lack of a place to sit in either of his two waiting rooms. Of course, two waiting rooms—one for whites, the other for blacks.

Thankfully, Fannie was able to find a seat, but despite the tall open windows, the August humidity had most patients glistening with sweat within minutes. The doctor provided access to drinking water via a very large stoneware jug, with a tin cup hanging beside it on a peg. A towel hung nearby so each person could wipe the cup clean before and after drinking from it.

It was close to noon before Fannie's name was called and she stepped into the doctor's office. Although she was obviously not feeling well, Josefson was acutely aware that her beauty could not be hidden. Her hair was jet black, yet her eyes were blue as a robin's egg, her skin flawless, and her figure thin but voluptuous. He almost forgot she was his patient, let alone that she was Irish.

She described her fever, headache, sore muscles, and dizziness, but did not mention her female problem, as she had finally decided that surely that particular issue either had not existed at all or was now resolved. Josefson asked her if she had been around anybody with yellow fever, and she replied, "I don't think so. But I work in the Peabody, and I have to clean up the most disgusting messes you ever saw. I never know if somebody's truly been sick, or if they were just dead drunk."

"Have you had the yellow fever before, Fannie?"

"Yes, sir. I had it five years ago when I was just a girl. My mama nursed me through it."

"That's actually a good thing. It's unlikely you'll catch it, but even if you do, you should have a much easier time of it." He pressed on her abdomen, and she couldn't help but flinch. "Does that hurt?"

"No," she lied, thinking the pain was related to the bleeding she'd experienced that morning, "you just took me by surprise."

He pressed again, asking if her liver was tender, then on her lower back, inquiring if she had problems with urination, or if her urine was dark-colored. "If any of those things happen, you send for me right away and I'll come see you. In the meantime, I want you to take this magnesia every night for two days, drink six or eight glasses of water a day, and stay in bed for a few days."

She bowed her head. “I’m afraid I’ll lose my job at the Peabody.”

“I’ll write a note to the hotel for you. Surely they don’t want to lose you.”

New Orleans

Shortly after noon, Nurse Emilie Christophe was keeping watch over four patients in the yellow fever ward at the Hotel Dieu when she was called into the hallway by one of the sisters. “We’ve just received an emergency patient who’s probably going to require surgery. Can you break away from your patients long enough to assist Doctor Brouchard?”

“Of course, Sister.” Emilie stepped back into the ward long enough to quickly determine that her patients were stable enough to be left alone for awhile, then met Brouchard and his patient in what passed for an operatory. Brouchard had been a recent volunteer at the hospital due to his immunity to yellow fever, but there was some debate among the nurses as to just how much benefit his presence lent to their work.

He could only be described as elderly, thin, severely stooped, and what hair he had left was white and sprinkled sparsely over his cranium. In fact, he had as much hair coming out of his ears as he did the top of his head. His voice, though understandable, was rather quavery. Emilie had not worked with him directly, but had heard enough remarks to make her question his abilities, particularly if he was required to deal with a difficult emergency.

Their patient was Isaac Turner, a black man of some fifty years of age. Mr. Turner drove an ice wagon, and had encountered three young boys at the head of Julia Street who had decided to steal a block of ice from the back of his wagon. Mr. Turner shooed them away, and had returned his attention to his horse when one of the young incorrigibles threw a rock at him, striking him on the side of his head.

Mr. Turner was knocked from the seat of his wagon and fell forward onto the rear of his horse. The animal spooked and jumped forward, pulling the front wheel of the wagon over Turner’s shoulder. He had some cuts and bruises on his head, plus his clavicle appeared to be fractured in two places, with one of the breaks being compound in nature.

Patrolman Hogan had briefly but unsuccessfully chased the boys, then returned to the accident and drove Mr. Turner and his wagon to the hospital. It was doubtful the patrolman had ever seen a compound fracture before, and the more he stared at the wound, the sicklier the shade of gray he turned. Emilie got him out of the room and seated on a bench outside, placing his head between his knees for a couple of minutes.

When she returned to the operatory, Dr. Brouchard was rummaging in a cabinet. “What can I help you find, Doctor?”

“Either chloroform or ether, some bandages, and maybe a short splint.”

Emilie found what was requested, then began cleaning the injured area as carefully as she could, as the patient was in a significant amount of pain. She turned to Brouchard. “I can get this cleaned up better once he’s anesthetized.”

“This shouldn’t take long. Let’s use the ether on this poor fellow.”

Emilie would tell her fellow nurses later that Dr. Brouchard, whatever his physical failings, was an excellent surgeon, having set both breaks in no more than fifteen minutes, without visible defects afterward. Dr. Brouchard would only comment he had unfortunately accumulated far too much surgical experience while being attached to Lieutenant General Leonidas Polk’s army during the war. After he awakened, Mr. Turner could only say thank you, and Officer Hogan was kind enough to deliver him and his wagon to his home. He would not be lifting any more ice for a month.

When Emilie returned to the ward, she was surprised to find an old black gentleman sitting at the bedside of Mamie Monroe. He sat in an erect manner, not slumped in any way whatsoever. His hair was almost white, but his face showed almost no sign of aging. He wore a coal black coat, and Emilie realized his skin color was a perfect match for his coat. There was no way he possessed a drop of white blood in his lineage. “Afternoon, Nurse. This here is my wife. I’d be Musa Monroe.”

“Mr. Monroe, we don’t allow family members in this part of the hospital.”

"Oh, I know she's got the fever. But wherever she goes, I go. Been that way for thirty-four years."

"Have you had the yellow fever?"

"Would it make any difference if I said yes or no?"

"If you've already had the fever, you're not likely to have it again."

"All right. Then the answer is yes."

Emilie looked at him, shaking her head. "What do you intend to do if your wife gets well, and then you get sick?"

"I ain't leavin' her. Besides, she 'pears to be awful sick."

"She's not doing well." Emilie handed him a cotton mask. "At least wear this." She helped him tie the mask behind his head, then began sponging his wife with ice water. She finally concluded that he was serious about remaining with his wife. "So how did you get a name like Musa?"

"My papa give it to me. He say Mansa Musa was the greatest king that ever was over in Africa—and he claimed we was his kin. So he give me his name. As fer the last name, he took it from the president in those days. He figgered he'd use the names o' big men from both sides o' the water."

"My grandmother says the same thing about herself. She claims to be a princess from Haiti."

"You sound like you don't believe her."

"I don't know. She's not the easiest person to believe."

"Maybe you oughta. You never know. She might be just what she say she is." He paused for a moment. "Lots o' people didn't believe me when I come back from the Mexican War and told everybody I was free."

"How did that happen?"

"Colonel Osborne took me with him to Mexico as his manservant. We was down there at that Chapultepec and he went and got himself shot. I put him on my back and carried him quite a ways to a doctor. He figgered I saved his life so he gave me a paper that said I was free, and he wrote on it that I was to have forty acres and a cabin on the southwest corner of his sugar cane plantation on the south bank of the Mississippi, down in Jefferson Parish."

"So he told everybody when you got back what he'd done?"

"Not hardly. He took the blood poison and died down there in Mexico. I showed my papers to everbody and their brother in that army, traded his saddle and guns and even his sword for a mule and wagon, then I brung him in his casket all the way back to Louisiana t' be buried by his folks. Took me the best part o' two months t' get here."

"What did his family say when you told them you were free?"

"First thing was, they was upset I got rid of the colonel's sword and guns. Wanted me to pay 'em back. I says, 'Y'all got this here mule and wagon. That's all I gots to pay you with.' Next thing I done was take the paper to Lawyer Holt. When he told the Osborne boys about it, they didn't care for it one bit, but they couldn't argue with their papa's mark on that paper.

"The way I see it, they got more land than they can farm as it is. Come October, it's common for them to have a good thousand hogsheads o' sugar stacked upon their dock to sell. You'd figger my little old ten barrels wouldn't make no never mind t' them Osbornes. Course, they ain't exactly used to sharin'."

"What about your wife? Was she freed as well?"

"She had to wait for the end of the war. I tried to buy her, but the Osbornes wouldn't turn her loose 'til they had to. Prob'ly done it just t' spite me."

Within three days, Mamie Monroe was dead, and Musa himself had been struck down with the fever. He came through the first stage of the disease fairly well, and Emilie had hopes that he would recover. But then his fever returned and he rapidly began to go downhill. Emilie suspected he had lost his will to survive with the passing of his wife.

On the day which Emilie believed would be his last, Musa's kidneys had failed, his skin began to yellow, his fever hovered around 105 degrees, and he had lapsed into a meaningless babble. She was surprised when the head nurse called her out of the ward, asking her to speak with two young black men in their early twenties who were waiting on the veranda.

"Are you the one takin' care of Mamie Monroe?"

"Are you related to Mrs. Monroe?"

"We're her sons. I'm Amos and this here is Abednego. Is our papa in there with her? We need to speak to him. It's sorta an emergency."

"I'm sorry to tell you that Mamie passed away a week ago, and Musa is terribly ill himself."

The boys lowered their heads, patted each other on the shoulder for a minute, then inquired, "Can we talk to him?"

"He's unconscious. It's doubtful he'll make it through the day."

"Did he happen to mention a paper that granted him ownership of a little piece of property?"

"Yes, he did. He said a Mr. Osborne had granted him his freedom and a forty-acre plot of land."

"Did he say anything about where he kept that paper?"

"No, that didn't come up."

"The Osbornes are tryin' to say they're takin' the property back when our papa dies."

"You two stay right here and I'll go back and see if Mr. Monroe is able to talk to you."

Emilie re-appeared in less than ten minutes. "I'm so sorry, boys. Your father is gone."

Both of them sank down on the steps of the veranda, first crying, then consoling one another. Amos finally looked at his brother. "I reckon that's the end of it, then. We gonna lose everything we got."

Emilie thought for a moment. "Why don't you just tell the Osbornes that Musa is in the hospital, looking after his wife? They won't know the difference. In the meantime, that will give you a chance to look for that paperwork."

August 7, 1878—"The sensationalists are circulating unfounded rumors as to yellow fever in Memphis. The Board of Health and this paper will publish, officially, every case occurring in the city. Treat all rumors as false, and rely only on official daily reports published in the columns of this paper."

"Quarantine Instruction by Board of Health Office: Dr. A.A. Lawrence will proceed at once to Quarantine Station, President's Island, and have full charge of the station. He will stop all boats passing up the river, and make a thorough examination of all passengers coming from infected ports. If he finds anyone sick with fever of a suspicious nature who intends to land at Memphis or vicinity, he will have him removed from the boat at once, quarantined, and treated. He will have all freight from an infected port, destined for Memphis or vicinity, landed at Quarantine Station and thoroughly disinfected for 10 days before being allowed to be moved to Memphis. He will

not give a certificate to any boat to land at the Memphis wharf if she has run from an infected port, by order of the Board. J.H. Erskine, M.D. Health Officer." Memphis Daily Appeal

August 7, 1878—"Yesterday a lively scene attracted a large crowd on Conti Street, between Royal and Bourbon. Two physicians, Drs. Felix Formento and A. Poincy, it appears, had each attended a sick yellow fever patient, and prescribed different drugs for him. This created an animosity between them, and on Monday, Dr. Poincy addressed a letter to Dr. Formento, in which he applied opprobrious epithets to him. On Tuesday Dr. Formento met Dr. Poincy, who was walking on Conti Street with his wife. From persons nearby, it was learned that Formento placed his hand on Poincy's shoulder, and said, "Sir, a word with you." Dr. Poincy turned around and Dr. Formento placed his hand in his breast pocket, drawing forth a cowhide thong, striking several blows. Poincy clinched and both men fell down, rolling over and over the stones, while repeatedly striking one another. Two bystanders finally were able to separate the two physicians, but both parties bear marks of the encounter." New Orleans Picayune

Memphis

Despite the uncomfortable summer morning, Annie Cook would not be caught dead on the streets without being decked out in her finery. After all, she had a reputation—of sorts—to uphold. In her short walk down Beale Street, she was quick to realize that both the roadway and the sidewalks were practically deserted. Even in the enlightened times of the 1870s, Beale was known as '*a mile of vice, owned by the Jews, policed by the Whites, and enjoyed by the Negroes.*' But with rumors of yellow fever circulating, practically no one of any race or creed was out and about on the avenue.

She found her destination, and was happy to find the shoe and haberdashery shop still open. However, she was disappointed at the skimpily stocked shelves. She called toward the short proprietor sitting at his desk. "Mister Schwab, I was hopin' to buy a gentleman friend one of those Stetson hats. He's from San Antonio, Texas, and he prefers a Western look. Besides, he's bald as a billiard ball, and I'd prefer to see that shiny head covered." She couldn't help but smile at the thought of slowly relieving the old sport of the wad of cash he was always showing off

Abraham Schwab looked up from his bookkeeping, peering over the top of his reading glasses. He sported a rather full mustache, with his hair already speeding toward gray. Like most store proprietors, he wore a collar and tie, even in the worst of the August heat, but also included a yarmulke in his daily dress. He struggled to keep the look of displeasure off his face.

After all, the woman owned the whorehouse down on Gayoso, her low-down customers referring to it as 'the Mansion House' and some wise-cracker calling it 'a palatial resort for the purpose of commercial affection.' The way she flounced around that morning, if forced to guess, he'd estimate she had on at least a half-dozen petticoats under her dress. Didn't she know it was hot as blue blazes outside? And her hat—it appeared to sprout at least half a peacock's worth of feathers. He briefly wondered at its cost.

"Good morning, Miss Cook." He motioned toward the river. "I believe my order of gentlemen's hats is sitting out yonder at the quarantine station, waiting for somebody to decide they're safe to come ashore. It's downright ridiculous. Whoever heard of a hat having the yellow fever?"

"Looks like the whole town is runnin' low of goods. I hope this blockade is only temporary. I don't mind tellin' you, it's bad for business."

Schwab held his tongue, wanting so badly to point out the huge difference in their two business strategies. "Indeed it is."

Annie opened the front door on to Beale Street, but quickly shut it, retrieved the lady's scent flask from her bag, dabbed a bit on her kerchief, and held it under her nose for a few seconds. "I swear, these streets smell worse every day."

She had obviously hit a nerve with the haberdasher. "I don't see how Mayor Flippin can justify this stench! As if that nasty sewage ditch isn't enough, there are ten thousand water closets emptying their foulness onto the ground every day. The streets being constructed of that Nicholson pavement—those decaying wooden blocks soaked in creosote—make their own contribution to the poisonous smell. And wouldn't it be nice if the city made arrangements to pick up the trash and garbage, not to mention the horse droppings up and down the streets? Maybe then we could pretend as though we were truly a civilized town."

"You are so right, Mister Schwab. How in the world our illustrious city fathers could justify firing the street cleaners and sanitation officers—let alone selling off the slop carts and mule teams—for the life of me, I just can't understand it. And it bein' a hundred degrees outside makes it twice as odoriferous as usual." She took another sniff from the scent flask to fortify herself, and went out the door.

August 10, 1878—"The Chamber of Commerce respectfully protests against the unreasonable and unnecessary quarantine proclaimed against our city by various cities, villages, railroad stations, and river landings. We look in vain for justification for this interference in the commerce of New Orleans." New Orleans Picayune

Mr. Bionda would not have come close to this place, except he had an emergency. Despite wearing a mask to protect himself, he stood at least ten feet away from the bed which held his wife, and would come no closer. It was shocking to see the weakened condition of the woman, and more or less confirmed the dreams which had kept him up half the night, as he argued with himself as to the pros and cons of going to the hospital.

"Kate, I got t' have some money t' buy some groceries. We 'bout run outa most everthin' since you been in here. We got no business a'tall. They come and put lime all up and down Front Street. It looks like snow out there! The devils used that carbolic acid in our restaurant, plus all the other businesses in the whole block. And if that warn't enough, they put policemen on both ends of the block. So everybody is pretty much stayin' away. But I still got t' buy food for me an' the girls."

Kate Bionda pulled the blanket tighter around her neck. Her eyes were bloodshot and her skin was clammy. She'd been in the hospital for three days with a high fever and a throbbing headache. The sunlight filtering through the gauzy curtains of the hospital window forced her to squeeze her eyes almost shut.

Kate looked around the almost empty ward before she answered in a weakened voice. “I keep some money in a hollowed-out cookbook that sits on the shelf right behind the cash box. You take what you need.” She tried to give her husband a reassuring smile, but had already begun to wonder if she would leave the place alive. She turned her head and vomited into a chamber pot, just as she had twice earlier that morning, but this time it was hard to ignore the blood. When she turned back around, her loving husband had disappeared.

August 11, 1878—(Ad) “Christian Brothers College here in Memphis affords ample means for a thorough, classical, scientific, and commercial education. Higher classes are offered per quarter of 2½ months for $18.00, intermediate classes for $13.00, and preparatory classes for $10.00.”

“FALSE ALARM—It was printed yesterday that Colonel Mike Burke of the Mississippi and Tennessee Road, received a telegram from Grenada, Mississippi, which stated there were 6 deaths in that city last night, and 35 sick people within a radius of 400 yards of the depot. The citizens were greatly alarmed, although others in Grenada say it is not yellow fever. No apprehension is now felt by sensible citizens that any yellow fever will appear in our city this season. The work of the Board of Health is having a good effect.

“The yellow fever continues to spread among the 1st and 2nd districts of New Orleans. The Board of Health continues the use of carbolic acid as a disinfectant, but will try lime in a few days. Arrangements are being made to irrigate the city by flushing the gutters with river water. 35 cases and 8 deaths (in New Orleans) *yesterday. Included in the 466 yellow fever cases reported to the Board of Health up to noon today are 121 children under ten years of age and 19 colored persons.”*
Memphis Daily Appeal

Chapter 4
Tragedy Strikes

Grenada, Mississippi

The Howard Association was established in New Orleans in 1842 as an answer to cholera and yellow fever epidemics. The association served to organize teams of physicians and nurses during times when these diseases overwhelmed, not only New Orleans, but other communities in the Southern states. Within a few years, there were Howard Associations established in many American cities, including Memphis. But the New Orleans Howards were the primary resource of emergency medical assistance throughout the South.

On Sunday, August 11th, the Memphis Howard Association, the Board of Health, the Masons, the Odd-Fellows, and the Knights of Pythias were staggered by the number of telegrams they each received from Grenada, Mississippi (ninety miles south of Memphis). Until then, most Memphis authorities had believed the report received earlier from Grenada was an exaggeration, if not totally untrue.

The Howards called an emergency meeting Sunday afternoon to decide on a plan of action, and by 7:30 PM a special train on the Mississippi and Tennessee Line had been obtained to go to the aid of Grenada. In the short time available to organize the relief, they had found seven nurses—largely inexperienced—who volunteered to go, plus old General W.J. Smith of the Howard Association (a veteran of two wars), and Dr. R.F. Brown from the Memphis Board of Health.

A large and enthusiastic crowd assembled at the railway station to see them off, with much cheering and waving of hats. But when General Smith stood on the platform and asked for a volunteer to step forward from among the men assembled in order to lead the efforts of the nursing corps, man after man gave one excuse after another, and repeated the phrase, "Pray thee, have me excused." It was widely acknowledged that, due to a lack of experience among the nurses, a solid leader was extremely important if they were to be successful. And so the crowd turned their heads almost as one to the man who all recognized as perhaps one of the finest men and noted leaders in their city.

As the locomotive built up steam in preparation for departure, Colonel Butler P. Anderson straightened his shoulders, then leaped onto the step of the first passenger car, saying, "I will go myself." The colonel's physique was imposing. He was taller than most men, possessed a broad chest, brown hair, a very full mustache, and a pair of gray eyes which had seen terrible things in the previous war. In the minutes before the train departed, he only had time to write a short message to his family; but the audience, though greatly relieved someone had finally volunteered other than themselves, had a terrible foreboding that their Colonel Anderson was heading to an almost certain doom.

The first victim in Grenada had expired on August 9th. Unlike Memphis and New Orleans, both of which possessed long histories with yellow fever, this was the first yellow fever case ever experienced in Grenada. The city's population had always taken comfort in their location some seventy miles from the Mississippi River, thus avoiding the river commerce which was associated with the spread of disease. Additionally, their small city was relatively sanitary compared to Memphis and New Orleans, but apparently the security of their town was no longer something which citizens could depend upon. There was even considerable discussion before Grenada physicians could actually agree on the cause of the death. But the confusion of diagnosis was quickly put to rest as the body count mounted and symptoms became more definitive.

Theories as to why the yellow fever had attacked their city were rampant. Some believed the recent opening of a sewer near the center of the town was undoubtedly the cause. Carcasses of dogs, cats, hogs, and other unknown animals in various stages of decay were discovered in the sewer. Another popular idea was that Mrs. Field had received a mail-order dress from New Orleans shortly before she became ill. Many blamed the garment itself for Grenada's misfortune.

The fever in the city spread like a wildfire. Compared to reports from New Orleans, apparently no patient was said to have recovered in Grenada. The nine local physicians did all in their power, but the high fatality rate of the disease destroyed any remaining confidence the citizenry had in their medical abilities. General Smith and Colonel Anderson worked at least eighteen hours of every twenty-four, and often did not see their beds for days at a time.

The local telegrapher, Thomas Marshall, sent out daily dispatches regarding the status of Grenada, and in one twenty-four hour period, he reported twenty-two deaths. Unfortunately, the telegrams ceased on August 23rd when Marshall died. Determined to stay at his post until the last, it was said his fingers were still upon the telegraph key when he passed on.

The citizens were terrified. They attempted to bury the ever-increasing corpses as soon as possible, but there was no one willing to assume responsibility for burials. And so in the first days of the epidemic, families and friends worked to accomplish this task. However, there had been very little rain since early July, and the ground, being composed of a great deal of clay, was hard as cement. Many bodies were buried in the only soft ground available—in private garden plots and flowerbeds. Yet corpses still began to accumulate in yards and alleyways.

Because there was such fear in the community of bodies left unburied, families did what they could to get their loved ones interred as rapidly as possible. This often meant burials occurred at night—immediately after death—and only with the light of lanterns to guide their sorrowful work. The flickering lights illuminating the picks and shovels engaged in the morbid task presented a frightening scene after dark.

More nurses and physicians were requested from both New Orleans and Memphis, as well as medical supplies from the Memphis Howards. And in Memphis, the Howards provided twenty-one more nurses, the Masons found four, and the Odd-Fellows designated two. Compared to the seven nurses who had been sent the day before, all twenty-seven of the new group of nurses were considered to be experienced.

They departed on the train the afternoon of the 12th of August.

August 13, 1878—Dispatch from B.P. Anderson—"Until today, no patients have shown signs of recovery. There are near 100 cases in a population that does not exceed 2,000. I saw eight cases and one corpse in a single dwelling today. The brave physicians in the town are terribly worn, though hard at work. All nurses were assigned to duty within half an hour of their arrival. The authorities have asked for forty more nurses from New Orleans and Mobile. The town badly needs pecuniary aid and a few physicians."

August 13, 1878—"All parties from New Orleans, Vicksburg, and Grenada or vicinity, coming to Memphis in violation of quarantine orders, without special permit, will be subject to arrest and fine. By order of the Board of Health.

"Hundreds of people commenced drinking Holland gin yesterday as a beverage and disinfectant, particularly as a precautionary measure against yellow fever, should it come to our city." Memphis Daily Appeal

New Orleans, Grenada, and points between

In New Orleans, the news from Grenada traveled rapidly in the medical community, and before the morning was out, had reached Emilie Christophe at the Hotel Dieu. She was certainly busy with her patients, but the fever in New Orleans did not seem nearly as catastrophic as that described in Grenada by the *Picayune.* Additionally, with its hospitals, New Orleans had a large reserve of skilled health care workers, whereas it was obvious the small city of Grenada was desperate for nurses—particularly those who had previously been infected with yellow fever.

Emilie discussed this at some length with the sisters at the hospital, and in her passionate description, they quickly understood how motivated she was to go to the area most in need. Reluctantly, they gave her their blessing. Now the only obstruction to departure was her grandmother.

When she began to try to discuss the matter with Vivienne later that evening, it quickly became apparent that nothing she could say or do would make the slightest impression on her grandmother's edict. She was not going. Period!

Emilie finally agreed that she would continue to work at the Hotel Dieu. She adjourned to her room and sat on her bed, looking at nothing but the wall for what seemed like hours. How long would her grandmother rule her life? Had she not proven she was a capable nurse? Did her desire to serve others not count for anything? And her final question—the one which helped more than any other—what would her mother have done?

Then she did the unthinkable, not to continue sulking, but to plan and to pack. The next morning she kissed her grandmother's cheek and departed the house as though she were going to the hospital. She then picked up her valise, which she had secreted at the side door, and made her way directly to the train station.

When the Chicago, St. Louis, and New Orleans train departed New Orleans Station just after eight AM, Emilie finally allowed herself the luxury of a smile—could it really be possible that she had escaped? Escaped from the life her grandmother insisted upon. Escaped from the thinly veiled looks of disapproval and prejudice from the old woman, just because of her darker skin color. Escaped from watching her grandmother bilk people out of their hard-earned cash, and even worse, fill them with concocted stories. But the most unacceptable sin of all was dealing in the true black arts for profit.

Almost unconsciously, her fingertips explored her pocket, finding their way to the locket dangling from a worn gold chain. She had taken the locket for good the night before from her grandmother's bedroom. After all, it rightfully belonged to her. In her dying breath, her mother had said so.

Her Grandmère Vivienne had reminded her regularly that the jewelry was an omen, a blessing from the spirit of her Haitian great-grandmother, a predictor of what Emilie could achieve, and a means to her fortune. But Emilie could only regard such a 'blessing' as a curse if she used the locket as her grandmother had. She intended to turn her back on that heresy, completely relying on the scientific training she had received as a nurse to guide her way forward.

The train headed in a westerly direction out of the city, running along the southwest bank of Lake Pontchartrain before turning to the north and crossing a long trestle over the shallow end of Lake Maurepas. By noon she had departed Louisiana, she hoped forever, and was enjoying a brief walk for exercise in Brookhaven, Mississippi, while they waited for a spur-line train to pass. Perhaps she was overstating it, but the very air seemed purer, unblemished by her grandmother's overdone use of lilac perfumery and strongly scented candles, and Emilie began to actually believe that she was free.

Before four PM she was in Jackson, where the delay was almost an hour, then still northward. There were other delays, first at Durant to wait for a crossing train, then another stop at Winona before reaching Grenada, Mississippi, at eight o'clock in the evening. They found the train platform, as well as the streets, completely deserted, save the local agent and General Smith, who had come to the station to meet them.

Emilie Christophe and the small number of Negro nurses were temporarily housed at the African Methodist-Episcopal church, while their white counterparts were escorted to more preferred quarters at a local hotel. Early the next morning, they rejoined forces and met for an hour with Colonel Anderson for a status briefing before receiving the assignments which would occupy them in the foreseeable future.

Due to the lack of a hospital in Grenada, each nurse was assigned to a particular family that had been stricken. In some cases, this might mean providing care for only a single patient, while in other households, sometimes every member of the family was ill. Although this seemed to be a poor utilization of skilled nurses, there apparently was no alternative at the moment.

Immediately after their meeting on August 14th, the medical team discovered all train service on the Mississippi Central and the Mississippi and Tennessee lines to the city had been discontinued. The word had passed up and down the rail lines that the fever in Grenada was impossible to stop, and so the trains rushed through the town, only slowing long enough to blow their mournful whistles to acknowledge the danger. The newly arrived nurses suddenly realized they now couldn't get out of the town, even if they wanted to do so.

The citizens were paralyzed by their fear. The mayor was very sick. There were no civil officers—state, county, or municipal—remaining in the town. All were dead or had fled. Into this vacuum, Anderson and Smith set about trying to organize teams of Negro men to gather corpses in all degrees of putrefaction, from all areas of the small city, in order to bury them with some sense of decorum at the cemeteries. At least it was a first step.

However, there was such a feeling of hopelessness and demoralization prevailing amongst the townspeople that Colonel Anderson and General Smith decided to make it known to a few of the town's leaders that they were considering leaving Grenada and returning to Memphis. After all, they had been sent with the idea of coordinating and organizing the response to the fever; but without cooperation from the townspeople themselves, this was an impossible task.

When the news of their departure was circulated, the following letter was presented to them:

"Dear Sirs: Having heard that there is a probability of your being called to Memphis, it is our duty to the afflicted people of this town to entreat you to remain with us as long as you see things in the deplorable condition they are now. You have seen how inefficient have been the responses of communities away from her for our relief, and that we are largely dependent on the generous benevolence of the Howard Association of Memphis to prevent men and women from dying here without having a single hand to administer even a glass of water to them in their misery. Memphis has thus far overwhelmed us with their generous charity, and we beg not to be deprived of the aid which has proven thus far to be our best stay and best friend. We trust, therefore, that you as representatives of your Association, will continue with us. Signed, John Powell, Robert Mullin, Thomas Watson—Committee"

Smith and Anderson assured the committee they had no wish to depart, but that the townspeople had to act with them and second their efforts if they were to be effective. Finally, on August 15th, General Smith was able to recruit enough volunteers to staff a local Citizens Relief Committee, which was organized with the first order of business to establish a hospital that would accept both white and colored, as well as to issue another wide appeal for assistance from Memphis, New Orleans, and Mobile. Thankfully, with the establishment of a hospital, the nurses would now have a more organized and equitable way of caring for their patients.

There had been a significant increase in the numbers of burglaries and thefts since the epidemic began in Grenada. General Smith and Colonel Anderson were able to prevail on the committee to set up a Grenada African-American Guard to patrol the streets at night in order to better protect their citizens. Along with having the Negro guards and a nighttime curfew, crime dropped like a stone.

On August 16th, there were seventeen deaths among the remaining population of the town. It appeared as though no family would be spared. The nurses who had not had the yellow fever previously began to go down, and a telegram went out to Memphis from Judge Thomas Walton: "*People dying today without an attendant.*"

Emilie Christophe paused for a second in her duties to scan the ward wherein twenty-six women were patients. Two days ago, there had been five nurses taking care of that number. Today there were only two others, besides herself. It certainly wasn't because the patients were getting better. Indeed, in that same length of time, six had died, and immediately were replaced in their pallets by six others. Four of those beds now contained Howard nurses who had volunteered, despite having no existing immunity. Two of them were in the last throes of the disease.

She remembered her conversation with the sisters at the Hotel Dieu less than a week previously, wherein she'd convinced them that she wanted to go where the disease was most virulent. She shook her head at the memory. Her wish had certainly been granted. A woman and her three young daughters had been brought in the previous day. Upon first examination, they all had appeared to be in the early phase of infection. But from the looks of them now, Emilie doubted that any of the girls could survive the night.

She had already decided to spend the next shift at the hospital so the little ones would at least have someone to hold their hands at the last, as their mother had already passed, and their father had fled the city at the first sign of his family's illness. All they had received from him was a get well note from Baton Rouge. What their absentee father would soon discover was that traditionally safe cities of refuge were not protected at all in the summer of 1878. The yellow fever would find and decimate Louisiana's capitol city as well, and he would be included in its deadly roll call.

Emilie could not ever remember being so weary. Although the scheduled shifts were twelve hours in length, in reality she and quite a few of the others were at the hospital for eighteen hours straight. The doctors constantly harangued the nurses about not getting so worn down, as they believed yellow fever to be opportunistic in attacking victims who were already in a weakened condition. Almost no one listened. How could they?

On August 21st, General Smith telegraphed the Memphis Howards: *"The death rate not so large today, but the fever continues to spread. There have been not less than 75 struck down in the last 24 hours. We have 12 colored in the hospital, where they are equally well cared for with the whites. Both of our New Orleans doctors are dumbfounded at the malignancy of this disease. Frequently, after the 7th or 8th day, patients die within a few hours. Our efforts are paralyzed for want of proper remedies. We are short of lemons, ice, beef-tea, and all kinds of nourishment for the sick."*

Later that same day, General Smith was himself taken down with the fever. He decided to return to Memphis. All the physicians argued against such a move, but Smith prevailed, asking his close friend, Major Burke, Superintendent of the Mississippi and Tennessee Railroad, to send a special railcar to Grenada, so he could travel back to his family. His doctors argued it would cost him his life to make the trip. He was determined, and none could stop him. If he was going to die, it would be with his wife at his side. Meanwhile, Colonel Anderson remained at his post.

Chapter 5
I've Tried to be a Good Girl

Memphis

Johnnie Rourke was Irish through and through—slightly built, but with an extra wide set of shoulders—and he possessed a head of hair so red it appeared almost like a halo of fire over his face, though halo was undoubtedly a holy exaggeration. Perhaps he was a bit self-conscious about his hair, as he wore a bowler hat a size too big for him, pulled down to his ears, whether he was outside or in. He put in substantial effort in growing a beard in the current style, but finally had given it up as a lost cause. However, over the course of several months, he had eventually been able to coax a thin, slightly pinkish mustache on his upper lip. His eyes, green as a cucumber, were set so close together there was barely room to squeeze a pointed nose in between. Although he had been surrounded and inundated by the Southern drawl in Memphis for almost ten years, he had lost not a whit of his brogue, and he wasn't bashful about displaying it.

He puffed prodigiously on a nickel cigar, blew a couple of smoke rings to entertain himself, then turned his attention across the bar of the Globe Saloon on Main Street toward his three most reliable customers. One of them, Jack Shannon, was a fellow Hibernian from County Cork, while the other two were the barely literate Royster twins. The three of them had assumed the heavy responsibility of holding up the northern end of the bar, each of them with one foot hiked up on the brass rail. Apparently, they had decided bar maintenance was a full-time job.

Willie Royster started rambling without much direction about the yellow fever, when Shannon abruptly cut him off. "Why don't you close that rattlin' trap o' yours, Ollie? You got no idea how to have a conversation in po-lite society. You and yer brother are just barely a step from yer monkey ancestors. I'd be worried about the state of yer offspring, was I you. So 'tis I who'll be doin' the talkin' here."

The brothers produced a pair of hard looks, but since it was Shannon's turn to buy, they kept their opinions to themselves. He held his glass up to the glow of the sunbeam passing through the window. "Good rum oughter be just as close t' food as 'tis t' drink." He looked with some skepticism at Johnnie. "Fact, a better grade o' rum would make ye think ye should take it with a knife and fork. But yer stomach got t' be ready fer that quality o' rum. Course, this here version be watered down somethin' awful. Did it never cross yer mind, Johnnie, t' sell rum without dilution?"

Rourke decided to let the insult slide. He had bigger things on his mind. "They say 'tis gonna be another one o' them fever years—a mild but wet spring, and now a summer hot enough t' make old Lucifer sweat."

"The papers say it ain't gonna happen."

"Hmmph! Ye best get yerselves prepared, Jacko. After all, it's willin' I'd be to let the three o' yis in on an old family secret. 'Tis a proven treatment I'm offerin' ye boys, and it might be best if ye'd show a bit o' respect. Mebbe the only obstacle standin' twixt ye and the gravediggers' shovels is me cure."

"Sounds like more o' yer blarney, Johnnie."

Rourke placed his hand on his chest. "It pierces me heart yis would question me recipe. 'Tis only the truth I'll be tellin' yis reprobates. On me mam's grave, I took it meself in '73, and I never had a blink o' that fever."

"What might your treatment be, Johnnie?"

"'Tis a mixture discovered by me old pap, and passed on to yours truly. I wouldn't be stretchin' the truth one whit t' say it was a blessin' on a man's gullet. But yis got to take it every day to escape the fever. Don't be givin' the fever the chance to slip betwixt yer lip an yer goozle without havin' to pass by this special medication."

The larger of the Roysters spoke up. "Awright, awright. Let's have a taste o' yer miracle, then."

Johnnie smiled and turned his back, presumably to prepare their treatment in privacy. He put a generous half spoonful of powdered sulfur in three glasses, then added two shots of whiskey and stirred each of them into a mustard-colored slurry before placing the 'medication' in front of his patients. "Down the hatch it is, gentlemen. And be sure you come in for a dose every day whilst the fever is in town."

As they tossed their glasses down, each of them sputtered, followed by vile looks on their faces. "What you tryin' to do to us, Johnnie? Tastes t' me like you put rotten eggs in our whiskey!"

"If yis don't prefer that mixture, it's another one I've got made o' gin and quinine, but it might be just a tad on the bitter side."

"Damn! I know good n' well what ye figger. We'll have t' buy a drink just t' fortify ourselves afore we take the medicine. Then we'll be buyin' another one or two afterward just t' get the putrid taste out'n our mouths."

"Aye, could be. But 'tis better by far ye'll be rather than takin' the dose o' calomel the doctors will be givin' yis when ye get the fever and then huggin' the thunder pot the live-long day. Just be sure yis come back every morning. I wouldn't be likin' it if me best customers ended up with the mortician." He looked at Shannon. "I bet the one down the street—the Presbyterian with only one eye—would be relievin' yis o' that fine gold tooth in yer head, Jacko, before he planted yis."

Shannon lovingly ran a short, pink tongue over his shiny front tooth before answering. "Another drink o' that nasty yeller brew o' yours an' we'll likely be laid out on his slab anyways."

Levi Royster was still sputtering. "We ain't got the money t' be spendin' it on the likes o' this." He looked at his brother for support. "We'uns is too poor to spend what little we got on yer poison."

The bartender shot a look at the both of them. Oliver Royster realized it might be a good time to stay mum when Johnnie rode his high horse. "Poor! The two o' yis got no idea what poor means. Me mam and da were terrible poor. They had to sell a pot full o' piss to the tannery in Clonakilty ever week just so's we could have food in the house. Thet's what folks refer to as piss poor. We had us some neighbors, the

McClatcheys, who lived in a mud and thatch hut—didn't own a stick o' furniture. They was so poor they didn't even own a piss pot. Everbody said they was so poor they didn't have a pot to piss in. And you two got the nerve t' come in here and say you was poor!"

Sister Agnes was perspiring heavily in the furnace of an August afternoon in Memphis. Partly to blame was her Dominican nun's habit—white, mostly woolen and multilayered, except for the white guimpe covering her head and neck, offset by a black veil, which was lined in white linen. But the primary reason sweat was running down her face, stinging her eyes, and dripping off her chin was that she had been half-walking and half-running ever since she left the hospital.

Her instincts told her there was very little time left. The poor woman was a member of St. Peter's Parish, and unfortunately, she was in immediate need of last rites. Sister could only hope Father Joseph Kelly or one of his assistants was at the church. If she had to go searching for them—well, there just wasn't enough time.

Briefly, Sister Agnes visualized the corpulent form of Father Kelly running down the street along with her, but quickly admonished herself for thinking of such a thing. She wasted a good five minutes looking for the priests in their quarters, until Sister Theresa confirmed they were all out and about on the town.

"Do you know where they went?"

"They each left here with a list of folks to visit all over the parish. No telling where they are."

Sister Agnes was unhappy, but resolute that she at least had to do all she could, even if it only meant holding the woman's hand at her last hour. She bent over the porcelain wash bowl and splashed tepid water on her face in an attempt to cool down a bit, then took off in a big hurry again back toward the hospital. It struck her that she had never been this scared before. The devil take those priests, anyway!

She had gone no more than three blocks when she heard a man's voice from the shade of a store awning. "What's the hurry, Sister?"

She turned quickly, hoping the voice might belong to Father Kelly or Father McGarvey, but immediately identified the short, pot-bellied little man with a neat black beard reaching from ear to ear, a smile almost as wide, and a skull cap with a mop of curly black hair protruding around the edges, as the leader of B'nai Israel Synagogue. "Hello, Rabbi Samfield. I can't stop right now. There's one of our parishioners dying at the Quarantine Hospital, and I can't find our priests."

With that, she was off again. With his short legs, it was all Max Samfield could do to catch up with her. "How can I be of help, Sister?"

She looked with some appreciation at the man, knowing that, despite his misguided religion, he was a truly fine person. "I'm sorry, Rabbi, but the woman needs last rites said over her. Of course, I can't do that myself, but the least I can do is be there with her when she passes on."

"You mentioned the Quarantine Hospital. Does your parishioner have yellow fever?"

"I think so, Rabbi. Don't endanger yourself."

He half-smiled at the woman. "I'll be going with you, Sister. I know Father Kelly would do the same if it was one of my people."

And so the unlikely couple stood, not without a reasonable level of trepidation, before the suffering Kate Bionda—thrashing about in her agony. Although she was making noises, there was no sense to be made of them. The bedding was saturated with her sweat, and there were remnants of foulness in her auburn hair as well as at the bedside. Her skin was clammy, almost the color of goldenrod, and as if in confirmation of her failing liver, her eyes were yellower still. Her breaths were shallow and seemed to be separated by a good ten seconds. In fact, with each of those long pauses, Sister Agnes wondered if she would breathe again, or if the previous breath had been truly her last.

The nurse wore a mask on her face, but it still couldn't hide her concern. She had handed both the sister and the rabbi a mask upon entry, and warned them as well. "This patient is highly infectious. Please keep your distance and don't touch anything she's touched, or you may be back here yourselves as patients."

Sister Agnes was trying to control her impulse to turn and run, when Rabbi Samfield's voice cut through the tension. "Oh, Jehovah—accept this woman to your heaven, according to her faith. She lies here alone, wrapped only in her belief in you. Relieve her pain and suffering, and show her your mercy. And please, have mercy on our city. Amen."

Kate's thrashing about stopped for a moment, her moaning ceased, and she opened her eyes. Whether she actually saw them or not, Sister Agnes would never know. The woman simply said, "Momma, I've tried to be a good girl." And then she was no more.

Chapter 6
Those Who Stayed—and Those Who Didn't

August 14, 1878—"The yellow fever found another victim in Memphis yesterday. Kate Bionda, a woman who superintended an eating house on Front Street, which was a resort of steamboat roustabouts, from some of whom, passing up from New Orleans, she no doubt contracted the disease. There are three possible cases of the fever on Poplar Street, near the market, but the Board of Health was not satisfied to pronounce with certainty that they were yellow fever. These may be decided upon today."

"Telegraph received from Grenada: Only about 700 white citizens remain in Grenada, and of these, about 125 have the fever. Twenty-six deaths occurred yesterday. Business is entirely suspended, and the trains pass by without noticing the place. The distress is truly appalling."

"Rumor, which is not a respecter of truth, and has no particular regard for facts, was busy on our streets yesterday, insisting upon all sorts of wild stories, which our reporters could not trace to any foundation of fact. The Board of Health has acted in good faith, and this paper has published the only two cases of yellow fever that have occurred. We trust our people will act with discretion, and frown down on sensationalism that can do no good, but is doing a great deal of harm."
Memphis Daily Appeal

(*Author's note:* While many people accept the premise that William Warren and Kate Bionda were the first two cases of yellow fever in Memphis in the summer of 1878, there is ample evidence that several other people traveling from Grenada, Vicksburg, and New Orleans had violated the city's quarantine at about the same time as Warren. There was the husband of Attorney General Turner's Negro cook, who had snuck into the city, already infected with the fever. There was Willie Darby, an employee of Farrell, the oyster dealer, and then there were three ladies, also from William Warren's ship, the *Golden Crown,* who had been brought ashore on the same night Warren arrived, and were taken to the residence of Esquire Winters. So the quarantine was full of holes.)

Treating physicians were not willing to make a diagnosis of yellow fever in early August. In fact, the disease was sometimes not easily differentiated from other illnesses referred to as generic "malarial fevers." Rather, the physicians talked, and conferred, and hesitated.

By the time there was consensus that Memphis was indeed experiencing an outbreak of yellow fever, perhaps twenty cases were in various stages of development. So when Kate Bionda's death was reported in the newspaper, there was substantial ammunition for the rumors in the city. In fact, there had been other suspicious fever cases in Memphis in early August. Professor Theodore Decker, the organist at St. Mary's Catholic Church, died from the fever the day after Bionda passed away.

In 1878, Dr. James Vandergriff was the president of the New Orleans Howards. It was to Dr. Vandergriff that the Memphis Board of Health Director, Dr. Erskine, directed his telegram requesting help. And so they came—physicians and nurses from New Orleans, but eventually there would be physicians from eleven other states, and nurses from many more—all converging on Memphis. The primary requirement was that each volunteer must have previously been infected with yellow fever. Painful experience in other outbreaks had shown that those who had no previous infection did not last more than a week or so after reporting to a stricken city. Time would tell if this precaution would work in Memphis. Unfortunately, many physicians, and literally hundreds of nurses, either lied about their disease history or insisted on serving, despite having no previous yellow fever infection themselves. Their insistence would take a heavy toll.

Physicians employed by the Howards were paid ten dollars per day, and usually provided a buggy with horse or mule. "Foreign" nurses (those from outside the affected community) received four dollars a day, plus board and lodging. Home nurses (from within the community), as well as all Negro nurses—regardless of their home of record—received three dollars per day plus board. All physicians and some nurses from outside Memphis were housed at the Peabody Hotel, a high-class place with running water, porcelain bathtubs, and flush toilets. The administrative offices of the Howard Association while in Memphis would be on Main Street, across from Court Square.

At the same time, the mayor, the chief of police, the president of the Board of Health, several prominent businessmen, and a few former military leaders, who had decided to remain in the city, formed the Citizens Relief Committee. This organization would allocate food and provisions for the needy, establish camps outside the perimeter of the city for refugees, and coordinate military supervision of the municipality if it became necessary. The Committee worked in tandem with the Howard Association.

The Committee assigned two of their white members, plus a Negro, to each of the ten wards in the city. It was their responsibility to assess the needs of their particular portion of Memphis and report back to the Committee, so that available resources could be as evenly distributed as possible.

Police were told to arrest anyone on the streets after nine in the evening, unless they could prove they were out and about on behalf of the Howards or the Citizens Relief Committee. In case more law enforcement was required, two Negro military units were on duty near Court Square. The Bluff City Grays (a post-Civil War para-military organization) was at Camp Williams, the Chickasaw Guards were on standby at Grand Junction (some forty-five miles to the east), and there was a company of volunteers seven miles to the north at Raleigh Station. All in all, there were more men in uniform than had been present at the infamous Battle of Memphis in 1862.

(*Author's note:* Unfortunately, in 1878 the Memphis Board of Health only functioned in an advisory capacity, thus its many recommendations to improve the health status of the city were often ignored or only partially observed.)

Memphis

Johnnie Rourke, the bartender, had been standing in line for over three hours before he finally worked his way to the ticket window. The hat band of his bowler was soaked with perspiration. He, as well as his attitude, was drenched. There were well over two hundred people behind him, and by mid-morning, none of them had a patient bone in their body.

Everybody was carrying as many of their possessions as was physically possible. Children were running amok on the platform. Mothers were pinching guilty ears, swatting behinds, and hollering for all they were worth. Everybody was talking with the next person in line, while at the same time trying to keep their distance. The most recent arrivals were finagling a way to break into the long queue of people. Only one subject was being discussed.

He couldn't help but hear a woman behind him on the platform, talking to an acquaintance. "I was so scared, I left my washing in the tubs and my dishes on the table. My husband was hurryin' me so much, I couldn't even take time to make the beds."

Johnnie gave her a glance. It appeared she hadn't taken time to wash her face, either.

Finally reaching the ticket window, he turned his attention to the haggard agent before pointing to the train sitting on the tracks, which was just beginning to build up a bit of steam. "Might ye have room on that train for one more, sir?"

"That train and the next one are filled up. No seats available until the seven o'clock train in the morning."

Johnnie reached inside his baggage, pulling a bottle of bourbon halfway out so the agent spied it, and asked again. "Might this little gift change yer mind, sir? I need to depart as soon as possible. Me mam is sickly, and I need to go see about her while she's still amongst the livin'."

The agent could barely hide his disgust for the obvious lie, but his honor didn't prevent his longing stare at the bottle. "Where are you going, sir?"

"Where is that train yonder headed?"

"To Nashville, and on to Louisville."

"Well, I'll swan!" He flashed the agent a broad grin. "'Tis an amazing coincidence. That would be perzactly where I'm headed."

The agent could almost taste the liquor, at least until he spied a fellow in a blue uniform coming his way. He turned back to Johnnie. "We might work something out, but you'll need another bottle for the conductor."

Johnnie almost spat on the man for his greed. Undoubtedly a damn carpetbagger, takin' advantage of poor innocent folk such as himself. But now was not the time to point out the agent's shortcomings. Johnnie squelched the response that jumped to his tongue and instead provided a half-hearted smirk. "Sure, I believe I can find another drink or so in me bag for a thirsty conductor."

Gunter the German slapped the reins on his mule's arse, and the old nag moved the wagon on down the street another twenty feet or so. He looked back at Lester Sellers, hollering at him, "Give it a go here, too."

Sellers replied, "Yes, suh," and resolutely bent to his work, pitching shovelfuls of lime off the back of the wagon, aiming for the disgusting slime of the Gayoso Bayou, which ran parallel to the street. There was an identical disinfecting wagon on the other side of the sewage ditch, performing exactly the same task.

Their boss, John Denie, had been tasked by the Board of Health to spread 500 barrels of unslaked lime in the Gayoso Bayou after he had reported to them that the ditch was filthy beyond all belief. Several men had threatened to leave his employment, so terrible was the stench, but he had finally prevailed upon them with an additional fifty cents a day to remain at their posts.

Gunter was a thick-waisted fellow, with reddish-brown hair and a similarly hued bushy mustache, which covered a good third of his face. On this day, he wore a twine necklace, from which hung twin cloth packets: one containing asafoetida and the other two bulbs of garlic, well mashed. His once-white muslin shirt was saturated in sweat, and at least every half hour, he gargled a mouthful of gin before swallowing it. The necklace had been his wife's idea, but the gin was Gunter's contribution toward immunizing himself against the fever.

Lester preferred the pungent smell of lime in the back of the wagon to the mixed and noxious aromas surrounding the drayman. Although he was still in his thirties, most would guess the Negro's age on the far side of fifty. His hair was very short, with an inch-wide stripe of completely white hair running from the middle of his brow to the back of his head. His mother had told him that stripe was the mark of the Cherokee, inherited from a father he had never met.

His frame was sparse, but his forearms appeared not to fit with the rest of his body. They were thicker than his calves, with ropes of muscle and sinew running from wrist to elbow. He never seemed to be able to stand up straight, almost as though his back was misshapen from birth. But his most remarkable characteristic he would wear to his grave.

Not long before the war, he and his mother had been slaves on Mr. Brantley's plantation, down by Brinkley, Arkansas. A couple of Brantley's more rambunctious colored possessions had run off, and it took a good month to run them down in Missouri. In fact, Brantley had a hard time convincing a do-gooder sheriff they truly belonged to him. Had the man never heard of Dred Scott?

As a result of his difficulties, when Brantley got back to Brinkley, he proceeded to identify every one of his twelve slaves, including the fourteen-year-old Lester, by cutting a triangular notch about an inch long and an inch wide in the bottom lobe of their right ears. No longer would there be any argument about to whom these people belonged. So fifteen years after the Emancipation Proclamation, and thirteen years after the war, Lester Sellers was still identifiable property.

Gunter and Lester had been at their work since shortly after daylight, and had only covered about two hundred yards of the winding three-mile ditch. The reek of the bayou, combined with the terrible heat and humidity, further magnified by the constant attacks by mosquitoes and horse flies, made for an extremely miserable day for the two men. Their work was compounded by the almost constant traffic of wagons, carriages, and buggies leaving the city in great haste.

The entire population—at least the folks with any money—appeared to be of one mind. Some conveyances were packed to bursting with household belongings, while other people had opted to simply flee, with no second thoughts about leaving their worldly possessions behind. It was said that a few of the wealthier families departed in such a panic that they left their sterling silver lying on the mantel and their doors wide open—quite the potential bonanza for thieves.

The owner of a cotton gin, a man of some wealth, "sporting diamonds and fast horses," was among the first to flee the city. He left behind three sisters and an aging father. Some weeks later, when the epidemic was at its peak, one of the sisters died, and his two remaining siblings telegraphed him, asking for money enough to pay for the fares of themselves and their father to leave the stricken city. Instead, he sent five dollars and an order for an undertaker to construct a cheap coffin for his dead sister.

Others, who possessed less means for escape, desperately pawned watches, jewelry, and anything of value to raise funds to get away. Small depositors withdrew their last nickel from the banks. Many left the city with no more than ten or fifteen dollars to their name and no prospects to greet them at the end of their journey, wherever that might be.

As Gunter and Lester slowly traversed the central portion of the city that morning, they passed by the Memphis and Charleston railyard. Hundreds of people were gathered near the ticket window. A veritable mountain of trunks, bags, boxes, and portable possessions was gathered on the loading dock, awaiting the arrival of the next train. There were two separate fist fights occurring—apparently vying for a more advantageous place in line at the ticket window.

The normal decencies extended on the streets were completely absent. Every soul who could afford to leave was hell-bent on getting away from the city, whether it meant being rude to their friends and neighbors or not. Any conveyance that tarried too long in the street was subjected to shouted threats, and even drawn pistols on more than one occasion. You could almost taste the terror of yellow-jack in the streets. The only thought was escape!

That is, Lester reflected, unless you were poor.

Grenada

Emilie Christophe was caring for the Bishop family, who lived in a small farmhouse just on the northeastern edge of

Grenada. The Bishop home stood on a small elevation of land overlooking the slow-moving Yalobusha River. Four of the five family members were currently quite ill, with only the father, J.M. Bishop, escaping so far.

Belle and Addie were four and six years old, while big brother Eugene was nine. The three of them had passed thru the initial stages of high fever and body aches, but Emilie could not convince any of them to drink enough fluids to be worthwhile. Mrs. Bishop was the sickest of the group, having lost her kidney function and beginning to experience the second phase of fever. Her forehead, neck, and chest were currently covered in towels packed with ice.

Despite these efforts, Emilie had little faith that the mother was going to live another twenty-four hours. In fact, in Grenada, it was rare indeed for white people to survive this terribly virulent form of the fever.

So it was totally unexpected to hear a knock at the front door that afternoon. The only people about on the streets were the doctors and the hearses. But their visitor was Reverend Hiram Haddick, the pastor of their First Baptist Church. Mr. Bishop answered the door. “Reverend, it’s a surprise to see you. I thought you were out of town.”

“I was, Mr. Bishop, but the Lord called me back home when I heard what was happening here in Grenada.”

“Well, we’re glad to see you, but you’d be a lot better off if you’d stayed away from this place.”

“For sure, when I re-entered the town, it did feel like I was walking into a living hell. They tell me your whole family is sick.”

“Yes, Reverend. I know the missus would love to see you, but she’s been out of her head since yesterday. We’ve got ourselves a good nurse, but it seems like it’s almost hopeless once folks get the fever.”

“Do you mind if I say a prayer over her?”

“Of course not.” He turned to the side and accepted a mask from Emilie. “But you need to wear one of these if you’re goin’ in her room.”

Reverend Haddick spoke his piece at the bedside, then bid his goodbyes. Emilie checked on her four patients and found no indication of improvement in any of them. “Mr. Bishop, I feel I’ve got to prepare you for some very bad news. Your wife is in a terrible condition. She may not survive. And the children desperately need to drink fluids; otherwise they're headed in the same direction."

"Thank you for being honest with me, Nurse Emilie. Do you suppose I could try to get some water or tea down the children?"

"I wish you would. All three of them are so listless, I can't get them interested in even sucking on ice chips."

The following morning, Bishop walked into town to the undertaker's place to ask that they come for his wife. The funeralist accompanied him back to the house in his hearse. Not only was his conveyance and horse black, but the man was covered head to foot in black—black coat and pants, black tie, black bowler, black brogans, black mustache and beard. In fact, he gave the impression that he was ready to mourn at even the suggestion of a possible fatality which might involve utilization of his services.

Once he and Bishop had placed Mrs. Bishop in her casket, and then into the hearse, he inquired about the health of the children.

"Thanks for askin'. They're all three in pretty bad shape," Bishop replied.

The undertaker began to rub his palms together as though he was anticipating feasting on a large slice of apple pie. "Not that I'm suggestin' anything bad is gonna happen, J.M., but you see, I ain't got many caskets for tots." Whereupon the undertaker retrieved a measuring stick from his wagon, walked into the children's sick room, and measured the three of them from head to toe.

Addie and Belle began to weep and called out from their sick room, "Papa, Papa—are we gonna die?"

Their nine-year-old brother Eugene spoke up, trying to appear brave. "He's measurin' all of us for our caskets. He don't wanta waste no adult caskets on little kids." This elicited a whole different level of crying from his sisters.

Realizing what the man had done, Mr. Bishop grabbed the undertaker by the nape of the neck, literally lifting his feet off the ground as he escorted him to the front door, then gave him a good push down the front steps to make his point. "You callous bastard! If somethin' happens to my little ones, I'll bury them myself. I don't want you back on this property."

When the man was gone, Emilie simply said, "Thank you, Mr. Bishop. I wanted to shake that evil little man so hard it would make the teeth rattle in his head."

There had been almost no rain in Grenada during the entire month of July and early August, hence burial was extremely difficult unless the packed ground had previously been tilled. Over the next four days, Bishop would utilize the garden plot behind his house to bury all three of his children.

(*Author's note:* Reverend Haddick died less than two weeks after returning to Grenada. He was thirty-three years old. They found a statement in his office, written in his own hand:

In my hands, no price I bring,
Simply to the cross I cling.)

August 15, 1878 —"Quarantine Notice! Bolivar, Tennessee is quarantined against all persons and baggage coming from all districts infected with yellow fever. C.A. Miller, Mayor, James Fentress, Jr., Recorder."

"The fever developed yesterday to the extent of twenty-two new cases, but only two deaths reported in the last twenty-four hours. The news found ready and early dissemination, and a panic was the result. The trains on the Charleston and Louisville railroad lines, as a result, went out crowded, and we understand every seat and berth has been taken on the trains on both roads for the next two days. Business is in great part suspended, and everyone that can afford it has left, or will leave before the week is out."

"The Board of Health has isolated the infected district, and literally saturated the buildings, streets, and alleys with disinfectant. Though the type of disease is virulent, and does not readily yield to treatment, the sanitary officials are not without hope of mitigating its severity, if they do not overcome it." Memphis Daily Appeal

August 15, 1878—Letter from Father Maternus Mallmann, OSF—"The yellow fever is spreading rapidly. Yesterday I had 400 confessions and five sick calls. I am sickly, but get along."

August 15, 1878—"'Twas a simple thing to observe that Columbus Wilson and I were different, he being a Negro, and

myself—according to my mother—being whiter than a snowman, but that wasn't the end of the comparison. My family had immigrated to America from Glasgow when I was still a boy, ending up in Louisville, Kentucky; while I believe you could say Columbus Wilson's forebears had arrived involuntarily on the same shores some twenty years before he was born. My father insisted I finish secondary school before he would allow me to 'go gallivanting off to the war.' Columbus claimed he could read and write, but I never saw any evidence to substantiate such. Of course, there were hundreds—no, thousands—of examples of my own race who frankly spoke no better, and still relied on the use of an 'X' to sign their names. Both Columbus and I worked for Mr. Flack, the cotton broker; I as his bookkeeper, and Columbus as a laborer on the docks or in his warehouse. We were both paid every Saturday at noon sharp. I had been hired in 1874, while Columbus had worked for Mr. Flack, first as a rented slave, then as a salaried employee since all that came to an end with the war. As I had access to the company books, it was not difficult to find that my income was approximately three times that of Columbus. To be sure, we were on friendly enough speaking terms, he and I, but could hardly be called friends. My family—wife, two daughters, and a son—live on the eastern outskirts of the expanding city in a modest home. Columbus, his wife, and two sons occupy an apartment above a carriage house on the south side. I am Presbyterian. Columbus belongs to that new African Methodist-Episcopal church. We are both in our early thirties. Each of us appear to be in relatively good health. But the real difference between us brings me no small amount of shame. You see, Columbus Wilson is a brave man. I have discovered I am not. When the epidemic began, he resolved to remain in the city and do whatever he could to help. On the other hand, my family and I intend to run back to Louisville as fast as the train can carry us." Diary entry—Alexander McHugh

Memphis

John Johnson had spent his entire life on the river. He had been born in 1854 in a little shack a few miles north of Memphis along Bear Creek—part of George Fenton's plantation. His mother and father were slaves, though come to think about it, so was he, but he had been too young for Fenton to get much work out of him before the freedom came. The little family, as well as the remaining eight or nine slaves owned by Fenton, relocated to higher ground on the Bluff Road, just west of Drummonds, Tennessee, each spring when the river flooded.

In early 1864, John's father had run off to join the Union Army up at Fort Pillow, as part of the 2nd Colored Light Artillery. But he'd picked a poor time to go. Fort Pillow was an earthen fort located on a bluff overlooking quite an expanse of the Mississippi. The fort's mission was to interfere with any Confederate boat traffic on the river. But by that point in the war, the only rebel boats were small craft intent on running contraband. Any Confederate vessels with an offensive capability were already sitting on the bottom of the river.

The personnel at the fort were unique in that over half of the 600 soldiers were Negro troops, many of them former slaves. Proud, courageous troops, who were advised if they were taken prisoner, they would likely be executed on the spot by the Rebel army. A thing like that was bound to wear on your mind.

The morning of April 12th, the fort was attacked by between 1,500 and 2,500 cavalry troops, led by Generals Forrest and Chalmers. The Yankee commander of the fort, Major Lionel Booth, was killed early in the battle by a sniper, while the Confederate General Nathan Bedford Forrest had three mounts shot out from under him.

After the engagement, there was disagreement related to whether or not the Yankee troops had been offered an opportunity to surrender, not to mention either the delay or the lack of response to that edict from the fort. In fact, much was debated about the battle (or massacre, depending on who you asked) for over a hundred years afterward, but as far as the small world of John Johnson was concerned, he never saw his father again.

April 24, 1864—"'The blacks and their officers were shot down, bayoneted, and put to the sword in cold blood. Out of 400 Negro soldiers, only about 20 survived. At least 300 of them were destroyed after the surrender.' This is the statement of the rebel General Chalmers himself to our informant."
New York Times

His mother had done the best she could for the boy in the closing months of the war, but in reality, John Johnson had raised himself. He trapped muskrats, beavers, and raccoons, and became an expert fisherman on the Mississippi. By the time he was twelve years old, he could handle a rowboat on the great river as well as most full-grown men. He knew every deep pool that held hungry catfish within at least a five-mile stretch along the river, and had learned to bait his long hoop nets with five pounds of rotten cheese or fish guts to attract a mixture of blue, yellow, and channel catfish.

As John grew to manhood, he had no desire to tie himself to the life of a sharecropper as so many other country blacks were doing. And so he relied on what he knew, perhaps as well as anyone on the river. And the Memphis waterfront had quite an appetite for his catch.

But life in a waterman's shack was not exactly what John's wife, Marissa, had in mind for their two girls. And so their nightly conversation almost always turned to the pros and cons of moving the family to the city. Where Marissa could only envision the opportunities of church and school and a social life in the city, the stories John had heard convinced him they would have a very unpleasant experience, with exposure to severe poverty, terrible housing, crime, and no small amount of bigotry. But like most of their disagreements, John was on the losing side.

So the little family moved into the south end of one of the old military barracks at Fort Pickering, which had been closed down at the conclusion of the war. The fort was constructed among several old Indian mounds on the bluff of the Mississippi, a short distance south of the Memphis waterfront. In fact, the Union army had disregarded any historical significance of the mounds, and simply hollowed out a number of the large man-made hills in order to protect their artillery guns and ammunition.

It was to this site that John Johnson returned the evening of August 1st, after secretly transporting William Warren from the quarantine area on President's Island to the Memphis waterfront. And on this night of August 15th, as he had the previous two nights since it was announced the city had its first homegrown case of yellow fever, John stood atop the bluff, looking over the river, and wondered for the hundredth time if his deed would be found out.

As far as he knew, only a skinny white woman had seen him deliver the sick man to the city. But maybe she had given his description to the police! Was it possible they were already looking for him? And then there was the terrible burden of the growing number of sick and dying people. His fault? His greed! And not a solitary thing he could do about it now.

There wasn't a member of the Memphis Department of Police who was clean shaven. Most sported a mustache and full beard. Patrolman Lucas McNair merely exhibited a well-groomed mustache—probably so the ladies' view of his dimples would not be blocked by a set of bushy whiskers. He wore a blue suit, festooned with a single line of brass buttons marching down the front of his coat. Only senior ranking officers wore jackets with a double row of buttons. Thankfully, in hot weather he was only required to fasten the very top button of his wool coat. He was proud of the yellow six-pointed star patch on his left breast pocket. His outfit was completed with a tin helmet covered in blue felt cloth, as well as a nightstick, hand restraints, Colt revolver, and whistle.

McNair was stationed at the southern end of the Memphis river landing, while his counterpart, Fitzsimmons Sweeney, manned the northern extreme of the docks, some two hundred yards south of where the Wolf River entered the Mississippi. Their assignment was to intercept any person or craft from landing at the half-mile long Memphis waterfront between the hours of 7 PM and 7 AM.

While all agreed this activity was necessary to protect the citizens of Memphis from any river traveler who might be infected by the fever, both McNair and Sweeney would describe their duty assignment as mind-numbingly boring. They spent the entire night peering into the fog and gloom which swirled over the river's surface. And all night long, nothing happened —nothing save the merciless onslaught of mosquitoes. Despite the stifling August heat, after the first night, both officers built fires in barrels, with a goodly bit of creosote added to improve the smoke's ability to repel the damned insects. Their success in this particular battle was limited.

After the embarrassment of learning of the night-time arrival in his city of yellow fever patient William Warren, the chief of police was making sure his orders were understood. Along with all forty-one members of the Memphis Department of Police, Officers McNair and Sweeney had heard the chief loud and clear when he proclaimed no one else would slip into the city past his patrolmen. But night duty guarding the Memphis waterfront was hardly what McNair had envisioned when he became a police officer and promised to protect and serve. So after ten days of this duty, he felt it was not unreasonable when he asked his sergeant to rotate that assignment among his fellow officers. His request was met with a snarled, "Just be glad you've got yerself a job, McNair."

Nicholas Helms had run away from home at the ripe old age of fourteen to join the Confederate Army. They took him—reluctantly—and made him a drummer boy. Before the end of the war, quite a number of Southern boys his own age would be expected to hold a rifle instead of drumsticks. But on the fifth of April, 1862, Nicholas had found himself on a long march with 40,000 men under the command of General Albert Sidney Johnston, trying to surprise the Yankees, who were led by General Ulysses S. Grant, at a forlorn spot along the Tennessee River. Early the next morning, surprise them they did, but that initial success unfortunately turned out to be only temporary.

In the bloodiest battle to that point in the war, the Rebels were finally forced to withdraw from the field the evening of April 7th and made a successful retreat to north Mississippi. Scattered across the woods, fields, and orchards of the Shiloh battlefield were 22,000 Union and Confederate casualties, plus the missing three toes separated from Helms' left foot by a Yankee musket ball.

His days of beating a drum on the battlefield were over, so he made his way back home to his family in the little settlement of Germantown, Tennessee. But the prodigal son was not entirely well received at home. With eight other children in the house, there were just too many mouths to feed—particularly when his father noted Nicholas' foot injury now made his contribution to the family farm somewhat unlikely.

"After all," as his father pointed out to his mother, "if the boy figgers on decidin' he's all grown up and runs off to be a soldier—well, he'll need to pay his own way from now on."

Fortunately, because so many men had joined the Rebel cause, there were jobs to be had in the nearby city of Memphis. Although Nicholas was absent the use of his toes, he had fully retained his ability to talk like a Philadelphia lawyer, albeit with a Southern drawl. So he was able to convince the editor of the *Memphis Daily Appeal* that, as a wounded combatant for the South, he deserved at least some consideration for the position of apprentice typesetter for the newspaper. Thus began his work life.

Helms was still using a cane in June of 1862, when a group of Union gunboats and rams arrived on the river directly above the Memphis waterfront. A small number of Confederate boats appeared around the big bend in the river south of the city to face them, but were outnumbered, severely outgunned, and flimsily armored compared to the enemy. The Battle of Memphis was a complete rout. From that point until the end of the war, Memphis was a Union-occupied city.

The editor of the *Appeal* recognized the implications of the arrival of Union troops in his town, and within the hour, he and his printing press, as well as four able-bodied employees and a boy with half a foot, caught the south-bound train to Grenada, Mississippi, where they set up temporary printing operations. The Yankees would have liked nothing better than to put him out of business permanently. By the time the war had ended, the printing press, along with Nicholas Helms, had relocated to six cities across the South, each time fleeing just ahead of the Union's forces.

It was said that General William Tecumseh Sherman himself hated the *Appeal* for its ability to rally Southerners to the cause—no matter how hopeless that cause might be. Sherman called it "that damn Rebel rag," finally catching up to the paper in the spring of 1865 and destroying all of its type. The press, however, was saved, and the *Memphis Daily Appeal* would eventually return to operations in Memphis in November of 1865, half a year after the conflict was brought to a conclusion.

On the morning of August 15th, thirteen years after the horrors of the war, the thirty-year-old Helms, sporting enough wavy brown hair on his head to adequately supply any three lads in the town, a poor excuse for a mustache, and a still noticeable limp, went in to see his editor, J.M. Keating. The newsman had left Ireland after the Irish Rebellion failed in 1848, and found his way to newspapering not long after he arrived in the United States. He was just entering the forty-eighth year of life. He didn't realize it yet, but the coming three months would prove to define him.

Keating's slicked-back hair and neatly trimmed mustache and beard were well on their way to turning silver. This was contrasted by very black thick eyebrows, which hung over his face, continuously imparting a look of seriousness to the observer, no matter what Keating's mood might be. One only had to read a few samples of his writing to determine the editor was truly brilliant.

"Mister Keating, I set the type on the piece this morning about the fever and how everybody was leavin' town. I just wanted to remind you that I had the fever myself five years ago, so I got good reason to believe I won't be infected again. Unless my wife goes down with it, you can count on me to be at my post every day, no matter what."

"Thank you, Helms. I understand you've always been a dependable employee, so I appreciate you telling me this. I'm afraid some of our folks, particularly those who came down here from the northern states, don't have any experience with the fever. Neither do I, for that matter. Maybe it won't be as bad this time as it was in '73. There's forty-two of us here at the *Appeal*, and I'd surely hate to lose anybody."

"The mood is awful dark on the streets."

"Helms, I think most people feel as though a curse has been put on the city. First they deal with the war, then the Memphis Massacre, Reconstruction, two bouts of yellow fever, cholera, and then smallpox. Folks have to wonder when it's all going to end. I see them walking around in a stupor—as though they're resigned to a terrible fate about to befall them. It's like they've lost all hope. The first two questions people ask in the morning is 'who lives?' and 'who died?'"

"My brother-in-law works at the post office. He says they're fumigating all the mail leaving Memphis. He says he uses a paddle, studded with nails. He dips it into a sulfur solution, then bats every letter and package with it. Sticks a half a dozen holes in everything."

"I hear most cities won't take our mail, no matter what precautions we take."

Nicholas tried to lighten the mood. "Did you hear the story about Brownsville?"

"I don't think so."

"Well, you know they put up a quarantine against Memphis the same day we published the story of our second case of the fever."

"I'd heard that. I suppose most towns have by now."

"Yes, sir, but the folks in Brownsville got a shipment on the rail line of several barrels of carbolic acid and a barrel of gin comin' from Memphis. Those geniuses decided they had to disinfect the carbolic acid and gin before they'd bring it into their town." Helms would swear later to the boys in the newsroom that he actually saw Keating smile.

Chapter 7
It Could Mean Your Life

August 16, 1878—"From and after this date, the banks of Memphis will open their doors at eleven AM and close at two PM. Customers are urged to exercise great prudence in all things, and especially to avoid exposure to the night air."

"From Grenada, Mississippi—Sixteen nurses and two doctors arrived in Grenada from New Orleans. So far, there is no organization among our citizens. All are panic-stricken. The mayor is dying. The sheriff and all the city officers, except the town marshal, have left. The jail is thrown open and the prisoners gone. New cases are developing all the time. Disinfectants are being used freely. All the stores are closed, except drugstores, undertaker parlors, and one or two saloons. Help us to pay nurses and bury our dead. The town is a graveyard."

"From Helena, Arkansas—Our city is quarantined and picketed. No person allowed ingress."

"From Little Rock—Our citizens are greatly excited. All adjacent towns are quarantined against Memphis."

"The Memphis Western Union office requests all parties expecting messages to call for them today. The messengers all having left the service of the company in the last two days, no delivery can be promised." Memphis Daily Appeal

August 16, 1878—Letter from Father Maternus Mallmann—"The yellow fever is causing dreadful havoc. Yesterday I prepared nine. There is hardly a tear-less face to be seen. I am not well, but feel a superhuman strength. Who knows how many of us will still be alive in a week."

In April of 1878, President Rutherford Hayes had signed the Quarantine Act, which gave the Marine Hospital Service authority to take all necessary actions to prevent infectious diseases from coming ashore at the nation's ports. Prior to this time, quarantine activities were assumed by local and state governments, and were not standardized in any way. With the passage of the Quarantine Act, this changed.

However, the nationalization of quarantine rules and regulations only applied to international shipping destinations. Quarantine activities in the nation's interior continued to be under the control and authority of local governments. The variations in quarantine found from one town to the next was often scientifically unexplainable. This was the case in all of the municipalities involved in the yellow fever outbreak of 1878, except for the Port of New Orleans, which was regulated under the newly assigned control of the Marine Hospital Service.

Memphis

When Dr. Josefson opened the door to his clinic at eight AM, he was appalled to see the line of over sixty people waiting to see him. His only nurse was his sister, Sarah, and although she was well organized, he feared the two of them would be unable to deal with so many patients.

The onslaught was due to the stories and rumors circulating in the city about the spread of yellow fever. Fortunately, a majority of the morning's patients had no symptoms that would indicate the presence of the fever, and he was able to deal with most of them in short order. But eight people, including a mother and her three children, were suspect for the disease. Once identified, Sarah hurriedly separated them from the remaining patients. As soon as this was accomplished, the potentially ill ones were given more than ample room by everyone else.

By noon, Dr. Josefson had sent those eight patients to the Quarantine Hospital and dealt with everyone else who had been in line when he opened his door. But they had been replaced by almost sixty others—all clamoring to see him. Among this crowd, he noticed Fannie Lester sitting off by herself. While she did continue to exhibit questionable signs of yellow fever, he was relieved in his belief that her symptoms, if that of the fever, were mild enough to be recoverable. In fact, at this point he had begun to doubt that she even had the fever, but decided to err on the side of caution.

"Fannie, I want you to take a powder paper of quinine twice a day. Be sure you drink six or eight glasses of water to flush your kidneys. There are still plenty of medical nitwits who prescribe calomel, but don't you take that, whatever you do."

"Why is that, Doctor?"

"Doctors have been using calomel for several hundred years, but actually, it's more of a poison than a medicine. Now I want you to go home and fumigate your whole house, and wash your clothes and bedding in water as hot as you can make it." He looked at the girl, recognizing how frail she was. His next question, while somewhat necessary in his medical interview, also served a personal curiosity. "Do you have anyone living with you?"

"No, Doctor."

He nodded, laboring to conceal his smile. "Do you feel well enough to be by yourself?"

"As long as I don't get any worse, I'll be all right."

"The quinine might make you a bit dizzy, and some people say it causes ringing in their ears. So don't be alarmed if that happens."

She stood to leave. Despite her sallow appearance, he was struck once again with her natural beauty, not to mention her figure. It took him a few minutes to collect himself and refocus on his remaining patients.

Albert Arnold sat at the window of the telegraph office on Madison Street in downtown Memphis, attempting multiple tasks at once. Normally the telegraph operator, his usual responsibilities were to send and receive messages to and from the city of Memphis.

Sitting close by was the cashier, Garry Rose, a black-haired rake for whom the ladies had a definite preference. Rose usually distributed telegrams to delivery boys and collected funds from anyone sending outbound messages. But since all the delivery boys had skipped out, Rose spent a majority of his time distributing telegrams directly to people calling at the window. And since the article in yesterday's paper had been published, there seemed to be a continual line of customers outside, asking after their telegrams.

Albert truly disliked interacting with people. His personal reminder of the Civil War—in particular the Battle of Parker's Crossroads, when his artillery crew had been hit by Yankee grapeshot—was the stub of his left arm, which hung lifeless in the empty shirt sleeve at his side. As a one-armed telegrapher, his vocation was difficult enough as it was, but when you compounded that with the stares which went along with it—well, that was downright unpleasant. Even worse were the questions from men who hadn't been in the war, and only wanted to taste it vicariously through him. The relative privacy of being a telegraph operator fit him to a fare-thee-well, but having to deal with the public—not so much.

Of the twenty-five employees who had worked the previous week, the staff now consisted solely of Albert, Rose, and their night-time counterparts, Jeffrey Dyer and George Putnam. The telegraph office was near the river, and the full force of river bottom humidity, the hungry mosquitoes attacking without respite through the open window, and the added workload, all made their jobs almost intolerable.

John Johnson looked up from his supper of beans, hamhock, and cornbread. "They say our people have some kind of resistance to the yellow fever—but you wouldn't know it around Fort Pickering."

Marissa tried not to look at her husband. "I know what you're thinkin'—that we'd be better off up in the country, 'stead of here in the city, right in the middle of this here epidemic."

"That's water under the bridge, Marissa. Cain't do nothin' about that now. Just be sure you keep a fire goin' in the stove all day."

"But it's so hot we can't hardly stand it."

"They say smoke keeps away the pestilence. Besides that, you got to hunker down and stay away from anybody thet's sick."

"That might work for me, but what we gonna do about the girls? All they want to do is play with their friends."

"You gonna have to be hard on 'em, Marissa. Last count I heard was four families right close by with the fever. Leisha and Ruthie will catch it sure if they keep goin' outside, mixin' with everbody."

"What about you? Runnin' them nets ever' day on the river, then sellin' what you catch in town."

"I done had the fever before. It's likely I won't catch it again—at least thet's what they say."

"How much money we got?"

He didn't like telling his wife, as she usually already had a place in mind to spend it. "Right at forty-five dollars."

"Why don't you stay away from all those people in town for a few weeks, see if this fever don't run its course? We got enough money to see us a while. You might not get the fever yourself, but you could bring it back here to the rest of us. I ain't never had it, and we know the girls haven't."

John lit his pipe and pondered this for a few minutes, puffing extra hard to try and calm the situation. "We still got to eat. Mebbe what I catch on the river will just be for us. And we got what's left of the garden—tomatoes, taters, maybe a few squash, an' them damn turnips o' yours."

Jack Shannon looked across the alley toward where the Royster boys lay. Never in his life had he experienced such a hangover. They had been drinking for the past three days, making sure, of course, to supplement their usual rum with a daily dose of sulfur and whiskey, as prescribed by that low-down coward, Johnnie Rourke. But Shannon had considerable experience in long spells of drinking and was sure he had never felt so bad.

He started to rise from where he lay in the alley between Main and Second Streets, but his head was throbbing as though he had taken a beating. He finally called out to the Roysters. "Hey, there, Ollie—and you, Levi, wouldst one o' youse fetch me a drink?" No answer from the east side of the alley. He decided to get their attention a bit more forcefully, and tossed half a brick-bat at Ollie, striking him square in the backside. "Hey, Ollie." Again no response.

Shannon was entirely too dizzy to stand up, so he crawled across the alley and gave both of his drinking buddies an un-gentle shake. "Hey, you Roysters!" Even Shannon was repelled by the stink given off by the two brothers, and he back-pedaled to his side of the alley. By then his head was about to spin off his shoulders, and he lay down, cradling his cranium as best he could on his arm.

August 17, 1878—Letter from Father Maternus Mallmann—"All are dying. Luckily the city is almost entirely empty. Entire streets, entire sections are almost abandoned. I am well. The others are pretty well. I do not fear for my own person, but probably we shall not escape entirely."

August 17, 1878—"Three persons were reported dead who had brought yellow fever upon themselves by indulging in drunkenness. After a drink, the stomach and entire system is out of order, which places the unfortunate inebriate in a too favorable condition to take the fever. Above all, acts of imprudence and drunkenness should be avoided." Memphis Avalanche

August 17, 1878—Letter from Dr. William Armstrong (who chose to stay in the city in 1873 as well as in 1878) *to his wife, who had fled to Columbia, Tennessee, some 200 miles to the east, along with their eight children—"You cannot conceive of the desolation in our good city. I do not suppose that one fifth of the white population are left in the corporation. On our street, counting even as far out as Mrs. Cochran's, there is no one left, until you would reach the poor families near Finnie's, except Mrs. Lithian's family and myself. Poor Mrs. Nelson stood watch over me, according to her promise to you, for one day, but she left last night, perfectly demoralized."*

Dr. Armstrong had graduated medical school from the University of Nashville in 1862, promptly joined the Confederate Army as a surgeon, and was widely recognized as a superb officer and physician. In the late days of the war, he'd married his sweetheart, and they moved to Memphis after the peace was signed. Well respected, he was an elder in the Presbyterian church in the city.

He was described as tall and rather slender, with a fine head of dark hair, although some would point out that it was becoming a bit sparse in front. He had a full, heavy beard and mustache, was black of eye, and possessed a well-shaped brow. In fact, he was generally regarded as so remarkably handsome as to attract attention in any crowd of gentlemen.

Chapter 8
There Ain't No Precedent For This

Memphis

At least a half-dozen fires were visible through the windows of the police station—all comprised of piles of bedding and clothing belonging to yellow fever victims which were burning in the streets—but Patrolman Lucas McNair's attention was otherwise occupied. He cut his eyes to the side, looking for a reaction from his fellow officers. What would be their response to Police Chief P.R. Athey's announcement? Unless he was badly mistaken in interpreting their body language, most of them were having a difficult time controlling themselves. Apparently Athey had made this decision because Patrolman James McConnell had died, eight others were sick with the fever—including McNair's partner, Sweeney—and five officers had skipped town. But could the chief really follow through with his outlandish idea to put coloreds in police uniforms and put them out on the streets of Memphis?

The patrolman immediately on his right spoke in a whisper. "Who the hell does he think he is? There ain't no damned precedent fer this!"

Indeed, thought McNair, there was no precedent anywhere in the South as far as he knew. Did Athey really believe those people would maintain law and order? More important, what self-respecting white man would allow himself to be arrested by a colored? And then what might happen next?

As far as McNair was concerned, he was not prejudiced. He treated every man he arrested exactly the same, more or less. But working beside a colored just as though he was an equal? He didn't see how that could possibly work. However, this was no time to pitch a fit. He had a family. He had to keep his job, no matter what.

August 20, 1878—"Your correspondent has just returned from Grenada, where the fever is striking down daily about the same number it consigns to the grave. The situation there is too appalling to be described, and the worst is, not a single case has recovered or promises a recovery. The doctors disagree as to treatment, but under different treatment regimens, the result appears the same. The grave swallows up all alike." New Orleans Picayune

Annie Cook had made up her mind—and once her mind was made up, nobody had better stand in her way. So at three o'clock in the afternoon, when she could be sure they were all at least sort of awake for the day, she hollered in the direction of the staircase in the Mansion House. "Y'all girls get on down here. We got to have ourselves a meeting, and you likely ain't gonna care for it." She stuck her head in the kitchen. "That means you too, Beulah and Princess. Get on in here."

Some of the more tawdry brothels in town required their girls to pay room rent in thirty-minute intervals, and it wasn't unusual for a girl to conduct business in four or five different rooms in the course of an evening. But the Mansion House was a cut above, and each of the whores had her own private bedroom.

The six fallen doves came down the stairs in various states of dress and composure, most wearing camisoles and bloomers, their hair-dos resembling a sextuplet of squirrel nests, with most of them still in the early stages of waking up. The Negro cook and maid accompanied the whores, wondering what in the world was up with the madam. It took them a few minutes to get settled, but Annie was not the most patient woman in the world, and besides, she had to run them off.

She eyed them all before beginning. Two of the girls had managed to retain their looks and their deportment, for the most part, but the rest were showing the results of too much alcohol and too much exposure to an unforgiving lifestyle. Just the same, she was going to miss them all, even the Empress. Oh, well, she thought, might as well get to it.

"We got ourselves a situation here that can't continue. They've put a curfew on the town every night. Almost everybody with two nickels to rub together has already lit out. What's left are the folks with either no money to spend or them with a parson's attitude. Instead o' y'all havin' four or five customers apiece per night, you're lucky to have one. I'm not makin' enough money to keep y'all fed. For a bunch of women, you eat like a herd of Percheron horses.

"Besides that, most of y'all haven't had the fever. And the way people are dying in this town, some of you are bound to be included before long." She paused, cocking her head to the side. "Y'all hear them funeral bells, don't you? It seems like they don't hardly stop ringin' all day long and half the night. Much as it pains me to say it, I want all you girls to leave town. Go someplace safe. When this all blows over, you're welcome to come back here and get your jobs back."

"Where we gonna go, Miss Cook? I doubt all those church people would embrace us in one of the camps outside the city. Particularly if some of the married men want to take up with us where they left off here at the Mansion House."

"You're probably right about that, Lilly. You may have to get farther away—maybe up to St. Louis or Louisville."

"The last time I was on a riverboat, it was insultin'."

"Now what, Jasmine?"

"There was a big sign at the top o' the gangway that read '*All gamblers and fancy women must sign up with the captain before the boat leaves for New Orleans.*' The boat was full o' women dressed ever' bit as fancy as me, but somehow I was the only one who had to go before the captain."

Annie snorted. "The steamboats aren't stoppin' here anyways. Get on a train, or rent yourself a hack and driver."

"That costs money, Miss Cook."

"Well, I ain't payin' your postage, Rosalee. Besides, you got more money than Croesus, and don't think I don't know it." She stared at the girl for a few seconds, remembering her disgusting personal hygiene habits, before continuing. "Can't make no money anyhow. So I've decided to turn this place into a hospital. I already talked to the Howards about it. They're gonna start puttin' patients in here tomorrow."

A hush fell over the room as each one of the women contemplated just exactly where she might go. Finally there was a quiet voice from a tiny, white-haired woman with surprisingly unwrinkled mahogany skin. It was the cook. "What you gonna do and where you gonna go, Miss Annie?"

"I suppose I'm gonna stay right here, Beulah. Somebody's got to look after all this." She spread her arms expansively, indicating all the expensive furnishings surrounding them in the parlor.

"With all them sick folks comin' in here, you gonna need a cook, ma'am."

"Beulah, I want you to get outa here and be safe, too."

"I got nobody to worry 'bout me no more, Miss Annie. I believe I'll just stay here with you."

The offer caught Annie off guard, and she had to dab at her eye before composing herself. "Thank you, Beulah." She turned again to the girls. "Well, what y'all waitin' on? You got to be out of here by morning. You best take all those fancy clothes with you. The Howards want nothin' but bare walls and beds in your rooms. They'll be sterilizin' the room every time a patient leaves here. In fact, seein' what goes on up there," she nodded toward the stairwell, "they might want to sterilize 'em right now!"

August 22, 1878—"We the undersigned, colored citizens of Memphis, desire that a mass meeting should be held at the Greenlaw Opera House at 3 PM today, for the purpose of considering the situation, and be advised as to our duty in this hour of danger and sorrow. We call upon all colored men who have the welfare of the city at heart, to cooperate with us in maintaining order and rendering aid to the sick and destitute."

"The Board of Health should compel the evacuation of every house on Poplar Street, on both sides, from Fourth to the stone yard and the grocery on the east side of the bridge. It is a pestilent breeding neighborhood that should at once be cleaned out."

"The yellow fever has claimed 50 fresh victims in Vicksburg and killed 22, and at New Orleans developed 107 new cases with 40 deaths, while in Memphis there have been 50 new cases and 12 deaths yesterday. The cause of this increase was the fact that we had damp and heavy weather, with rain on Tuesday night—a condition of atmosphere said to be favorable to the disease. Exposure to the night air, sleeping in rooms poorly ventilated and not thoroughly disinfected, sleeping in an area of the city where the very air, and especially at night, is laden with the poison of malarias, are causes to which may be attributed much of the increase. The report should be a warning to people, and should induce every person not sick to leave the infected districts and seek the camps outside the city for safety, where you will find pure air, pure water, and pure soil."

"A gentleman who had wandered from the city to the country every evening for the past week writes: 'It is preferable to occupy a comfortable room and have the yellow fever in Memphis, than to sleep with ten in a room and three in a bed out in the country, and where the water-dipper is always disinfected and looked upon with suspicion after you handle and use it.' He will go to the country no more." Memphis Daily Appeal

"Picture yourself at home, living in luxury and good health, enjoying every comfort and receiving the caresses of your children; then, on the contrary, find yourself away from the busy walks of life, living in an old barn or corn crib, almost away from civilization, with starvation staring you and your family in the face, and lying on the floor, without bed or cover, and in constant dread of the disease reaching you; to see whole families down sick at one time, and in one room, with no relative or friend to even pass them a glass of water to quench the thirst caused by the burning fever. Then you will have a partial insight to the effects of the scourge. This was not only with the poor, but with the rich whose wealth was not readily convertible to dollars, perhaps tied up in property or inventory. Living in huts, stables, outhouses, and barnyards, their riches were nothing to them. They were so overcome with fear that they dare not visit the city to even purchase the necessities of life. Rather starvation than take the chance of an introduction to the fever." Letter received by the officers of the Hebrew Hospital Association.

There was a large bell at the cottage in Elmwood Cemetery, and for every corpse which was brought there, the bell was rung six times by eight-year-old Lucinda Dawson, the loving, tow-headed daughter of one of Elmwood's long-time employees. Some would say later it seemed the funeral bell at the cemetery, as well as those at the few churches which remained open, almost never stopped.

On the late afternoon of August 21st, Lucinda spied a funeral wagon, accompanied by a man and two children in a carriage, all headed toward the cemetery. By the time the little procession had crossed the railroad tracks, Lucinda was at her post with the bell. What transpired next had to be one of the worst exhibitions of callous indifference Lucinda had ever witnessed during her short life. The two conveyances arrived at the gate at fifteen minutes after five, a full forty-five minutes before the cemetery would no longer accept caskets to be buried that day.

Six Negro gravediggers met the hearse at the gate, and noticing the little family of Mr. Ben Pullen, all removed their hats in a show of respect. As the hearse entered the cemetery, making its way to the family's plot, the gravediggers followed along behind, ready to prepare a grave for the deceased.

About that time, John Flynn, the white man temporarily in charge of the cemetery, hurried up to the spot where the grave was to be dug, and berated the gravediggers in an unkind manner, that they would not receive any overtime pay whatsoever for labor performed after six o'clock, in an attempt to prevent any further work for the day.

The Negroes were obviously repelled by his statement, particularly as it was said in front of the grieving family. One of them stepped forward, turned his back on the supervisor, and spoke directly to Mr. Pullen. "Sometimes, suh, we works for friendship." As Flynn stalked off, furious that he had been ignored, the men began to dig.

They had finished the hole, lowered the casket to its final resting place, and almost had it completely covered, when Flynn reappeared to make one last remark—again right in front of the grieving husband and his two children. "You've worked after six o'clock, and you will receive no pay for it.

Hereafter no work shall be done after that hour, no matter how many damned carcasses are brought here."

Mr. Pullen was stricken that his son and daughter had to hear such an insult about their dear mother, but kept his tongue and retired to his home. The next morning he filed a complaint with the Howard Association, and reported the event to the editor of the *Daily Appeal*. "*You know, Mr. Keating, it pains me to say this about my own people, but the coloreds could teach us all a lesson. They exhibit a generosity of spirit—which is often lacking among our own race. In fact, many whites seem to first count the cost of a matter before showing a willingness to do what is right.*"

The Howards and the newspaper fulfilled their obligations. Within two days, the man who had insulted Pullen's family at the cemetery was discharged, and he left the city in disgrace—perhaps lucky not to depart straddling a rail and wearing a garment of tar and feathers.

August 23, 1878—"Chief Athey requests the pastors of colored churches to cease night services. General Wright and Mr. Turley of the Citizens Relief Committee appeared and consulted with the Board in regard to requesting compulsory depopulation. Action postponed. Resolved—that undertakers must bury all persons, reported to them as having died of any infectious or contagious diseases, within six hours after said report." Minutes of the Memphis Board of Health

John Johnson sat in the huge meeting room of the opera house, along with over two hundred other Negro men, listening to a white man, Reverend J.T.C. Collins of the Collins Chapel Church, whose members were almost exclusively black. The preacher talked about their responsibility to fellow members of their race, but also to people of all races, citing passages to support his plea. "From Paul's letter to the Philippians: '*Let each of you look not only to his own interests, but also to the interests of others.*' And from Jesus himself in the book of Matthew: '*For I was hungry and you gave me food, I was thirsty and you gave me drink, I was a stranger*

and you welcomed me, I was naked and you clothed me, I was sick and you visited me ...'"

But then Dr. Erskine of the Board of Health stood up and gave them a dose of reality. "I know many of you have come to believe that the Negro has a special resistance to yellow fever. Some say this resistance comes from many generations being exposed to the fever in Africa and the West Indies, and that you have inherited this resistance from your ancestors. This may be true; but then again, medical science has learned every yellow fever outbreak has its own special characteristics. So you may have safely avoided being infected in previous epidemics, but that does not necessarily mean you will have the same safe outcome this time."

He waved a copy of the daily newspaper in his hand. "You can look at this morning's copy of the *Appeal* and read the dispatch from Grenada, Mississippi to get an idea about what you might be facing this time." He began to read, "'*The fact that the colored people are dropping down in Grenada like sheep, should warn the Negroes of Memphis that they have no immunity from this terrible disease, and should put their houses in order. A number of colored people of all shades have been taken down with the fever.*' And so, I believe each and every one of you should leave this city as soon as possible, and move your family to safety in one of the camps."

Then Bishop Henry Brown of the First Beale Street Baptist Church (the sanctuary of which was only about half completed in 1878) pulled himself to his feet and tottered to the podium with his cane. He was a small man, shrunken with age and bent with rheumatism, but spoke with a booming voice that filled the hall. "You men represent the only hope for our city. Without your service, this city will degenerate into a hell on earth. I know that all of you are scared—scared of this terrible fever. Well, brothers, so am I!

"But this is our once in a lifetime opportunity to show this city—indeed, to show the entire country, that we black men are worthy of being called men, of being called equal, of once and for all finally discarding the shackles of inequality, racism, and yes, even slavery itself."

August 24, 1878—"Colored Persons' Meeting: The Board of Health Director tried to convince the colored people that they

should leave the city and seek refuge in the camps. Their response: Resolved: That we offer our services to protect the property of all, and the lives of those remaining in the city, with the assurance that we will not shrink from any danger that may be incurred. We earnestly recommend that the Citizens Relief Association furnish citizens who are not able to leave to a place of safety, with comfortable shelter and wholesome subsistence. Resolved: That we have unqualified confidence in Chief of Police Athey, who merits our gratitude for his recognition of our race, for selecting among the colored people an equal number of policemen. Resolved: That we will render him every assistance in our power to guard and protect the property left to the care of city authorities."

August 24, 1878—"The Howard Association asks and enjoins all citizens as a special and personal duty, to report to us all nurses who fail of their duty in the least particular, or who give any evidence of being addicted to drunkenness, neglect, or any other failing that would interfere with the proper performance of a duty to which the members of our Association have pledged their lives." Memphis Daily Appeal

John Johnson had not dared to tell his wife, Marissa, about his involvement in bringing the first yellow fever victim to the city, nor did he intend to. He was too ashamed of himself for that. So he was having a hard time convincing her that he should join with other members of his race in helping to keep the city safe, now that a majority of the whites had left town. "You should have heard the bishop the other night. He had the whole opera house standing. The place was filled to the rafters with the sounds of stamping feet and huzzahs. Not a single soul shrank from his call."

"Now let me get this straight—you want to run out and help those same white people who don't want you in their businesses, who look down their skinny noses at you, who call you all kinds of disgusting names, who wouldn't give you a job in one of their stores if their life depended on it?"

"Don't you see—this is our chance to show them we Negroes belong here as much as they do?"

"And aren't you the one who said we needed to keep the girls inside, have a fire all day long, hunker down and keep to ourselves—stay away from our neighbors—so's we don't catch the fever?"

"Look, Marissa, I got no intention of bein' a nurse, or drivin' a hearse, or diggin' graves. I ain't gonna come in contact with the sick ones."

"Just what you think you gonna do, then? Fish?"

"No, no." Johnson shrugged. He knew what was coming, but might as well tell her. "I'm gonna be a policeman."

He thought for a moment her eyeballs were going to explode. "You mean you gonna join up with them men what drag our people on the street and beat hell outa us with them nightsticks?"

"Chief Athey says he wants as many colored men on the force as they is whites. This is our chance, I tell you."

She looked at him hard. "If you gonna be out in the town, dressed up in one o' those uniforms, don't you be bringin' that fever back to this house, you hear? I ain't never gonna speak to you again if one of our girls suffers from it."

"They puttin' together camps outside the city for people to go so's they can stay away from the fever. Camp Joe Williams is south at the Webb place, Duffy is up at Raleigh Station, Wright is on the Cuba Road, mebbe more before long. Might be you and the girls need to go out there."

"Any o' them camps for us coloreds?"

"I don't know, Marissa. That's sure 'nough a deservin' question. But I'll be findin' out tonight."

Grenada

Emilie Christophe used cool water and whiskey to bathe the face, neck, and shoulders of Miz Lou, mother of Delia, Dinah, and David, and loving wife of James McLean. Originally assigned to the household to care only for the mother, within a day of Emilie's arrival the other four family members had become ill as well. In normal circumstances, the Howards would have assigned two nurses to a family of this size, with one working days and the other on night duty. But circumstances were not normal.

All of Grenada seemed to be an infirmary. Not only were almost all the white residents either sick or already dead, but a significant number of Negroes were ill, as well. To complicate matters, many of the Howard physicians and nurses had fallen victim themselves. And so Emilie, and several others like her, had to do more than what most would say was humanly possible.

The mother, with her two young black-haired daughters, were in a single room, and the father was just down the hall with their six-year-old son David. All of them had been very ill, and no more than twenty-four hours earlier, a Howard doctor had warned Emilie that none of the family would live to see another day. But the McLeans had themselves a stubborn nurse.

She now had hopes that both parents, as well as ten-year-old Delia, had a chance of surviving. But David and his three-year-old sister Dinah were so dehydrated and so weak that none of her heroic efforts were making any difference for either of them. In fact, Emilie was already seeing the beginnings of jaundice, no urinary output, and the return of high fever in both of them.

The windows remained covered with drapes because the light was painful to her patients. If not for the early morning delivery of food and ice from the local Citizens Relief Committee, and her self-rationed single cup of coffee at daylight, it would have been difficult for Emilie to tell whether it was day or night. But on what she figured was the sixth night of her assignment, David and Dinah had no kidney activity whatsoever, and then began the black vomit. Their fevers peaked to over 105 degrees, they were completely out of their heads, and by five o'clock in the morning they were gone.

It was a shock to Emilie when she picked up their lifeless bodies. They were light as a feather pillow. Perhaps because of their dehydration, the thought struck Emilie that neither child was much more than dry husks. It was her goal to get the corpses out of the two sick rooms without alerting her other patients, as she knew how the shock of a death could send another family member spiraling downward themselves. But she was not successful. Miz Lou saw the whole thing—saw her completely still babies being carried away. And she began to cry in deep, wrenching sobs, her whole body shaking with the pain of it all.

Delia, awakened by the weeping, quickly realized what had happened, crawled to her mother's bed, and pulled the covers over both of them. Although Emilie attempted to comfort them, tried to offer them something to drink, they resisted her every effort, and the sobbing continued for well over a half-hour.

Finally they were quiet. Emilie decided to let them rest for a while, and seated herself in an uncomfortable rocking chair beside the bed. She had been awake all night long and much of the previous night. She decided to close her eyes—for no more than fifteen minutes. Then she would make them drink fluids—maybe try some beef tea.

The knock at the front door startled her awake, and through the haze of her sleep-addled state, it dawned on her that their food delivery had arrived. She rose stiffly from the cramped chair, realizing she needed to pass a message to the Citizens Relief Committee that the children's bodies had to be picked up for burial. She hurried to the door to make her request.

When she came back to the sick room, Emilie hesitated, not wanting to wake her patients, but also knowing she needed to keep them hydrated. "Miz Lou—Miz Lou—wake up, now." She gently pulled the cover back from mother and daughter, and despite numerous face-to-face encounters of a similar nature over the past month, her knees buckled when she saw their gray skin color and fixed expressions.

The sight struck her so hard, Emilie fell to her knees and wept. How had she let this happen? If only she hadn't allowed herself to fall asleep! She was prostrate with her guilt. Both Miz Lou and Delia had been getting better. How could she have ignored the danger involved when they found both Dinah and David were gone? Emilie remained in this mode of self-recrimination for some minutes before realizing she had a responsibility to tell the husband.

McLean was a robust fellow under normal circumstances, but after doing battle with yellow fever for the last eight days, robust was hardly a valid description. He had lost at least twenty pounds, his eyes were bloodshot, his lips cracked and raw, and he was a mental wreck, having constantly worried about the survival of his wife and children.

He spoke up before she could begin. "Where is my son?"

Emilie hoped she could retain control of her emotions when she answered. "Mr. McLean, I have terrible news for you."

His eyes searched from one side of the room to the other, and his voice ratcheted up an octave. "Where's my son?"

"David passed away early this morning."

With significant effort, he pushed himself to a sitting position. "Where is he?"

Emilie held her hands out in protest. "Don't get up, Mr. McLean. There's more."

He looked at his nurse, his body's posture collapsing right in front of her. "Tell me."

She tried to hold his gaze. It was almost impossible not to look away. "David and Dinah went first, then just a little while ago..."

"What? What are you telling me?"

"Delia and Miz Lou—they both passed just a few minutes ago."

"All of them? Every one of them? Except me?"

"Yes, sir. They're all gone."

He tried to rise, but what little strength he possessed was crumbling before her eyes. "Where are they?"

"David and Dinah are downstairs. Miz Lou and Delia are in the room right next door."

"But—that's my whole family!"

Emilie stepped over to his bedside. "Can I help you walk in to see them?"

McLean went to his knees at Lou's bedside. He wrapped his arms around both his daughter and his wife. "I can't live without my wife and family." His shoulders began to shake as the sobs took his breath away. "I have to be with my family." Finally he looked back at Emilie. "Can I be alone with them?"

"Of course, Mr. McLean. I'll be downstairs." As she closed the door behind her, the air was rent with the most hideously pitiful scream she had ever heard in her life. She started to go back in the room to sit with him, but made her decision on the side of his privacy and went downstairs.

The undertaker's wagon arrived a few minutes afterwards. "The Committee say you got two dead chillun for us."

"The news is far worse than that. There are two more upstairs you'll need to take. The father just found out he's lost his entire family. Can you give him a few minutes with them before you go up there?"

Before her request was answered, a gunshot rang out from upstairs. They rushed up to the room, finding the three of them, all in the single bed, awash in McLean's blood. His old cap and ball revolver had done its job. He would not be separated from his family.

Memphis

Lester Sellers had a new employer. Working for Mr. Denie, he had previously earned a mere seventy-five cents a day, spreading lime around the city. But with the lime job finished, there was no cement business to be had in the city, and Denie temporarily closed down his operation. Thankfully for Lester, the call had gone out just the day before from undertaker John Walsh on Second Street, who had obtained the contract from the city to bury all paupers in Memphis and Shelby County. Due to the horrendous working conditions, Mr. Walsh offered the fantastic sum of two dollars per day, plus ten cents an hour for overtime, for drivers of the death wagons.

Unfortunately, Lester's former partner, Gunter the German, would not be able to take advantage of the higher wage. All his steps of fever prevention—the asafoetida, the garlic, and even the gin—had failed him.

During the early days of the epidemic, the procedure recommended by the Citizens Relief Committee was that once yellow fever was diagnosed in a house, the family was to place a square of yellow cardboard near the front door. If there was a death, then a black piece of cardboard was to be set beside the yellow piece, along with a note about the length of the casket needed.

Someone was to record the address and the size of the casket needed, then the wooden coffin would be delivered to the house, with the expectation that the family would place the body into the casket, along with a mixture of tar and carbolic acid, and then fasten the lid. At that point, Lester Sellers and his counterparts would stop by and pick up the corpse and the casket. At least, that was the plan. But it was quickly found to be unworkable.

Often the family could not manage their end of the bargain. Perhaps the father was ill or dead. Sometimes the whole family was in various stages of illness. Additionally, so many people were dying, and the demand for rapid burial was so great, that it was not irregular for Walsh to inter people who were not poor in the least. After all, he got paid for every casket delivered to the cemeteries.

Immediately after a death, the neighborhood would begin to clamor for instant removal of the body, but if someone was not present who could vouch that the victim had adequate means to pay for private interment, or that he or she already owned a burial plot in either Elmwood or Calvary Cemetery, or perhaps the B'nai Israel Cemetery on Hernando Avenue, then rapid removal took precedence, and the previously well-to-do person found themselves inside a plain pine box, relegated to a common burial trench in the potter's field of one of the cemeteries.

There was often an uproar from families after the fact, appealing to Mr. Walsh to dis-inter their loved one so they could be buried in a separate plot. But these pleas went unresolved, as no records were kept, either by Walsh or the different cemeteries, of where individuals were put in potter's field.

And so the original process fell by the wayside, in favor of Walsh's workers taking care of the corpse. Lester drove what had formerly been a large furniture wagon, pulled by a pair of stout mules, which was loaded up with empty coffins on Second Street. As his morning progressed along the city's streets, Lester would call, "Bring out your dead. Bring out your dead." To facilitate recognition of their duties, employees wore yellow armbands, and a crude sign was mounted on the funeral wagon: "Walsh Funerary Company—Caskets and Burials."

In many cases, the dead had already been laid out at the side of the street, and he and his new helper, Israel Jackson, simply filled one of the coffins with the deceased party. In other cases, someone would carry or drag a corpse to the street when they heard his call. But the worst times were when someone would simply shout out to them that there was a dead body in such and such a residence, and they would have to go and retrieve it themselves. It was for this occurrence that both Lester and Israel wore leather aprons—hopefully to prevent getting the most unspeakable of bodily fluids on their persons as they went about their tasks.

Their third day on the job found them on Jefferson Street in the elegant neighborhood known as Victorian Village. Lester made his usual appeal. But rather than a corpse, he was accosted by an Irish maid who stuck her head out of an imposing front door. "Say, you. Check next door at the Flack house." She pointed to the home on the east side. "We ain't seen sign o' them folks in several days. An' they's a powerful stink comin' from over there."

Lester tipped his hat to the woman and stopped his wagon in front of the residence next door. He knocked—repeatedly. The maid was certainly right about the odor. After his experiences of the previous days, he had no doubt that a body was inside. He knocked unsuccessfully again. He finally tried the door, and finding it unlocked, stuck his head inside. "Halloo in here." No sound issued from the house. "Halloo."

Lester had seen all sorts of terrible situations in just two days of employment with Walsh, but he wasn't prepared for what he found. Thousands of green flies were everywhere, all interested in the bodies of a man and woman, as well as five children. The woman appeared to have been dead the longest, as her belly had burst open, and maggots were having a feeding frenzy on her innards.

He called out to Israel that he needed help, and the two of them loaded six of the corpses in pine boxes. But they had no more coffins on their wagon, and Mr. Walsh had made it clear that he was only paid for burials when there was a separate casket for each body. "Israel, I really hate to do this, but we got to leave that littlest girl here in the house fer right now. We'll make a run to the graveyard, then fetch us some more coffins and come back fer her."

Israel looked around the large house. "You mean we gonna leave thet little baby here all by herself?"

"She won't know the difference, Israel. We'll be back in a couple hours."

"Reckon I oughter stay with her?" He looked over his shoulder. "Her ghost is likely to be awful scared in there by itself."

"I cain't handle all them coffins by my lonesome. We won't be gone long."

They made their delivery to the graveyard, the gravediggers accepted the load of ten coffins and their occupants, and the two returned to Second Street to pick up more caskets. Mr. Walsh was waiting on them. "You boys get on down to Union Street. You got a load waiting on you there."

Lester looked quickly at Israel, giving him a subtle shake of the head to make sure he wouldn't say anything. "Yes, suh, boss."

When they had gone no more than two blocks, Lester turned back to the north. "We'll drop by thet house an' pick up the baby. Walsh don't need to know nothin' about it."

What was supposed to take a few minutes turned into an unpleasant half hour. Not thinking anyone was in the house—alive, at least—Lester and Israel stepped through the front door, carrying a coffin. A woman of about twenty-five was there, crying uncontrollably and bent over the corpse of the little girl. She looked at the two men. "What have you done with the rest of my family?"

"Miss, we took the others to the graveyard. We came back for the little one there 'cause we run outa caskets."

"You mean all of them are dead?"

"Yes'm. Seven in all—including the little babe." Lester nodded toward the little girl.

She wrung her hands and Lester thought she was going to start crying again. "When are they going to be buried?"

Lester took off his hat. "Well, miss, I reckon they's already buried."

"Are they in the Flack family plot in Calvary?"

"No, miss. They warn't nobody to tell us about no plot. We took 'em to potter's field in Elmwood."

"Mister Flack was a cotton broker. Surely you would know not to take them to potter's field!"

"No, miss. 'Less they's somebody to tell us different, we take 'em all to potter's field."

"What will happen to little Bonnie here? Will she be buried with her family?"

"Miss, most everbody is put in a common grave out there."

"You mean she won't be buried beside her mother and father?"

"I reckon there ain't no way to tell, miss."

"Then Bonnie has to go to Calvary. At least she can be beside her grandparents."

August 24, 1878—Letter from Dr. William Armstrong to his wife—"I had to send to Mrs. Porter Monday to get something—no butcher stalls, no groceries, no food stalls open anywhere. We live on bacon and coffee and milk. Be of good cheer and God will provide for us both."

The chief of police had finally decided there was no point in stationing his officers on the waterfront at night. After all, the sickness was already in his city, and a man would have to be crazy to want to sneak into a fever town. So Patrolman McNair had gone back to patrolling near Court Square. Because of all the vacancies on the force, his area of responsibility was some three times larger than it had been before the epidemic, and there were several incidents which occurred that he just could not get to in time—burglaries, robberies, assaults, and public drunkenness mostly. So he understood why he needed help. But the chief's solution was hard to take.

He and his new partner, Patrolman John Johnson, were to cover the same area, but they were not to patrol together. Each of them carried a steel whistle, which they were to blow if they needed assistance. It was understood Patrolman Johnson could not arrest a white man by himself, so if he encountered a crime being committed by a white person, he was to blow his whistle so that his partner could show up and technically make the arrest. Likewise, if Patrolman McNair needed help in subduing someone, or multiple persons, he was to summon Johnson with his own whistle.

They had not said more than two words to one another since being introduced at the station. That didn't really bother either one of them, as neither had a habit of speaking to members of the other race unless it was necessary. But as their first shift came to an end, each of them had begun to wonder if he could truly count on his partner if one of them really needed help.

The third night of their partnership, McNair was patrolling near Third and Madison Street when he spied a white man on the other side of the street, climbing out of the side window of a house which he knew had been vacated by a family fleeing the fever. The man was carrying a bulging gunny sack. McNair and Johnson had already been briefed about several hoboes and ne'er-do-wells who had apparently come to the city to prey on the homes which had been left unattended by their owners.

McNair started across the street at about the same time a young girl came out of the house next door, apparently headed for the necessary in the back yard. When the suspected burglar saw McNair headed his way, he grabbed the girl, held her in front of him, and pulled a small pistol from his waistband. "Stay right where you are, lawman! Now, you just back off, and I'll let this here girl go when yer outa sight."

McNair was torn between standing his ground and trying to shoot the man, versus doing what he was told and disappearing down the street. Nobody had discussed this kind of situation before, and he couldn't see any good solution. So he took a few dozen steps down Third Street, and blew his whistle loud enough to be mistaken for a steamboat. Then he stepped behind a fence post and waited.

Daniel Davis had been happily burglarizing empty houses for the past two days. Up to this point, he had not encountered a police officer. But apparently his strategy to take a hostage was working like a charm. The copper had taken his bluff without a peep and walked away, so he and this girl were just going to take a little walk, and then he could disappear.

McNair could see the suspect from his position of concealment, but there still had been no sign of his so-called partner. He decided to try one more time and blow his whistle again, but as he lifted it to his lips, he detected a slight movement behind the burglar. Damned if it wasn't Johnson!

Realizing what his partner had in mind, McNair stepped back into the street, making sure the burglar saw him. Davis shouted at him. "I thought I told you to git!"

"I changed my mind. You need to lay down your gun and let that girl go."

"If you don't back off, I'm gonna have to shoot this girl."

The girl was no more than ten years old, and she cried out, "Please don't shoot me, mister. My mama needs me real bad."

McNair watched his partner approaching the burglar from the rear. "This is your last chance, my friend. Lay down that gun."

"The hell you say. I'm gonna..." Johnson was no more than five feet from the burglar when he pulled the trigger.

Davis screamed in pain and hit the ground. Immediately Johnson stepped forward, shoved his gun barrel in the man's face, and kicked his pistol away. "Don't move or I'll finish you off."

McNair was there in two seconds. He noticed the little girl was hugged tight to her savior's leg. "Did you kill him?"

"No. I just shot him where it would hurt."

"Where's that?"

"In the arse. I figgered it wouldn't be good for a white man to be killed by one of us new Negro police. So I did the next best thing."

McNair looked at the thief and kidnapper, writhing on the ground in pain. He couldn't help the grin that spread across his face. "You done good, real good—partner."

Chapter 9
Stacked Bodies

August 25, 1878—"We have reached the end of the second week of the fever, and find that for the third time in her history, Memphis is paying fearfully in loss of life for sanitary neglect. One hundred eight deaths out of four hundred twelve cases is an awful summary. How much trade we have lost besides, is impossible to enumerate, but it is safe to assert that half that sum would straighten and cover the death dealing bayou, and give us other sewers to carry off the filth that has been allowed to accumulate in that ditch of abominations. We urge the Citizens Relief Committee to finish the work of disinfecting the bayou."

(Ad) "Flaherty and Sullivan Undertakers—317 Second Street—Metallic and wooden burial caskets, Elegant robes, Gent's suits, Coffin trimmings, Special attention to embalming. COD."

"The Jews set the example for good work. They organized at first sign of the yellow fever, and proposed to send every poor Israelite out of the city, and to furnish him with sufficient means to support him for a reasonable time. In fact, they seemed to lose sight altogether of the money required or the labor entailed. They had only one objective—the relief of suffering humanity."

"From Bartlett, Tennessee (20 miles northeast of Memphis)*—Our little town did not enact the farce of quarantine, and is therefore full of Memphis refugees. We do not exclude any who desire to come, provided they do not bring bedding. We have hearts full of sympathy for your stricken city. The brigade of noble brave men and women, who are there day and night fighting the yellow fever, and helping the sick and*

destitute, display a moral courage and heroism worthy of any age of chivalry." Memphis Daily Appeal

In contrast, Collierville, Tennessee (25 miles southeast of Memphis) immediately set up a shotgun quarantine against Memphis. In fact, anyone who went to Memphis for business was not allowed back into Collierville without a permit. The streets in the little town were described as like a zebra—white with lime and black with carbolic acid. The whole municipality smelled to high heaven, but so far they were fever-free.

Memphis

Nicholas Helms tapped on his editor's door before entering.

"What's up, Helms?"

"Have you heard anything from your correspondents about the bodies piling up at the cemetery entrance, Mr. Keating?"

Nobody could say Keating didn't have a reporter's nose for a story. "Tell me what you know, Helms."

"My auntie told me about it yesterday, so this mornin' I rode my horse out to Elmwood before I came in to work, and the bell was already ringing. The undertaker's wagons are runnin' non-stop. Some of them carry up to eight or ten coffins at a time. They drive in the gate there on the north side, unload their freight, and the gravediggers say the stack keeps gettin' higher and higher every day. It looks like there's a good two days' collection in there this morning. A body or two don't even have a casket. They're just wrapped in a blanket. And with the wind outa the south, I could smell the place at least a half mile before I got there."

"What do the families have to say about it?"

"That's the strangest thing. There's no mourners out there. Probably the families don't even know their loved ones are still above ground. The only people out and about on the streets are the doctors, ambulance drivers, funeral wagons, and o' course the nuns and the reverends. Everybody else is either sick or too scared to go outside. The only time regular folks are out is around noontime, when the commissaries open up to distribute food and supplies."

"I thought the Board of Health decreed bodies were supposed to be buried within six hours?"

"It appears they don't have enough gravediggers to come anywhere close to that."

"Maybe they need to hire more men."

"Coming into contact with the corpses like that—it could be it's hard to find men who're willing to take the chance." Helms paused before continuing. "There's another problem right here in the center of the city."

Keating glanced at his pressman, not sure if he wanted any more bad news. "What's that?"

"You know that narrow alley betwixt the two undertakers—Hinton and Sons on the one end, and T.J. Collins on t'other?"

"The one that's only about five feet wide, laid with cobblestones?"

"Yes, sir. Now they're callin' it Dead Man Alley. I reckon the two undertakers got more than they can say grace over—and they're both stackin' bodies out in the alley. Might be they're waitin' on a supply of caskets to come in on the train. I hate to say it, but there was a whole bunch of vermin in that alley when I passed by."

Keating winced at the thought of why the rats were congregating. "Hinton is one of our advertisers. Tell you what, I'll talk to him. Maybe warn them they need to do something about it before the Board of Health hears about it. However, we probably need to publicize the problem out at Elmwood—try and get some men to volunteer as gravediggers. But Helms, it's easy to understand their problem. Our own staff has almost been wiped out."

"I know, sir. There's but seven of us left at work out of forty-two. Barely enough to set the type and run the press."

Camp Joe Williams had been established some five miles south of the city on the Hernando Road, adjacent to the Mississippi and Tennessee Rail Line, with the idea that Memphis residents would leave the infected areas in the city and relocate to a healthier area. The location was well chosen. It had ample fresh water, plenty of shade, perfect drainage, and quick access to supplies via rail communication. As it would turn out, the major negative aspect of the camp was that it was too easy to get to the city, thus presenting too much of a temptation to its members to go back and forth into the dangerous area. This would all too soon translate to cases of yellow fever traveling into the camp. Fifty-two campers would eventually die there of the fever.

It was a large operation. A thousand tents and forty thousand rations had been sent to establish the camp by the Department of War in Washington. The site's inhabitants were assigned to a tent, supplied with cooking utensils and bed straw, and given rations from the commissary every other day, as well as being able to draw shoes and blankets if they were needed. The camp's rules—which were many—were stringently enforced.

The camp employed two surgeons, a pharmacist, a head nurse, two stretcher-bearers, and eventually two gravediggers. The head nurse was assisted by campers acting as nurse assistants. There were also three bakers, a butcher, a carpenter, and a wheelwright. All campers were required to work for the greater good of the members.

Finding their way to Camp Williams shortly after it opened was seven-year-old Jimmy Winters, his twelve-year-old brother Thomas, Jr., and their mother. Tom Winters, the father, had chosen to stay in the city to take care of their livestock and look out for the household. It had been a hard choice, and one which pleased neither mother nor father.

Worried to death about the health of her husband, on the evening of August 21st, Mrs. Winters asked Tommy to sneak out of the camp that night, return to the city, and fetch their father. The boy departed soon after dark, while Jimmy and his mother looked forward to the reunification of their family—certainly by the 23rd of the month, if not sooner.

That day came and went, and the two set their hopes on the following day. Again they were disappointed, not daring to allow themselves to think too hard about what might have happened.

On the 25th, Mrs. Winters appraised her younger son. He was big for his age, and just as desperate as she was to see his brother and father. She asked Jimmy if he remembered the road they had taken out of the city. He replied that he did. She then asked if he remembered where to leave the

Hernando Road and head back to the west in order to reach their home at the corner of Linden and Fourth Street. Again he replied in the affirmative. She recalled how well Jimmy had fared on the walk down to the camp, and had to admit he'd been still full of pep at the end of their journey a week previously—certainly more energetic than she had been herself.

So her youngest son was tasked with returning to their home in the city and bringing back his brother and father. "You be sure and tell your pa how safe it is here. Tell him we got plenty to eat and a nice place to stay."

Was the boy scared on his journey? We'll never know the answer, but what is fact is that seven-year-old Jimmy Winters was found early the next morning in Memphis. He had obviously missed the appropriate left turn leading to his house in the middle of the night, and ended up on a doorstep at the corner of Exchange and Front Streets, some fifteen blocks beyond his home.

Israel Jackson spied the huddled-up bundle in the doorway as he and Lester Sellers made their way in a death wagon toward the Pinch District, their assignment for the day. They stopped simply because they assumed the solitary bundle of clothes was yet another body which had been deposited on the side of the street.

The two men retrieved a small empty casket from their wagon and set it down before the "corpse." When they grappled with the body, Jimmy awakened.

"Oh, lawse! We got us another live one."

Lester peered closely at Jimmy. "You sick, boy?"

Jimmy placed his hands on either side of his head. "I don't feel so good."

"How long you been sick?"

"Just now, I reckon."

"You live here?"

Jimmy turned his head inquisitively toward the door. "No, this ain't our house. I was lookin' for my pa and my brother."

"Where they s'posed to be?"

"We live on Linden—right across the street from St. Patrick's."

"Linden! Boy, you a long ways from Linden." He looked hard at Israel. "Don't say nuthin' 'bout this. We gonna take this boy down to the Howards. They kin tell if'n he's sick. Mebbe find his folks. Then we'll just hurry back here. Won't take no time."

When Jimmy presented at the reception table at the Howards Association, he was flush-faced and clammy. After a quick assessment by a tall, distinguished gentleman with a head of white hair and an unlit pipe clenched between his teeth, it was decided to send him to the infirmary. But the boy would not be denied his quest. "Sir, can you help me find my pa and my brother?"

"Where is your mother, son?"

"She's waiting for us at Camp Williams, sir."

"What's your pa's name?"

"Thomas Winters—and my brother is Tommy."

The old doctor bit his lip, then turned to the clerk. "Look on this morning's list. Or maybe it was yesterday. I believe I recall one or the other." He looked again at Jimmy. "Where do they live?"

"Linden Street, sir."

The clerk scanned several sheets of paper, then looked at the doctor and nodded his head slightly.

"The father?"

He spoke in a low voice. "Last night, and the brother is in the infirmary, Doctor Parrott."

The physician turned to Jimmy. "Son, we'll send for your mother. She'll want to know where you are."

The boy squinted against the bright sunlight flooding the room. "Sir, what about my pa and Tommy?"

"We'll figure all that out when your mother gets here. Right now we've got to concentrate on getting you well."

*August 26, 1878—(Ad) "Remember Your Loved One Forever—Family Keepsakes—*Memento Mori *Photographs—Royal Photographic Studio, 609 Rue Royale, French Quarter"* New Orleans Picayune

(*Author's note: Memento mori* {remember you must die} photographs were those taken of the dead as a way of remembering them. The recently deceased was often propped up near a window so their countenance was bathed in a heavenly light. Sometimes pupils were painted on the closed eyelids in order to impart a lifelike appearance. *Memento mori* could also include poses by other family members sitting or standing beside the deceased, who might be leaned against a wall or seated in a chair. With the advent of photography in the mid-1800s, photographs of the deceased became a much simpler and cheaper way of memorializing loved ones, rather than having a portrait painted.)

Grenada

Dr. P.F. Fitzgerald stood, arms folded across his stomach, at the bedside of Christopher Ferrell. He was accompanied by Emilie Christophe, who had been caring for the Ferrell family. "He brought it on himself. No matter how many times you tell people that there is no prophylactic for yellow fever, fellows like Ferrell here have got their socks stuffed with sulfur, they're wearing necklaces of onions and garlic under their shirts, taking three or four doses of quinine a day, and they drink so much gin they begin to slosh when they walk. None of those things has any scientific value in the treatment of yellow fever."

He gestured at his patient. "I've known Ferrell for some years. He's always enjoyed good health. In fact, a month ago I would have described him as fat and happy as a town dog. However, he decided he was smarter than all the doctors and figured he could flit around this town any way he pleased, because he knew a secret that all of us didn't. Unfortunately, you can't expose your body to irritants like carbolic acid and creosote and alcohol without making yourself more susceptible to the fever—not less."

Emilie had come to much the same conclusion several weeks previously. "It seems that the people who escape the fever—or at least have the mildest cases—are those who live in moderation, aren't unduly frightened, don't try to saturate themselves with the things you've mentioned, and have a strong relationship with their God."

"Nurse, you've struck at the heart of the matter. If Ferrell had just continued to live in relative good health, breathed plenty of fresh air, gotten a regular amount of sleep each night, eaten nutritious food, bathed freely, read his Bible regularly, and avoided all these toxins and stimulants, I doubt he would be lying before us right now. Conversely, strong men of irregular habits, who weaken their constitutions with quinine and alcohol, are stricken down every day. In fact, I'd say the two items responsible for the most illness are lack of sleep and champagne!"

"Doctor Fitzgerald, are you the only local physician still on your feet?"

"It's worse than that, Nurse. I'm the only one still alive. The others are all dead and buried. Grenada had about 2,500 people when the epidemic started, but just within a few days only 125 whites and 1,000 Negroes remained. Our local Presbyterian church has been decimated. We've lost our pastor, all three elders, two deacons, and some thirty members in just a month. My wife says the entire Grenada church has been transferred to heaven."

Fitzgerald continued to mutter under his breath as he left the household, while Emilie returned to her task of sponging Christopher Ferrell and begging him to drink water. Like so many other patients in the city, she saw no positive outcome for the man.

(*Author's note:* Dr. Fitzgerald's theory of healthy, temperate living would fail him, as he, like the rest of his fellow Grenada physicians, would sicken and die within a week. The newspaper would say of him that "*he died with his harness on.*")

Emilie's next assignment was to a very small cabin on Pearl Street, not more than thirty yards from the waterfront on the Yalobusha River. Due to the lack of recent rainfall, the river was little more than a trickling creek. It was obviously a bedraggled area of town. Standing in the yard of the cabin, there was no mistaking the smell of a nearby stagnant body of water. She knocked at the door, which seemed to be hanging on by a single hinge, and received no answer. The note she carried from the Howards only stated that the two patients were Sally Butler and her seven-year-old son, Exodus.

She knocked a second time, and finally a young boy answered, his finger over his lips, shushing her. His tattered clothes were little more than rags. Despite his small size, she couldn't help noticing how grown up he acted. There were two pallets laid side by side in the front room—one of them occupied by a young black woman, who appeared to be asleep. The smaller pallet was empty.

Emilie spoke just above a whisper. "Are you Exodus?"

The boy nodded. "Yessum".

"I thought you were sick."

"I been poorly, but I reckon I'm better now."

She nodded toward the pallet. "How is your mother?"

"She ain't much interested in eatin' anything. I been tryin' to feed her some bacon, but she won't have it. Mostly she just drinks a few sips o' water when she wakes up."

Emilie couldn't help noticing the boy's pallor. "When is the last time you had a meal?"

"I had me a couple slices o' bacon a while back. Been savin' what's left for when Momma gets hungry. I ain't really had no meal since Momma took sick."

"Have you been taking care of your mother all by yourself?"

"Yessum. My pa ain't here. He's off workin' over in Tupelo."

"When did he leave, Exodus?"

"Four, maybe five weeks back. He went over there to build a couple fireplaces for a white man."

"Has anybody tried to contact him?"

"No'm. I guess my momma knows how. But she ain't been herself for a week or so." He paused, his lip quivering, before he could continue. "You can help her get well, cain't you?"

Emilie bent to her knees and felt the woman's forehead. She reached into a bag, withdrew a small towel and some ice, and motioned to Exodus. "Let me show you how to keep your mother's fever down. While you do that, I'll see what I can do in the kitchen about a meal for you and some thin soup for your mother."

The boy smiled for the first time. Whether it was in anticipation of a meal, or the opportunity to finally do something positive for his mother, it was hard to say. "Yessum."

Despite doing what she could, by the next morning Emilie was fairly certain Sally Butler would never rise from her sickbed. The woman had ignored all attempts to get her to take anything by mouth except an occasional ice chip. Her pulse was rapid, her breathing ragged, and she had said not a single word since Emilie's arrival.

Emilie knelt down in front of Exodus. "I need to walk back into town to get some more ice for your mother, and some food for you and me. Can you swab your mother's neck and forehead with this cool water? I should be back in less than a half hour."

"Yessum. Do you want I should go instead?"

"You're just getting over the fever, Exodus. I think you should stay here and not get out in the sun. I'll be right back."

The Howards had no ice. They were waiting on the evening supply train from Memphis. She collected a few items from their commissary and headed back.

She had picked the wrong time to be away. Exodus met her at the door, his eyes full of tears. "You best hurry. I don't think she's breathin' much."

Emilie checked her pulse, then placed her ear directly over her mouth and nose, then re-checked her pulse. Finally, she gently closed the woman's eyes. Exodus stood watching behind her. She turned and pulled him into an embrace. "I'm so sorry, Exodus. Your mother has passed on."

"Are you sure? She looks like she's just sleepin'."

"I'm sure, Exodus."

The tears turned to deep sobs and his shoulders shook. "I did everything I knew to do. I couldn't save her."

"Son, it's not your fault. Nobody could have saved her—not me—not even one of the doctors. She was just too sick." Emilie held him at arm's length. "I'm going to step out on the porch—give you a few minutes to say goodbye to your mother. Her spirit is probably still here in the room, so you talk to her."

"Yessum."

In a few minutes, the little boy came out and sat on the front step. He said nothing, but simply put his head in his hands, trying to hide his tears. Emilie's heart went out to the child, and she knelt down in front of him. "Exodus, I want you to go with me into town. We need to make some arrangements for your mother." They made quite the pair—the nurse and the boy—walking down the middle of the deserted streets in the stricken town to ask for an undertaker and a casket on Fourth Street.

They also stopped at the Howards' office.

"Colonel Anderson, this is Exodus Butler. He just lost his mother to the fever. In fact, he had it himself, but is just getting over it. He was taking care of his mother all by himself when I got there."

Anderson looked at the boy, surprised at his obvious young age. "It takes a brave boy to do that, Exodus. In fact, there's many a grown man who's turned tail and run when his family has gotten sick. I only hope a son of mine could be so brave." He put his big hand on the boy's shoulder. "Do you have any relatives here in town, son?"

"No, sir. My papa is up to Tupelo, workin' on a man's house."

"What's the man's name, Exodus?"

"I don't know as I ever heard it, sir."

Emilie took a deep breath, steeling herself. "Is there a place in town for orphans? Maybe he could stay there until his father comes back home. We could leave a note at the house, telling him where his son is."

"We're keeping a record of all the children at the orphanage, Nurse. We'll get it all figured out when he comes back."

"Thank you, Colonel." Her initial plan had been to leave the boy with the Howards and proceed to her next assignment, but she realized he needed closure. "I'll bring Exodus back in a little while—after the undertaker comes for his mother."

The sight of the raggedly dressed little boy, seated on the front step of his house with his head buried in his hands, as two men carried his mother in her casket to their funeral wagon, seared Emilie's heart in a way she had never experienced before. She just had to do something more. "Exodus, would you like to follow the wagon down to the cemetery? Maybe you'd like to see where your mother is to be buried."

He looked up at her, wiping his tears with the back of his hand. "Yessum."

The cemetery in Grenada resembled every burial ground in every city where the fever held sway. Fresh mounds of earth were everywhere. Emilie sat with him under the slight shade of a sycamore while the grave was being dug—with Exodus watching the whole process.

When the two gravediggers lowered the casket into the earth with ropes, they called to the small boy. "Come over here, son. Your momma will want to see you one more time.

You come and tell her goodbye. If you listen real close, maybe you can hear her, too."

Exodus walked over to the grave, mimicking the two men when they removed their hats. "Goodbye, Momma. I won't never forget you."

One of the gravediggers picked up his shovel and turned toward the pile of dirt. The taller of the two placed his hand on the man's shoulder and shook his head, then turned to Exodus, holding his shovel out to him. "Since you're her son, it's your responsibility to shovel the first dirt on your mother's grave."

Exodus looked at the two men, nodded his head, and took the offered shovel. "Yessir." He performed his responsibility, then returned the tool.

The man nodded his head. "That's the way it oughta be done. Your mother is bound to be proud of you."

Memphis

Father Patrick McNamara had made a promise which was impossible to keep. Like all of the Catholic churches in Memphis, St. Patrick's was overwhelmed with requests from parishioners for assistance—hearing confessions and receiving the sacraments, as well as providing nursing care. In these difficult circumstances, McNamara had contacted the mother superior of the Sisters of St. Joseph of Carondelet in St. Louis, asking that she release her nuns to come to Memphis to assist his church.

The mother superior had been unwilling to send her sisters yet again to Memphis. During the epidemic of 1873, miraculously none of their order had perished of the fever, even though six of the sisters had aided the sick across the city. The mother superior realized how fortunate they had been and had no desire to flirt with fate again. Yet Father McNamara persisted in his responding telegram, finally taking the reckless step of personally guaranteeing the safety of those nuns if they would but come to Memphis. And so she relented. Yet one of their number was stricken within days of her arrival. McNamara was so distressed at this that he immediately knelt and prayed that God spare the life of Sister Irene, and if necessary, he offered his own life instead of hers.

Father McNamara took to his bed with the fever on August 29th, and steadily declined. The young priest died on September 4th. Unfortunately, Sister Irene worsened herself, to the point that four days after McNamara's death, the physician and her fellow sisters declared that she had breathed her last.

Father Weiver from St. Mary's administered extreme unction, and Dr. Cavanaugh was called. He reported the body to be stiff and cold with no pulse. Her fellow sisters wrapped and shrouded the body, but decided to postpone the burial until the following day, when several more of their fellow nuns were expected to arrive from St. Louis.

One of the newly arrived sisters brought a crucifix on a chain from their mother superior, and when she affixed the necklace around Sister Irene's neck, she gasped in surprise, saying that she had seen the corpse's eyelids flutter. Although dubious, Dr. Cavanaugh immediately returned, and this time did indeed detect a faint pulse.

The nuns began to pray and care for Sister Irene, and within a very short time, the woman was talking. She revealed that she remembered all of the actions that had taken place since she had been declared dead, including the presence of the priest and the doctor, as well as the affixing of the crucifix and chain. She stated that she had tried to object when her body had been prepared by the sisters, but had been unable to move a muscle. Thankfully, she recovered. Father McNamara did not, but his guarantee had been kept.

August 27, 1878—"161 new cases of the fever in the past forty-eight hours, and 52 deaths. 573 cases reported thus far to the Board of Health, with 160 deaths. Our only hope for abatement lies in the ability of city government to compel people—white and black—who remain here to depart for the camps."

"Experienced female nurses are earnestly requested to call at the office of the Howard Association immediately."

"From Grenada, Mississippi—For heaven's sake send us a few nurses. Our nurses are worn out, and all our physicians are taken down." Memphis Daily Appeal

In the priests' rectory at St. Peter's Catholic Church, it was deathly quiet. Sister Agnes wrapped chunks of ice in a towel and lifted Father McGarvey's head so the cool bandage could rest against the back of his neck. She averted her gaze from the black vomit on the bedding and the floor. Her eyes were red and puffy, as she had spent the last two days weeping over her favorite priest.

When the short, plump Father Kelly entered the room, she tried her best to hide her emotion. But the priest had already seen far too many people in the throes of death these last two weeks to have any doubt about McGarvey's fate. He placed his hand on her shoulder. "Don't weep, Sister. He wouldn't want that."

"I know, Father. But he's such a treasure to us."

"Yes, I feel the same. He is undoubtedly a treasure." His voice broke and it took a moment for him to recover. "A treasure to our Father in heaven, as well." He looked down on the pallid face of his best friend and placed his hand on McGarvey's forehead. The poor man was moaning, out of his head, and flailing about. He turned to Sister Agnes. "Have you been able to get any fluids down him?"

"Just a few pieces of ice, Father. He really hasn't had anything to drink since yesterday afternoon."

"Has Doctor Josefson been by today?"

"Yes, Father. He just said to try and make him comfortable." She gathered herself again before speaking. "I don't think the doctor believed he would survive the day."

Kelly removed the cross from around his neck and reached in his pocket. "I never thought I'd be giving last rites—" His voice cracked again and this time he began to weep along with the nun. Finally he was able to finish his sentence. "—giving last rites to McGarvey."

After a period of deep thought, Kelly and Sister Agnes finally rose slowly to their feet and moved away from the bedside. Sister pointed toward the far side of the room. "Father, this is a terrible time, but we should probably do the same for Father Bokel—I fear he's just as bad as Father McGarvey."

"I know, Sister. I was hoping there would be some sliver of good news." He paused for a moment. "I hear that three other priests in the city are very sick."

"Fathers Meagher and Martin Walsh, and the Franciscan, Father Erasmus, aren't expected to survive."

He bowed his head yet again. "None of us may survive, Sister."

August 28, 1878—"The sale of watermelons should be interdicted, and this death-dealing fruit should be withheld from all who will not leave the city. The Board of Health continues to recommend disinfecting with lime, and today they will commence the burning of tar in the infected districts, followed by the firing of gunpowder and the maintenance of large fires in the streets."

"While our people are, with heavy hearts, battling with the fever, which claims every day its scores of victims from a population greatly reduced, the people from all sections of the country are sending us contributions of money, provisions, and medical stores, as well as their nurses and physicians. How grateful we are for these manifestations of generous, neighborly feeling, words cannot tell. Overwhelmed by a calamity that every moment confronts us with death in its most terrible form, we are greatly appreciative of the good work that warm hearts in every part of the nation are doing for us."

(Ad) "Happy tidings for nervous sufferers, and those who have been dosed, drugged, and quacked. Pulvermacher's Electric Belt effectively cures debility, weakness, and decay; as well as memory loss, fainting, fullness of blood, moping, and melancholy." Memphis Daily Appeal

August 28, 1878—Letter from Dr. William Armstrong to his wife—"The fever is assuming a most fearful form—distress and death are on all sides. Our best citizens are going by the dozens; and we poor doctors stand by abashed at the perfect uselessness of our remedies."

The Peabody, located at the corner of Main and Monroe Streets, just three blocks south of Court Square, was the only hotel in the city to remain open during the epidemic. In fact, almost all the boarding houses had closed down, as well. Prior to the fever, the hotel charged the almost unheard-of fee of four dollars per night, to include two meals per day in the dining room. Some would say this was justified by the gas lighting and private bath in each room, plus the availability of a huge ballroom, ornate lobby, and bar, which normally served as an intriguing place to socialize in the city each evening.

The writer David Cohn was widely quoted as saying that the unbelievably rich farmland known as the Mississippi Delta originated in the lobby of the five-story Peabody Hotel and stretched all the way to Catfish Row in Vicksburg. Anybody who was anybody, if passing through the Delta on business, was almost expected to make an appearance in the lobby of the Peabody during their travels.

However, as the city's commerce and thus the hotel's normal business disappeared, the Peabody had decided to change their billing procedure to the European plan, charging only a dollar a night for a room and fifty cents for each meal, rather than just offering both for one price. After all, most of their current boarders were with the Howards, and often depended on an early morning breakfast or late evening dinner as their only opportunity for a meal.

Fannie Lester was in the middle of a nightmare at the hotel. As the out-of-town doctors and nurses had moved in over the previous week, she'd assumed her duties as a chambermaid would not really change. She couldn't have been more wrong. When a few of the new occupants began to fall ill, it was decided to isolate them all on the top floor in a makeshift infirmary and try to care for them right in the hotel. Because Fannie had already survived the fever, the top floor became her assignment.

She spoke to her friend. "Whatever you do, don't go up on that floor, Leah. The fever is likely in every corner by now. You wouldn't believe the messes in those rooms—vomit like you've never seen before. Half the time they can't get to the chamber pot, or they're so out of their heads with fever that they don't know what they're sayin', let alone what they're doin'. And the rooms are so dark! They all complain that the light hurts their eyes, so the drapes stay pulled all day long."

"Fannie, if you gonna be up there with all that, why don't you be a nurse?"

Fannie looked at her friend. "I'm no different than you, Leah. I'm just a chambermaid."

"They all takin' on 'bout how they need nurses what's had the fever. What them nurses do that you ain't already doin'?"

"Well, they have to clean those folks up five or six times a day, try and get them to drink water, put ice on their face and neck, clean out their bed pans, and give 'em a little medicine every now and then. Some of the poor patients have sores and pustules on their faces, arms, and legs. So they have to try and keep them from scratchin' those places to a fare-thee-well, with pieces of ice or poultices and such."

"Why cain't you do that?"

"What's the difference, Leah?"

"Why, hell, girl. It's money! They be payin' them nurses three dollars a day. You an' me only makin' six dollars a week!"

Father Lucius Buchholz was the senior pastor at St. Mary's of the Immaculate Conception Catholic Church. St. Mary's was the second-oldest Catholic church in the city, and had been established primarily to minister to the ever-growing German immigrant community. For this reason, the priests assigned to St. Mary's were fluent German speakers. The sermon in the church was delivered in that language, and priests heard confessions in both German and English.

On the morning of the 29th, Buchholz approached his young associate Father Aloysius Weiver, who, as usual, was dressed in a plain brown habit with a faded white knotted cord, his bare feet only partially covered with sandals. This "hermit priest" was appreciated throughout the Catholic community. In 1873, he'd had a terrible case of yellow fever, and was thus acknowledged as being immune to the current scourge. In fact, because of this, he had been designated to perform last rights to other priests and sisters in the city.

Buchholz was a man on a mission. "I'm convinced we can no longer handle the demands made on us without help."

"I agree, Father. Have you considered appealing to the Franciscan sisters in St. Louis? I know that many, or perhaps most of them, are German speaking."

"My thoughts as well. I'll telegraph the reverend mother immediately. If she's supportive, we'll need to arrange housing for them. Our school may be the best option."

August 29, 1878—"Although there are scarcely 4,000 white people, and perhaps 16,000 Negroes left in Memphis, new cases of fever yesterday numbered 119, and deaths were 58. Of the new cases, 88 were white and 31 Negroes, and of the deaths, 47 were white and 11 were Negroes, showing that the black population is also being attacked by the scourge."

(Ad) "Colden Liebig's Liquid Extract of Beef has been extremely beneficial as a preventive to those exposed to yellow fever in New Orleans."

(Ad) "Yellow fever can be prevented by the Medicated Fever Bath. It can be moved from room to room, and managed by a child, with no danger in operation. No family can have yellow fever if its members use it. It has proved more effective than a Turkish bathhouse in eradicating rheumatism, asthma, catarrh, dyspepsia, and all nervous maladies. The entire apparatus, including medicinal agents, can be obtained for ten dollars."

(Ad) "A new remedy for yellow fever has been announced by Parke-Davis and Co, manufacturing chemists, which is an extract of the leaves of boldo, an Alpine shrub found in the Andes in Chile. The firm has shipped this new drug to the physicians of Memphis, free of expense." Memphis Daily Appeal

August 29, 1878—Letter from Dr. William Armstrong to his wife—"You will see by the papers, the inhumanity of John Donovan, an old Irish politician, who was only fifty miles away from Memphis, and when his wife and family were taken down, would not come, but sent word, 'take care of my family.' The newspapers and people are giving him fits, and justly too—an old dog—he is a type of what many others are doing. I reported as you will see, in my district 127 sick. One doctor has been given me as a help, but none work like me. Nutall sitting right beside me reported 33 sick in all, and receives the same pay—but I am so rejoiced that God has given me health and strength to do this work."

(*Author's note:* The Donovan family lived in a large home on Washington Street—one befitting the well-to-do status of John Donovan as a local businessman. When the epidemic began, he was in Brownsville, Tennessee, and upon receiving word that his wife and son were near death, he did not return to Memphis, but sent a small sum of money, along with a note to take care of them. His perceived callousness was widely discussed in the city.)

Reverend Charles Parsons had called a morning meeting of the staff at St. Mary's Episcopal Cathedral. As he looked around at their faces, he saw an exhausted yet always willing group. He shook his head at the prospect of the work which faced them. "We have a request from the Citizens Relief Committee. They're asking us to open up the Canfield Asylum out on the Old Raleigh Road to receive orphans."

Sister Constance spoke quickly. "The Asylum was previously for colored only. Are they asking us to restrict our work to colored children?"

"No, Sister. Dean Harris and I made sure the Committee understood we would tolerate no discrimination if we ran the home. They asked that we start taking epidemic orphans as soon as possible. I know we're all stretched thin. But thank goodness, two days ago I sent a request to Bishop Quintard to send us more sisters. Between them and the Howard nurses, we should be able to answer this request. Now, Sister Frances, I'd like you to be in charge of the church's orphan home operation. As soon as the new sisters arrive, at least two of them will be sent there to assist you."

"Yes, Reverend. Can I assume the Citizens Relief Committee is going to send provisions, clothing, and bedding?"

"I have a commitment from Benjamin Babb, of that committee, to deliver the supplies we need."

Fannie Lester had decided the best approach to figuring out whether or not switching professions was a good idea was to simply talk to some of the Howard nurses. She was finding, however, there was no such thing as a common opinion. To be sure, several had spoken about "the calling" in such a way that it made Fannie believe she should join their ranks. These nurses seemed to impart a special dignity to those patients engaged in the fight of their lives, and were truly saddened, if not stricken, when the struggle failed.

On the other side of that coin, there were enough stories bandied about that some of the nurses in town were only "called" to Memphis so they could take advantage of people during their most vulnerable time. Her last interview was with Nurse Charlotte, who was nothing if not honest.

"We all heard the call from the Howards down in Shreveport, and me and a girlfriend decided we needed to come. We left on Sunday, arrived on Monday, and they put me to work on Tuesday. On Wednesday, my patient was lovely, couldn't have been no nicer. By Thursday he was only tolerable; that night he got restless, kept me up the whole night through with all kinds of hell-raisin'. Friday mornin' he was cussin' me and ever'body within shoutin' distance. Friday night he was dead. I figger Saturday mornin' he showed up in hell with a first-class ticket. Folks like him, he went to hell by telegraph, and not over no wires neither.

"Honey, you want to be a nurse around this here fever, I'm here t' tell you, it ain't easy. You got to be soft as a mother's love when they need it, and hard as a brickbat when you have to be."

Chapter 10
Don't Waste Your Life

Memphis

With the deaths of Fathers M. Walsh and Meagher on August 29th and 30th, Bishop Feehan reassigned Father William Walsh from St. Patrick's Church to St. Brigid's. The bishop was acquainted with Walsh's connections with Catholic societies, as well as the Temperance Unions, and he needed a man who could reach out across the country to raise funds to establish a safe-haven camp for Catholics—specifically the Irish Catholic members of St. Brigid's—who seemed to live right in the middle of the most infectious area of Memphis: north of Market Street and surrounding the Gayoso Bayou. The bishop picked the right man.

Father Walsh immediately began sending letters and telegrams across the nation, asking for funds. At the same time, he contacted Washington, D.C., requesting tents and rations for a camp that would eventually house 400 people. In his efforts, he was aided by Brother Maurelian, as well as other brothers from the temporarily closed Christian Brothers College. The camp was to be called Camp Father Mathew—named in honor of the Franciscan in Ireland who preached abstinence from alcohol.

In a matter of days, they received the miraculous sum of $40,000 through Walsh's fund-raising requests, and the Secretary of War sent seventy or eighty tents, as well as rations to accommodate their immediate needs. They were able to secure a plot of two hundred acres some two and a half miles north of the city on farm property owned by Napoleon Hill, a wealthy Catholic businessman. (The site was in what has become north Memphis, near Vollentine and McLean.) The land was well watered by a bubbling spring and surrounded by forest. While it was convenient to receiving supplies from the city, the property was far enough from the infected area to be considered safe.

The tentage was laid out in long rows, referred to as streets, and they were generally named after saints and Catholic holy men. Facilities available included a commissary, butcher shop, drugstore, and a large kitchen.

That first morning, as the camp began to receive would-be residents, Tim Considine, the vice president of the Father Mathew Society of St. Brigid's, met them at the entrance. "All of you are welcome here, as long as you have full understanding that this camp will permit no intoxicants of any kind within its borders—excepting only that which is prescribed by our physician. The camp will be fully picketed, and no one is allowed to enter or leave without the written consent of Father Walsh." He paused to nod toward the priest. "We will hold a Catholic Mass here—" he paused to gesture toward the altar, upon which stood a statue of the Sacred Heart "—every morning at seven AM. All able-bodied men and women will be expected to perform work for the common good." Considine paused again for effect. "Before you go to your campsite, the leader of each family must sign an agreement, promising to abide by all camp rules."

A gentleman of dubious gentility, accompanied by a broken-down woman and an abundance of children, looked toward Father Walsh when he made his appeal. "Yeah, eh—yer holiness, my doctor in town tole me I needed a dram now and then fer my nerve condition. You'd be permittin' that, would ye not?"

Acknowledgement must be given that Father Walsh had perhaps the most difficult job in all the land—convincing several hundred Irishmen it would be in their best interest not to drink any spirits for several weeks or months. Regardless, he was resolute. "Sir, Camp Father Mathew has been financed by Temperance Unions and good Catholics across the United States. We would be violating their trust if we allowed any alcohol other than that prescribed by our Doctor

Cavenaugh. And finally," he gestured toward the altar, "we are placing our faith in the Sacred Heart and believe strict adherence to our tenets will deliver us all from the fever. If you cannot live with this agreement, there is a secular location, Camp Burke, just north of the Wolf River near Frayser Station."

The man said not another word to Father Walsh, but simply turned his brood toward the west with the directive, "Come on, Ma, this foolishness ain't fer us."

Report of Father William Walsh to the Howards: "Out of our population of 400 at Camp Father Mathew, we had only ten deaths from the fever. In each case, the fever was contracted in the city. It did not spread in the camp. In fact, we had not one case of a fatal or unfavorable result, contracted in our camp. With the help of three of the Sisters of St. Joseph, we established a school for the children in structures near camp, thus we were able to provide for every necessity."

August 30, 1878—Letter from Dr. William Armstrong to his wife—"A sad case is that of Mrs. Croker, whose husband died a few days ago, leaving her and five or six children, and a little infant that I delivered since the beginning of the epidemic, and last night the mother went, leaving all those children without a relation in this city. I feel sometimes as if my hands were crossed and tied and that I am good for nothing. Death coming upon the sick in spite of all that I can do. Alex Lytle had been hunting me all day—just to see how I was. We talked of the troubles we were going through, and both cried right in my office. I tell you it breaks the stoutest hearts."

August 30, 1878—"The sale of watermelons has at last been prohibited."

"Tar barrel bonfires are in abundance every night now, as well as explosions of fireworks in the streets. Fire is a purifier."

"The committee charged with caring for homeless orphans are now prepared to receive orphans and destitute children and transfer them to the Canfield Asylum on the Raleigh Road." Memphis Daily Appeal

Entries in Belle Wade's diary—On August 30—"There were 140 new cases yesterday and 73 deaths." On August

31—"The fever is so bad, the doctors haven't time to report new cases."

Father Kelly found it difficult to prepare the telegram to his bishop that morning, but he had no choice. He had to ask the diocese for assistance. After all, whoever Bishop Feehan might send to Memphis could very well be walking into almost certain death. But there were so many people in need; it was undeniable he had to have help.

Kelly had been able to prevail upon the undertakers, Flaherty and Sullivan, to send a hearse to St. Peter's on the morning of August 30th to carry the bodies of his two assistants to Calvary Cemetery. And despite the fact that the entire load had now shifted to his shoulders until the bishop was able to recruit replacements, he was determined to accompany the caskets of Fathers McGarvey and Bokel to the Catholic burial ground.

They traveled in a southeasterly direction from the church before reaching the Hernando Road, where they headed directly to the south. Father Kelly was reminded of how different the countryside was from the horrors of the city. Instead of piles of burning bedding, the acrid smell of lime, the deserted businesses, bodies in various states of putrefaction, and the constant pleas for help at every turn from desperate people, just a mile outside Memphis he could almost convince himself that the fever was no more. The dirt road was bordered by pastures of cattle and sheep, and men going about their everyday labors. For the first time since the epidemic began, he noticed birds singing. He wondered how it was possible that there was anything to sing about.

However, as they approached the horse trolley stop on the southwestern corner of the cemetery, the full impact of the epidemic struck him from every direction. The majestic willow oaks were surrounded by at least a hundred plots of freshly turned ground. And as they turned to the east into the burial grounds on the Carriage Road, he could see a large work crew of Negroes digging a mass grave on the hillside off to his right. Unfortunately, it was only the newest of four long mounds of earth, all of which appeared to be over a hundred feet in length. More depressing, he could see a second crew of men beginning to dig another long trench on the swale beyond the hillside. He had the impression that the ground itself had been attacked and severely wounded by the yellow fever.

But his destination that morning was almost straight ahead. The Priests' Mound was by far the highest elevation in the cemetery, and as the wagon reached the burial site, Kelly noticed two graves had been freshly prepared, awaiting his dear friends.

They would not be the first to be buried on the mound. There were other priests there from the yellow fever epidemic in 1873, and their gravestones were arrayed in the beginnings of a circle near the top of the mound. A brand new grave—already covered over—was there as well. Father Martin Walsh, from St. Brigid's Church, had been buried just the day before. And upon reaching the mount, Father Kelly was gratified to notice that the newest graves, those for McGarvey and Bokel, had been positioned as part of the circle of burials begun in 1873.

Kelly paused to gaze over the cemetery. He had presided over numerous burials here under normal circumstances in the past. The vista of rolling green hills might be described as soul-stirringly beautiful and even inspiring. But today, with the multitude of examples of unexpected death confronting him, he was struck with fear when he contemplated what the place might look like before the fever finally departed his city.

Father Kelly spoke over the graves of the two priests, and their caskets were lowered away. Four gravediggers began to cover the two graves, whereupon Kelly turned to the hearse for his return to the city. But before the work could be completed on the graves of his friends, another workman approached, said something to the gravediggers, and two of them stepped to the side and began to dig yet another grave in the ever-expanding circle for martyred priests.

Kelly shook his head. He knew that Fathers Meagher and Erasmus were both very ill, and wondered if one of them had already been designated to lie in this honored spot. It was hard to think about such things as honor at the moment. The sight of the new grave taking shape in the earth made Father Kelly sick to his stomach. He was forced to turn away.

For the tenth time that morning, Fannie Lester tried to push a handful of dark curls under her new nurse's cap. She was headed down the stairwell to the basement to get more ice for her feverish patients, and hoping to steal just a bit for herself, when she was startled to meet Dr. Saul Josefson heading in the opposite direction. "Doctor Josefson, what are you doing here?"

"Why, Fannie, is that you? I might ask you the same thing."

She briefly wished she had spent a moment trying to make herself more presentable before coming downstairs, but at this point that couldn't be helped. "I started working for the Howards just yesterday. They needed nurses who'd already had the fever, so I thought I could help."

"That's very brave of you, Fannie. Most people are running away from the fever, but here you are running toward it."

"I figger the brave ones are those who haven't had the fever, but they're still here." She looked inquiringly at the young physician. "What about you, Doctor Josefson? Have you had the fever?"

"Well—no, I haven't, Fannie. But there are many doctors working for the Howards who haven't had it either. And we all took an oath to help." He hesitated for a minute before finishing. "If they can do it, so can I."

"I got four patients up there," she pointed up the stairwell, "who thought the same thing. Doctor Madison says it's not likely any of them are gonna pull through."

Josefson thought for a moment. "Madison? I think he and I are supposed to be paired up to treat everybody in the district just south of downtown, but I haven't met him yet. Is he from Memphis?"

"No. He's from Charleston. Anyway, he's already had the fever. He keeps sayin' people are crazy to come here if they've never had yellow fever. Most of 'em are gettin' sick within a week." She looked at Josefson again, and decided she had to say something. "Please don't stay around here and get sick, Doctor Josefson. You can come back when all this is over. You're too good a doctor to waste your life here."

In fact, he was enduring his own private struggle, coming to terms with his decision. His parents had basically mirrored Fannie's admonition before they left town, and now his sister had followed them. He thought for a second he was going to tear up. "Why, thank you, Fannie. I appreciate your concern." For the third time that day, he reminded himself of the resolve he had possessed just the evening before. "But my mind is made up. I'm staying. Since I signed up for the Howards myself, I'll probably see you around."

She impulsively grabbed his hand before he could pass her by. "Just don't end up being one of my patients. I doubt I could stand that."

August 31, 1878—"We understand some of our physicians do not report the yellow fever cases under their care, owing to professional disagreements either of a personal nature or differences of opinion as to what the fever is to be called that is decimating our city. The reports of cases of fever is not a personal matter—but a public duty, in the discharge of which doctors should be as careful as they are with their patients."

"A yellow fever remedy from a constituent: As soon as you feel the fever coming on, take a foot bath of warm water and mustard. Then mix two tablespoonsful of powdered charcoal, one and a half tablespoonsful of sulfur, one-half tablespoonful of calcenated oyster shell, and two teaspoonsful of white sugar. Mix well and give patient a teaspoonful of this mixture every half hour in chamomile or other herb tea. All others in the household should take a half teaspoonful three times a day."

(Ad) "Hall's Vegetable Sicilian Hair Restorer is a scientific combination of some of the most powerful restorative agents in the vegetable kingdom. It restores gray hair to its original color. It makes the scalp white and clean. It cures dandruff and humors, and falling out of the hair. It makes the hair moist, soft and glossy, and is unsurpassed as a hair dressing. It is officially endorsed by the State Assayer of Massachusetts."

(Ad) "Robinson Druggist—Open all night. Corner Second and Madison Streets." Memphis Daily Appeal

August 31, 1878—"Complaints are being received on the subject of noises made by bells, machinery, etc. Such complaints have been made to municipal authorities of the rice mill at 109 Julia Street. It is stated that the machinery at this mill runs all night, and there are 18 cases of fever in the neighborhood. The Administrator of Police will request the noise be abated in the daytime and stopped altogether at night. There is some talk of street car companies removing the bells from the car mules, as their jingling is considered injurious to yellow fever patients along the rail lines."

"From Vicksburg: 160 new cases in last twenty-four hours and 13 deaths."

"During yesterday, the Young Men's Christian Association took care of 51 new cases. Five deaths were reported, which had been duly cared for. The Young Men are doing good work and the results of their labors are found in all parts of the city. In our city, 915 deaths and 3,111 total cases to date." New Orleans Picayune

Beulah found Annie Cook rummaging around the pantry of the Mansion House that morning, trying to calculate whether or not they would have enough food to last the day. She was surprised to find her boss dressed in a stained camisole and a cast-off, faded blue house dress. Beulah had not even known her boss owned a house dress, and she couldn't help but speculate that when the whores were still around, the missus wouldn't have been caught dead without her fine clothes on—but times were different now.

"Miss Cook, them Howards done brought in another four sick ones. I don't know where to put 'em. We run outa beds two days ago."

"We've just about run out of everything, Beulah. We've got no more ice, we're down to a couple pounds of ham, and maybe four or five potatoes that aren't mushy. There's no milk. And the chickens must be on a work stoppage. I only found four eggs this morning."

"Since them Howards makes us burn the bedding when somebody dies, we hardly got a single sheet on some o' them beds. And I cain't keep up with the washin'—no way, no how! Course, lots o' these folks got such a fever, they don't want no covers a-tall. A couple of 'em are layin' in the bed buck naked—and they still be burnin' up."

Annie made a note to herself. "I'll see if I can get any sheets at Lowenstein's—or maybe from Southern Dry Goods."

Beulah paused and gave her boss a long, appraising look. "You ain't gettin' sick, is you, Miss Cook?"

Annie wiped the perspiration from her brow. "I think it's just this humidity. I don't have time to get sick right now."

"Please don't you be gettin' the fever, Miss Annie. I don't know what these sick folks would do without you."

"It seems like the doctors don't know what to do for their patients anyhow. All they know is laxatives and ice and foot baths and various teas. Every now and then they might give a dose or two of quinine. I don't know why they don't try somethin' different. At least half these poor people die anyway. Or maybe they die because of it!"

"I knows what you mean. Thet Doctor Sohm is 'bout the onliest one thet saves anybody."

Annie looked around quickly. "Don't let anybody hear you say that, Beulah. These doctors got a pretty high opinion of themselves."

Beulah sniffed. "Yes, ma'am."

Annie lowered her voice. "Just the same, if I was to get sick, be sure you get Doctor Sohm for me."

Beulah half-smiled. "Yes, ma'am, Miss Annie. I'd want him to look after me, too."

Nicholas Helms spoke to his boss that morning. "We're down to Bartel, Moode, Broom, Hollomon, you, and me, Mr. Keating."

"That pretty well convinces me that we've got to make a big change, Helms."

Nicholas tried not to show his concern. Surely he wasn't going to close down the *Memphis Daily Appeal.* "What have you got in mind, sir?"

"We've been printing a four-page paper six days a week since right after the war. But this has turned into a dire emergency. Starting tomorrow, we're going to reduce the paper to two pages."

Nicholas pondered this for a minute. "Well, if I've only got to set type for two pages, maybe I can help with other things."

"That would be wonderful, Helms. What can you do?"

"Back during the war, I set up the pages—doin' the composing. It was harder then 'cause we moved around so much, tryin' to stay a step ahead of the Yankees. We didn't really have regular advertisers. But now almost half the two pages won't change from day to day. And I ran the press, too. A couple of pages should be a piece of cake." He thought again. "How many papers are you sendin' out by mail?"

"Since everybody left town, over a thousand."

"Mebbe I could help Chester Hollomon with that, too."

Sister Constance finally found Reverend Charles Parsons, rector of St. Mary's Episcopal, standing at the bedside of a very weak little girl in the infirmary. (Sister Frances was sending the sick ones from the Canfield orphan home to the church infirmary.) Constance spoke in a whisper. "Reverend, we've got a little problem I'd like to discuss with you."

"Certainly, Sister."

"We've got so many doctors coming and going here and out at the orphan home, it's hard to keep up with all their treatment ideas, let alone all of their bills, and different charges for everything. What if we were to get a doctor in here that would be in charge, and he could set the example for these other doctors, sort of keep them all in line?"

"Did you have anyone in particular in mind, Sister?"

"Actually, I do. That Doctor Armstrong is just about the hardest working man I know. He's very sincere about taking care of his patients—and I believe he's a godly man, to boot. Now I have to warn you, he is a Presbyterian, but just the same, he's a godly man."

"How do the other sisters feel about him?"

"I haven't asked, but I can't imagine they would object to Doctor Armstrong."

"I'll ask Dean Harris."

She pointed over his shoulder and spoke again in a low voice. "How's little Carrie?"

Parsons shook his head. "Not good, I'm afraid. I'd best go ahead and say last rites for her while I have the chance." He looked at his senior-most nun. "We've got so many sick ones now, I hardly know who needs me first."

Dr. James Madison saw Fannie Lester step into the broom closet, leaving the door slightly ajar. He glanced up and down the hallway of the Peabody Hotel and made the quick decision to follow her. He stood in the half-open doorway and peeked in the poorly lighted closet. She was bent over at the waist, retrieving the mop bucket. At the sight of her round bottom and small waist, he paid no attention to his better judgment, quietly entered the closet, and pulled the door closed behind him. The room instantly turned completely dark, but he was caught up in the moment and would admit to his mirror later that he couldn't help himself.

He placed both his hands on either side of her hips and gave her a small squeeze. She jerked away in surprise, turned quickly toward him in the darkness, and swung her fist. She struck him a blow full on the cheek, then a glancing uppercut to his chin, before he could locate and grab her wrists. She began to struggle against him, kicking him with her brogans twice in the shins until he finally spoke in a whisper. "Fannie, it's me, Doctor Madison."

She stopped fighting, but didn't totally drop her guard. "Doctor Madison, what are you doing in here?"

"I saw you come in here and wanted to talk to you."

She tugged at her wrists. "Then why have you got hold of me?"

He laughed and released her. "Because I didn't want to get hit again."

She smiled at that, although it was too dark for him to see her. "I've got a mess to clean up in Doctor Lawrence's room. What did you want to tell me?"

"I just wondered what you thought about seeing one of the doctors after hours."

"Who might that be?"

"Why, me, Fannie. What would you think about seeing me?"

She was thankful for the darkness of the room, as she was unsure of the look on her face. "I'm bone-tired when I leave here of an evening. It's all I can do to walk home and fall into bed."

"Maybe you need a day off."

"I probably do, but these folks need me a lot worse than I need a day off."

"Just think about it for a couple of days. Maybe we can figure something out." He opened the door behind him, and light streamed into the small space. As he stepped out into the hallway, she reached for her bucket and mop again, then backed out of the broom closet and hurried down the hall.

Standing behind a stanchion, Dr. Saul Josefson swore under his breath. "Damn it! That s.o.b. Madison is after Fannie." He had not missed the fiery red mark on the doctor's face, nor the new limp in his walk. Maybe she wasn't particularly willing, after all. At least, he hoped that was the case.

August 31, 1878—"They called me at twelve to go to Reverend Harris (Dean of St. Mary's Cathedral). *He had a chill and terrible fever. No doctor could be had for ten hours. Mister Parsons did what I told him, and Doctor Armstrong was satisfied when he did come. I could not have had a more overwhelming blow in the midst of my work. So much depended on his daily supervision." Note written by Sister Constance*

Chapter 11
Recognized?

Memphis

September 1, 1878—"The region of the city known as the infected district is now nearly depopulated by death and desertion. But the great increase in cases is in the ninth ward, the seventh ward, and the fifth ward—where the fever is making frightful havoc among the colored people. Piteous appeals are made for doctors."

(Ad) "We see that J. Robinson, druggist, who just yesterday advertised to stay open day and night, merely for pay, has jumped the town. However, we will stay open in the future unless we fall in Jordan's cold stream. We do this through philanthropic motives. Morrison & Humes, Druggists" Memphis Daily Appeal

September 1, 1878—Letter from Dr. William Armstrong to his wife—"Our dear Memphis—the sights that now greet me every hour in the day are beyond the much talked of [epidemic of] *1873, as that year was, to me, something beyond anything I had ever known. What it is going to do with us all is something which only God, in his wisdom, can reveal. It is appalling and makes the very bravest quake."*

September 1, 1878—Letter from Rev. Parsons to Rev. Charles Quintard, Episcopal Bishop of Tennessee—"I have just received your letter of the 28th, addressed to Harris. We cannot tell you how he is, because his case is not yet developed. The doctor promises it shall be very light, but Sister Constance and I are not so hopeful. Our pastoral duties extend from one end of the city to the other, and include all classes of people. It is incessant. I must hasten this letter to its close, because I have so many visits to make. Sometimes they pass away, or into a final state of unconsciousness, before we can reach them. A large number of those to whom we minister are utter strangers to us until we reach their bedside. Last night I rode in haste to Mosby Street to communicate a dying girl. You know how short the distance is, and yet before I reached the house there were three instances of persons dying unknown given me, with piteous appeals to procure their immediate interment. My dear Bishop, the situation is indescribable. The Sisters are doing wonderful work. It is surprising to see how much these quiet, brave, unshrinking daughters of divine love can accomplish in efforts and results. One of the most important of their duties henceforth will be to maintain the Asylum for all the destitute children and orphans of the city. In two days, already, thirty-two have been sent to them, and in a short time the number will be near a hundred. Harris and I were charged by the Citizens' Relief Committee with the duty of organizing this charity, and we took immediate advantage of your authority to locate it in the Canfield Asylum. For our general work we have several excellent nurses in our employ, and for the Home and the Asylum one of the best physicians in the city. We need all the contributions we can receive in money, clothing, and provisions. I am well, and strong, and hopeful, and I devoutly thank God I can say that in every letter."

John Johnson was dead on his feet when he arrived home at thirty minutes past eight that morning. He had worked twelve-hour shifts every day since joining the Department of Police, all spent on his feet, walking a beat in downtown Memphis. Thank goodness, crime was actually down. Whether it was because so many people had already fled the city, the presence of a strict nighttime curfew, or perhaps would-be criminals were afraid to be out and about when the infectious vapors were said to be most prevalent, it was hard to tell. But the reduction in robberies and assaults was certainly welcome among Johnson and his fellow policemen. The epidemic's impact on cases of public drunkenness, however, was less than desirable.

John finally had gotten the information related to moving Marissa and the girls to one of the refugee camps. From all he had heard, it sounded as though both whites and coloreds were living under equal conditions in the camps. In fact, at Camp Joe Williams, some five miles south of the city, the camp was being policed by both a white and a colored military company—the Bluff City Grays and the McClellan Guards.

John had spent the better part of his nightshift rehearsing just how he was going to convince Marissa that she and the girls needed to go. But he wasn't prepared for what greeted him in his dwelling. His wife heard him enter, and when he saw her, it was obvious she had been crying. "What's wrong, Marissa?"

"Both the girls went to bed early last night, right after you left for work. They was complainin' before bedtime, then got me up around three o'clock. They both had a headache, and now they's burnin' up with fever."

The two of them walked back to the girls' pallet. Marissa put her hand on her oldest daughter's forehead. "Ruthie said it felt like she was sore all over."

"Have they been around any sick folks?"

"Not that I know of. For the last three days they been playin' outside in the washtub. I let 'em put a few buckets of water in the pan so they could splash around and stay cool in this miserable weather." She wrung her hands. "If only we'd stayed in Drummond—maybe they'd be safe up there, away from all these sick people."

John decided not to have that discussion. Marissa was feeling bad enough as it was. "Any of their little friends sick?"

"I don't think so, but there's people sick all around."

John hung his head and leaned over the girls' pallet, hoping against hope his wife's description was overstated. It wasn't. Seeing his daughters like that, hair matted against their scalps and drenched in sweat, he almost lost his self-control. "I should have sent y'all to one of the camps before it got so bad here. Fact is, I just found out last night they was fair to black folks. I'll walk down to the Howards' office—see if they's a doctor to come see about them."

"I hardly ever see a doctor around here. Are they takin' care of the Negroes the way they are the white folks?"

"They's supposed to. The money they get is fer all of us. I'll see what I can do 'bout a doctor."

When Johnson arrived at the Howard Association's office on Main Street, he was still wearing his policeman's uniform. The building appeared to be deserted, save one woman sitting at a desk, facing the front door. "Ma'am, I got two sick little girls, three and five years old. They 'pear to have the fever. Can I get a doctor to come see about 'em?"

The woman was white, and he was worried she might not pay any attention to his request. Perhaps she took note of his clothing, and responded somewhat favorably. "All the doctors are out right now. Where do you live?"

"Down in Fort Pickering. We're in Barracks Number Four, the south end of the building."

She made a quick note. "The doctors are working all day and half the night with the patients they've already got. But maybe one of them will be back in here late this afternoon. I'll ask if they'll come see your little girls."

"Thank y'all. My name is Johnson—John Johnson."

The knock at the door came just as Johnson was getting ready to leave for his night shift. Marissa answered, holding a handkerchief over her face. When she saw the white man with a black satchel in his hands, accompanied by a white woman in a nurse's cap, she dropped the kerchief and invited them in.

"I'm Doctor Josefson, and this is Nurse Lester. We're with the Howards. They said you had two sick children?"

"Yes, Doctor. They took sick last night." Marissa nodded toward the back of their home. There were no partitioning walls in the structure, save a sheet hanging from the ceiling which served to separate the children's pallet from their own. "They're back here."

The girls were somewhere between asleep and awake when Josefson examined them. "How much have they had to drink today?"

"Not much. I got a little sugar water down them, but probably not more than half a glassful."

"Have they eaten anything?"

"They usually love my hoecakes, but I couldn't get them to take a bite."

Josefson and Fannie herded Marissa back to the door before removing their face masks. The doctor dug around in his bag and produced two glassine powder papers of magnesia. "You've got to get them to drinking. They're already dehydrated. They really need six or eight glasses of water a day. Mix one-half of one of these powder papers in water and get them to drink it once this evening, and again tomorrow afternoon. It's not going to taste very good, so you might have to put a spoon of sugar in, as well.

"Have you got any ice in the house? The most effective treatment for fever is to put ice in whisky, and use that mixture to rub on their chest and back. It will cool them down, and help them sleep, too. Keep them as quiet as you can—and stop the hoe cakes. Don't try to feed them anything stronger than beef tea. I'll be back tomorrow to check on them."

By this time, John Johnson had finished putting on his uniform and faced the two medical people. But his focus was on the nurse. She looked exactly like—but surely he was mistaken! Then again, she had a puzzled look on her face as well, apparently trying to place where she had seen him before. Johnson turned to face the doctor, trying to avoid looking directly at the nurse. "Do you know where I can get some ice?"

Josefson replied, "Check down at the Howards' headquarters. They usually have some."

Fannie twisted around, trying to get a better look at Johnson. "If they don't have any, come by the Peabody. I'll be sure you get some."

When Fannie and Josefson departed, Marissa turned to her husband. "I see you're goin' to work, despite our girls bein' so sick."

"I doubt there's much I can do for 'em besides what you'll be doin'."

"Do you really believe these white folks are gonna care one whit about you pertectin' them and their town after this fever is over?"

"I'm hopin' they will, Marissa. One thing is for sure—they won't never forget if us Negroes turn tail and run."

"They got no good memories where we're concerned. I figger they'll go right back to hatin' in no time at all."

"I ain't gonna think that way, Marissa. I'll be back shortly with some ice."

As Fannie and Dr. Josefson headed toward their next patient visit, Fannie remarked, "I can't shake the feelin' that I know that man from somewhere."

"It looked to me like he recognized you, as well."

"Well, a colored man sure couldn't get himself a room in the Peabody, so I can't figure where I would have seen him."

That little mystery was the farthest thing from Josefson's mind. He was secretly ecstatic that Fannie had agreed to make this house call with him. Surely they were making a connection.

When John Johnson reported for duty, he spoke to McNair before they left the station house. "My girls got the fever. The doctor just told us to try and cool them off with towels soaked in ice and whiskey." He looked pleadingly at his partner. "I got to ask a big favor." He stuck a hand in his pocket and pulled out some money. "I got to pick up some ice at the Howards, but there ain't no saloons close by what'll sell to a black man. Would you buy a bottle of whiskey for me?"

McNair looked at the three dollars, then nodded. "Sure. Meet you back here in ten minutes."

Johnson let out a breath of relief. "Thanks so much—I didn't know how I was gonna make do without your help."

"Where do you live?"

"Fort Pickering."

"Just don't let anybody on the force see you down there this evening. That's way out of our patrol area."

Johnson turned to go. "Thanks. I'll hurry."

As he headed toward Main Street, he couldn't believe the twist of fate which had brought him together with the only witness to his crime of bringing the first yellow fever victim to the city. He was almost sure she had recognized him—or at least there had been some level of recognition. Whether she connected him to that event of a month previous, he had no way of knowing. If she was able to recollect his deed that night, his whole life might collapse. He'd certainly miscalculated when he'd spied Fannie Sellers on the riverbank a month earlier. He wouldn't have figured her for a nurse. Not in a million years. But what in the world was he going to do about the fix he was in?

Chapter 12
Voices

Grenada, Memphis, and points between

September 2, 1878—"No nobler spirit lived than that of Colonel Butler P. Anderson. He was the stuff of which heroes are made. He went down to Grenada when the call was first made to us for help. He went cheerfully and willingly to the people of that once happy town, and for them, during three weeks of unparalleled misery, he was as father, brother, and husband, filling all places of relationship, allowing the citizens a dependence on him, though dazed in the presence of the awful fact of the yellow fever. He went among them, carrying judicious advice for the sick, bearing cheering hope to the despondent, and inspiring those who, nerveless from despair, were giving way to the gloom which had settled over a once beautiful town. He was everything to the Grenadians, and must be to them the one specially cherished name above all others, bright and luminous as that of a hero who dies for his fellowman." Memphis Daily Appeal

"Grenada is no longer a city. It is only a morgue. The police, fire, board of health, and relief committee have all been stopped by death." New Orleans Picayune

September 3, 1878—From Port Gibson, Mississippi—"Out of only 550 citizens remaining in the town, 400 are sick, and 55 are dead." New Orleans Picayune

Emilie Christophe was almost in shock, and many of her fellow nurses could do no better than stagger aimlessly

through their workday, after news of the death of Colonel Anderson began to circulate around Grenada. Emilie had tried her best to ignore all the indications that the end was coming quickly for their selfless leader. But he had been so tired, so used up by the time the fever took hold of him, that he was scarcely able to mount any fight at all. From the time he took to his bed until his demise was less than three days. Perhaps the suddenness of it all—the lack of adequate time for them to prepare for the inevitable—or maybe that his tragic ending was so unexpected was what made it so painful. Then again, they all loved him. Loved him for his goodness, loved him for his courage, and loved him because he loved all of them.

Everywhere Emilie went, she could see reminders of what Colonel Anderson had achieved in Grenada. Although there was still fear, at least there was no longer panic. He had been successful in developing common goals and organization in the little town, despite so many civic leaders fleeing the city or falling to the fever. The number of cases was now greatly reduced, with most of the patients now in the convalescent stage. Of course, that could very well be because there were few victims left for the fever to feed upon. The only pharmacist still open for business in the town had told her the streets of Grenada were pathetically black, in reference to the wearing of black mourning clothes by the few who remained.

So when word came from Memphis that their daily death rate was approaching 200 per day, Emilie knew she had to move on where the needs were greatest. And so she made arrangements to head further north.

She collected her pay from the Howards, donned one of the two civilian dresses she had brought with her, and obtained a ticket on the Mississippi and Tennessee Line for that afternoon. As she sat in the station, waiting on her train, her hand idly closed on the locket and necklace, which she had left in her pocket when she departed from New Orleans.

The northbound train was called and she made her way to the passenger car. It was very crowded, and she finally found a seat directly opposite an elderly Chinese gentleman. He wore a long cream-colored shirt which extended well below his waist, a shiny pair of green pants, green slippers, and a corresponding green cap not much bigger than a yarmulke on his bald head. He looked at her with a piercing eye, perhaps trying to determine if she was sick with the fever. She decided to relieve his concern. "I am a nurse, on my way to volunteer in Memphis. May I sit here, sir?"

"Of course, missy. I spend last two weeks here, try to save my brother and his two sons. Treat them for liver fire in old Chinese way—acupuncture alla time, ginseng and jasmine tea all day, all night." A single tear ran down his cheek. "I fail. All die."

"I'm sorry, sir. I'm afraid I didn't do much better."

He nodded, appreciating her attempt to erase the guilt he felt. "My name Tsen Szen."

"Hello, Mr. Szen. My name is Emilie Christophe."

He sniffed. "You got good ear. Call me Szen." He turned up his nose. "Most peoples call me Chin Chin—stupid peoples."

She smiled at that. "Are you traveling to Memphis?"

"No. Go back my grocery in Senatobia. Wife there now."

"Is there yellow fever in Senatobia?"

"Not so far." He rearranged himself on the seat. "Go sleep now. Long day."

Emilie turned slightly to her right so she could look out upon the town where she had worked these past three weeks. There had been very few success stories, and she wondered if she had accomplished anything worthwhile during her time in Grenada. She suddenly wanted very much to speak to her mother. She pulled the locket from her dress pocket, gazed at it for a moment, looked to be sure Mr. Szen was asleep, then quickly affixed the chain around her neck. Despite her earlier conversation with her mother, this time, the experience was something she would never forget for the rest of her life.

The effect was immediate, and absolutely horrifying. The voices—none of which belonged to her mother—came from every direction, seeming to bounce off the very walls of the railcar's interior and reverberate inside her cranium. Until that moment, she had assumed the locket would enable her to speak only to her mother. What an error that had been!

When she quickly turned her head from side to side, studying Mr. Szen and the other passengers, it was hard to believe they were all sitting there as though completely unconcerned with the multitude of voices, let alone the uncountable and insistent pleas for assistance. It was impossible not to feel their pain, let alone not to heed their calls.

Particularly difficult was an emotional plea from the little seven-year-old Peacock girl, who begged that her momma come to see her in the cemetery, giving explicit directions to her unmarked grave. Next was the also deceased father, James Peacock, asking that someone tell his wife, Josephine, how much he loved her, as he felt he had been neglectful in his last days and had not taken the opportunity himself when he'd still had the chance.

Next there was a voice which she had hoped to hear before the woman died. Sally Butler spoke to her. "Exodus—he a good boy. Please write a letter to his pa—Joshua Butler. He over in Tupelo workin' for Mistuh Burrow. Tell him I said come home and take care of his son."

"I will, Sally. You raised a fine son."

"Joshua ain't the best pa in the world. Be sure you tell him he all the boy has got now."

She was startled when the conductor interrupted the conversation with his last call. "All aboard!" It began to dawn on Emilie that the voices were not part of some dream, or an unknown facet of her imagination. They were real. And the most terrifying thing was, they were all speaking to her—just her. It was as though they recognized someone was in their midst who could hear their voices from beyond the grave. And every one of them was taking full advantage of that realization.

As the engine built up steam, she heard the most heart-rending request of all from Butler P. Anderson himself, asking Emilie—specifically Emilie—to tell his dear wife how sorry he was to have left her so early, and how he would love her until the end of time. He explained that, when he went to Grenada, he'd had no time to properly tell his wife goodbye. He had only been able to warn her to flee to the small town of Hernando, Mississippi, in order to escape the coming epidemic.

Although it had not occurred with the other voices, suddenly a tall figure, covered head to toe in a white burial shroud, stood before her. The top of the cloth fell away, revealing Colonel Anderson himself. He appeared to her just as though he had died seconds earlier—gaunt, sunken-eyed, yellowed skin, an unshaven beard, and his hair and nightshirt in disarray. He was almost unrecognizable compared to the genteel, heroic figure he had presented when Emilie first arrived in Grenada over two weeks before his death. However, his voice was strong and insistent, with no intention of letting her go without a promise to seek out his wife. Indeed, by the time the train had left the Grenada depot behind, Emilie surprised herself by giving the colonel a promise to find his spouse and deliver his message.

She wondered why her mother's voice had not been among those seeking her out. Could it be that the woman no longer felt compelled to speak to her? Was the distance too great from Grenada to New Orleans? And why did all the voices this time seem to originate from people who'd perished in Grenada?

As the small city disappeared from view, Emilie was startled when she looked across at the figure of Mr. Szen in the opposite seat. His eyes were open, staring directly at her. He shook his head slightly, and spoke in a quiet voice. "No worry, missy. I not tell your secret."

She tried to conceal her surprise. "Why, Mr. Szen, I didn't realize you were still awake."

"My mother tell me story 'bout a woman who can do this. I not know to believe her or what. Today I finally know she tell truth."

"I—I didn't know myself until just now."

"Thought you look confuse. My mother say—for people like you, it your duty you use only for good."

"My mother told me the same thing. I think I understand, Mr. Szen."

Emilie had known she had an ability to understand the sometimes deeper meaning behind people's words, their posture, the rhythm of their speech, the movement of their eyes, and even those almost invisible changes of expression. This trait she had possessed for as long as she could remember, and the capability had served her well, not only in interacting with her grandmother, but also in many of her recent bedside conversations with critically ill patients. But the locket—well, that was on an entirely different level. She gazed out the window for some time, thinking about what she had experienced.

Mercifully, Emilie's lack of sleep, combined with the rhythmic music of the rails, finally lulled her to slumber, and she roused only briefly during the next five stops when the conductor walked through the car announcing the stations. That is, until she reached the little town of Hernando, some twenty-five miles south of Memphis. It was only then she realized Mr. Szen had left the train.

Although not nearly so numerous as those in Grenada, the voices in Hernando were every bit as insistent in their requests for her help. At that point in the epidemic, Hernando had only recorded six deaths from yellow fever among her small population, but that number would soon enough reach forty-five. Emilie tried to occupy her mind in some other fashion during the brief stop, but that proved impossible. Suddenly, she heard a voice rise above the others, from Mrs. Butler P. Anderson, asking Emilie to convey to her husband that her heart would always be full of love for him, for without that assurance she could never finally rest.

Emilie looked around her, this time with extra caution, and was satisfied the other travelers were either out of hearing or still asleep. So she spoke quietly to the woman, who had died just two days after her husband, neither knowing that their beloved was also dead. Emilie's message gave the woman immediate peace.

"Now I can go on to heaven with a full heart, knowing my sweet Butler will be there also. There are no words to tell you how important this is to me. Bless you, dear child."

Emilie suddenly was overcome with a feeling of contentment, feeling as though she had actually accomplished something beyond anything she had imagined before, and she resolved to return to Grenada as soon as it was feasible to share this new message with Colonel Anderson. Could it be possible this strange gift actually had value after all? She resolved to pray about it.

The train continued to the north in the fading twilight, with the Hernando voices quickly fading away, but as she neared Memphis, the number and volume of voices began to increase. They began earnestly at White Haven Station, then just a couple of miles from the depot, the train passed close to Calvary Cemetery, where there arose such a cacophony of anguished and distressed voices that they were like a continuous, urgent rumble of thunder. As the railcar proceeded northward, the voices reduced for only a few minutes, then began to build again, finally to another crescendo, as the train reduced its speed to a crawl and snaked its way alongside Third Street, then made a series of turns to arrive at the switchyard in Memphis, which was close to the riverfront, near the intersection of Poplar and Main.

What in the world was she to do? Two hundred people were dying every day. Did that mean she would have that many more tormented souls asking for her help? How could she possibly assist everyone? Worse—how would she convince anyone she now possessed this ability? She decided to remove the necklace until she could get some professional advice.

Chapter 13
Not Even a Rumor of Yellow Fever Here

Holly Springs, Mississippi

A.W. Goodrich, mayor of Holly Springs, Reverend J.N. Craig, pastor of the local Presbyterian church, W.J.L. Holland, editor of the *Holly Springs Reporter,* and Colonel H.W. Walter were making their argument to a large group of citizens. Colonel Walter had the floor. "Holly Springs has never in our history had a single case of yellow fever, and there's no reason for us to expect such now. Unlike Memphis and New Orleans, we've got ourselves a sanitary city. We have no river traffic to bring the fever to us. Our city owns the highest elevation in the entire state of Mississippi—a full 800 feet above sea level. We have no swamps or bayous or ditches. There is no place in our city which could hold the miasma which everyone says is the cause of the fever."

The most knowledgeable man in the room regarding infectious diseases was Dr. Francis Dancy, who had practiced medicine in Holly Springs for several years. "Better to err on the side of caution. The news from Grenada is of a fever much more malignant than previously known. I say protect our own loved ones and our city. I'm for a full quarantine."

Holland recognized Stephen Apple as soon as he stood up to speak. Son-in-law of one of the town's oldest citizens, marrying well was his sole claim to fame, but he did enjoy being seen and heard. "The doc is the only one of us who knows anything about the fever. Why do we want to tempt the devil? We've got ourselves a fine town here—considerin' what the war and the carpetbaggers left us with. So if this partic'lar fever is the worst they ever seen, why bring it here?"

Reverend Craig spoke up. "We're not bringing the fever here. We propose simply bringing innocent people here to get them away from the fever. And we're doing it because it's the charitable thing to do. God has indeed been good to this city, and we should consider sharing our prosperity with those who have little. Those poor people in Grenada have nowhere to run—nowhere to hide. Why not bring at least some of them here so they can survive? If they stay in Grenada, it appears that they have no chance."

Another man in the audience stood up, pointing his finger at the reverend. "Are you and your family gonna stay, Preacher? We hear most o' the holy men run off when the fever comes to their town."

"First of all, the fever is not coming to our town. But no matter what, I will be here, whether it comes or not."

Goodrich, Craig, Walter, and Holland prevailed in the argument. No one mentioned the suspicious fever at the military encampment outside the city, which had been responsible for the deaths of two soldiers. But, like in other cities, physicians were hesitant to speak the words yellow fever in initial cases—particularly when they had no previous experience with the disease.

W.J.L. Holland traveled to Grenada, inviting the locals to come with him to the healthy environment in Holly Springs. Two young men accepted his offer, and actually stayed at the editor's home. Unfortunately, they were undoubtedly already infected, because almost immediately after arriving in Holly Springs, both of the travelers took to their beds.

When the first one died on August 25th in Holland's back room, it was decided his friend, who was in terribly dire straits in a front room, should not find out about the death, as the resulting depression might push him into a decline. Rather than troop through the house with a casket, Holland prevailed on the undertaker to sneak the wooden box through a side window under cover of darkness.

The corpse was placed inside, the casket whisked back out the window, from there into a waiting wagon in the narrow carriageway, then straight to Hill Crest Cemetery. Unfortunately, their precautions had no positive effect on the patient in the front room, as he also succumbed before the night was over. The same procedure of removing the body was utilized, this time in an attempt to not panic the townspeople. Holland's home, often called the Bachelor's Quarters because it seemed only bachelors like Holland lived there, was only one block east of the town square, and certainly a hearse at his front door would have easily been seen by a number of people.

At about this same time, Reverend Craig helped to nurse a sick refugee from Grenada for several days. Despite this personal exposure to danger, he was determined to remain in Holly Springs. But thinking of his family, he sat down and wrote out his will "*between the hours of 11 and 1 o'clock.*" He had a chill not more than thirty minutes after completing the document, and took to his bed.

Almost concurrently, Mayor Goodrich died "under suspicious circumstances," and became the first Holly Springs resident to die from yellow fever. Within three days of his death, some sixty citizens fell ill, with a majority of them dying soon after, and the town was declared to be in epidemic status.

The Marshall County Courthouse, having no business to conduct, was turned into a yellow fever hospital. It was staffed, for the most part, by the Catholic Sisters of Charity, who were based in Nazareth, Kentucky. Beds were nothing more than simple piles of straw, which could easily be swept up, removed, and burned when a patient expired.

Wire from W.J.L. Holland, Chair, Holly Springs Relief Committee, to the Memphis Howards —"*The situation is growing worse. The hospital is full, and it looks like every man must go down. Only 10 of the first 100 cases live. Two days ago, 30 new cases, 10 deaths. Yesterday, 23 new cases, 11 deaths. After having recruited for members five times, the Relief Committee now numbers 1. Of our population of 3,500, 1,500 remain in the city—300 white and 1,200 black. 500 persons lie stricken. We pray for friends and frost. Rows of ghastly coffins line the courthouse lawn, waiting for the ghastlier bodies. The only sound, other than those in the cemetery,*

is the dismal howling of dogs, making a gruesome requiem for the dead."

There was a large ante-bellum home on the south boundary of Holly Springs, which was owned by C. Joseph Herr and his wife. They both came down with yellow fever at about the same time as their infant daughter. They were nursed by "Aunt" Minerva, a Negro woman who had been with them for many years, first as a slave, then after the war as a household servant.

As the Herrs continued to worsen, the husband asked Aunt Minerva if she would promise to care for their two sons, Edward Herr—two years old, and William Herr—aged three, if both he and his wife died. They promised she would be able to live in their home while she raised their sons, and that she would always have a place in the household for the rest of her life.

She replied in the affirmative, and within two days, the two adult Herrs, as well as their baby daughter, passed away. The very next day, the local police arrived, advising Aunt Minerva they were going to confiscate upholstered furniture and clothing in the house so it could be burned. Thankfully, they did not take anything from the pantry or the smokehouse, for Aunt Minerva and her two young charges would have to rely on those provisions to survive until the plantation could harvest and sell a crop.

Aunt Minerva found two sticks of about the right size, tied them together in the shape of a cross with a piece of twine, and with that symbol, each night at bedtime she would trace the shape of a cross on the boys' chests, saying, "white chillun, this be all y'all got to believe in now." (She would successfully raise the two boys to adulthood, and true to their father's word, Aunt Minerva was able to live in the house until she died.)

From time to time, Reverend Craig would rally a bit from his fever and ask his wife, Lydia, for a status report as to his church members and his city.

"There's hardly a person on the street, excepting someone hurrying for a doctor. They say every store and shop and office is closed, if not for a single pharmacy down on the square."

"Are none of our parishioners about?"

"Only those riding in the back of a hearse. As far as I can tell, only you and Elder Scruggs survive in our neighborhood, and I may be the only lady alive in the south end of Holly Springs."

Craig was deeply affected by this news, and paused to collect himself before asking, "What of our other members?"

"Miss Mary and Miss Annie Stewart made up their minds to stay in their home, despite everybody trying to get them to leave the city. I think they had too much affection for their dishes and doilies."

"Even at the risk of their lives?"

"It's worse than that. Miss Mary died five days ago, and Miss Annie begged the undertaker not to take her, but to leave Miss Mary in the house with her."

"Surely they didn't allow it."

"No. But before the day was out, Miss Annie was sick herself, and no one would go near her."

"I don't doubt it. She has a well-deserved reputation of being extremely hard to deal with. Was she left to fend for herself?"

"You've heard her speak out regarding her low opinion of the Catholics?"

"Not more than twenty or thirty times."

Mrs. Craig smiled at her husband's weak attempt at humor. "It seems that the Sisters of Charity were the only ones who would enter Miss Annie's house."

"So it appears our Lord does have a sense of irony! I'd love to have witnessed that first conversation."

"Annie must have been desperate indeed, as the Catholics took her straightaway to the courthouse and nursed her until she died just yesterday."

(*Author's note:* In Holly Springs, six of the sisters at St. Joseph's Catholic Church—Stanislaus, Stella, Margaret, Coninthia, Victoria, and Laurentia—as well as their only priest, Father Anacletus Oberti, died during the epidemic while caring for not only Catholics, but any others in need.

In addition to their assignment at the church, several of the sisters ran the Catholic girls' school—Bethlehem Academy.)

Thomas Falconer was the editor of the *Holly Springs Southern Herald,* and lived in the town with his sons, Howard and Henry. When first Thomas became sick, followed closely by Howard, a third son, Major Kenloch Falconer, who was safe in Jackson, Mississippi, immediately went to see his boss, Governor John Stone. Kenloch was not an imposing man. He was slightly built, of less than average height, possessing dark curly hair and a short beard. But if one looked at his eyes, it was evident there was unquestionably an intensity dwelling therein.

Kenloch had been a distinguished officer in the Confederate Army, then after the war obtained a law degree and was selected by Governor Stone to be his secretary of state for Mississippi. Many acknowledged that this position was merely the first step in what was believed to be a great future for Kenloch in politics.

However, on this sixth day of September, Major Falconer asked that the governor release him from his responsibilities so he might return to Holly Springs to the bedside of his father and brother. Realizing just how dangerous this might be, Governor Stone begged him not to go. After some discussion, Kenloch prevailed, telling the governor he wanted him to select a new secretary of state in his stead, and acknowledged he might never see the governor again.

Major Falconer reached Holly Springs the afternoon of September 8th, and was only there in time to hold his father's hand as he passed away that very evening. He then spent the next week nursing his brother, Howard, before he himself had to take to his bed. Howard Falconer died on September 20th, and his brother, the secretary of state for Mississippi, died three days later.

On September 25th, *The Jackson Weekly Clarion* published the following anecdote from a letter Kenloch Falconer had penned from his deathbed. *"Oh, the scenes here are beyond human power to describe. I realize that there is but One alone who can save us."*

W.M. Hull, a relatively new resident of Holly Springs, related a conversation he'd had with old Colonel H.W. Walter during the worst days of the epidemic. "Walter and his three sons done everything possible to help the people of Holly Springs. All four of them nursed the sick—even opened up their home to folks who had nowheres else to go. Their house was full o' sick and dyin' citizens. The undertaker wagon stopped there twice a day to see what new baggage there was. When I seen Walter last, I asked him what I could do to help. I'll not soon forget what he said to me.

"'Get on your horse and leave this town, and take all your kin with you. It's not your town, nor your people, but it is mine, and here I must stay—and will stay. And I'll do all I can to relieve my stricken people.'"

Hull wiped an invisible speck from his eyes before continuing. "Now that there is a real man."

(*Author's note:* Colonel H.W. Walter and two of his three sons—Frank and Jimmy—died helping their fellow townspeople in Holly Springs. The colonel had sent his wife and daughters away at the beginning of the epidemic. After the yellow fever departed the city, Mrs. Walter returned and reared her daughters in Holly Springs.)

Chapter 14
Have I Sinned, Father?

Memphis

September 2, 1878—Letter from Dr. William Armstrong to his wife—"The Sisters (at St. Mary's Episcopal Church) *are very kind and attentive, and seem to trust implicitly in all my instructions. I told you already they have employed me as Physician to their* [Orphan] *Home—amounting already to near a hundred children, and still more to follow. I hope they will all have a light attack, but it is impossible to tell—it is the most treacherous disease we've known. I wish I could see my little ones so much. The number of deaths reported is pitiful—yesterday 208. I wish I could go to some secret spot where there would be no burning heads and hands to feel, nor racing pulses to count—for the next six months. It is fever, fever all day long, and I am so wearied."*

After her arrival in Memphis, Emilie Christophe reported to the Howards' office on Main Street the following morning in her nursing uniform, providing them with a list of her recent assignments as well as her personal history with yellow fever in 1873. They were ecstatic to find someone with her qualifications, and immediately assigned her to a family in that area of the city referred to as Victorian Village. This particular neighborhood was home to the most prosperous families in the city, and it was evident in the girl's background, as well as the demeanor she displayed, that she would be a good fit.

Before reporting to 680 Adams Avenue, Emilie found her way to a nearby Catholic church, as she possessed an urgent question which had to be answered before she could continue in her work. She entered the church, lighting a candle before she sat in a rear pew. Within a few minutes, a priest approached her.

"Father, will you hear my confession today?"

"We've seen very few parishioners here in the church for the past two weeks." He paused for a moment. "Most of the confessions we hear now are at the death bed," he couldn't help noticing her nurse clothing, "but I suppose you know that, given the occupation you're in."

"Yes, Father—but I have a question I cannot resolve by myself." She was obviously in a bit of distress. "Will you help me?"

He smiled at her. "Let's step into the confessional. Perhaps it will be easier there."

When they were both seated, Emilie glanced sideways at the wooden-slatted screen before crossing herself. "Forgive me, Father, for I have sinned. It's been four weeks since my last confession."

"Given the times, child, I'm not surprised. Very few people are out and about."

"I'm not sure where to begin, Father."

"Maybe the beginning would be a good place to start."

"I suppose so. My grandmother, and her mother before her, came from Haiti. They each practiced the Creole arts of fortune telling, holding séances, casting spells, and the like."

"Tell me, child, were you raised as a Catholic?"

"Yes. My mother did not participate in my grandmother's profession. She raised me in the church."

Expecting to hear an obscure, rural church as her answer, the priest inquired, "And what might be your home parish?"

"St. Louis Cathedral in New Orleans."

That was indeed a surprise—although he could not argue that the girl certainly spoke well and carried herself like a lady. "And what is your question for me?"

"I inherited a locket from my great-grandmother, which my grandmother always wore when she was engaged in her business dealings. She put a great deal of store in what she called the special powers of the locket. Just yesterday, I put this locket around my neck as I departed Grenada."

Thankful for the protective screen between them, the priest rolled his eyes, but endeavored to keep his voice serious. "And did you find it to have any special power?"

"Yes, Father, I did. As soon as I fastened the clasp, I began to hear a multitude of voices, which I immediately recognized as belonging to the dead."

"Are you sure you weren't simply imagining these voices because of stories your grandmother had told you?"

"Although she always said the locket had special powers, she never described those powers. So it was a complete surprise to me when I heard the voices."

The priest reflected on all the important work he needed to be about. Surely this girl wasn't serious. "Did anyone else hear the voices?"

"No, Father—and I was surrounded by others when this occurred."

"And what is the sin for which you wish absolution?"

"I am fearful that using this locket to speak to the dead is somehow a sin."

He thought about that for a moment. "Just where did you hear these voices?"

"I put on the locket in Grenada. So I heard voices there, then again in Hernando when my train arrived, and finally in Memphis last night."

"And do you hear them now?"

"No, Father. I took the locket off last night, and the voices immediately stopped."

"What did the voices say?"

"All of them seemed to be pleading with me to give a message to someone they had left behind. They appeared to be tormented because they had neglected to reach out to a loved one before it was too late to ever speak with them again."

He thought briefly of his coffee, suddenly wishing he had never left his cup in the senior pastor's office before he'd wandered into the nave. "Did any of the voices give you their names?"

"Yes, Father. There must have been over a hundred of them, sometimes all speaking at once. It was overwhelming. I only concentrated on a few, but I believe all of them were telling me who they were, who they wanted me to communicate with on their behalf, and why it was important."

"Can you tell me their names?"

"Well, I spoke to Butler P. Anderson in Grenada, who wanted me to speak to his wife. And then I spoke to Mrs. Anderson in Hernando."

All of a sudden, the priest was giving her his full attention. "How did you find her?"

"I didn't find her—she found me, Father. She is also dead. If I'm not mistaken, she had just passed on yesterday before my train arrived."

"I want you to say ten Hail Mary's a day for a week, child. Now go in peace and sin no more."

Reluctantly, Emilie realized she would receive no resolution to her question. "Thank you, Father."

She exited the confessional, knelt quickly, crossed herself, and turned to go. But before she reached the exit, the priest spoke to her from the door of the confessional. "I think this matter requires more wisdom than I have, child. Please come with me and perhaps together the vicar and I can give you some advice."

When they reached the vicar's office, the priest bade her wait outside for a few minutes. She could hear them talking through the door before the priest beckoned her inside. The senior reverend, a fellow of some fifty years, took over the questioning at that point. "Let me be sure I understand. Are you saying you spoke to Colonel Anderson or perhaps his ghost in Grenada? His death is certainly information known and mourned by everybody in this city. But his wife, you say she found you in Hernando?"

"Yes, Father. I believe she had died earlier on the day I arrived. I was able to pass on the message from her husband—he wasn't a ghost as far as I could tell—and it seemed to give her great comfort. She said she could now go to heaven since she knew her husband was there waiting on her."

"Are you saying she was ready to leave purgatory once she knew her husband was in heaven?"

"I don't know, Father. Maybe all of them were in purgatory—at least those who wanted to speak to me."

"All of them? How many is all of them?"

"I couldn't begin to tell, Father. The voices were all talking at once. Perhaps as many as a hundred in Grenada."

"Young lady, it sounds as though you are trying to convince us you can communicate with the dead using some kind of black magic." He indicated the priest beside him. "I believe Father indicated your Haitian background. But surely you know we cannot accept this blasphemy."

"Are you saying I've committed some kind of terrible sin, Father?"

"Have you recently had the yellow fever? We have seen many people who now have a damaged mental capacity after the fever. Some have even had hallucinations. Perhaps this is the explanation?"

"I haven't had the fever since 1873, Father."

"Then I hope this is nothing more than your imagination, and that you did not intend to mislead people into believing you had some special power."

"I've told no one, Father. I came here to you because I didn't know what else to do."

"Then go and practice your healing profession. And pray for understanding."

"Thank you, Father."

He opened another door for her. "You can leave through here rather than going back the way you came."

Emilie slowly made her way through the side garden of the church and stepped out on to the street, ready to walk on to her nursing assignment, but something held her back. She couldn't escape the feeling that she had been completely misunderstood. She had a hard time accepting what the reverend had said, making it sound as though she was some kind of fake—or even a charlatan, like her grandmother. She paused just long enough to build her confidence, then did the only thing she could. She retrieved the locket from her pocket and once again fastened the jewelry round her neck.

A strong voice immediately accosted her, and she stood there listening for a couple of minutes. "Of course, Father." Emilie then turned and walked back through the garden, again finding the door to the reverend's office. She wasn't surprised to find the two of them still together when her knock was answered. She stepped inside without invitation, as she was not to be deterred.

"Excuse me, Fathers." She had her hand on the locket. "Someone spoke to me just outside the church."

They looked a bit surprised. "Yes?"

"One of your priests passed away here two days ago. He took to his bed immediately after the shock of witnessing Reverend Martin Walsh's funeral procession, and never rose from that bed."

The vicar looked at the priest before answering. "Yes, but you could have heard that anywhere here in the city."

"Have you examined his effects?"

"No. But what business is this of yours?"

"The priest spoke to me not five minutes ago. He asked that I express his regret at leaving you, and he wanted to be sure you found the note he left on his Bible."

The vicar's voice hardened. "So you have decided not to be repentant after all."

Emilie ignored this. "The priest owed a small debt to a Reverend D.A. Quinn, whom I gather does not reside here in Memphis. He had no money when he died, and so his note bequeaths his entire library to Reverend Quinn to clear his name and his debt."

"His entire library?" The vicar turned to his fellow priest. "Wait here with this girl. I'll be right back."

And he was. "How did you manage to know about this note? Have you or an accomplice broken into our quarters?"

"I arrived on the train from Grenada last night and came straight here this morning after reporting to the Howards. Why do you assume I am lying? Is it because you don't understand? That's why I came here this morning. I don't understand either, but somehow the dead are seeking me out."

The vicar's voice left no doubts about his feeling. "That's just not possible."

She turned her attention to the priest who had heard her confession, perhaps because he had at least been willing to listen to her without making a harsh judgment. "The church celebrates hundreds of miracles. Maybe this is one. I don't know. But if I can help someone who is obviously in torment, I intend to do so. Surely our interest in a person does not simply end at their death.

"I feel as though I owe the dead a debt. After all, who speaks for them?" She exited the side door again without further comment, leaving the two holy men standing there. It was hard not to notice the look of hesitation in the younger priest's eye. Harder still not to see the tears of frustration in her own.

Chapter 15
He's the Best of Us All, Y'all

Memphis

Sister Hughetta answered the door at the Episcopal Sisters' House in early afternoon, and was heartened to see, standing on the stoop, Sisters Helen and Ruth, who had just arrived from New York on the morning train, and with them Sister Clare, from St. Mary's in East Grimstead, England. "Oh, Sisters, come in, come in. You can't imagine how we've been praying for your safe arrival." Hughetta brushed away tears of relief. "We've got so much to talk about, and so little time to do so."

Mrs. Bullock came in with cups and a teapot, and after Sister Hughetta had given them a short status report, the housekeeper whisked them away to their rooms so they might rest up for the battle they were about to enter the next morning.

Sister Thecla came in, asking for clothing in which to bury a girl. "I've given everything I have away. This is the fourth I have seen in the same family die, and I've commended the soul of each into the hands of God. The father is still up and doing all he can. I promised to prepare the body for burial."

Sister Hughetta hugged her briefly. "Dear sister, you must not do too much in that way; promise me you will not."

"I will do just what you think is right." As she turned to go, she reflected. "One can do so little."

Sister Hughetta spent the afternoon visiting a long list of sick families, one of which was that of a friend. All six in the house were ill with the fever. Finally returning to the residence near sunset, she remembered not having visited Dr. Harris that day.

She was distraught when she discovered Reverend Parsons had been taken ill that very morning, and so she visited him first, trying very hard to conceal her fear for his welfare. They had decided to open up an infirmary in the St. Mary's school which had closed a week after the epidemic began, and it was to this facility that Parsons had been put to bed. He was very cheerful. The room was uncomfortably warm, and she offered to do him some little service, perhaps fanning him, or putting up a mosquito net.

"No, no, I beg you will not; indeed, I could not let you so fatigue yourself."

His nurse whispered to her, "Let him have his way. I never saw anyone as unselfish as he is."

On her way back to the Sisters' House, Hughetta couldn't help but realize that, up until this time, Reverend Parsons had led the daily celebration of the Holy Eucharist in the cathedral, but with he and Dean George Harris both ill, they had no reverend on duty.

September 3, 1878—"The people of New Orleans yesterday applied to the Secretary of War for rations, representing their distress and suffering as terrible beyond description. Total deaths in New Orleans up to yesterday were 1091, including 461 children. Baton Rouge—11 deaths from yellow fever. All business is suspended. Port Gibson, Mississippi—55 deaths. Memphis—582 deaths."

"Another of the noble Howards was buried Sunday. Ed Mansford, 35 years old, who, in 1873, and thru this epidemic, until two days before he died, was conspicuous for his untiring energy in a work, but for which the poor would have no succor, passed away as Sunday morning dawned. He fought the good fight, henceforth there waits for him the crown of martyrdom. He went to his grave, acknowledged as a leader among those not afraid to die that others might live."

"Innumerable complaints were made at the health office yesterday about corpses lying unburied, some for 36 to 48 hours. Undertaker Walsh declared his inability to get coffins built or enough laborers to dig graves."

(Ad) "Dr. T.H. Durdynaud, of Paris, residing in New Orleans will, by paying five dollars in advance, send to any person in Memphis all the medicines which are necessary to cure the prevailing epidemic, the so-called yellow fever. Not one patient shall succumb by using this medicine on first symptom. The money must be deposited in advance with Harry Seches, 128-130 Union Ave." Memphis Daily Appeal

"The fever has spread rapidly to the southern part of the city. Fort Pickering is full of it. There is now no part of the corporate limits of the city not thoroughly infected with the fever poison. All of Sunday and yesterday, hearses followed each other at a trot to the cemeteries, unattended by any but the drivers." Memphis Avalanche

September 3, 1878—"The recently elected mayor of our city (Vicksburg), *who was to have been installed yesterday, was instead buried this morning. Father McManus, of St. Paul's Church, was buried yesterday, and two other priests are in critical condition. At a meeting of the Board of Aldermen, only the City Clerk and two aldermen were present—all others being sick, dead, or having fled the town. This truly has been the saddest day Vicksburg has experienced for fifty years. No pen can picture the dreadful state of existing affairs. We cry Help! Help! Anyway! Everyway! Send us doctors, nurses, money, provisions, anything. There is no way of getting an accurate count of cases. The death list—Oh! Horror! Exceeds any during previous epidemics. No person seems to be exempt from attack this year, not even those who have had the fever before—and some of them have died." Telegram received by* Chicago Daily Tribune

Lester Sellers and Israel Jackson were making their last trip of the day just south of the city in Fort Pickering. The old military quarters, plus a number of new homes and new streets, made it difficult to locate addresses, but they continued, as they were fairly sure there would be other customers in the neighborhood.

Israel looked long and hard at his co-worker before finally finding courage to ask his question. "Lester, do you ever have trouble sleepin' at night?"

"My woman claims I sleep like a dead man."

Israel tried to clarify. "Do this business ever give you the bad dreams?"

"You mean seein' all these dead folks?"

"Yeah, the dead families, the bodies what been eaten on by them rats, the little babies."

"I reckon not. How 'bout you?"

"I sees 'em all night long, Lester. They wake me up, an' when I finally get back to sleep, here they come again."

"Mebbe you need t' find yerself a woman. Course, it's a whole lot cheaper to just take a drink or two afore bed."

Israel held his head between his hands. "I had myself a wife once—and a boy, too."

Surprised, Lester looked sideways at his friend. "You never told me that. What happened?"

"'Bout five years ago, Reesa—that's my wife—she was gonna have a baby. Gonna be a boy—leastwise thet's what I had my head set on. She was prob'ly a month or so from havin' my boy. Skinny as can be, but she was all swole up, ye know. I went off to Mr. Denie's to work, and when I got home that evenin', she was gone."

"Where'd she go?"

"That's just it. I got no idee. What little clothes Reesa had was still in the house. The neighbor lady says she never saw nothin'. I spoke to the midwife. She didn't know nothin' neither. I went to the police, but they didn't pay me no mind. I reckon they figgered, jest 'nother problem amongst the coloreds. I spent the better part o' two years lookin' for her. Not no trace. So up til I took this job, I spent ever' night havin' fearsome dreams 'bout Reesa an' my boy. But now these here corpses done took over most o' my nights."

Lester put a hand on his friend's shoulder. "Not too many men kin do this kinda work, Israel. Take a drink or two. You'll be all right."

"The worstest is when some little chile comes out the house and asks us to come in and see if they momma is still alive. I swear it feels like my heart gonna tear in two. The money is good. But I never figgered it would 'fect me so much."

As they turned a corner and made their way through the newer little houses, they were flagged down by an Irishman and forced to come back to the reality of their jobs. “Sure, and it’s thankful I am that I’ve found you boys. ’Tis a friend o’ mine, Dennis O’Leary, a son of Tipperary County, what’s ready for your wagon on the street behind me.”

“This here load is headed to potter’s field. He ain’t got himself a plot over at Calvary Cemetery, does he?”

“Dennis would be tickled to be there, with all the saints an’ such, but ’tis unfortunate it is that he’s poor as I am.”

Lester clucked at the mules. “Lead the way and we’ll pick him up.”

They arrived at the humble dwelling, withdrew a casket from the wagon, and went inside. The Irishman chose to stay outside. “’Tis hard t’ see me old friend put in that box. I’ll be waitin’ out here.”

In a few minutes, they emerged from the house, carrying their load, and Israel went to fetch a wooden lid and hammer to close the casket. At that point, the Irishman finally decided to look upon his friend one last time, and he bent over the casket. “Well, it’s damned I’ll be! The idjit nurse put the wrong clothes on old Dennis.”

Lester looked in the casket at the corpse. “Well, we figgered he was all dressed up fer a party or somethin’.”

“Dennis left five dollars for the nurse to put his Order of Ancient Hibernians regalia on him for his burial. But the stupid idjit has put a harlequin costume on the old sod. That’s what poor Dennis wore for Mardi-Gras three years back.”

Lester shrugged his shoulders. “Look here, mister. We got to get this load to the cemetery afore six o’clock. They be closin’ the gate, an’ won’t take no more corpses after that.”

“But what would poor old Dennis say?”

Lester glanced briefly in the casket. “I doubt he’s gonna say too much about nothin’ from here on out.” Lester turned back to face the dead man’s friend. “Mister, we ain’t got time to wait fer his other clothes. Once we nail down this lid, ain’t nobody gonna know what he’s wearin’.”

The Irishman stuck his head over the casket one last time and patted the corpse on his shoulder. “Well, Dennis, old son, it’s to Glory you’ll be goin’ in colors and spangles.”

Dr. Armstrong gathered his bag together before departing from St. Mary's infirmary. As he opened the door, Sister Hughetta pressed a small envelope into his hand. "Doctor, please don't open this until you get to your home."

Armstrong looked at it, supposing it to be perhaps a description of symptoms for either herself or someone else at the church, and thrust it into his pocket as directed. "Yes, Sister—good night."

"God bless, Doctor Armstrong."

When the doctor reached his quarters, he pulled the small envelope from his pocket and read the note on its cover. 'An expression of gratitude and affection from the Sisters.' Neatly folded inside were two fifty dollar bank notes. Tired as he was, this touched him greatly, as he knew the ladies of St. Mary's had very little money. His first inclination was to put his coat back on and go back to the church to return the money. But then he realized it was a sincere gift, and it would be uncharitable to return it. Perhaps one day, if they survived, he would make a gift to their order as a way of expressing his gratitude. They were certainly deserving.

As Emilie Christophe proceeded east toward her assignment on Adams Street, she couldn't help but notice the dramatic increase in the impressive size and quality of the homes. Obviously, this had to be the most prosperous neighborhood in the city. The two-story mansion she stood before at 652 Adams was larger than any home she had ever seen, whether in Memphis or New Orleans.

In the front yard, she spied a man, dressed in rough clothing and wearing a tattered straw hat, who appeared to be heading a huge bed of yellow and red chrysanthemums. She walked up to the front gate and called out to the man, who she assumed must be the gardener. "Excuse me, sir, I'm looking for the Dickinson house."

The man rose awkwardly from his kneeling position, brushed the dirt from the front of his britches as best he could, and strolled over to her. She noticed he was very tall—well over six feet—and sported a trimmed salt-and-pepper beard. She guessed his age at around sixty. His gray eyes quickly appraised Emilie before he pointed. "The Dickinson family is in the very next house. You must be the new nurse.

Their maid ran off first, and then they lost their doctor yesterday. I'm sure they need you in the worst way, as I understand several in the family are sick."

"Thank you, sir." Emilie presented herself at the back of the house next door, which was large, but significantly smaller than its outsized neighbor. She knocked repeatedly until the door was finally answered by a young girl, who had a kerchief tied around her auburn hair. She looked as though she was completely exhausted. "I'm Emilie Christophe, the new nurse from the Howards."

The girl gave an audible sigh of relief. "Thank goodness. Please come in. We need your help." She held the door open and Emilie entered an anteroom off the kitchen. "Would you like a cup of tea?"

"No. Please don't go to any trouble."

"That's okay. I surely need a cup myself. Come back in the kitchen and I can tell you what's happened with us." The girl stirred the coals, then put a pot on the stove before turning back to Emilie. "There are six of us here now. My brother Donnie passed away two days ago. My father and three sisters have had the fever for a week or so. Then right after Donnie passed, Mama took to her bed. We were able to keep up with everything until she got the fever. Then Doctor Nugent left us when he took sick just yesterday morning. That's when I had to ask the Howards for help."

"So you're the only person in the house to take care of everyone else?" The girl nodded. "What is your name?"

"Victoria Dickinson."

"How old are you, Victoria?"

"I'll be eleven in November."

"You're a very brave girl. I doubt many girls, or women for that matter, could have done what you have. Your mother must be very proud of you. Now, sit here for a moment and tell me a little about each one of your patients, how they're getting along, what they're able to eat or drink, and what kind of treatment each is receiving."

At the conclusion of this conversation, Victoria led Emilie through the home, opening five separate bedroom doors, and telling which family member was in each of the rooms. Emilie then turned to Victoria. "Have you had the fever yourself?"

"No. For some reason I've been spared."

"All right. Starting right now, you are going to keep your distance from all of them. I'll take care of the nursing duties. What I need you to do is take over the kitchen. You'll need to prepare their broths as well as whatever you and I eat. You must wash every dish and every utensil in very hot, soapy water, and keep our dishes separate from theirs. In the meantime, I'm going to put your three sisters in a single room. It's far too difficult to keep up with everybody when they're separated. We will continue to keep your mother and father apart. I'm sure you realize Mr. Robert is very ill, and we can't have him preventing your mother from getting her rest."

"You mean I can't go in to see about my family?"

"I mean the last thing we need is six people sick. We need to keep you well. I'm going to get those girls moved to the largest room, and you put together a chicken broth for them, and something more substantial for us. Then you're going to take a good long nap." Victoria started to object and Emilie shushed her. "No arguments. I'd guess your bed hasn't seen you in about thirty-six hours. Get some rest. I'll need your help soon enough."

Before turning to her new patients, Emilie reflected once more on her conversation with the priests. She had a premonition her new capability would be required again someday soon. There was nothing to do except utter a short prayer for understanding. She could only hope it would come.

The morning of September 4th, Sister Hughetta and Mrs. Bullock, of St. Mary's Episcopal Church, stood together in the infirmary, both wearing cloths tied around their head and covering their nose and mouth, their arms wrapped around each other. Lying in front of them was Reverend Charles Parsons, in the midst of an attack of high fever, his eyes flicking from one corner of the room to the other. It was unlikely he knew they were even in the room. His face and chest were splotched with a red rash.

Sister Hughetta sniffled. "If only his Margaret could be here with him. Maybe she could at least give him some comfort."

"Ah, she's going to have two boys to raise by herself now. If she did come up here, she'd likely catch the fever, too."

Mrs. Bullock bent down, dipped a towel in some icy water, and sponged Parsons. He was so hot, it seemed like the cold water evaporated almost instantly. She immersed the towel in the cold water again, then wrung it out and placed it around Parson's neck.

Finished, Mrs. Bullock sighed and spoke again, quieter now. "It doesn't seem possible our Lord would take Reverend Parsons from us. Nobody has given more of himself in this city. And he's only forty years old." She paused for a moment, reflecting on all the terrible things she had witnessed over the last three weeks.

They spent a few minutes praying over the reverend before retreating to the Sisters' House just after the noon hour. What they discovered was terrible indeed. They found Sister Superior Constance in the parlor, resting on a sofa. It was obvious she was ill, and Hughetta asked her to please go up to bed.

Constance's face was bathed in perspiration, and her eyes revealed she was in pain. "It's only a slight headache. Besides, I've got so much to do. Mrs. Bullock, would you be kind enough to let me dictate a few notes to you?"

"Of course, Sister." Mrs. Bullock filled her ink pen, took her place on a chair beside the sofa, and Constance began to dictate her way through a list of thank you notes for donated money and goods which they had recently received. It was a task to which she attended at least twice a week since the epidemic had started.

Hughetta spied Dr. Armstrong, on his way to Reverend George Harris' home, and hurried to catch up with him. "Doctor, I fear Sister Constance has come down with the fever. Would you look in on her, please?"

Even during the epidemic, Armstrong was surprised to see Constance reclining during the middle of the day. Indeed, he had never seen her so much as sit down from daylight until long after dark. "Sister, tell me how you're feeling."

She looked him square in the eye, speaking with as convincing a voice as she could muster. "I have not the fever. It is only a bad headache, and it will undoubtedly disappear by sunset."

"Just to be on the safe side, I want you to go to bed. No excuses."

"Mrs. Bullock, will you help me?"

When Sister Hughetta pulled a comfortable mattress into the school infirmary, Constance shook her head, saying, "It is the only down mattress you have in the house, and if I have the fever you will have to burn it."

Within the same hour, Sister Thecla came in, having sat at the deathbed of a poor woman in the neighborhood. When she saw Sister Hughetta, she calmly and quietly said, "I am so sorry, Sister, but I have the fever. Give me a cup of tea, and then I shall go to bed." When Hughetta attempted to give Thecla the comfortable mattress, she also refused, possessing the same generous yet practical spirit as the sister superior.

When both Thecla and Constance were settled in the infirmary, Hughetta spoke privately to Mrs. Bullock. "How in the world are we going to keep the Canfield orphan home going now? Doctor Armstrong said poor Reverend Parsons wasn't likely to make it through the night. Now there's Sister Constance and Sister Thecla down with the fever. What are we going to do?"

"There's the two of us, and Sisters Ruth, Helen, and Clare; and I think Sister Frances is doing much better. Maybe we can borrow a priest from St. Louis or somewhere. The bishop is going to have a conniption when he gets a telegram from one of us instead of a priest. Besides that, we'll have to rely on Doctor Armstrong as well as some Howard nurses if we're going to keep up with the orphan home." She paused, looked at her friend, and the tears flowed. "I'm scared, Sister."

Hughetta held her friend as tightly as she could, then released her. "So am I. For the first time, I wonder if I've got the courage to do what we're called to do."

September 5, 1878—"Black as the dead list is today in our city, it fails to represent all those ready for burial yesterday. The county undertaker has four furniture wagons busy all day. Upon each the coffins are stacked as high as safety from falling would permit. These four vehicles, doing the wholesale burial business, failed to take to the potter's field all of the indigent dead. As the officer made his report, sixty bodies were waiting interment." Memphis Avalanche

September 5, 1878—From Collierville (25 miles east of Memphis)—*"Great excitement here on account of the yellow fever which appeared last Monday. Two deaths so far and*

several suspicious cases in town. The greatest panic prevails, people are fleeing to the country in all directions. Fifty-one families have left, others are leaving hourly. The country all around is wild with rumors and the town is almost completely destroyed." Memphis Public Ledger

When Dr. Armstrong visited Reverend Harris' home that evening, he found the dean somewhat better, but still ill enough that he could see no positive outcome for the man. Dean Harris, however, was adamant the doctor not waste his precious time on him, but rather he should go immediately to the Howards' Court Street infirmary, where Reverend Parsons had been moved earlier in the day.

After a five-minute buggy ride to the infirmary, Armstrong found Parsons to be quite ill. He was feverish, his skin had begun to yellow, his eyes were filled with blood, he had an unrelenting case of hiccups, and, although he tried to hide it, there were smears of corruption on his bedding. Armstrong hoped he could put on a positive face for the reverend.

For his part, Reverend Parsons was fully conscious, and despite the fever, his mind seemed to be quite clear. As was his custom, he seemed to spend all of his time thinking about others, though his voice was strained. "Thank you for coming, Doctor Armstrong. How is Dean Harris this evening?"

"It's hard to believe, but he is stable, Reverend. He's stronger than most men, that's for sure."

Parsons was taken with a prolonged shiver, but made no mention of it. "And how are Sisters Constance and Thecla?"

"Constance is weaker today, but I'm optimistic that Thecla can pull through." (In truth, both sisters had very high fevers, and Constance had just remarked "I shall never get up from my bed." She also had asked Sister Hughetta to send for Sister Clare at the Canfield orphan home, so she could assist at the infirmary as well as with nursing Harris. Perhaps Dr. Armstrong had purposely decided to spare the reverend any more alarming news than he was already dealing with.)

"That's indeed good news, Doctor." Parsons paused, grabbed for the emesis basin, and gagged several times without any results. "I'm sorry, Doctor. I don't mean to be rude." He paused long enough to be sure his stomach had quieted.

"I would imagine you've seen plenty of this sort of thing lately. Would you mind telling me what is the situation at the orphan home?"

"There are almost a hundred children at the home now. Sister Frances has done a wonderful job in getting everything organized. It would make you very proud to see how well the operation is being run. If I'm not mistaken, we've only sent six children to the infirmary here, but there will undoubtedly be more."

"I suppose that was to be expected, given the reason all of them became orphans in the first place. And frankly, I expected nothing less from Sister Frances. By all rights, she should be administering all of our functions. No one is better qualified—and that includes Dean Harris and myself. Strangely enough, she is our newest sister, having just recently joined the order."

"Are you able to drink anything, Reverend?"

Before he could answer, Parsons was struck with a violent bout of vomiting, all flecked with dark blood. He took several more minutes to gather himself before answering in almost a whisper. "Not so much this evening, Doctor."

"Reverend, I want you to know how much I respect you. And it's because of that respect that I must be honest with you." He cleared his throat and dabbed at something in his eye. "You are very ill tonight. Your prospects are very dangerous," his voice caught, "and I fear we may not see each other again in this life."

Parsons looked at the doctor for a full minute. "Bless you, Doctor. I trust that I have done my duty." The two men's handclasp lasted for some time, neither of them wanting to face the fact that this was undoubtedly the end. Dr. Armstrong departed, sad as he had ever been in his life.

Sister Hughetta was on watch that evening at the Howards' infirmary, and she was not surprised when Reverend Parsons calmly spoke to her. "Sister, we have no clergyman available. If you would hand me my prayer book, I'd like to read the last Commendatory Prayer for myself."

She knelt at his bedside while Parsons spoke the prayer that she had heard a hundred times in the last month. She held the book open to the appropriate page for him, but it was unnecessary for him to read the text. He had spoken it so many times in the last three weeks, it had become a part of him. But as to Hughetta, she had never heard, nor had she imagined hearing, it spoken for oneself.

"O Most Gracious Father; I fly unto thee for mercy, in behalf of this thy servant, Charles, here lying under the sudden visitation of thine hand. If it be thy will, preserve my life, that there may be place for repentance. But, if thou hast otherwise appointed, let thy mercy supply to me the want of the usual opportunity for the trimming of my lamp. Stir up in me such sorrow for sin, and such fervent love for thee, as may, in a short time, do the work of many days. That among the praises which thy Saints and holy Angels shall sing to the honor of thy mercy through eternal ages, it may be to the unspeakable glory, that thou has redeemed the soul of this thy servant from eternal death, and made me partaker of the everlasting life, which is through Jesus Christ our Lord. Amen."

Sister Hughetta wept like a young girl when she closed his prayer book. Reverend Parsons folded his hands across his chest, looked toward the heavens, and simply said in a quiet, clear voice, "Lord Jesus, receive my spirit." In just a few minutes—at half past ten o'clock—he passed over.

When Sister Hughetta arrived at St. Mary's that Saturday morning, she quickly gathered everyone together. When she delivered her terrible message, there was not a dry eye amongst them. They had hoped against all reason that Reverend Parsons would survive his ordeal. But the news of his death, let alone the courageous way he died, was a knife which pierced every heart. Mrs. Bullock said what all of them were thinking. "I believe Reverend Parsons was the best of us all, y'all."

It was under these circumstances that Sister Hughetta greeted Reverend William Dalzell at their door, just arrived via the Tennessee and Mississippi Line from Shreveport, Louisiana. He had answered Bishop Quintard's call for assistance, and since he possessed previous personal experience with yellow fever, he did not flinch from volunteering.

They had finally received assistance in the form of someone whom they could count on to survive. There was much to do. The sisters didn't hesitate to put him to work.

September 6, 1878—Letter from Dr. William Armstrong to his wife—"I have just a few calls ahead between eight and

nine, and then to bed. I have quite a hospital in and around our home. Dean Harris and Reverend Parsons are both quite ill. (When Armstrong wrote this, he didn't realize Parsons was already dead.) *Sisters Constance and Thecla, at the school are down. Jim Tighe's family are ill, two are sick at the Goldsmiths', and two at old Linde's. You may think after a while that you have a pretty fair husband, compared with some others."*

September 6, 1878—Letter from Dr. William Armstrong to his daughter—"My Dear Sweet—you think of your poor tired papa, I know. He is here risking life, that he may be able to give you a home and comforts in life. Will you not love him for it? I know you do—and I want you to be a good girl and get on your knees every night and ask God to save your papa from the pestilence —for only He can do it."

September 6, 1878—"D. Sussman, a nurse who came from Chicago, has been acting very badly and has imposed on every organization in town. He is totally worthless and irresponsible. He was sent to nurse Dr. Brown, on Chelsea, and managed to break the doctor's watch and thermometer, and drank all the liquor in sight. Such characters had better give Memphis a wide berth, or they will find themselves in a warm place."

September 6, 1878—"Another sickening case of desertion has come to light. A man named Townsley lost a child by fever, immediately after the funeral of which, his wife and little daughter, Florence, twelve years of age, took the fever. In despair, he told his neighbors he was going to make away with himself, and has not been heard of. Since he deserted his wife, she died, and has been buried, and his little Florence, as well as his youngest child, a boy, are wards in the infirmary. If he isn't dead, somebody ought to kill him."

"Drs. Baskerville, Meade, Williams, and S.H. Brown were taken down by the fever yesterday. Postmaster Thompson passed away yesterday. Rev. Dr. A. Thomas, of the German Free Protestant Church, died of the yellow fever yesterday. Dr. Thomas was one of the noble martyrs, devoting himself entirely to the sick and afflicted of his parish."

"Mrs. C.S. Hart, of Winchester, Virginia, writes that a teaspoonful of prepared willow charcoal taken every morning will act as a prophylactic in yellow fever. She says she tried it in New Orleans during the epidemic of 1867."

"Dr. Chappin, President of the New Orleans Board of Health, does not think the mortality rate from yellow fever will exceed one in ten of the cases in that city. In Memphis, so far it exceeds five in ten. Total cases in Memphis to date is 1511, deaths 858."

"Dr. Bartlett, of Buffalo, inventor of the ozone generator, proposes to kill yellow fever by his invention. We hope he will try it."

(Ad) "E.F. Bevens, druggist, will fill prescriptions at all hours, day and night. James P. Merritt sleeps at the store all night long, and will attend to night calls promptly." Memphis Daily Appeal

Chapter 16
Dr. Sohm

Memphis

Annie Cook was struggling on the stairway with an armful of clean bedding and a bucket of ice. She had never been so exhausted in her life, but the patients never seemed to stop coming. Every day the Howards brought more sick people to her. There were seven bedrooms in the Mansion House, and at last count she was caring for thirty-four yellow fever patients. It seemed as though no sooner did one patient die than the Howards would show up with two more. It was a rare event to see someone get well enough to stand up and walk out of the house. The number of people who had died in her home was appalling.

When she'd offered to open the Mansion House to the Howards, she'd imagined taking perhaps six patients—one for each of the whores' rooms. But the reality was four people in a room—including her own—and six more in the drawing room. She and Beulah slept on improvised pallets in the kitchen and the pantry.

To be sure, the Howards brought stores to her when they were available, but in order to provide at least some measure of predictable sustenance and supplies for the patients, a significant portion of her day was spent trying to obtain bedding, food, and ice. She hadn't planned for this kind of demand on her resources, and had begun to wonder just how long her money was going to hold out.

Beulah spent all of her time cleaning up the terrible messes made by patients, preparing two meals a day composed of what little these poor people could eat, then washing all of those dishes, as well as any towels and bedding which could be saved and recirculated. Annie caught a quick look at herself in the drawing room mirror that morning, and had to acknowledge she looked like a scarecrow. Truth be told, Beulah looked even worse. Annie was frankly ashamed of herself for allowing the woman to stay, but nevertheless, the reality was she couldn't make it without her.

After putting clean sheets on the three pallets which had been occupied until the previous evening, she made sure the five nurses on duty were making good use of the ice—let alone proper utilization of the whiskey. Annie had to suppress a chuckle. The very idea that she was supervising a bunch of nurses instead of a house full of whores! Her, with just a fourth grade education!

She started back down the stairs, but was stopped before she reached bottom by a mournful cry from out on Gayoso Street, the same sound she had heard twice a day for almost three weeks. "Bring out your dead. Bring out your dead." Annie walked to her front door, opened it slightly, and gazed out on the street to see if any other neighbors had passed away during the night. There were remnants of bedding and clothing smoldering up and down the roadway, although none seemed to belong close by. Her nostrils were assailed by the twin odors of acrid smoke and the sweet, sickening smell of death, which had become far too familiar.

A young colored man was sitting on the seat of the wagon, making his appeal. Behind him lay six occupied caskets and four others awaiting customers. While Annie watched, a man who looked to be a doctor or nurse hailed the driver. The wagon stopped, the driver supposing he had another corpse to be loaded.

The medical man referred to a piece of paper in his hand. "Do you know where 244 Gayoso might be? I'm looking for a patient by the name of James Sampson."

The driver didn't miss a beat. "You won't find him at home, your honor."

"I was told he was sick. Where is he?"

"I got him in his coffin in the back o' my wagon."

"Oh. Thank you." The doctor slumped a bit, then resignedly looked at his paper again, searching for the next name on the list.

Annie sadly watched the exchange, then said a short prayer for poor Mr. Sampson before returning to her duties. When she reached the kitchen, she called out for Beulah. Not getting a response, she stuck her head in the almost empty pantry. There on the floor was her cook. “Beulah, are you all right?”

The woman was curled into a ball, with her back to Annie. She was holding her head in both hands. Annie touched her shoulder. “Beulah?”

She turned her head just enough to see Annie, opening her eyes barely a fraction. “I cain’t go no mo’, Miss Annie.” She started to cry. “I cain’t do it. I’m sorry, Miss Annie.”

“Oh, Beulah, maybe you just need some rest. Let’s get you in bed.”

“That ain’t it, Miss Annie. You best get Doctor Sohm.”

When Dr. John Sohm arrived at the Mansion House that afternoon, he wondered yet again just how he was going to explain to his wife that he was apparently the favorite doctor for the whorehouse. He had yet to figure out what he could say that would not imply he’d had previous dealings in the building. The reality was the Howards had sent him there, plain and simple. But now apparently Miss Cook was asking for him by name. He decided it might be wise to keep this particular assignment to himself.

The good doctor did not cut what might be described as a debonair figure. He was a bit thick around the middle, shorter than most men, possessed a rapidly receding hairline and a bit of a jowly, double-chinned look, with glasses riding well down on his nose and a tendency to mumble when he spoke. His blue-gray eyes were perhaps his redeeming external feature, as they gave the impression of a man who had seen and heard far too many stories of misery and suffering. Despite his physical shortcomings, a finer man, let alone a more caring physician, would be very difficult to find.

He discovered Beulah on a pallet in a small room off the kitchen. She had a severe headache and high fever, despite toweled applications of ice on her neck and chest. She turned her bloodshot eyes in his direction. “Doctor Sohm, I swear it feels like I is back to bein’ a slave again.”

Sohm gave her an inquiring look. “Why do you say such a thing, Beulah? Why like you’re a slave again?”

"My back and shoulders hurts so bad, it feel like the overseer been at me with his cane."

The thought of such a thing was repellent to the doctor, but he made no direct response to her statement. "Well, muscle aching is fairly common with the fever." He turned to the nurse. "Give Beulah two ounces of castor oil, followed by two large glasses of water. Once the bowels have thoroughly been emptied, the idea is to allow the digestive organs to remain as quiet as possible. You'll also need to keep her temperature as near normal as you can.

"I see you've got some ice. Keep sponging her neck, chest, and back as much as every hour. Keep up the flow of fluids, preferably water or tea. But if her urinary flow should stop, use a poultice of ice and salt on her loins. When the fever subsides, probably by tomorrow evening, give her chicken tea or beef broth. You can add a shot of whiskey if she's restless. But keep her away from solid food for a week. She should stay in bed this whole time. Too many people have had a relapse simply because they decided they were well enough to be up and about, resuming their normal activities."

He then turned his attention to Annie. The woman looked terrible. "How are you feeling, Miss Cook?"

"Oh, I guess I'm just worn to a frazzle. I spend my time between nursing patients and nursing a headache." She gestured toward her cook. "Don't worry about me. What about dear Beulah?"

He stepped away from his patient so she wouldn't overhear his concern. "We won't know for several days what's going to be the result. If she relapses—well, we won't talk about that unless it happens. But tell me about you."

Annie reflected for a minute. "For sure I'm worn out. I guess I've gotten too old to work this hard. But," she motioned toward the stairs, "there's so many sick people to take care of. It seems like they never stop. With Beulah sick, I don't know how I can keep this place going."

"I'll get you two more nurses. And I'll make sure the Howards know you need help with the house. But, pardon me saying this—you don't look good—not good at all. When is the last time you had a decent meal? I don't mean the thin soup your patients are trying to keep down. I mean a meal?"

"I honestly don't remember."

"Maybe I can get one of the Howards to find you a decent ham and some sweet potatoes. You've got to keep your strength up, or you're going to be lying on a pallet in there just like Beulah." He looked at her again, a bit more dubiously this time, rested his hand on her forehead for a moment, and finally began to paw through the contents of his medical bag. "Just to satisfy my curiosity, let's take your temperature."

Her routine was constant and never ending. Sit with Natalie, Naomi, and Rebecca Dickinson while encouraging them to sip chicken broth and drink, drink, drink. Interspersed with this activity, Emilie Christophe visited their mother, Elizabeth, to sponge her with the ice water and whiskey mixture.

Finally, she tried to clean up after the father, Robert. He'd stopped producing urine, his pulse was racing, breathing ragged, and she suspected he had almost no chance to live through the day.

Emilie had hopes that at least two of the girls would survive. Certainly they were co-operating with her efforts to feed them and take in fluids. On the other hand, it appeared that Rebecca, the oldest of the three, had lost all interest in attempting to live. Although Emilie had avoided any discussion with the girls about the status of their parents, it was impossible to ignore the sounds emanating from their father's room. Perhaps Rebecca had decided living without him was not worth the daunting effort required of her to survive.

Dr. Franklin had been sent over by the Howards, and he dutifully stopped to see the family once a day, but over the last couple of weeks, the reality of the death rate had taken its toll on the physician. He was a man who was just going through the motions. All he was able to do was simply endorse Emilie's efforts and promise to come back the following day.

Sometime between the hours of midnight and 2 AM, when Emilie made her rounds, Robert Dickinson passed away. She found him lying half in bed and half on the floor, where he had apparently ended up during his final battle. She woke no one in the household, realizing how important it was that each of them get as much rest as possible.

The next morning, she found ten-year-old Victoria in the kitchen, still in her nightgown, trying to invigorate the coals in the cookstove. "Victoria, I want to ask you a very big favor. I need you to keep this to yourself for a little while, at least until we've had time to see what effect the news will have on your sisters and your mother." The girl looked at Emilie with expectant yet cautious blue eyes. "Mr. Dickinson—your father—passed away just after midnight last night."

A sob escaped from Victoria, and she allowed herself a few private moments to mourn her father, but she didn't have the luxury of spending much time on her own grief and quickly composed herself, nodding toward Emilie. "I knew in my heart we were going to lose him. He didn't have a chance. He was so sick!"

"The doctor told me two days ago he couldn't survive. I'm surprised he made it as long as he did. But now I'm very worried about Rebecca. The other two girls have a good chance of recovery, but Rebecca seems to have given up, despite my doing everything for her that I've done for the other two. I don't know what will happen when she hears about your father."

"Becka has always been the sickly one, and both Mother and Father doted on her. Sometimes I used to wonder if she said she was sick just so they would sit with her and spend extra time with her, but with everybody ill in the house except me, she's gotten no more attention than anyone else. I wonder if she's not strong enough all by herself to get well?"

"That's what I'm getting at. I have to tell your mother what's happened to her husband, but for now, help me not to say anything to your sisters. There will be plenty of time to mourn when they begin to feel better. Doctor Franklin should be here before noon. I'll ask him not to mention your father to your sisters. When he goes back to the Howards' headquarters, perhaps he can send a hearse out for Mr. Dickinson."

September 7, 1878—Letter from Dr. William Armstrong to his wife—"Everything with me tonight is terribly blue, on every side death and sickness. I do feel so often, as if I can stay no longer—but like a coward, run—then 'duty points with outstretched finger' to the work before me, with the little good,

under God's blessing, that I may accomplish. We will be so broken up here, when this cruel malady is over, that society will have to begin anew. I hope something is yet bright in store for this poor unfortunate city."

September 7, 1878—"Major Willis, general superintendent of the Southern Express Company, is left alone. Of his thirty employees, who a month ago were assisting to conduct a large business, he alone is in good health. The last two clerks he had were taken with the fever yesterday."

"The Howard Association appeals to citizens to furnish horses and vehicles of any kind for use by our medical corps. They cannot attend to more than one call in ten on foot. With conveyances they could do far more work."

"Sister Alphonsa, Mother Superior of St. Agnes, died on September 6th. She was the seventh of her order to succumb to the dreaded scourge." Memphis Daily Appeal

September 7, 1878—"Total new cases reported in the city—95, deaths—100. These new cases were reported by eight physicians only. Verbal reports from twenty-three other physicians indicate at least 300 more cases. Dr. Mitchell (Howards' Medical Director) *gave it as his opinion that the new cases would actually aggregate to fully 600. It is terribly dark as the record reads today."* Memphis Avalanche

(*Author's note:* Dr. Mitchell would later acknowledge that physicians who were not housed at the Peabody—usually those who were local Memphis physicians—had difficulty in reporting their numbers each evening, as they frequently returned to their home after completing their house calls. So the number of cases they saw, as well as the dead, were sometimes missed. Worse were those physicians who sickened and took to their beds with the fever, and thus their current numbers were often never known or included in the Howards' tally.)

When Fannie Lester and Dr. Josefson returned to John Johnson's household for the fourth time, they were surprised to find Leisha and Ruthie lying on the floor, playing jacks. Their mother was watching them with a huge smile on her face. "I got my babies back, Doctor."

Josefson felt he needed to issue at least a word of caution. "Just don't let them get very active too soon. We've seen many cases where people tried to get back to their usual level of activity before they were completely well. And more often than not, they had to take to their beds again. Sometimes, they were even sicker than they were before. They may not look like it, but their health is extremely precarious right now."

The looks of relief on Marissa and John's faces were visible for all to see, and they quickly agreed to Josefson's directive. "I'll keep 'em inside for another week or so, Doctor. We're just so happy they're gettin' better."

John stuck his hand out for the doctor. "We cain't begin to say how much we 'preciate you savin' our girls. Thank you, suh."

John noticed once more that Fannie was giving him more than a glance. What did the woman know? At the same time, Fannie wondered why the colored man would not look her in the eye. If only she could remember...

On Sunday morning, Reverend Dalzell celebrated the Holy Communion in the Sister's Chapel at St. Mary's Episcopal Church. He stood beside Sister Constance's bedside, bent low over her, and asked, "Dear Sister, I have come to bring you the blessed sacrament of our dear Lord. Do you desire to receive it?"

Despite her dire condition, she spoke in a clear voice. "Oh, so very much!"

At the conclusion of the communion, Sister Constance became weaker still, but continued to have moments of lucidity, interspersed with long periods of unconsciousness. During the times she was awake, she was heard to repeat, over and over again, "Oh, God, make speed to save us, O Lord, make haste to help us."

This was followed by *The Gloria,* sometimes spoken, and other times she attempted to sing it. "Glory to God in the highest, and on earth peace to men of good will. We praise Thee, we bless Thee, we adore Thee, we glorify Thee. We give Thee thanks for Thy great glory." At times the voice would fail in the midst of her celebration, and she might pause for a bit before continuing or sometimes starting over. Other times, she would lose consciousness, then come to herself, until she became completely exhausted.

September 8, 1878—Letter from Sister Emerita to Reverend Mother in Emmittsburg—"We arrived in Vicksburg at 5 PM and went straight to the bishop's. His door was opened as we entered the house. O Mother, if you could only have seen the delight of the poor bishop! We only had minutes to stay as the boat was departing for Port Gibson. As we passed Canton, I asked if they had a priest, and was told that one had already died, and the death of the second was expected at any moment. So many dying and no one to offer them the consolations of religion. Every place looks desolate in poor Mississippi. Last night, Sister Mary Elizabeth and I went at the request of a doctor to see a dying woman. She had never been baptized. We baptized her; she died making Acts of Faith and Love. And what shall I say to yourself, dearest Mother? I feel so thankful to you for sending me, yes, more so every hour. How sweet it is to help these poor people to die well."

When Dr. Sohm returned to the Mansion House to check on Beulah, the morning of the ninth of September, his knock on the front door was not answered. He thought that a bit strange, but assumed Miss Cook was probably seeing after her duties upstairs, so he stepped into the entryway. He called out unsuccessfully for Miss Cook twice before remembering she had not looked well herself the last time he'd seen her.

He found her in the kitchen, sitting on the floor and propped against the wall. The unmistakable evidence confronted him and made diagnosis a simple matter. Although Sohm had seen these symptoms hundreds of times in the last month, he still had not gotten used to the feeling of helplessness they evoked, nor the knowledge of what was to come.

He bent down, took her pulse, listened to her breathing, patted her hand, and called her name. Although she was slow to respond, at least she was still cogent. "I've got myself in a mess, Doctor Sohm." She tried to wipe the perspiration from her face. "I'm sorry you had to see me like this."

"Don't give it another thought, Miss Cook. Let me fetch a nurse from upstairs and help you get into bed."

"Don't worry about me. Look there in the pantry and see how Beulah is doing."

The doctor did as he was asked and peered into the almost dark pantry. He found Beulah, surprisingly still alive, and appearing to be no worse than she'd been the day before. Her first question was to inquire about Miss Cook, followed by a request for some ice, and maybe a biscuit.

"If you please, Doctor Sohm, reach up there on that top shelf, way in back. I got me a jar of muscodine jelly I been savin'. Thet sho' would be good on a biscuit. These Howards, they'd let a body starve to death on beef broth and watermelon seed tea. I bet some o' these peoples passed on for want of a good biscuit."

Sohm grinned for the first time in at least a month.

Walking from the train station to the Episcopal cathedral at St. Mary's, on Sunday afternoon, September 8th, the young reverend was sweating like he'd never dreamed possible. Rivulets ran down his face, soaking his collar and then his shirt. He would swear even his hair was sweating. Was that even possible?

Coming from a church in Hoboken, New Jersey, the reverend had almost no experience with the extreme humidity produced in late summer in the lower Mississippi River Valley. More than once in his half-mile trek, he asked himself how people could survive in such an environment. For that matter, why in the world would a human actually choose to live in this kind of hell?

So when he presented himself at the door to the Sisters' House, his appearance was somewhat disheveled. Sister Ruth answered the door, seeing before her a priest of no more than thirty years of age. He towered over her, standing at least six feet in height. He was thin, cleanly shaven, with curly brown hair, and would undoubtedly be called handsome by most young women.

He tipped his hat. "Good morning, Sister. I am Reverend Louis Schuyler. I understand your Reverend Parsons has passed away, and that Dean Harris is quite ill. Bishop Quintard sent out telegrams across the country to his brothers in Christ, asking for help for St. Mary's. I was at St. Gabriel's, in Peekskill, New York, on a retreat, and our dear Lord spoke to me. So I've come."

"Forgive my manners, Father. Do come in. We're all still reeling from Reverend Parsons' death."

"I understand, Sister. He was a well respected man in the Episcopal church." He paused for a moment, afraid of the answer he might receive. "And Dean Harris, how is his health?"

"He is still very ill. And at his age—well, he's putting up a fight. Now we all are praying he'll survive."

"And I also understand two sisters are ill?"

Sister Ruth's voice caught, and she had to struggle to regain her composure. "We fear we're losing our dear mother superior, Sister Constance. And Sister Thecla is terribly sick."

"That's more awful news, Sister. Please tell me anything I can do to help you in your work."

Ruth felt duty-bound to ask the question. "Before you unpack your things, tell me, Father—have you ever had yellow fever?"

"No. They have cases at the Marine Hospital on Staten Island every year, but Hoboken, New Jersey is quite a distance to the north. As far as I know, Hoboken has never had a case."

"I'm asking because people who have had the disease previously have immunity, and people who haven't will very probably fall ill themselves if they're exposed to yellow fever. When you volunteered, Reverend Schuyler, did anyone in the church warn you how dangerous this might be for you?"

He shook his head slightly and worked mightily to keep the tremor out of his voice. "It would have made no difference, Sister. My vows are sacred to me, too."

Sister Ruth would say later that his smile seemed almost beatific.

September 9, 1878—Letter from Dr. William Armstrong to his wife—"I have concluded that I must write you again, and it is only to recount to you the horrors with which we are surrounded. I hate this, but there is nothing cheerful or hopeful, or that has one ray of sunshine attached to it in our whole city. Such a fearful plague, oh, none but eyewitnesses can appre-

ciate its horrors, or can tell of its ravages. Sister Constance is dying tonight, and I now think Sister Thecla will get well." (It is believed Dr. Armstrong wrote this letter sometime after he arrived at his home the night of September 8th, but dated the letter the next day when it would be mailed.)

September 9, 1878—"Let it be recorded to their credit that the Negro militia and policemen have discharged their duties zealously and with discretion. We are proud of them. They have proved their title to the gratitude of the people of Memphis." Memphis Daily Appeal

Elizabeth Dickinson finally felt well enough to sit up in bed and enjoy a visit from her three surviving daughters. All of the girls were sitting on her bed, alternately hugging their mother and talking about their departed sibling, Rebecca, as well as their father. Emilie kept her distance, standing at the doorway. She was still cautious about the full recovery of Natalie and Naomi, but knew they each needed some time with their mother.

As the tears began to dry, Emilie decided this was a good time to speak up. "I just wanted to be sure all of you knew how important Victoria has been over the last week. When I arrived, she was taking care of all of you. While the doctor only visited for a few minutes each day, she was up taking care of you day and night. She spoon fed each of you, fought to keep your temperature down, cleaned up after you, bathed you with cool water, and cooked your broth.

"After I got here, I made her stay in the kitchen, hoping she wouldn't get sick as well. She spent these last few days cooking and keeping everything clean for you." She spoke directly to Elizabeth. "You have a very brave daughter. Adults all over this city are running away, in fear of their sick families. But she chose to stay. I would be proud to have her nurse with me anytime."

Victoria ran over and embraced Emilie for all she was worth. "Thank goodness you came. I was so scared until you got here."

Elizabeth smiled. "Naomi and Natalie and I would not be here if it weren't for the two of you. Thank God for you both." She looked at her daughters. "I have something important to talk to Emilie about. Would the three of you go back to your rooms so we can have that conversation?"

When they were left to themselves, Elizabeth picked at her bedclothes. "I know we must owe you quite a bit of money for your time here." She spread her arms wide. "And from the looks of this house, you would think we were rich, but the truth is I don't know if we have any money at all. My husband took care of all of that, and never told me a thing concerning our finances."

Emilie held up her hand. "You really don't have to tell me about this. The Howards will pay me for my time here. I think some well-to-do families just make a donation to the Howards instead of paying the doctors and nurses. But if you aren't able to do that, then please, don't worry about it."

"I'm sure the girls and I owe you our lives, and I did so want to pay you. I'm terribly embarrassed. If I just had a chance to talk to my husband, perhaps he could tell me about our money."

Chapter 17
The Rescue

Memphis

Sometime around midnight, between Sunday and Monday, Sister Constance could be heard to exclaim, "Hallelujah, Hosanna!" repeating it again and again, more faintly each time. These were her last words, and she continued through the remainder of the night in an unconscious state, although uttering a soft moaning sound. This lasted until seven AM, when the bell of St. Mary's sounded. At that familiar, well-loved ring, her moaning ceased, and the sudden quiet was deafening to her fellow sisters.

Although he knew it would be a message painfully received, Reverend Schuyler felt it was his responsibility to tell Dean Harris that not only had Reverend Parsons died, but also Sister Constance was gone. Hearing the terrible news, the old man was too weak to raise his white head from the pillow, and all he could muster was a whisper. "*My work here is done. The whole of Memphis was not worth those two lives.*"

Reverend Schuyler could only pray he had not contributed the straw which might finally break the old reverend. He sat at his bedside for a little while, but realized his presence was not helpful. He left Harris sobbing into his pillow.

September 10, 1878—Letter from Dr. William Armstrong to his wife—"A letter from you dated the 5th just received today, and for that I had to go to the Post Office, as in old times—no mail, no groceries, no ice—you cannot conceive what a fearful-

ly desolate place this is. One by one the Howards and doctors are falling, but up to this good time, God is sparing me. Mr. Torrance died today, alone and unattended. I offered to do anything for him, but he was so averse to my profession I could not serve him. I am trying to stay this month out, if I remain in health. But I am so wearied tonight I do not know how I can go two days longer, let alone twenty."

September 10, 1878—"Reverend E.C. Slater has gone to his reward as a faithful servant of Christ. No man did more on behalf of the sick. He carried consolation to the afflicted, and bore the blessed assurance of Jesus to the dying. Night and day he traveled from one bedside to the other, knowing no relief as long as there remained one unattended. A faithful minister of the Methodist church, he went wherever called, knowing no divisions among faiths. He was at all times an example of the true Christian minister." Memphis Daily Appeal

September 10, 1878—"From Canton, Mississippi: Fever spreading all about in surrounding county. The sick are dying and we are unable to attend to them. Send me 12 to 15 nurses—particularly those willing to care for colored people."

"New Orleans deaths yesterday—87. Total deaths—1638. Total cases—5,211."

"From Plaquemine, Louisiana: The epidemic in our town has assumed such a form that organization to fight the fiend has become impossible, and outside assistance is imperative. We want someone to come here and take charge of the town, organize the panic-stricken population, and regulate the assignment of nursing. Everything is in confusion." New Orleans Picayune

It was well after sundown and thankfully near the end of a very long day. Dr. Sohm drove his buggy back to the Mansion House, realizing it was his twenty-second house call since eight o'clock that morning. Having not eaten a bite since daybreak, it suddenly struck him that he was famished. Unless somebody was around to remind him, he had a tendency to miss too many meals.

Perhaps he should start taking his own advice—but there never seemed to be enough time. He paused for a moment, briefly considering the events of the past week in his own household. He struggled to push those thoughts aside. Sometimes it was very hard to remember. Duty comes first.

He was shocked to be greeted at the front door by Beulah. “Come on in, Doctor Sohm. Miss Cook, she in a bad way.”

Sohm was so weary he just barely had strength enough to hold up his end of the conversation. “You shouldn’t be up and around, Beulah. You need at least a week of bed rest.”

Beulah looked him up and down. “Doctor Sohm, ’scuse me fer sayin’, but you a man of few words.”

He smiled slightly. “That could be because, if I’m to be honest about yellow fever, there are no words I can use in polite conversation. Now tell me how you and Miss Cook are doing this evening.”

“Don’t make no never mind ’bout me. She in here in the parlor. You got to do for her what you done for me.”

Sohm shook his head helplessly at the thought of that. “I wish it was that easy. Most folks aren’t as lucky as you were.” He paused for a moment before revealing his own pain. “I couldn’t even save my own sister. Margie passed with the fever three days ago, and we lost my wife’s sister the day after.” It was the first time he had actually verbalized his loss. He had to stop and compose himself. “My mother has what I believe to be a light case. She should be able to survive, but we just never seem to know.”

Beulah instinctively placed her hand on his arm. “I’m awful sorry t’ hear that, Doctor Sohm. We ’preciate you takin’ care of us, ’spite what’s happenin’ in your own house.”

They reached the bedside. He could see immediately that Annie Cook was in terrible condition. She had lost at least ten pounds. Her yellowed eyes followed the doctor’s every move, until she seemed to finally recognize him. Her voice was so quiet, Beulah had trouble matching the woman in bed with the outspoken, gregarious madam she’d known for so long. “Doctor Sohm—thank you for coming.” She tried to brush the matted hair from her face, but was unsuccessful. Her forehead and cheeks were marked with numerous red lesions. “I fear I look a fright.”

“Miss Cook, it’s so nice to see you this evening.” He looked at Beulah for confirmation when he asked his question. “Have you been taking your medicine and drinking enough fluids?”

Annie looked around the room for a moment before finally discovering Beulah. "She won't let me get by without it." She tried to muster a smile for her cook through dry, cracked lips. "I think Beulah gets too much enjoyment out of watching me choke down that watermelon seed tea."

"We're trying to get your urine flowing again, Miss Cook."

"I don't believe it's helped one iota, Doctor."

Sohm hesitated to ask, but knew he had to. "Do you have family, Miss Cook?"

"Not really." She closed her eyes. "They all disowned me a long time ago. I wish I could call for a priest, but it's not likely any of them would come near me, seein' the life I led. I reckon Beulah is my only family now."

Sohm looked at the old colored woman, tears running down her face. He turned his attention back to the madam. "Miss Cook, I expect you're very fortunate to have someone like Beulah who cares so much about you." He once again gave directions to the nurse, then put his arm around Beulah's thin shoulders. "You two take care of each other."

Sohm departed the Mansion House with a burden hanging over him. His buggy had traveled no more than two blocks before he reversed direction and headed to the corner of Main and Exchange Streets. The B'nai Israel (Children of Israel) congregation had purchased an old bank building and converted it into their synagogue at that location. Dr. Sohm strode up to the door, hoping his friend would be in his office, despite the late hour. He had good reason to hope, as the man seemed to be everywhere in the city since the epidemic started.

"Good evening, Reverend Samfield."

"And to you, Doctor Sohm." The rabbi gave the doctor more than a cursory glance. "You look like you haven't been to bed for a week. Can I offer you a glass of sherry?"

"Just another very long day, Reverend. But I believe I'll take you up on that sherry."

Rabbi Samfield had been elected by his congregation to serve as their spiritual leader in 1871. He was the son of a rabbi, and had been born in Bavaria before his family migrated to America. At the time of the epidemic, he was thirty-four years old.

The two men walked back to Samfield's office. As the rabbi poured, the doctor wandered around the small space.

He paused before a roll-top desk, which was constructed of beautifully stained white oak and sported a brass commemorative plaque on its front. "Is this new, Reverend?"

"My congregation gave it to me a couple of years ago. As pretty as it is, I almost hesitate to use it."

"That it is." Sohm gratefully accepted his glass of wine. "As if you don't have enough demands on your time, I have a favor to ask. I just saw a woman—actually a very good woman—who, because of her past, is undoubtedly no longer welcome in the church where she was raised. She has very little time left on this earth, and I was wondering if you would be willing to see her and perhaps say a prayer over her? I guess I'd better tell you that Miss Cook is the owner of a house of ill repute on Gayoso Street. But to her lasting credit, in the last several weeks, she has turned her business into an infirmary for yellow fever patients and has probably spent her last dime on taking care of them. Unfortunately, she now has the fever herself and is in the final stages."

Samfield picked up his hat. "From your description, it sounds like we should go now, rather than wait until tomorrow."

"I'm afraid so, Reverend."

When they arrived at the Mansion House, the doctor leaned over the bedside, calling Miss Cook's name. It took her a few minutes to respond. She turned her head in his direction, a slight smile working its way across her face when she saw him. "I thought you'd gone, Doctor Sohm."

"I brought someone to see you, Miss Cook, my good friend, Reverend Max Samfield."

The rabbi was dressed head to toe in black, and he bent down so she could hear him. "I understand you are a very special lady, Miss Cook. Would you mind if I gave you a verse from the Book of Psalms and then said a prayer for you?"

Annie looked from the doctor to the rabbi, her eyes beginning to overflow. "I would dearly love to hear it, Reverend."

"'*Hear my cry for mercy as I call to you for help, as I lift up my hands toward your Most Holy Place.*' Oh wonderful Jehovah, we have here a woman most precious in your sight, as she has given all that she possesses, including now her own life, to the sickest and the poorest of your children. Please take her unto your bosom according to her own faith, and cease her suffering and her pain. I ask this in Your Holy Name."

Annie was still crying when she thanked Rabbi Samfield for his visit, then she grasped Dr. Sohm by his shirt sleeve, fixing him with her bloodshot eyes. "I surely wish I could've met you twenty years ago, Doctor Sohm." She turned slightly, as though to embrace the contents, as well as the baggage of her house. "Before all this happened."

Sohm reached out and grasped her hand. The skin was as dry and fragile as old newsprint. His voice caught. "It would have been my privilege, Annie."

"Doctor Sohm, could I ask you for one last favor? I don't suppose I have the time to find myself a lawyer. Would you be a witness for me?"

"Why, of course, Annie."

Annie called to Beulah. When the old woman was standing close to her bedside, Annie spoke, but so softly both she and Sohm had to bend over to hear. "I expect I don't have much time left, Beulah." The cook started to protest, but Annie feebly waved her comments aside. She motioned to her neck, pausing for a minute to catch her wind. "Help me with the clasp on this necklace, Beulah." The cook did as she was told, and handed the silver chain to her boss. Annie turned to Sohm, saying "I imagine there's some folks who wouldn't believe this without your word to support it, Doctor Sohm." She then held the chain out to Beulah, along with the brass door key affixed to it. "I don't have much left in this world, Beulah, but when I'm gone, the Mansion House is yours."

September 10, 1878—Sister Ruth's note from the Episcopal orphan home—"Sister Frances is well. At the church infirmary there are about twenty cases of fever. Sister Clare will go back as soon as possible, and there are two good nurses here. We have sent four of our sick children there. One very bad case died here, and was two days unburied. We have difficulty in getting the undertaker to come all the way out here. We try to be careful, but with the hard work and such dirt—with the children coming from the fever districts and taken ill here—it is quite as bad as if we were in the city. It does not seem possible any human power can shield us from the fever,

but if we can only keep up a little longer, until the others are better, or taken safely home, I shall be so thankful."

September 10, 1878—Mississippi Board of Health—"That no regular trains will be run on the Vicksburg and Meridian Line, except for those carrying supplies, physicians, and nurses to Vicksburg."

Sister Agnes was perspiring heavily in the heat and humidity of a September afternoon, and paused for a few minutes to sprinkle a bit of water on her face and fan herself when she reached St. Peter's Catholic Church. Upon finding Father Kelly in his office, she noticed he looked every bit as overheated as she was, although he had been stationary for undoubtedly the entire day.

"Father, I have a serious situation that only you can solve. I've just come from one of our parish families, the Maroneys. The family is almost entirely destroyed. The mother and two youngest children passed earlier in the week, and last evening the father followed them to the grave."

"I know, Sister. I was at the home yesterday afternoon. The nurse on duty assured me the father was dying. If I'm not mistaken, one of the children survives."

"Yes, Father, and that is the problem you must solve."

"And what is preventing us from taking the child—a girl named Myra, I believe—at our St. Peter's Orphanage?"

"We can, Father. But first we have to get her back. She's been taken by Mr. Maroney's employer, a Leo Gustafson, if I'm not mistaken."

"I don't recognize that name, Sister."

"Nor I, Father. I believe he calls himself a Congregationalist. He told the nurse at the Maroney home he intended to take the girl into his own household and adopt her as soon as possible."

Kelly was not sure he'd heard correctly, and found the volume of his voice rising. "But the girl is one of ours, Sister. None of our good Catholic children belong in Protestant households. Every reverend in the city recognizes the importance of keeping children in the faith of their families."

"Yes, Father, hence I have come to you for your counsel."

"But we must have her back!"

"Yes, Father."

"Where does this Gustafson live?"

"I believe on Union Street, where it intersects with Fourth, Father."

"I'm leaving straightaway, Sister." He paused for a moment. "Perhaps you'd best come with me, in case there are difficulties." He paused for a moment before adding confidentially, "Some say I have a bit of a temper when it's necessary. So there's a wee possibility I might be in need of a witness."

Father Kelly was on the portly side, so hurrying was not an option. However, they arrived at Gustafson's residence within about fifteen minutes, and the priest knocked loudly on the front door.

A Negro woman answered the door and Father Kelly offered what would have to pass for a smile in her direction. "I'd be looking for Mr. Gustafson. Would you please tell him I'd like to talk to him?"

"Sure will, Your Worship." She closed the door behind her, and they waited a good three minutes before Kelly knocked repeatedly on the door. It was finally begrudgingly opened by Gustafson.

He was a tall, thin fellow of about fifty, with smallpox scarring on his face and neck, thinning hair, a pot for a belly, and a smirk of a grin which was about six teeth short of a worthwhile smile. "What's on your mind, Pastor?"

"I understand you have a young lady here, a Myra Maroney, whose mother and father recently passed away. The family were all good Catholics, members of St. Peter's for many years."

"Her father worked for me for the last five years, and I owe it to the good man to take care of his orphan."

"Now that's a worthy reason, 'tis indeed. Do you intend to bring the child up in the religion in which she was born, christened, and raised?"

Gustafson straightened the slump in his shoulders. "I certainly do not. There's no room for a Papist in this household. She'll be raised and baptized a good Congregationalist, and that's the end of it. This whole city is awash in orphans, hunerts of them I understand, mebbe thousands. Plenty of them for you to worry about, if you're so concerned. I intend to do the good Christian thing with little Myra."

"I'll have to insist you turn her over to me so she can flourish in the religion of her forebears."

At all the commotion, Myra herself stepped from behind Gustafson and called out hopefully, "Hello, Father. Did you come to get me?"

"Indeed we did, Myra. If you'll be kind enough to fetch your things, we'll take you with us now."

Gustafson slammed the door, and they could hear him with voice raised. "Get to your room. We'll talk about this later."

Father Kelly and Sister Agnes looked at one another. "Did you happen to notice, Sister, Myra is not exactly what I would call a little girl. She appears to be well on her way to blossoming into a young woman."

"Yes, Father." She decided, under the circumstances, that she should be clear about her opinion. "I couldn't help but notice a certain gleam in Mr. Gustafson's eye when he spoke about his plans for Myra. I wonder if he didn't happen to notice the blossoming, as well, and that perhaps had something to do with his new paternal instincts."

The priest returned her suspicious look in kind, giving an almost indiscernible nod, but said nothing. They retreated west at a quickened pace on Union Street, but did not turn north toward St. Peter's.

"Beg pardon, Father. Where are we going?"

"To see an old friend of mine."

When they arrived at the Department of Police, in no time they were ushered in to Chief Athey's office, where Father Kelly outlined the problem.

"Well, Father, I don't believe my department has a part to play in this situation." Athey looked from priest to sister before smiling knowingly. "It definitely sounds like a matter for the church."

Kelly grinned himself. "Then you would have no objection to my contacting a few good Irishmen at the Fire and Police Benevolent Societies, as well as some of my old friends at the Temperance Union, in order to find a few like-minded individuals who might accompany me to my next meeting with Mr. Gustafson."

Athey was an imposing fellow, and it was easy to imagine the effect his size had on any would-be criminal who faced him. His sparse hair was combed straight back and he was in possession of a full goatee. He placed his large hands on the desk, studying his steepled fingers before replying with more than a knowing smile. "Now, Father, you know the Department of Police can't officially endorse such a plan, nor can I attend such a meeting."

The next evening, twenty determined men were in his company when Father Kelly again knocked on Gustafson's door. Without a threat being voiced, the message was crystal clear. Thus twenty-one men departed the residence, plus one much relieved Myra Maroney. The march back up Union Street was a bit loud, and when the group arrived at St. Peter's, there was a short hullabaloo. Someone recommended a celebratory taste of the grape, and this met no resistance whatsoever from the members of the Temperance Union.

After an appropriate sampling, which went on for at least an hour, all of the rescuers returned to their homes, although some took the precaution of disguising their breath before being confronted by their wives. When Sister Agnes approached Father Kelly for an explanation, he grinned. "Another fine Catholic lass rescued from the Protestants."

The following day, Myra accompanied Sister Agnes to St. Peter's Orphanage. It had been temporarily relocated by the Dominican Sisters well east of the city limits on Poplar Street, in an attempt to avoid the most dangerous areas of the epidemic.

Police Chief Athey was struck down with the fever that very day, and it was as yet unknown whether he would survive. Father Kelly regarded the chief's delay in becoming ill as a heavenly intervention, having directly contributed to the freeing of Myra Maroney.

With her patients on the road to recovery, and Victoria remaining untouched by the disease, Emilie Christophe spent one last night at the Dickinson home, planning to report to the Howards the next morning. Despite her nightly prayers, asking for understanding of what she should do regarding her locket, there had been no heaven-sent illumination. But after nine days spent nursing the Dickinson family, and the new information about their precarious finances, her conscience now showed her the path to take.

Although she was still struggling with the Catholic priest's admonition to simply go and practice her profession, she had come to a decision. When the house was completely quiet, she dug around in her personal belongings until she recovered the locket. She didn't hesitate.

Robert Dickinson's voice reached out to her immediately. "I need to talk to my wife."

"I'm sorry, Mr. Dickinson. It doesn't work that way. I wish there was a way you could speak to your wife again, but I'm afraid you have to speak through me. I'll be happy to give your wife a message from you."

"I must speak only to her."

"If it's about the location of your money, she has already explained to me that she has no idea whether or not you even have any money. Elizabeth says you chose to never talk to her about finances. She knows nothing about it, and now believes she and the girls are paupers."

"Surely she knows better than that. You're asking me to trust you with everything my family needs to survive. I don't even know you."

"I can understand it must be hard for you. I can only promise I would never betray your wife and daughters—for any amount of money."

There was a pause as the voice transitioned into a physical presence—the wraith appearing with the very sheet which Emilie herself had wrapped around his corpse. His distorted, haggard countenance appeared, and he studied the Negro nurse for some time, seemingly arguing with himself regarding the wisdom of sharing his most precious secrets. "I suppose you'd best fetch paper, pen, and ink."

In a few minutes, Emilie settled herself at a desk, and Dickinson began. "I have made my living by buying and selling cotton. There's no reason why Elizabeth can't do the same."

"As far as she's concerned, she has no money."

"She has plenty of money if she will continue my business. If not, she'll run out of funds within three or four years."

"What does she need to do?"

"In December or January, when the cotton crop is completely harvested, and the supply chain is full from Memphis to Manchester, England, she should purchase at least 500 bales—that's 250,000 pounds—of the low-middling grade or better, at about eight cents a pound."

"Goodness, that's $20,000."

"Correct. She stores that cotton in a warehouse for between four and six months, until all of the previous year's crop is exhausted. Then she sells it for eleven cents a pound between April and August. Depending on the crop and the demand, that price can fluctuate from ten to thirteen cents a pound. But eleven is pretty common if she'll be patient. After subtracting for storage, that gives her a profit of almost $7,000.

"She can do that every single year, as long as she's careful and pays attention. But you must stress that she cannot become extravagant just because she has money in her pocket. She will need to retain at least $20,000 every year to make the following year's investment. If she starts spending her principal, she'll quickly not have enough funds to make an adequate purchase the following year."

Emilie paused, pen in hand. "Five hundred bales—where does she store that much cotton?"

"She needs to talk to our next-door neighbor, Benjamin Babb. He's probably the biggest cotton broker in the city, and has several warehouses available up and down the waterfront. I rent a small one from him every year within three blocks of the Cotton Exchange. He can point the site out to her."

"Are you speaking about the huge home next door? Is that where Mr. Babb lives?"

"He and his wife, Mary."

"I met his gardener a week ago on my way to your house."

"Gardener? Ben has no gardener."

"He was very tall, a bit stooped, maybe sixty years old, black beard with quite a bit of gray, shabby clothes, old straw hat..."

She didn't expect to hear a dead man laugh, but that was what Dickinson did. "Believe it or not, that was Ben. He's like an old shoe. You'd never assume he's one of the wealthiest men in the South. Unlike most fellows who are always scheming to make a big impression, Ben saves his silks for the office."

Emilie shook her head at her false assumption. "So where is Elizabeth going to get $20,000 to buy that cotton?"

"How can I be sure I can trust you?"

"Mr. Dickinson, I have this unexplainable ability to talk to the dead. I don't know why. I don't know how. If you think your wife can figure out where your money is without any help, then don't tell me. I'll share with her what you've already given me."

Another long pause. "That's the crux of the problem. I doubt seriously that she can find it."

"Does your neighbor know where it is? Maybe he can tell her."

"Nobody knows. All right, it seems I have no choice. When the epidemic started, I withdrew all my money from the banks in town. I was worried they would go broke or the bankers would run off. After all, it's not like it hasn't happened before. So I brought the money here. There's a root cellar in the back yard. In the northeast corner of the cellar, she'll find two ten-gallon clay crocks hidden underneath several boards. In those crocks, she'll find a little over $24,000 in gold and silver. That should give her $4,000 to live on until she can buy and sell her cotton. Ben will help her arrange to not only pay for the cotton, but I'm sure he can advise her about the most opportune time to sell."

"I'll tell her as soon as she's awake in the morning. And Mr. Dickinson, thank you for trusting me."

"Just make sure my family is taken care of." There was a pause. "The devil will prey on you if you break this trust."

Emilie was surprised at the amount of money involved in a single transaction. She rose from her notes at the desk, removed the locket from around her neck, and took only a single step toward her bed when she was brought up short by a familiar voice from her doorway. "Who were you talking to?"

Emilie turned to face ten-year-old Victoria Dickinson. "I didn't intend to tell your mother about this until morning." She studied the serious look on the young girl's face and quickly made up her mind. "But you've earned the right to hear this, too. Come on, let's go wake your mother."

September 11, 1878—"Total cases reported to the Board of Health—1,913, and deaths—1,360. All physicians are notified the ordinance requiring them to report cases will from this date be rigidly enforced, by order of the Board of Health. Given the extremely high death rate, there is a belief among members of the Board that some physicians are neglecting the reporting of cases."

"To the Knights of Honor of Memphis—Brothers: Out of twenty members comprising your relief committee, only three remain on duty. If possible, come to our aid."

"Seven men in Olive, Finnie & Co.'s store were stricken down in one day, when the establishment, of course, closed."

"To the Howard Assn—Permit me to call your attention to a case which knows no parallel of destitution, that of the family of Mr. Anderson, No. 102½ Linden Street, with two deaths, four sick, and the mother with an infant child. The mother is nearly insane over her great troubles, and the father and remnant of the family are prostrated with the fever. I beg you, in the name of Christian charity, to give them succor." Memphis Daily Appeal

September 11, 1878—Letter from Dr. William Armstrong to his wife—"My heart bounds with joy at the mere hope this cool night will possibly end our labors to a great extent, if not altogether in this fearful scourge. No one knows but the weary doctor what a delight that would be—an end to this dreadful suffering and distress. I am feeling splendidly today—the cool breeze has braced me up. I wish we could have an inch of frost tonight. God grant you health and a full share of His grace."

Chapter 18
The Magdalene of Memphis

Memphis

Along with Sister Hughetta, Reverend Schuyler stood at the bedside of Mrs. Bullock. The woman had worked alongside the sisters all hours of the day and night since the epidemic began. Frankly, they regarded her as a full member of their sisterhood, having witnessed so many examples of her kindness and bravery. As recently as the last twenty-four hours, Mrs. Bullock had unselfishly spent most of the previous night sitting up with Sister Thecla to give the rest of them some much-needed sleep.

However, as morning dawned, she experienced a chill, as well as a severe headache, and when the sisters came down to check on Thecla, Mrs. Bullock took Sister Hughetta aside and confessed to her that she was past all going. Hughetta spoke to her in an encouraging manner, but Mrs. Bullock waved her away with the admonition not to waste time on her, rather to see after the others.

The next morning, Hughetta and Reverend Schuyler stood before Sister Thecla. The poor woman was obviously in the final days of her battle. She had come through the early stages of fever and had appeared to be improving. But Dr. Armstrong's optimism had proven to be in error, as she had relapsed on the sixth day of her infection.

She was speaking, but neither of them could make sense of what she was saying. Her eyes darted about the room, apparently recognizing nothing. The nurse tried repeatedly to restrain her from tearing her bedding off, as well as her nightdress. Armstrong had prescribed two doses of quinine per day after the relapse, but it had no positive result. The effect of almost constant ice water and whiskey compresses was short-lived, if it had any benefit at all. When Hughetta touched Thecla's wrist, it was so hot she jerked her hand away, thinking she might be burned.

Sister Hughetta spoke softly. "You might not know it, Reverend, but Sister Thecla is an accomplished woman. She taught music, grammar, and Latin in our school. She has a beautiful singing voice, and an even more beautiful heart. Along with Sister Constance, they were not only the most educated, but perhaps the most courageous among us. The rest of us are cowards by comparison. Nothing would stop them from their service—that is," she motioned toward the prostrate patient, "that is, nothing but this."

Thecla roused slightly, looked at the small group gathered round her, and whispered, "Oh, I want to see Jesus." She then looked from one to the other, as though questioning whether the end was near, and finally closed her eyes again, this time with a smile on her face.

Reverend Schuyler removed the crucifix from around his neck, retrieved the Book of Prayer from his pocket, and lightly touched Sister Hughetta on her shoulder. "You were her good friend. Let's do this together."

J.M. Keating gathered what was left of his staff together in his office at the *Memphis Daily Appeal*. "Gentlemen, I've called you in here because our old friend and employee, Al Plummer, is fading fast. In losing him, we're going to be forced to readjust responsibilities."

Hollomon spoke for the rest of them. "Good night! First his mother and father died with the fever, then his two sisters, and last week his brother Frank passed away. He's even got another brother and sister who are trying to recuperate, and now poor Al. His whole family dead or dying. Al has been here almost as long as Helms. How bad is he, Mister Keating?"

"I hear he won't last another twenty-four hours." He gathered himself before continuing. "Al was the only reporter left on staff. Do any of you have experience in writing?"

The men looked from one to the other before Mark Bartel spoke up with his usual self-deprecation. He was an imposing, broad-shouldered fellow, with thick forearms and hands the size of small hams. To look at his thick fingers, it was difficult to imagine them holding pen and paper, let alone crafting a story. "I did some writing in school. Nothing fancy, but a couple of teachers said I had a talent for it."

"Well, it's going to be impossible for me to write and edit everything we print." He nodded at Bartel. "Why don't you take over reporting from the camps and the police department?"

"Be glad to, sir. And I'll keep up with my duties in the press room, as well."

"Good man. Let me ask all of you for your opinion about another idea. We don't have the staff to connect to all the small towns around us, but we know they've got plenty of yellow fever news to report. And our customers are clamoring for that information. What if we used the paper to ask for volunteers in the towns hereabouts? They could act as our correspondents in the field, and send us a telegram when they had something important to report."

Though uncomfortable speaking in any public forum, Steven Broom took a half step forward. He was taller than everybody else in the room, with thinning gray hair and an even thinner beard, which unsuccessfully camouflaged a ragged scar that traced the path of a Yankee minie ball across his cheek from chin to ear. Unlike many veterans who had seen a great deal of battle, Broom had apparently been able to confine his scarring to the external only. "Sir, how do you know the volunteers will be decent writers? Even worse, how can you be sure their stories are truthful?"

"I've thought about that problem, Broom. We may have to dress up their prose a bit before we print it. And if their story sounds too outlandish, we'll have to try and check behind them. What we'll do for any of those stories from volunteers is quote them in the paper, preceded by a note that says *a correspondent*. In that way we're telling the reader the reporter is not one of our staff, but simply someone from the town who voluntarily is submitting information."

"Then I'll volunteer to go fetch the telegrams, sir. Although I hear the telegraph office has had even more sickness than we have here at the newspaper. There's only two men left during the day at the telegraph office, and just one at night, so if they experience any more reductions, they'll probably open for only a part of the day."

"Thank you, Broom. My proposal may end up not working anyway if we don't have a functional telegraph office. Hard to believe they had twenty-five employees just a month ago."

September 12, 1878—"Annie Cook, the woman who, after a long life of shame, ventured all she had of life and property for the sick, died yesterday of yellow fever, which she contracted while nursing her patients. If there was virtue in the faith of the woman who but touched the hem of the garment of the Divine Redeemer, surely the sins of this woman must have also been forgiven her. Her faith hath made her whole, made her one with the loving Christ, whose example she followed in giving her life that others might live. Amid so much that was sorrowful to an agonizing degree, so much that illumined the graces of a common humanity, the example of that brave woman stands by itself, singular but beautiful, sad but touching, the very expression of that hope, the realization of which we have in the words 'In as much as ye have done it unto the least of these my brethren, ye have done it unto me.' Out of sin, the woman, in all the tenderness and truthfulness of her womanhood, emerged, transfigured and purified, to become the healer, and at last to come to the Healer of Souls, with Him to rest forever. She is at peace." Memphis Daily Appeal (Annie Cook would later be named "The Mary Magdalene of Memphis.")

September 13, 1878—"The following physicians, employed by the Memphis Howard Association, have been taken with the fever: Brown, Erskine, Hodges, Brown-Dawson, Watson, Robbins, Green, Green-Avent, Saunders, Summer, Nutall, Mode, Williams, McKim, McCormack, Reum, Rodgers, Nugent, Smith, Collins, Baskerville, MacGregor, Donahoe, and Wise."

"The Wenham Ice Company in Boston has generously sent fifty railcars loaded with ice to this city."

"The New York Chamber of Commerce transmitted $5,000 to New Orleans, $1,000 to Vicksburg, and $4,000 to Memphis by way of the Howard Assn."

"Mr. Herbert Landrum, editor of the Memphis Avalanche (a competing newspaper)*, died yesterday morning of the fever. He knew no fear where duty was to be performed. He stood to his post and braved all the terrors of the epidemic, until he fell. He was the last member of the* Avalanche *staff remaining."*

"Tom Best, reported dead from yellow fever, was murdered. Yesterday morning his body was found in front of the Olympic Park Stable, perforated by a pistol ball." Memphis Daily Appeal

September 13, 1878—Minutes of the Hernando, Mississippi Citizens Relief Committee—"The claim of Dennis Avery for digging Miss Johnson's grave was audited and warrant ordered to issue for $1.50."

September 13, 1878—Letter from Sisters of the 3rd Order of St. Francis to Reverend Mother in St. Louis—"In the course of the last three days, we have buried three of our dear sisters in Calvary Cemetery, and the fourth, the corpse of Sister Gertrude, is still in the house. Please don't send anyone else, dear Mother. They die so quickly."

Lester Sellers and Israel Jackson were perched on the seat of their death wagon, waiting on the conveyance in front of them to unload their cargo of caskets at the gates of Elmwood Cemetery. A rather well-dressed man with a bowler hat on his head was standing there at the gate, trying to talk to the gravediggers, who were focused on unloading caskets. The man was holding a bouquet of zinnias in one hand, while securing a piece of sponge to his mouth and nose with the other. He looked like he was in desperate need of going somewhere, but had forgotten how to get there.

"What's that he's holdin' up to his face?"

Lester snorted. "He's prob'ly got it soaked in gin or some such, tryin' to keep them fever spores from gettin' to him."

The two men couldn't help but overhear the conversation between the white man and the gravediggers. "Please tell me where you've put my wife, Victoria Stanton. I purchased a grave site for her on Chapel Hill, but I've walked all over the site, and can't find any sign of her, or of a fresh grave on the hill."

"When was she buried, sir?"

"Two days ago."

"Might you know who brung her out here, sir?'

"She was delivered here by T.J. Collins, the undertaker."

The black man turned to his workmates, asking in a loud voice so as to draw them from their interminable task, "Any you boys recomember a Collins hearse two days ago—woman name of Stanton?"

His query was met with universally negative responses. He turned back toward Mr. Stanton. "Mister, we buryin' way over a hundred people a day. Less'n the undertaker tells us they belongs in a plot, the bodies go in a trench, along with everbody else."

The man looked at his bouquet. "But I brought these flowers to put on her grave."

"We're sho' nuff sorry, mister, but we ain't got no way of tellin' where she is. You best speak to Collins about it. He be the one responsible fer tellin' us if somebody gots a plot."

The last Lester and Israel saw of the man, he was wandering over the areas of freshly turned earth, searching for some unknown evidence that Victoria was interred there. He finally began to lay down a single flower from his bouquet on each mound of dirt, hoping one of them would find its way to his wife.

Chapter 19
Downriver

From Canton, Mississippi—"A week ago there was a population of 3,500 here. Now only 75 whites are to be found. The mayor and his family are sick. The Board of Aldermen have fled. The courthouse is locked up, and law officers have gone to a safe place. There is nothing left but the hearse and coffins on the streets. Many Negroes have died in the last few days. Not a single case of yellow fever has been doctored successfully. No person attacked has recovered."

From Jackson, Mississippi—"Panic is prevalent in Jackson. At least half our population of 6,000, and 75 percent of the whites, have fled, or at least are now ready to go at a moment's notice. The city is now completely quarantined—not only against New Orleans, but to all localities surrounding it." New Orleans Picayune

September 14, 1878—"Vicksburg has buried 335 yellow fever victims. It is estimated they currently have over 3,000 cases of the sickness." Memphis Daily Appeal

September 14, 1878—"The Negroes, who had been slaves such a short time before, have displayed a loyalty and devotion that is monumental. With the passing of each white clergyman in Vicksburg, Negro pastors, such as Reverend Abram Donald, humbly did the work of their office. Before each white body was given back to the dust, a prayer from black lips recommended the soul to a common God." Vicksburg Herald

September 14, 1878—Letter from Sister Emerita in Vicksburg to Reverend Mother—"I have been all day yesterday and last night helping to take care of a poor young priest, Father Vitelo, only one year from Italy. He said two masses last Sunday, and died today, Saturday. I feel sad just watching

that poor priest die. He would not take his medicine unless I would taste it, to see if it was right. Poor Bishop, he regains his strength very slowly. We did not want him to know that fine young priest had died; but he said we might as well tell him, he had learned to take things as God sent them. He is so grateful to you, dear Mother, the tears come when he speaks of you."

Dr. David Booth, Vicksburg physician, became so ill that he offered his private hospital to Sister Ignatius and the Sisters of Mercy. The sisters asked that the Howards administer the facility while they provided nursing services. In addition to their normal contributions, the Howards paid for most of the burials in the city, paying five dollars per corpse for a wooden casket, to include interment in a mass gravesite.

Sister Ignatius coordinated care for twenty yellow fever orphans in the city, purchased burial shrouds for men, women, and children, prepared bodies for burial, and shared her rations with the sick. Her mealtime prayers were generally preceded by her exhortation, "*Let us pray like there is something to eat.*"

Sister Ignatius had a significant reputation, having worked in the Douglas Hospital in Washington, D.C. during the Civil War. During those days, the sister had made multiple requests for food and supplies for her patients, but had become exasperated with the authorities for their lack of responsiveness to her requests. Rather than continue to beg the immediate chain of command, she decided to take matters into her own hands, went immediately to the White House, and was able to have an audience with President Lincoln. The president provided her with a letter when she departed, which stated, in part, "*The Sisters of Mercy shall be given exactly what they request for the sick and wounded, and it shall be charged to the War Department.*"

By the close of the epidemic, Vicksburg and the immediate vicinity had some 5,900 of its citizens who had been sick with the fever, and by some accounts, between 1,450 and 2,000 deaths. (The official count was 1,006, plus another 90 in Warren County, where Vicksburg was located.) But even this was widely acknowledged as under-reporting. Much of that was due to private burials in the countryside.

A steamboat voyaged upriver to bring money to the citizens of Greenville, as they could purchase nothing without funds in hand. What savings they had were safely locked away in the local bank's vault, but the bank officers were all dead. The steamboat's pilot sent his observations back to Vicksburg. *"Lime filled the drains and ditches, and carbolic acid was scattered in every direction and filled the air with its offensive odors, while the black cloud of burning sulfur brought to mind Dante's description of the Inferno."*

Reverend Duncan Cameron Green, Episcopal minister of St. James Church in Greenville, sent his wife and two sons to the safety of the countryside. He remained behind to minister and care for the sick. He died on September 15th. As it happened, Reverend Green's father, also an Episcopal minister, was very good friends with Henry Wadsworth Longfellow. When the elder Green wrote Longfellow a letter, expressing his great grief over the death of his son, the poet penned *The Chamber Over the Gate* as his way of addressing his friend's grief. The first verse reads as follows:

Is it so far from thee
Thou canst no longer see
In the Chamber over the Gate
That old man desolate,
Weeping and wailing sore
For his son, who is no more?
O Absalom, my son!
H.W. Longfellow, 1879

On September 19th, a passing steamboat was flagged down on the Mississippi near the runout to Greenville by a couple of citizens, and they reported 100 deaths, 200 sick, and only 450 white citizens remaining in the city, but were unable to leave due to illness in their families. No boats were running, the telegraph lines had been out for ten days, and they were shut off from the world.

On September 27th, another passing steamer reported 237 deaths, and only 15 of the 450 whites in the town had not had the fever. Greenville would eventually suffer 903 cases of yellow fever and 301 deaths.

At about this same time, Sister Mary Vincent led a group of sisters to Meridian, Mississippi on the Vicksburg and Meridian Rail Line to answer an appeal for help. Unfortunately, there was a shotgun quarantine surrounding Meridian, and they were forced off the train several miles short of their destination at the tiny settlement of Chunky in the middle of the night. Not to be deterred, Sister Mary Vincent found a man with a wagon who was willing to take the sisters the rest of the way. Despite the sisters' heroic efforts, the small town of Meridian would lose 55 of her citizens to the fever.

Within a week, the Vicksburg and Meridian Line resumed normal operations between Vicksburg and Meridian. Unfortunately, some railroad crews on the route reported over-zealous citizens firing their weapons into the side of the trains to prevent their stopping.

By epidemic's end, six Catholic priests and twenty sisters assigned to Vicksburg would die of yellow fever. The small remainder of their order would all fall ill, but survive.

In Pascagoula, Mississippi, the editors of the *Pascagoula Democrat* learned that two of the town's ministers had left the city along with other fleeing citizens, and published the following observation: "*When the preachers are afraid of death, what is to be expected of ordinary mortals?*"

"From a correspondent in Canton, Mississippi—Total cases 435, deaths 75. Dr. A.H. Cage is dead. The people are very gloomy." Memphis Daily Appeal. (In Canton, the eventual death toll would reach 180 of 924 total cases.)

Chapter 20
Reverend Louis Schuyler

Memphis

September 14, 1878—"The white people of Memphis appreciate and are proud of our colored fellow citizens. Whenever and wherever they have been called upon, they have manifested a disposition that has won the admiration of the members of the Howard Association and of the Citizens Relief Committee. Looking back through the gloomy vista of the past five weeks, and recalling all we have passed through, how near to anarchy we have been several times, we are thankful that the Negroes, forming as they do, just now, the great bulk of our population, have manifested a patience worthy of all praise." Memphis Daily Appeal

Reverend Schuyler found Sister Ruth kneeling before the cross in the chapel. He sat quietly behind her in the first pew, awaiting the close of her prayer. He was having trouble concentrating that morning, and couldn't seem to put his thoughts together enough to say his own prayer. The chapel seemed inordinately hot, despite it being only an hour after sunrise. He'd slept poorly, not being able to get comfortable the whole night. The reverend had soon discovered that the nights were almost as humid as the days in Memphis. Maybe that was why he ached from one end to the other. If only he could slip back to bed for just an hour or so.

When Sister Ruth finally rose, he noticed she stumbled a bit before regaining her balance. “Are you all right, Sister?”

The woman turned toward him, and he couldn’t help but notice the pained expression on her flushed face, as well as her bloodshot, rheumy eyes. She grabbed hold of a nearby pew before answering. “Is that you, Reverend?”

“Yes, Sister. How are you feeling?”

She rested both hands on the side of the pew to steady herself. “I fear I’m about to become another burden to all of you.”

Schuyler put his arm around her shoulder. “You’re no burden, Sister. Let’s walk over to the infirmary together.”

One of the nurses got Sister Ruth into a bed, then took her temperature, before calling for a doctor. When Dr. Franklin came over to look at her, Reverend Schuyler thought the doctor didn’t look much better than she did. He was sweating profusely himself, and his eyes were every bit as red as his patient’s.

Reverend Schuyler knew the house physician had just come down with the fever and was occupying a bed down the hall in the men’s ward. But by appearances, this replacement physician appeared to be in need of a bed himself. He decided to visit Dr. Armstrong in the other ward for a few minutes while the nurse got Sister Ruth in bed in the school infirmary.

As Schuyler made his way down the hall, he was reminded again of just how hot it was, and he finally had to acknowledge that his roaring headache perhaps wasn’t just a result of poor sleep. He wasn’t the sort who normally had aches and pains of any kind, but the severity of this particular headache, now seeming to spread to his neck and shoulders, was not something he’d experienced before. He was sure he could even hear the pulse of his heartbeat throbbing in his ears.

Dr. Armstrong was obviously sick. He appeared to be feverish and couldn’t seem to get comfortable in his bed in the infirmary. But sick or not, he was still a doctor. So when he eyed the reverend standing before his sickbed, it was Armstrong who first asked the question. “How are you feeling, Reverend?”

“I brought Sister Ruth over to the infirmary. It looks to me like she’s got the symptoms of the fever.”

"I mean you, Reverend. How are you feeling?"

"Oh, I'm all right. Probably just tired."

"Appears to me like you don't look a bit better than I do, and unfortunately, that's not good. I'm betting you've got an awful headache, and your neck and shoulders are aching something fierce."

"I guess so. I'm not used to this heat."

Armstrong turned in his bed and spoke in the more authoritarian tone to which they had become accustomed. "Nurse!"

The entire staff in the infirmary had become quite familiar with that voice in the last several hours. As a result, an older nurse hurried to his bedside. "Yes, Doctor Armstrong?"

"Stick a thermometer in the reverend here."

Schuyler held up his hands. "No, no. I can't possibly have the fever. I've just been here for five days."

Armstrong lay his head back on the pillow to stop the room from spinning. It took him a moment to reply. "I've heard that exact expression at least fifty times in the last month, Reverend, and it's always been from someone who's never been exposed to the fever before."

The nurse squinted as she held her thermometer up to the light. "A hundred and four degrees. Come on, Reverend, I've got an empty bed waiting on you close to Doctor Armstrong." She gave the man a closer inspection. "You need any help gettin' shut o' all those reverend clothes?"

September 14, 1878—Telegram from R.W. Mitchell to John S. Becher—"Dr. W. Armstrong very sick but doing well today. Tell Mrs. Armstrong she must not come here under any circumstances."

On September 15th, six friends of Ed Worsham did the unthinkable. They followed his casket to Elmwood Cemetery. Other than immediate family members, it was very unusual to see friends and acquaintances out and about, particularly considering they were exposing themselves to what many said was the most dangerous of all settings, the burial grounds. Upon arriving, they saw Reverend George White,

Rector of Calvary Episcopal Church, who was there with his wife and a Negro servant to bury his son, Eugene. When Reverend White learned that his old friend Worsham was about to be buried, the pastor asked if he could say a few words at the grave.

As that burial was completed, a man came forward and asked Reverend White to please do the same for his dead wife. White consented, but seeing his wife standing by in anguish, asked that he might bury his own son first. These two burial ceremonies had just been completed when Ed Beasley asked Reverend White to please speak over his friend William Willis' grave. Within a half hour, the minister performed his sad task for four separate souls.

September 15, 1878—Telegram from W.E. Rogers to John S. Becher—"Dr. Armstrong doing well."

September 15, 1878—Diary entry by Belle Wade—"Today is my birthday. I am fifteen years old. Mama says these are very sad times to be having birthdays, and I think so, too. There were 117 deaths yesterday."

Fannie Lester was on her way back to the John Johnson household; but, inexplicably, this time the Howards had paired her with Dr. James Madison rather than Dr. Josefson. They were met at the door by the man of the house, who was surrounded by his two daughters. The request for a physician this time had been not for the little girls, but their mother.

Once again, Fannie was conscious of the manner in which John Johnson would not look directly at her, but put that aside as she and Madison were led to Marissa's pallet. The woman was obviously ill, but not so much that she wasn't aware of her two daughters—both with inquisitive looks on their faces. She turned toward her husband. "John, take the girls into the other room. They don't need to be in here."

Madison turned his attention to his patient. "Marissa, what have you been able to eat and drink?"

There was a pause until she was sure her daughters were out of hearing. "My head hurts so bad, I cain't hardly think about eatin' anything." She nodded toward Johnson. "My husband ain't the best cook they is, anyways."

"If you don't drink lots of water, you're going to get even sicker—at least six glasses a day. Tomorrow you need to try some beef tea or chicken broth to keep up your strength."

She wiped the perspiration from her brow. "I'll try, Doctor."

"There's something else. Is your husband able to stay home and take care of both you and your daughters?"

"He's a policeman, but he gonna tell them after tonight he has to stay home 'til I get well."

Fannie looked first at Marissa, then at her husband. "In the meantime, do you need a nurse?"

Johnson spoke before his wife had an opportunity to make her wishes known. "We'll make do."

Fannie wondered briefly if Johnson was refusing the offer of a nurse because he supposed it would be her. But surely that couldn't be the case. She remembered the frightened look on Johnson's face when they'd entered the domicile. She turned to Dr. Madison. "Would you agree to send them a nurse?"

Madison shrugged. "That's fine with me." He turned his attention to Johnson. "Until that happens, I want you to give your wife sponge baths at least every hour with whisky and ice to see if we can get her fever down." He reached into his bag and produced four powder papers. "I want her to take a dose of calomel every day with a glass of water."

Fannie tried to hide her surprise at his prescription. "Excuse me, Doctor, did you say calomel?"

He gave her a strange look. "Of course. She has to get the yellow fever miasma out of her stomach before she can begin to get better." He turned to Johnson. "I'll be back tomorrow."

Sister Helen was on duty that night in the infirmary. Along with the two nurses present, she was dividing her time between Sister Ruth, Reverend Schuyler, Mrs. Bullock, Dr. Armstrong, and seven other patients. Almost all of them were quite ill. In the two weeks Helen had been in Memphis, she'd come to admire all of the men and women serving beside her; but she had become extraordinarily fond of Mrs. Bullock.

The sisters and the reverends had taken a sacred vow to serve, while the Howard nurses—though volunteers—were being paid for their service. Mrs. Bullock, however, was there simply because she had a beautiful heart. She had been involved in practically everything the sisters had done throughout the ordeal, rejoicing with them for small victories, crying beside them with every loss, and working as hard as any one of them.

So as Sister Helen made her rounds well before daylight on September 16th, perhaps she subconsciously decided to spend a little extra time at Mrs. Bullock's bedside. It was obvious the poor woman was suffering mightily. She had been mostly unconscious and moaning for much of the night.

Thank goodness, Reverend Dalzell had seen her the day before, when she had been fully cogent, and had been able to provide her with last rites. Even so, Sister Helen sat with her for a while, praying in a whisper. She was surprised when Mrs. Bullock roused and spoke to her. "Sister, I have my daughter, my poor little Bessie, on my heart. I don't want her sent to an orphan home. I want her brought up in the church. I want her to live where she will be loved. It is my wish that she become a sister."

Sister Helen held her hand. "Sister Hughetta and I have already talked about such a thing. Don't you worry any longer. The sisters will take her here at St. Mary's and raise her and love her as our very own."

With the comfort of that response, Mrs. Bullock closed her hands as though in prayer, and whispered in a beseeching voice to the sister, *"It's a hard thing to die and appear before God."*

Sister Helen enclosed her friend's hands in her own and simply said, "I know He will welcome you to His side with open arms."

Mrs. Bullock then closed her eyes, and within the hour she was gone.

September 16, 1878—"The Very Reverend M. Riordan, vicar-general of this diocese, and pastor of St. Patrick's Catholic Church, died after two weeks' illness from yellow fever. Like

those of his brethren of the priesthood, who preceded him, he fell at his post. He contracted the disease while in the discharge of the duties of his sacred office, and fell as the brave soldier of the cross loves to fall." Memphis Daily Appeal

Letter from Dr. William Armstrong to his wife—"My dear wife—I have passed through the fever stages and have only to get the stomach right. Hope I can do this and see you soon. Husband" (*Author's note:* Upon review of the communications to his wife in the Memphis Public Library, the appearance of this letter was striking. Rather than his typical smooth penmanship and well-ordered prose, this was written in an extremely shaky hand, with only the most basic information transmitted.)

September 17, 1878—"Dr. R.W. Mitchell, Medical Director of the Howard Association, recommends the following treatment for yellow fever: a daily dose of castor oil, or ten grains of calomel for an adult. The patient should be sponged every thirty minutes with ice water and whiskey (half and half), until permanent reaction is produced. This sponging has an immediate and free effect upon the kidneys, and induces sleep."

"A lady from Memphis, Mrs. Evans, who lost her husband on August 30th, and who had the fever herself, fainted and fell on the platform of Waverly Station, on the Chattanooga Rail Line. She had a sick child with her. The announcement of the fact stampeded the town, and the people fled to the mountains."

"The Board of Health reports 4,127 cases of yellow fever to date, and 1,991 deaths."

"The New Orleans Picayune *warns convalescents they must not return to work too soon. Induced by many sad cases of fatal relapse, we join our warning to those of doctors and nurses. The disease is subtle, insidious, deceptive, and treacherous."*

"Al Plummer, a faithful employee of this paper, who has been employed in our press room for six years, died on Sunday. He is the tenth employee of the Appeal *who has crossed the Rubicon during this epidemic. We are slowly but surely passing away."* Memphis Daily Appeal

At St. Mary's Episcopal Church, Sisters Helen and Hughetta had been on their knees in the infirmary, praying fervently for Sister Ruth for the last half hour. They were interrupted by the voice of the nurse standing behind them. "Sisters, I'm so sorry, but I'm afraid she's gone."

Both Helen and Hughetta raised their heads. They had wept so much over the last month, they'd begun to wonder if it was possible to become completely cried out. But they discovered that wasn't the case when they saw the nurse placing a sheet over Sister Ruth.

The nurse spoke again. "Sisters, I know this is a terrible day for all of us, but I must ask something else of you. I hate to add to your troubles. Perhaps you can both come to the men's ward. I'm afraid Reverend Schuyler is slipping fast. He's in need of your prayers."

Their passage across the rear of the church was halted almost before it began by a breathless young black man. He looked from one to the other before he spoke. "'Scuse me, Sisters. I got a message from Canfield for the reverend in charge. Kin you tell me where I might find him?"

Sister Helen shook her head. "Our only reverend is out making rounds in the city." She looked at Hughetta for confirmation. "If you've got a message, you'd better give it to us."

"The doctor at the orphan home tole me don't give it to no one but the reverend."

"That's just not possible."

The messenger looked at the two sisters and made up his mind. "This here from Doctor Sohm out at the orphan home."

Helen took the paper from his hands before he could change his mind. She knew Dr. Sohm by reputation only, as he and his family were long-time parishioners at St. Mary's Catholic Church. "Go down the hallway there to the kitchen. Tell them I said give you a biscuit and something cool to drink."

"Yes, ma'am. Thank you, ma'am."

The note was short and to the point. "Sister Frances went down with the fever yesterday. Send someone to manage the orphanage."

Helen looked at Hughetta. "How in the world are we supposed to run the infirmary here and the orphanage out there? There's only Reverend Dalzell, Sister Clare, and the two of us left."

"We don't have any choice. We'll have to send another telegram to the bishop in Nashville to ask for help."

"I expect we need to ask for somebody who's had the fever before. Otherwise they'll send some poor soul like Reverend Schuyler to us."

"I wonder if the bishop realizes how bad things are here."

"It's up to us to let him know."

The nurse came out into the hallway again. "Sisters, if you want to see Reverend Schuyler again, you'd best hurry."

As the sisters entered the ward, they were painfully aware of the sights and sounds of six men engaged in individual struggles with yellow fever. Some were in the early stages of the disease, and one man was lost in his own feverish visions. The smell was almost overwhelming.

Two nurses were engaged in sponging patients, changing bedding, and trying to get them to drink. Two patients were in convalescence, fever free—at least for now—and seemed to have their wits about them, although both had sores on their face, neck, and arms, and one of them seemed determined to scratch himself almost constantly.

When they arrived at Reverend Schuyler's bedside, his advanced stage of illness was obvious. He was tossing and turning almost constantly, completely unable to stay quiet. There were too many signs of impending death surrounding him. He seemed to be in a panic, his eyes seeing nothing, but continuing to dart about.

Helen and Hughetta found themselves leaning against each another, trying to prop one another up. "Only eight days! Reverend Schuyler has only been here eight days. What a waste of a beautiful heart."

The two women sank to their knees at his bedside, Helen holding the reverend's clammy hand, while they both began to pray, summoning their God to be with his servant. Each of them was absorbed in her own prayer and thoughts, and it struck Hughetta that it seemed only a few minutes had passed when the nurse spoke to them in almost a whisper. "Sisters, the reverend passed about thirty minutes ago. I'm so sorry, but we need this bed."

When Helen and Hughetta attempted to rise, they both experienced a dizzy spell and reached out to one another to steady themselves. The dreaded thought struck them both almost simultaneously when they acknowledged that each of them had a terrible headache and had begun to shiver with a fever. Helen gazed appraisingly at her friend before speaking. "Nurse, I think Sister Hughetta needs a bed herself."

Nurse Annie Ruth placed her hand on Hughetta's forehead, then turned toward Helen, repeating the movement before shaking her head. "Sisters, you've done all that's humanly possible. Now you both are going to need to concentrate every ounce of your strength on taking care of yourselves." She motioned for another nurse to assist her, and they escorted their new patients back across the hallway to get them both settled in the women's wing of the infirmary.

Despite their daily experiences in handling the dead, Lester Sellers and Israel Jackson were struggling in the late summer heat and humidity with the powerful odors coming from the rear of their wagon. "It can't get much worse than this, Israel."

"I'm just thankful we ain't the ones what has to bury these folks."

The wagon's progress stopped briefly, and Israel looked around for signs of another body to pick up. But finally Lester clucked to the horses and they began to move again. He nodded toward the corner ahead. "About three years afore the war—reckon I was eleven or twelve—it was right there in sight o' both that fine Catholic church an' the Calvary Episcopal right across the alley. I hates to even drive by this here corner."

"What be wrong with the corner?"

"Why, right here at the southwest corner o' Third and Adams—you see that spot there in front o' that big house?"

"Sho, what about it?"

"Thet's where that Gen'l Forrest had his slave auction. Me and my momma was both sold there, off a wood platform—had a fence around it in them days. Forrest hollerin' the whole time, tryin' t' make another dollar. Ain't seen Momma now in twenty years. She went one direction and I went t'other." As the wagon passed, Lester spit a gob of tobacco juice on the spot. "I hope nobody never forgets what happened here."

Chapter 21
Calomel

Memphis

Fannie Lester had been looking everywhere for her favorite doctor all day, and had begun to fear he might have joined the long list of sick physicians, until she spied him in the hallway of the Peabody Hotel. She hurried up to him. "Doctor Josefson, I need to speak to you for a minute. Do you have the time?"

"Of course, Fannie. Any time." He steered her to a quiet corner. "What's on your mind?"

"Yesterday, I had to go back to the Johnson household in Fort Pickering. Maybe you remember the one where we went a week or so ago to see the two sick little colored girls?"

"Sure, I remember. We went back and they were doing much better. Have they taken a turn for the worse?"

"No, the girls are fine. This time it was to see the mother. But the Howards sent me with Doctor Madison."

Josefson tried to conceal his distaste for the man, as he had no idea what Fannie thought about him. "I remember her. Let's see, the husband is a policeman. You said you thought you remembered him from somewhere."

"That's the one. I still can't figure him out. But remember when you told me not to let anybody prescribe calomel for me, that it was poison?"

"Sure. Unfortunately, a lot of doctors in town are using it."

"That's what I want to ask about. Doctor Madison prescribed calomel for Mrs. Johnson." Josefson slowly shook his head, but Fannie hurried on before he could speak. "I didn't say anything at the time, but I can't help but feel obligated to go back and warn Mrs. Johnson. Then in this morning's newspaper, they quoted Doctor Mitchell himself as recommending either castor oil or calomel for everybody with yellow fever."

Josefson took her by the arm. "Yes, I heard about the newspaper story. But Fannie, you need to be very careful who you talk to about this. There are quite a few of us younger doctors who won't use calomel, no matter what Mitchell or anybody else has to say about it. But at least half the physicians here—particularly the older ones—will prescribe it, come hell or high water."

"So I shouldn't say anything to Mrs. Johnson?"

"Let that come from another physician. If you get in the middle of it, you'll only find yourself in trouble, and knowing some of these doctors, you'll probably lose your job if you question what they prescribe. But since this has happened, let me explain my problem with calomel."

Josefson glanced up and down the hallway to be sure he wouldn't be overheard. "Physicians have been using calomel for hundreds of years. In fact, for a long time, about the only options physicians would prescribe for any illness was either a strong laxative—like calomel—or bloodletting. They figured every single disease was due to a build-up of toxic substances in your bowels or in your blood. So they emptied your bowels or drained your blood. Sometimes they even did both. But early in this century, some physicians started to question the wisdom of giving a poison like calomel, as well as the whole idea of either giving a strong laxative or taking your blood."

"So how is calomel a poison, if half the patients are getting it?"

"You might be thinking if something is a poison that it would probably kill people right away."

She nodded. "That's what I was figuring."

"Calomel is a form of mercury—mercurous chloride. It usually takes a while for its toxic effects to show up. But because some of these yellow fever patients are taking fairly large doses for several days, the mercury keeps building up in their system. Of course, the first thing it does is what is expected. It causes explosive diarrhea for hours and hours.

Some call it the 'thunder-clapper.'" Fannie couldn't help but snicker at that description. "And it's such a powerful laxative, it usually completely saps the strength from anyone under its treatment. By the time someone takes two or three days of calomel, they're generally weak as a kitten. That's awfully hard on a patient who's trying to recover from something as serious as yellow fever."

Josefson shrugged. "They next get a metallic taste in their mouth. But as time goes on, the patient's saliva gets thick and stringy, their gums become red and swollen, they get mouth ulcers, the tongue gets swollen and stiff, and their teeth actually start to loosen. If they take calomel long enough, their teeth simply fall out. And we don't know what other side effects are going on."

Fannie had her hand over her mouth. "My own papa didn't have a tooth in his head from the time I was a little girl. And he had the worst time trying to eat. He could just barely open his mouth."

Josefson nodded his head. He wasn't about to mention that calomel was often the main treatment for gonorrhea and syphilis, and because it was prescribed for months or even years at a time in treating those diseases, most patients ended up losing their teeth and their sense of taste, and having permanent damage to their gums and tongue. "Look, Fannie, I really believe one day soon, all physicians will realize what damage calomel is causing, and it won't be used any more. But right now—particularly since we don't have an effective treatment for yellow fever—you're going to see it used a great deal just because we doctors will try anything rather than stand there and do nothing while our patients die on us."

"Thanks for taking the time to explain it to me, Doctor Josefson. I just hate it that I can't warn Mrs. Johnson. I only wish we had a drug that would work all the time. It's so hard to not be able to help these poor people."

"The doctor comes with free good will,
But ne'er forgets his calomel." Folk saying, 1800s

September 18, 1878—"A passenger from Memphis on the Memphis and Charleston Rail Line, developed the symptoms of yellow fever upon his arrival in Stevenson, Alabama, and got off the train to receive medical treatment, but there was no one, not even a physician, who would go near him. Some citizens drew their pistols on him, and threatened to burn him and his clothing. Captain John Grant, Superintendent of the M & C RR, ordered the patient to be placed in a box car, with a bed and whatever might make him comfortable."

"From a correspondent in Grand Junction, Tennessee (50 miles east of Memphis)*—Our town is almost deserted due to the epidemic. Times are distressing. The merchants have closed their businesses, taken to their horses, and fled to the country."*

"What an example of devotion to duty the Catholic priests set. As fast as one falls, another takes his place. Fathers Scanlon, Thoma, and Van Troostenburg recently arrived to take the places of those who died at their posts." Memphis Daily Appeal

September 18, 1878—Letter from Sisters of the 3rd Order of St. Francis to Reverend Mother in St. Louis—"We are all on the way to recovery. Sister Bernadine and I sat up for the first time last evening. You have no idea how this disease takes all our strength at once, and one has to be so careful not to get a relapse like Vicar General Riordan who was up. Sisters Mechtildis and Armella were very sick. They had prepared for death. Sister Mechtildis already packed our trunk, ready to be sent back to St. Louis after we were all dead, because she was sure none of us would survive. Dr. Nugent (physician taking care of St. Mary's priests and sisters) *died September 4th. He received the sacraments, but not Holy Communion, because he vomited so much."*

September 18, 1878—Telegram from Dr. W.E. Rogers to John Becher—"Friend Armstrong doing 1st rate."

Sister Frances apparently had only been struck with a mild case of the fever, as she was up and about, again working as hard as any of her peers. Her responsibility of running the Canfield orphan home on the Old Raleigh Road was beginning to turn into an impossible task. They now had over

seventy children at the home, with at least ten sick and six who had already passed away.

Frances' responsibilities had been difficult, but as long as Dr. Armstrong had been able to visit the home every day, the load was not impossible. However, now Armstrong was sick—not expected to survive, according to the sisters at the infirmary—and her only support at the orphanage was Sister Clare, three good nurses, and a cook.

So it wasn't surprising that she was kneeling before a small altar which they had constructed after taking over the asylum. However, on the morning of the 18th of September, her prayers were interrupted by a calm, small voice behind her. "Sister, I'm sorry to do this to you."

Frances wearily pulled herself to her feet and turned to face Sister Clare. The woman was obviously ill. "Don't worry yourself one bit, Sister. The most important thing is for you to get well. You need to go back to the infirmary. The nurses and I can carry on."

"Please let me stay. As soon as I'm on my feet again, I want to help in any way I can."

"No. You need a doctor, and we don't see one often enough out here. If Doctor Sohm comes out today, we'll send you back to town with him."

Fannie made it her business to see the next visit to the Johnson household was assigned to Dr. Josefson, with her accompaniment. John Johnson answered their knock, and it didn't take much of an assessment for the doctor to realize he was worn to a frazzle. Fannie noticed he no longer made any attempt to avert his face from her.

Josefson spoke first. "How is your wife this morning, Johnson?"

He looked down on his daughters, each of whom were hanging on to one of his pant legs. "Ya'll get back there an' play on yer pallet." When he was satisfied they were out of the way, he turned back to Josefson and Fannie. "I cain't get much out of her. Me or the nurse been spongin' her night an' day, but she ain't interested in drinkin' anything a'tall. And them bowels been goin' non-stop fer two days. She be weak as a kitten."

Josefson exchanged a look with Fannie before responding. "Has she complained about a bad taste in her mouth?"

"Yes, sir. She say everthin' tastes like an iron skillet. Mebbe that's why she ain't interested in eatin' anything. Now she got spit in her mouth thet's thick as grits."

Josefson nodded. "Let's stop the calomel altogether. At this point, there's no reason to continue giving her the strong laxative. She'll just get weaker the longer she uses it. That should also help her get rid of that taste in her mouth. Maybe try letting her suck on a piece of ice every half hour, or more often if she'll accept it. Have you noticed whether or not she's still producing any urine?" He noticed the blank look on Johnson's face. "Is she still able to make water?"

"Not much. Maybe just a smidgen this mornin'."

"Let me check her temperature." He retrieved the thermometer from his satchel and looked at Johnson. "How are you feeling?"

"Don't worry yerself 'bout me. Just do everthin' you can to get my wife well. Whatever it takes. Is thet calomel expensive? Whatever it costs, I don't care. I'll spend ever' dime I got to save her. Reckon she's the best thing thet ever happened to me." He gestured toward the sound of play in the back of the home, trying mightily to hold himself together. "Me an' the girls—we cain't make it without her."

September 19, 1878—"Farmers are urgently requested to send in donations of wood for the destitute citizens of Memphis, in order to accomplish the disinfection of the city. All living near should haul it to 31 S. Court Street, to the J.C. McCabe Commissary. All in the country should haul to the nearest rail station, where it will be brought to Memphis free of charge."

"Fresh beef and mutton is distributed for the benefit of convalescents every morning at Seessel's Butcher Shop, corner Second and Jefferson Streets."

"From a correspondent in Holly Springs, Mississippi—Our first yellow fever victim was on August 31st. In the next two weeks, our small city has suffered 61 deaths, among them 58 whites and 3 colored. We fear the worst is yet to come." Memphis Daily Appeal

Emilie had completed her assignment in Victorian Village, making sure the Dickinson family had recovered physically, and also had the information they needed to get by financially. She was on her way back to the Howards' office to be given her next duty assignment when she decided to once more visit the Catholic church on 4th Street. Perhaps the father would be ready to give her some much-needed advice.

When she entered the narthex, hoping to see the young priest, the sexton approached her.

"Is the younger reverend available this morning? He's helping me with a complicated problem, and I'd like to speak to him if possible."

She could tell immediately by the man's reaction that something was very wrong. The sexton tried unsuccessfully to hide his raw emotions. His voice broke. "I'm so sorry to tell you this. Father passed away early this morning. He'd only been ill a few days."

Emilie felt an unexpected tear come to her eye. She had been convinced that the reverend had showed some empathy with her situation, and perhaps would offer her some needed understanding, but now that wasn't possible. "And what of the vicar? When I saw him last, he didn't look well himself."

The sexton bowed his head. "He passed away two days ago."

Emilie nodded. "I'm sorry to hear that. I won't bother you any further." She exited the church and stood for a moment on the front steps. She looked up and down the street, and seeing no one, furtively pulled the locket from her pocket, placed it around her neck, and waited.

The sound of the young priest's voice came almost instantly. "I did so hope you would come back—in spite of me not helping when you asked for my advice."

"Father, I put my locket on because I sensed you might have need to talk to me."

"Indeed, child. The fever came on me so suddenly, I had no opportunity to write my old mam in Ireland. Might you do such a thing for me? I promise not to take too much of your time."

Emilie removed a pad from her bag, which she used to record her nursing notes, then retrieved a pen and filled it with ink. The priest dictated a short message to his mother, telling her he had been taken quickly, and that a nurse was writing the letter for him.

Knowing the woman lived in poverty, he apologized to her for not being able to send her any money, saying humbly that neither he, nor any of the priests he knew, possessed even enough silver to cover their eyes when they died. He ended by telling her that she should not mourn him, but that he would see her soon one day in Paradise, and they would be reunited in the presence of the Holy Father and His Son.

When Emilie turned to go, the reverend suddenly appeared before her, not in his priestly garb, but wrapped in his burial shroud. "Emilie, I'm sorry for not helping you when you came to me. I realize now how wrong that was. I should have remembered that in times of great trouble, the Lord has a way of sending emissaries. We're all familiar with His angels and prophets and saints, but sometimes we forget others can be sent who also have the ability to offer great comfort to us. I now understand your own gift will be able to bring solace and understanding to many suffering people. Thank you for helping me. I can see nothing sinful in what you are doing. Just be sure your motives are always to do good."

She bent her head for a few seconds, trying to hold back the tears of celebration. It was the third time she had been told to use her "power" to do good, and she intended to follow that directive. She was now convinced it couldn't possibly be wrong to help someone just because they happened to be on the other side of death's curtain. When she lifted her eyes to speak to him again, he was gone.

Chapter 22
Ain't You Dead?

Memphis

Lester Sellers and Israel Jackson had almost a full load in their funeral wagon, and were about to head down to Elmwood Cemetery when they were hailed by the sexton at St. Patrick's Catholic Church. "You men—I've got a corpse at my back door—one of our parishioners from the neighborhood. I hate to wait until the next time you pass. Can you pick him up for me?"

"Yes, suh. Has he got himself a plot over at Calvary?"

"I doubt he'd have the money for such."

"I reckon we got room for one more." Lester drew back on the reins, engaged the brake, and helped Israel carry their remaining empty coffin through the garden to the rear of the church. The sisters had placed a shroud over the man's head, so the two of them loaded the corpse into his box. Lester picked up the lid and positioned it in place while Israel grabbed a handful of nails and a hammer, preparing to fasten the casket shut for all eternity.

But upon hammering in the first nail, Israel thought he heard a noise inside the box, and peered at Lester. "Did you hear anythin'?" Just to make sure, the two of them apprehensively slid the still unsecured lid aside.

The corpse stared back at Israel with a terrified look on his face, and asked, "Might you be the one they call Mr. Lucifer?"

Israel tried to stifle a scream of fright, but was only moderately successful. Lester bent down close to the box himself. “Ain’t you dead?”

“I suppose I am. I’m in my casket, ain’t I? Which one o’ you is Mr. Lucifer? I never figgered you t’ be colored.”

“You ain’t in hell, y’ idjit. We were just fixin’ t’ fasten the lid on this here casket o’ yours.”

“Well, I’ll swan! I reckon I was dead, but it was so doggone lonesome bein’ such, I s’pose I decided to come on back to life. I sure am glad I ain’t down there in hell with all that wailin’ and sufferin’ goin’ on—at least not yet.” The man then seemed to remember something, raised his hand to his mouth, and inquired of the two, “Did you’ns happen t’ notice my teeth when you put me in this casket?”

“No, sir. All we seen was bare gums.”

“Didja happen t’ notice a red-headed feller hangin’ around?”

At this query, the portly sexton tentatively stuck his head over the edge of the casket. “I did see a man, very thin, and he had a crutch with him. He walked like one leg was held together with hinges. He was leaving the garden when I answered a knock at the vicar’s side door and found you laid out here.”

“That’s my brother, all right! He’s always coveted my Waterloo dentures. Caught him wearin’ ’em on more’n one occasion. I reckon the fool figgers he got ’em for good this time. I’ll have my teeth back or burn up that crutch of his.”

(*Author’s note:* Waterloo dentures were composed of human teeth which were originally harvested from the thousands of dead on the battlefield at Waterloo. The teeth had then been modified by trimming the roots and fitting them into an ivory denture base. The lifelike dentures were very popular, and long after Waterloo, the same practice continued on other, more recent battlefields.)

At that point, the sexton intervened, helped the man climb out of his would-be final resting place, and took him into the church so he could make arrangements to send him to the infirmary on Court Street.

Lester looked at Israel, who still had not stopped shaking. Israel’s question said it all for the both of them. “You reckon we buried any others that warn’t quite dead yet?”

"My ma told me how they laid people out after they died in old times, and somebody always sat up with the body for a night or two. The reason was jus' in case the corpse warn't dead. Thet's why they said they was holdin' a wake—in case they waked up."

"I just thought my dreams was bad up to now, Lester. This here is a whole 'nother set o' nightmares."

(*Author's note:* Before the days when corpses were embalmed, the dead were disinterred from time to time—sometimes to relocate the body, often for medical education, and every now and then for criminal investigation. People began to notice in horror that in about one burial out of twenty-five, there were scratch marks on the inside of the casket. In an abundance of caution, families began insisting that a string be tied to the finger of the deceased before they were put in the ground, then a small bell was attached to the other end of the string above the grave. This would allow a supposedly dead person to be 'saved by the bell,' and the family member who sat by the graveside overnight, watching for the bell to ring, was said to be serving on 'the graveyard shift.' Even George Washington stipulated that he not be placed in his tomb until two days after he had been declared dead.)

September 20, 1878—"When the fever began here, there were four Episcopal ministers on duty. All fell ill, and only two have escaped death. The plague has no terrors for these men, pledged at the altar to a duty that embraces sickness as well as health, and all the changes and chances of life. All honor to them. Of the Methodist ministers, both have succumbed to the epidemic. Of the three Presbyterian ministers, only Rev. Dr. Boggs is still on duty. Rev. Daniel, of First Church, fell early in the action, but has currently relapsed, and is unable to continue his service. Of the Baptist ministers, only Rev. Dr. Landrum remains. Of the two German Protestant ministers, only Mr. Holmes survives. Of the Catholic church, seven have passed on, and only three priests remain on duty—Rev. Father Kelly of St. Peters, Rev. Father Aloysius of St. Mary's, and Rev. Father Walsh of St. Briget's. The record of the ministry in Memphis is bright and luminous with a personal courage and devotion that would do credit to Christianity at any period in its history."

"The following is a copy of a telegram sent to New York to be read at Booth's Theater on the 21st: 'Deaths in Memphis to date, 2,250; number of sick now, about 3,000; average deaths, sixty percent of the sick. We are feeding 10,000 persons—sick and destitute—in camps in and about the city. Fifteen volunteer physicians have died, twenty others are ill. A great many nurses have died. We are praying for frost; it is our only hope. A thousand thanks to the good people of New York for their kind aid.'"

"Of the sisters of St. Mary's Episcopal Church, Sister Frances continues to run the church's orphan home on the Old Raleigh Road. She has only lately risen from her sick bed, having been prostrated by the fever. She is the only sister of the six assigned to St. Mary's who is not sick or dead. Thirteen of the children at the orphanage have died, thirteen are convalescing, and six are quite ill." Memphis Daily Appeal

Nurse Emilie Christophe had been reassigned yet again to a family in need, and it was she who met Dr. Josefson at John Johnson's home. "Come in, Doctor." Turning to be sure she was not overheard, she lowered her voice. "Marissa has only been briefly conscious today. Her fever is so terribly high, I doubt she'll survive the night."

"What about her husband? Is he well?"

"He says he had the fever when he was younger, and it's hard to tell the two little girls were ever sick. However, they're both smart enough to know things are bad for their mother."

They walked back to where Marissa lay on her pallet. John was sitting cross-legged on the floor beside her, holding her hand. Josefson placed his hand on her forehead, then placed his stethoscope on her chest. Her heart was racing, her breathing ragged, and he didn't need his thermometer to recognize a very high fever. The highest temperature he had measured so far during the epidemic was 106.5 degrees, and he was confident Marissa's was very close to that mark. The poor woman was speaking off and on, but it was unintelligible gibberish. Thankfully, the little girls were not where they could see the remnants of their mother.

Josefson hated this aspect of his profession, but finally he turned to the husband. "Johnson, nothing is certain with this evil disease, but I'm afraid your wife is not going to live another twenty-four hours."

He rubbed his eyes. "Are you sure 'bout that? I swear she 'pears to be better this evenin'."

"I can only tell you that I haven't seen anyone survive when they're sick as your wife is."

"Ain't there some medicine you kin give her?"

"I wish there was." He nodded toward Emilie, smiling as best he could. "You've got one of the most experienced nurses in the entire city, and she's already doing everything possible for your wife."

"What about thet calomel? She warn't near this bad til you stopped her takin' them calomel powders."

"There's no reason to keep giving her a laxative, particularly one as strong as calomel, after the first day or two."

"But thet Doctor Madison said she had to have it."

"As weak as she is, I think more calomel would finish her within the hour. The only thing you can do now is try to get her fever down by sponging her with ice and whiskey. If she's conscious, let her suck on ice chips, and try to keep her quiet."

"So you ain't got no medicine a'tall for her?"

"I'm sorry, but there is no medicine that would do her a bit of good at this point."

"But you saved my girls. Why cain't you do the same for my wife?"

"Your wife was probably worn to a frazzle taking care of your girls. So when she got sick, her resistance was already compromised." He shook his head sadly, knowing there was literally nothing he could do to relieve the suffering of the patient or the husband. "She didn't have the strength left to fight it off." Josefson paused before asking the question. "Do you folks have any close relatives nearby who your girls might stay with? It's going to be very difficult for them to be here when their mother passes."

"My family is all dead. Marissa don't know where hers is. They was sold off down in Mississippi durin' the war. She ain't seen or heard of 'em since. We is all each other has got."

"I know you're a policeman. And I know how valuable you are to the city since you've already had the fever, and so many of the police have been taken already. Have you thought about what you're going to do if your wife passes away?"

John held his head in his hands. "I got no idea." He raised his head. There were tears of realization in his eyes. "What should I do?"

"Since the girls have already had the fever, they should be safe if you choose to send them to one of the camps."

"Yeah. I'd give anything if'n I'd done that a month ago."

"Maybe a better alternative is the Canfield Asylum. The Episcopal sisters have taken over the place and turned it into an orphanage out north of the city. If the girls went there, they'd be well taken care of."

"I ain't 'Piscopal."

"No, no. The sisters are taking children of any religion. When things get back to normal, you could have your girls again."

The man sat on the floor, wringing his hands. "Right now I gotta concentrate on my wife. She's just too fine fer this to happen." He looked pleadingly at Josefson. "Won't you please get her started back on calomel?"

The doctor shook his head. "It would be cruel to do that to her, Johnson. It just wouldn't be right."

Well after the doctor left, Johnson sat vigil in the sick room, only succumbing to sleep after Emilie promised to wake him if his wife awoke. Emilie held Marissa's hand well into the middle of the night, keeping up the sponging efforts and trying unsuccessfully to give her ice chips. Sometime after three o'clock in the morning, her patient experienced a hard but brief seizure, and she was gone.

Emilie quietly retrieved her locket. She instinctively knew Johnson would be troubled by questions, and so for the first time since she took over nursing duties in the household, she held a cogent conversation with the woman, before her husband and daughters awakened to their grief.

The Howards' clerk looked across his desk at the young Negro nurse standing in front of him. "Let's see—Emilie Christophe, isn't it? Yes, you were with the Dickinson family for eight days, and then with the Johnsons for four. Isn't that correct?" He looked up and acknowledged her nod. "We'd like to send you to work at St. Mary's Episcopal Church. They've got patients there at the church, as well as a hundred children at their orphan home. Three of the sisters have died, several more taken sick, and they desperately need more nurses."

"Does it make any difference that I'm Catholic?"

"Not to them. Does it make any difference to you?"

"I'll go wherever I'm needed, particularly if it includes children."

"Fine." He looked at his paperwork again. "I don't know who to tell you to report to. So many of them are sick, I don't know who is still working."

"I'll find my way."

As Emilie approached St. Mary's, she decided to once more test the power of the locket, and placed it around her neck before she ascended the front steps to the church. Knowing there had been a number of deaths at that location, she was prepared for another auditory assault, but it was surprisingly subdued.

She wondered if the lack of anguished pleading was due to several deaths being those of the sisters. Perhaps, Emilie reasoned, in their commitment to love and prayer, the sisters would have passed away with less distress and anguish than the average person. But she did hear two clear and distinct requests.

Dr. William Armstrong, who had just passed away the previous afternoon, requested she write a letter to his wife, Louise, who could be contacted via her family member, John Becher in Columbia, Tennessee. Emilie requested pen and paper as soon as she entered the infirmary, and she immediately wrote out the following letter:

'(Dictated to a nurse) Dearest Louise: When you return to our home in Memphis, you must immediately seek out the Bible on my desk. Look particularly to the 23rd Chapter of Psalms, where I hope you will not only find strength from our Lord, but also the savings I have accumulated for you and our children. Love always, Your Husband.'

Reverend Charles Parsons asked for little, save giving a message to his wife. He explained that she, and his two children from his earlier marriage, had been sent to Annandale, Mississippi when the epidemic began, and they were staying at the Britton family plantation. He requested that Emilie tell his wife of his love for her, as well as his enduring appreciation that she would take care of his sons.

Emilie remembered passing through the small town of Annandale just north of Jackson, on her train ride from New Orleans; so she had yet another reason (besides the Grenada visit to give a message to Colonel Anderson) to head back south after the epidemic was concluded.

September 21, 1878—"The members of the Citizens Relief Committee are now few in number. The clerical staff is reduced to one other than myself. We are endeavoring to do all we can to alleviate the suffering of the living as well as inter the dead. Hoping you will appreciate our position, and in future make your communications short and to the point. I remain, R.B. Clarke."

"The closing of the undertaker's establishment of Holst and Bros. was compelled by the sickness of Theo. Holst, the only surviving member of the firm, and Mr. Sutton, the only assistant remaining." Memphis Daily Appeal

September 21, 1878—Telegram from W.E. Rogers to John S. Becher—"Dr. Armstrong died yesterday afternoon."

September 22, 1878—"The Jews are so thoroughly organized as to be equal to any emergency of disaster or disease. They seldom ask relief, even of each other. But the demands of this epidemic have been so exhaustive, as to deplete the treasury of the Hebrew Relief Organization, hence an appeal has gone out to their co-religionists throughout the U.S. for pecuniary aid."

"Policeman John Getzendaner is on duty at the station house, though announced as dead by an exchange." Memphis Daily Appeal

Chapter 23
I'll Be Back to Get Y'all

Memphis

John Johnson wondered for the hundredth time if he was doing the right thing. He'd give anything if he could just ask Marissa for her opinion one more time. At the very least, he needed her permission for what he was about to do that morning. If he could only explain to her, maybe she'd understand.

It was over a mile from their home in Fort Pickering to St. Mary's Episcopal Church, and Leisha was perched on his shoulders the whole way, while Ruthie marched along with her father, determined to show how grown up she was. Johnson was carrying a gunny sack with a change of clothes for each of the girls, the two precious stocking dolls their mother had made for them, and their game of jacks.

But more than one problem was eating him. He was positive Marissa had been improving until Dr. Josefson took away the calomel. As far as he was concerned, that decision had killed his wife. Everybody said Negroes seldom died of the yellow fever. Why had that damned Jew changed her medicine? More to the point, what was he going to do about it?

When Johnson tapped on the church door, it was with a guilty heart. How could he ever justify to Marissa that he was leaving their girls at an orphanage? However, he was surprised when his knock was answered by a familiar face, one that quickly displayed a big smile. "Now, what are my favorite girls doing here?"

Both Ruthie and Leisha's faces went from tears to grins in an instant. "Nurse Emilie! We didn't know you'd be here."

"I didn't know myself until yesterday morning. I'm supposed to go up to the Canfield Asylum later today." She smiled at the two girls. "Maybe we can travel together."

Emilie plucked Leisha from her perch, then knelt and spoke directly to the sisters. "I'm so happy to see you two." She fingered the ribbons their father had awkwardly tied in their hair. "I don't think I've seen such pretty girls before." She gave them each a quick hug before looking up at Johnson. "Are you going back to work?"

"Yessum. They need me real bad."

After hearing just the day before about the heavy workload shouldered by the two sisters at the orphanage, Emilie wondered how much longer they would be able to continue taking more and more children. "I believe you said you didn't have any relatives close by."

"No, ma'am. We're all each other's got." He bent down and gave both girls a long embrace. "Course, you know Ruthie and Leisha done had the fever, so at least they won't be gettin' sick on y'all."

Emilie looked again at the girls. "I had the fever, too. It looks like we've got something in common." She smiled at them before returning to the father. "Just so I can make sure the paperwork is accurate—do you want to put the girls up for adoption, Mr. Johnson?"

He shook his head almost violently. "Oh, no, ma'am. I'll be comin' back for 'em as soon as the fever leaves the town." He looked searchingly at the nurse, then spoke quietly so the girls wouldn't hear. "You're sure there ain't no way somebody'll give 'em away on accident?"

"I'll make sure everybody knows you're coming to get them. We'll take real good care of these pretty girls so you can have them both back, good as new."

John knelt on the porch, drawing both girls into his arms. "Now, you two be real good for Nurse Emilie. Papa will be back soon to get y'all." It was unlikely he could ever forget the hugging, crying, and pleading that went on between them. He looked up at Emilie, a tear on his cheek. "If I could just talk to Marissa again. You know, to be sure this is all right with her."

Emilie kept her voice as neutral as she could. "Well, Mr. Johnson, it just so happens Marissa and I had a private conversation about that very thing while she was still—" she glanced at Ruthie and Leisha "—while she was still herself. She was afraid of what might happen to the girls in case something, uh, unexpected happened to her."

"What did she have to say?"

"She was upset, but we talked about the Canfield home, and once she understood the girls would be in a safe place, and you would come and get them after the fever was gone, she gave you her blessing."

Johnson kept his head turned so the girls wouldn't see his emotion. "You don't know how much that helps. Thank you."

There was more hugging and crying for a couple of minutes, with Johnson himself fighting to maintain control of his own waterworks, before Emilie spoke again to the girls. "You know, I bet we could get the cook to give us some sugar biscuits. Why don't you come with me, and we'll let your papa go on to work."

September 23, 1878—"Dr. R.H. Tate, of Cincinnati, Ohio, who volunteered his services here three weeks ago, succumbed yesterday to the fever. Dr. Tate was the first Negro physician to come to the aid of the Howard Association of Memphis. His assignment—west of Lauderdale and south of Union—was described by other physicians as 'Hell's Half Acre.' We are forever grateful for his sacrifice." Memphis Daily Appeal

September 23, 1878—Minutes of the Hernando, Mississippi Citizens Relief Committee—"President Bullington reported that, in view of the number of cases in our city, he telegraphed the following to the Howards in Memphis: 'We need money. Have had 27 cases of yellow fever to date, 8 deaths. 8 new cases in last 24 hours. Physicians now declare the fever epidemic.'"

September 23, 1878—Letter from Sisters of 3rd Order of St. Francis to Reverend Mother in St. Louis. "Please if it is not too much trouble, send us some oranges or any kind of fruit; we would be so glad to have it for the sick. We can't get anything at all here. Please address it to the Catholic church, as there are Protestant sisters here who have the same name."

Mark Bartel found the editor in his office. "Good morning, Mr. Keating. I've got a story that's a little outside what you asked me to do, but I think it's worth tellin'."

Keating looked up from a huge pile of paperwork. The man looked as though he had not slept in a week. He frankly didn't sound all that interested, but it was difficult to keep one's focus from becoming numbed when inundated on all sides by terrible stories of death and suffering day after day. "Let's hear it, Bartel."

"My sister sent me a copy of the *Jackson Tribune and Sun.* There's a story in there about a ten-year-old boy from Memphis by the name of Howlett. His family put him on the train and sent him to Milan, Tennessee to stay with his grandfather in order to get him away from the fever. Apparently, Milan is quarantined against people from Memphis, so his grandfather had to send him a few miles out in the country to stay in a log cabin with an old colored woman until his quarantine period was completed.

"I guess that wasn't good enough for the townsfolk, because the first night, several men gathered outside the cabin. They had themselves quite a bonfire. Apparently there was a bit of drinkin', they started hollering curses at the boy, threw brickbats at the house, and then began shooting into the building. The little fellow jumped out through a window and ran into the woods. Then these people started firing wild shots after him into the trees.

"Well, the boy was scared to death and stayed curled up and hidden in a stump hole in the woods all night long, wondering if they might find him and murder him on the spot. At daybreak, he crept back into Milan, and his grandfather took the poor boy to what he hoped would be another safe place."

Keating sucked on his pipe. "My God, shooting at children! This fever has turned folks into fiends. Have the local authorities done anything about it?"

"It appears the Jackson paper is trying to get the ones responsible hunted down and punished."

"Thanks for telling me about it, Bartel. I almost hate to publish the story. Fear is everywhere on our streets. I'm afraid this might give folks around here the same kind of ideas."

September 24, 1878—"The colored policemen have been very efficient, and are decidedly earnest in their efforts to show that their arrests are in the interest of law and order. The most remarkable thing about the court is the absence of lawyers. Owing to the absence of the legal fraternity in our city, His Honor discharges business rapidly and understandingly."

"While the northern states with lavish hand are soothing the fevered brow of southern suffering, she is building a monument to gratitude which will be luminous forever."

From Sioux City, Iowa—"My wife and I want a little girl, between the ages of four and ten, to raise and educate. Can we get a pretty little orphan girl of American parentage? We have no children, and being in the prime of life think we could rear and educate one. Mr. Editor, please hand this to someone who will give it attention, and I will forward the means for the child's transportation to anyone you suggest. My wife's people are southern." Memphis Daily Appeal

Sister Armella sought out Father Weiver in early afternoon. "Father, I have a special request of you, and it involves quite a long walk to the community they call Fort Pickering." She looked at him for confirmation. "I'm sorry. It's at least a mile to his home."

The twenty-nine-year-old Franciscan smiled at her. "If it involves the business of our Eternal Father, I'm always ready."

"I'm sure you remember dear Sister Mary Vincent, who came with us from St. Louis."

"Of course. I administered extreme unction to her not forty feet from where we stand."

"Yes, Father. Sister Mary Vincent was not only the youngest sister among us, but she was the first one of our order to volunteer to come here. And I think there were two reasons for that. Of course, she wanted to do everything possible for the poor people of Memphis, but she also wanted to help her own father. You see, he lives here in the city, but he left the church several years ago, and it pained her greatly to think that he might lose the joys of heaven if he remained thus.

"When we arrived at the train station, she actually saw her father in the crowd, but the press of people was so great she was unable to get to him before he gave up finding her and departed. She lacked an address for him, and sadly, she became sick within days after we arrived in Memphis, and passed away on September 11th, before being able to locate her father.

"As luck would have it, the man had discovered that his daughter was with us here in the city, and he endeavored to find her. But he was too late for a reunion in this life, as she passed on not three hours before his arrival."

Father Weiver clasped his hands behind his back. "This fever is so cruel."

"Yes, Father. He arrived here at St. Mary's as the undertaker was preparing to remove her corpse. The poor man fell to his knees at her side and exclaimed, 'Oh, God, I know it all now. I know what brought my daughter into this place of danger. It was the thought of her careless father, and the salvation of his soul.'

"We were all terribly distressed by this, both for him and for our dear Sister Mary Vincent. But when she was placed in her casket, her father rose immediately and went in search of Father Bucholz. He confessed his sins, received the sacraments, and made his peace with God."

"I'm so glad to hear that, Sister. I know that would give Sister Mary Vincent so much peace. But what need do you have of me?"

"Father, word has come to us this morning that the man has come down with a terrible case of the fever himself, and is now near death at his home in Fort Pickering. I know Sister Mary Vincent would be eternally grateful to you if you would administer last rites to her father."

"Then let's leave immediately, Sister. This fever possesses no mercy, and waits for no man."

September 25, 1878—"May we reasonably hope the fever is on the decline in this city? Since the 18th, when the daily death rate fell below ninety for the first time, there has been no return to that terrible number. For the past seven days, the average has been fifty-three per day. We look for further decline, to be accelerated, we hope, by any early frosts that will utterly destroy the germs of the disease. This decrease is felt in the city, but out in the county towns and camps, where there is now a population of perhaps 40,000, who ten days

ago felt themselves safe from the disease, the fever is raging with the same violence which characterized here in Memphis from the 3rd to the 17th. Taking the whole county into account, the fever is as bad today as it was when we in the city had our highest mortality."

"Thousands of destitute people in New Orleans went to bed supper-less last night—and all because some intermeddling busybody has influence with the Secretary of War, thus inducing him to discontinue sending rations to that suffering city."

"The Gregg family has been swept from the face of the earth. The father and six children have already died, and last night the mother passed through death's door."

"The fire department is suffering terribly. The force consisted of forty-five men, of whom seventeen have died, and fifteen are down sick." Memphis Daily Appeal

Dr. Josefson was going about his rounds in Fort Pickering when he came upon a man in his mid-thirties, sitting before a pine knot fire in front of a squalid dwelling. He noticed the fellow's ragged clothing, as well as the toes protruding through the front of his shoes. His eyes were cast down, as though he was unwilling to look upon the physician. "Would you be the doctor?"

"Yes. I understand there's a sick child on this street, but I don't have an address."

The man gestured with a glance behind him. "Yeah, he'd be yonder there in the house."

Despite the chill in the air, Josefson noticed there was no smoke at the chimney and no light in the dwelling. "Who might be with him?"

The man kept his eyes averted. "Just me. His ma lit out with the other younguns yestiddy, soon as she figgered he had the fever."

"Are you giving him any medicine?"

"I ain't been in the house since his ma left. He's awful sick. I heard him throwin' up all day in there."

"Are you saying nobody has given him any water or medicine since yesterday?"

"Thet's why I called fer you. What took you so long?"

Josefson shook his head at the man's cowardice, pulled a brand from the fire, and entered the house. The floors of the front room and the kitchen were smeared with the remnants of black vomit and excreta, with flies so numerous that the hum of their wings was enough to raise the hair on the doctor's neck. The stench was beyond description. With only the torch for light, it took a few minutes to find the boy, no more than eight years old, rolled into a ball on the floor behind the stove. When Josefson touched his shoulder, the boy called to him in a raspy voice. "Water—please, sir, I need water."

Josefson found a jug of water on the table and gave the boy a small drink. He looked around the room and opened a cabinet, but discovered not a whit of food, or anything else that might help the youngster. The boy was smeared with the foulness of his disease, so Josefson took off his coat, bundled the child in it, then gathered him in his arms and picked him up. The doctor was surprised at how light he was.

Josefson realized that, with this close exposure to the elements of the fever, he was about to risk his own health significantly more than he had previously. Perhaps his involuntary shudder was a premonition of what might lie ahead, but he forced himself to cast the fear aside. After all, how many nurses accepted this risk, or worse, every single day?

"Come on, son, I'm taking you to the infirmary. We can't wait on an ambulance."

Josefson walked outside, carrying the limp figure in his arms. The father looked away again. "Is he dead yet?"

"No. And no thanks to you! I'm taking him to the Howards' infirmary, in case you're interested."

"Did you bring any food?"

Rather than loading the child in his buggy, Josefson felt like placing his bundle on the ground and striking the man, but his duty to deliver the boy to the infirmary as soon as possible overcame his desire for punishment, and he simply responded, "No."

The father never stood up, never raised his head, nor even said a comforting word in his son's direction, but simply focused his attention on stirring the coals of the fire with his stick.

Chapter 24
The Canfield Orphanage

Memphis

Dr. Sohm usually was issued a wagon and pair of horses by the Howard Association, principally because he often had to transport children, nurses, and sisters back and forth to the Canfield orphanage. Too often, his passengers coming from the orphanage were sick and on their way to one of the infirmaries, so a wagon, rather than a buggy, was better able to accommodate their need to travel on a sleeping pallet.

On the morning of September 26th, Nurse Emilie, accompanied by Leisha and Ruthie Johnson, hitched a ride with the good doctor. He immediately began apologizing before they had traveled a single block. "This seat is awfully uncomfortable, Nurse. At least a buggy seat has got some give and take to it. But the way this wagon bangs and bounces will certainly give your bowels a good shaking."

Although Emilie had a firm hold on the seat with her left hand to keep from falling off, and a good grip on the girls with her right, she was able to smile at his expression. "Don't give that a thought, Doctor Sohm. I'd just as soon bounce a little bit as spend the next two hours walking."

"We've got ourselves a fine day this morning. The roads are mostly dry, so we ought to be able to make the five-mile trip in an hour. But after a rain, the horses move at not much more than a slow walk. The same trip has taken me over two and a half hours." He steered around a still-wet puddle from the rain several days previous.

"What happens if you get stuck in the mud?"

He gestured toward the back of the wagon, at the bundle lying beside Ruthie and Leisha's blanket. "The Howards always send a stout tow rope and a shovel. You probably noticed there's no cover on this wagon, so we've also got an oilcloth and an umbrella to keep us dry if it starts to rain. They even give me a lantern to use if I'm out after dark. I have to confess, I've been out late and gone to sleep half-sitting on this seat several times. Thank goodness the horses know the way back to their livery stable."

"Do people help if you get stuck?"

"Usually they do. But a couple of trips I've had sick children in the back, and nobody would come near us."

They plodded along in silence for a half mile or so, until Sohm pointed ahead in the roadway. "You see those dogs at the head of that lane? Those two try to spook the horses every time I pass by."

"They don't look that dangerous."

"I've had horses run off the road into a ditch and the wagon turned over. The team has even tried to run through a fence to get away from the dogs." He glanced at his passengers in the back of the wagon. "You girls hang on real tight when they start barking." He turned to Emilie. "Hand me that wooden box in back. I hate to do it, but I can't have anybody hurt if those dogs act up."

Emilie struggled with the awkward box, but did as she was asked. "This is heavy."

When the wagon was no more than fifty yards from the mutts, they stood up, began to prance around, and started to bark. Sohm responded by slapping the reins on his horses' backs three times in quick succession. The wagon lurched forward, quickly doubling its speed. Emilie grabbed the girls with both hands. The wagon wheels jumped into and out of the road ruts, threatening to throw all of them out of the wagon and into the roadway.

The dogs darted in and out, nipping and biting at the horses' hocks and fetlocks. The horses kicked, but ineffectively. Sohm switched the reins to his left hand while reaching into the box with his right. Emilie was surprised to see him withdraw a fist-sized rock. He leaned precariously to his left, threw the rock, and missed. With his third attempt, he managed to impart a glancing blow to the larger of the two dogs. Luckily, the animals fell back at this, and the wagon continued northward, slowing to its original speed as it rounded the next turn in the road.

Sohm turned to Emilie with a sheepish look. "The rocks are almost as important as my medical bag."

Emilie snickered. "I think you need to practice your aim."

As they entered the grounds of the orphanage, they could see ten or twelve children working on the grounds, weeding the almost dormant flower beds and trimming bushes. Dr. Sohm glanced at the back of the wagon, noticing that both girls were paying a great deal of attention to the goings-on at their new home. "The older children all are required to work—some outside and the rest inside. They don't have enough staff to get all the work done without the orphans' help."

Emilie was struck that black and white children were seemingly getting along with one another, even having fun together. "Do they have problems here with prejudice, Doctor Sohm?"

"I noticed that right away myself the first time I came here. I figure there's no racism at Canfield because there are no parents."

"I don't understand."

"Children don't become racist of their own accord. Somebody has to teach it to them. Fortunately, the only adults the children see here are the Episcopal sisters and a few nurses. As far as I can tell, all of them are blind to color and religion. Any child that exhibits any symptoms of prejudice is quickly corrected. So what you see before you is a result of an environment where all are treated with the same level of love and respect."

"I think I'm going to like it here!"

Leah Feathers was in a hurry to fetch one of the Howard physicians when she ran into Fannie Lester. "You got to come help me, girl. That Mr. Furbish just passed out cold in the hallway. The fool been sick for two, mebbe three days, and he keep sayin' he ain't got the yellow fever. Now he lookin' a whole lot like he dead. Mebbe he 'bout ready for his coffin."

Fannie spied Dr. Michael Martin ahead of them and called to him for help. Just as Leah had said, Furbish was unconscious, lying spread-eagled on his back in the hall. Fannie made sure Leah kept her distance while Martin checked his runaway pulse, then placed his hand on the man's forehead. "He's burning up." He turned to Fannie. "Let's get him up to the infirmary and see what we can do."

Once they had Furbish settled, Fannie began applying compresses of ice water and whiskey, and tried to get the man to drink something. But he didn't respond at all, the ice chips simply dribbling down his cheek. While Fannie went downstairs to retrieve more ice, Dr. Martin bent over Furbish's cot.

Behind him, a voice scoffed. "These ignorant folk are their own worst enemy. So many of them foolishly decide they'll treat themselves with either some country remedy or a big dose of gin, and by the time they realize it's not working, they're too sick for us to save. A goodly number wait so long they die in their ambulance on the way to the hospital."

Martin glanced behind him, recognizing Dr. James Madison. "Did you ever stop to think these 'ignorant folk,' as you call them, have watched their sick friends and neighbors and family members voluntarily enter an infirmary or a hospital, and they see that those people don't survive anyway? After all, we're losing a good fifty percent of our patients right here in the Peabody. They've probably figured out those aren't very good odds."

"Fifty percent! I'll have you know I'm saving close to eighty percent of my patients."

Martin gritted his teeth, but continued searching for a pulse on Furbish. He was unsuccessful and closed the man's eyelids, then pulled the bedsheet over his head before standing up and turning around. At about the same time, Madison turned on his heel to walk away. Martin spoke sharply, and plenty loud enough to be heard by others in the ward. "Madison! Come back here. I want to talk to you."

Madison turned quickly, with an angry look on his face. He was a good five years older, four or five inches taller, and thirty pounds heavier than Martin, but he was taken aback by the look on the smaller man's face and found himself taking a half step backwards. Usually a sociable and friendly fellow, Martin had something of the bulldog in the stare he exhibited. "Madison, it's time you heard what several of us think of you constantly bragging about your treatment success. You have a habit of hand-picking your patients, always selecting the ones who aren't seriously ill. And once they become ill, for some reason you're not in the vicinity when one of us has to take over at the end."

"That's preposterous!"

"All of us have had to pronounce patients of yours who didn't recover. All of us have had to include those deaths on our own reports. You've been elsewhere. As a matter of fact, very few of the patients you began treating have walked out of here alive."

Madison looked from side to side, realizing several nurses and a physician were watching the argument. He lowered his voice to something between a whisper and a hiss. "Perhaps, whelp, your medical care would profit from another year of medical school." He then turned and left the ward.

September 26, 1878—(Ad) "Collins Voltaic Plaster—Cures aches and pains, equalizes the circulation, subdues inflammation, cures ruptures, strains, and kidney complaints, strengthens muscles, cures rheumatism and neuralgia, invaluable in paralysis, cures nervous shocks, cures epilepsy and fits, cures spinal weakness. Prescribed by physicians. Endorsed by electricians."

"Judge L.V. Dixon, of the law firm of Adams and Dixon, died of the fever. Judge Adams died a couple of weeks ago. The law firm is no more." Memphis Daily Appeal

Although it did not involve Madison, Dr. Martin had a similar case that same afternoon on Market Street. A Mr. Schley had a severe case of the fever, but had improved enough in his two-week convalescence that he volunteered to go to the commissary for his wife. He picked up a few supplies, including a small sack of potatoes, and was on his way home sometime around one o'clock when he apparently decided he could go no further and lay down in the middle of the street. Whether he fell, or simply decided to stop and rest, no one would ever know.

Dr. Martin found him, purely by accident, while making his rounds. Schley was lying face down, his head nestled on the potatoes, less than a hundred yards from the loving arms of his wife. He was dead. Martin cited the case later that evening during a medical discussion at the Peabody, as representative of how fragile the thread of life was for patients who were convalescing. A short walk of no more than four blocks, and a sack of potatoes which could easily have been carried by a child, had been enough to completely break that thread forever.

September 27, 1878—"From a correspondent—Whenever you imagine you can smell sulfur, camphor, and asafoetida, you can bank on casting your optics on a Germantownite, with sulfur in his boots and a ball of camphor in his bread basket, and immediately on discovering you, he pulls out a bottle of turpentine and sticks it to his proboscis. He will stand and talk to you at a considerable distance, but suggest a handshake or embrace and he will immediately take off like the first section of an express train."

"Dr. G.W. Lawrence, of Hot Springs, suggests that spectrum analysis be made, by means of a spectroscope, in all yellow fever districts, to learn the vitiated state of the atmosphere, and an effort be made to compare all alterations in the air that may exist. The spectroscope should reveal marginal changes in the atmosphere. Organic tests, barometric pressure, electrical relations, phonetic conductive power, and all meteorological conditions should be noted to further our knowledge of the cause of the fever." Memphis Daily Appeal

John Johnson was patrolling Main Street, south of Court Square, around nine o'clock on Friday evening. His mind was not really focused on his job. He couldn't stop thinking about his little girls at the Canfield orphan home. He wanted to visit them, but he'd been working seven days a week, with no opportunity to travel out the Raleigh Road. Besides, when it came time to leave, parting would be just as difficult as it had been after Marissa died.

Thank goodness there was that pretty black nurse who would be there for them. Surely the girls would feel better around one of their own kind. But no matter how many times he ran it through his mind, there seemed to be no good solution to his quandary.

His thoughts were interrupted when he spied a light inside the Armstrong and Byrne Grocery. The store had been closed for two weeks after half the partnership passed away, and certainly no lantern belonged there, let alone a lantern which appeared to be moving around inside the grocery.

Johnson started to blow his whistle to alert his partner, Lucas McNair, but was afraid whoever was prowling inside the store would hear him and take off. He could find no sign of entry at the front of the store, so Johnson moved through the narrow space between the grocery and a millinery shop to the alleyway at the rear. The padlock on the back door was smashed off its hasp, so he pulled out his revolver, entering the business as quietly as he could.

He crouched down behind some shelving and waited for the intruder with the lantern. When the two were separated by no more than ten feet, Johnson rose up. "Put up your hands or I'll shoot."

He could read the hesitation in the intruder's movement—probably considering a run for it. But he took the lantern from the white man's grasp and held it up to his face. The fellow was vaguely familiar, but he couldn't place him. Maybe he was one of the vagrants he had arrested previously. "Who are you?"

"None o' yer damn business. I ain't about to talk to the likes of you."

"Lay yourself down on the floor, face first." Johnson knelt, placing a knee in the middle of the man's back, pulled his arms behind him, and attached a set of iron cuffs. "Stay put. I don't mind shootin' you." Johnson retreated to the open doorway, retrieved his whistle, and blew three long blasts.

Within a couple of minutes, McNair pushed his way through the alley door. "What've we got here, Johnson?"

"I seen this feller in here, holdin' a lantern. The back door was broke open, and when I come in, he was fillin' up that gunny sack with groceries."

At that point, the man on the floor rolled over on his side. "Say there, McNair." Lucas peered at him in the dim light. "Don't you recognize me? I'm Patrolman C.H. Smith."

"What the hell are you doin' in here, Smith?"

"I was walkin' down Main Street when I seen this here colored boy robbin' the grocery. I come in to stop him, and he got the drop on me. It happened just the opposite o' what he said."

McNair looked at the two of them. "You ain't in uniform, Smith. So where's yer whistle?"

Smith didn't even hesitate. "I used his whistle."

"Was that before or after he got the drop on you?"

"Before. I wrestled it away from him."

Johnson stuck his hand in his pants. "So how did it end up back in my pocket?"

Smith looked at McNair. "You ain't gonna believe this here boy over me, are ye?"

McNair grabbed Smith's elbow and jerked him to his feet, then nodded approvingly toward Johnson. "That's exactly what I aim to do. It's a shameful thing when one of us pulls this low-down stuff." He looked back at Smith. "You'll be sittin' on yer sorry ass in lock-up 'til you see the judge on Monday."

September 28, 1878—"We learn that Becton, the mayor of Grand Junction, (Tennessee) *who ran away from his people when the fever broke out there, and carried away the donated funds subscribed by the people of many of the states, has not been heard from. A traitor to his trust, a robber of the dead and suffering, he should be hunted down and put in the penitentiary."*

"On September 17th, John Dawson died at Elmwood Cemetery, where he had been an employee for the last six years. His wife soldiered on, caring for their four little girls, ages one, three, five, and eight—one of them the faithful bell-ringer at Elmwood. But on the 23rd she was attacked by the fever, and despite her struggle, passed away yesterday morning. The little girls have no relatives in this country, so they were taken to the Orphan Home, where they will be cared for with a mother's tender, watchful guidance. Hopefully, the

girls' relatives in England can be contacted for further instructions as to what better might be done for them."

"Three nurses, sent from Norfolk, Virginia to Memphis, attempted yesterday to return to Norfolk, but were put off the train seven miles from their destination by sanitary authorities. They were arrested, taken to the pest-house, and the clothes they brought with them from Memphis were burned. They will be strictly guarded for ten days." Memphis Daily Appeal

Chapter 25
A Raving Lunatic

Memphis

September 29, 1878—"Of the fifty Howard physicians detailed for duty here during the epidemic, twenty-one have passed away and eleven are currently sick. And all of those eleven claimed to have previously had yellow fever."

"To the Editor—I see in your paper a note from your correspondent in Germantown, who maligned our residents with his snide remarks. I would like for you to see your so-called correspondent. He loves too much that John Barleycorn."

(Ad) "For the speedy cure of seminal weakness, lost manhood, and all disorders brought on by indiscretions or excesses of youth. Any druggist has the ingredients. Contact Dr. Jaques & Co. 130 W. Sixth Street, Cincinnati." Memphis Daily Appeal

Fannie Lester had been assigned to nurse the entire Rawlins family, who lived in a house near the corner of Third and Union Avenue. Despite every effort by Fannie, as well as their physician, in less than three days the mother and her three small children were dead. Although he had been ill as well, Jacob Rawlins, the father, appeared to be convalescing.

When Fannie thought he was strong enough, she sat by Rawlins' bedside and told him about the fate of his family.

When he heard her fateful words, his eyes darted wildly around the room, and he simply said, “Mother’s dead?” Whether he was then attacked by another bout of high fever, or because of the sudden and traumatic news of the loss of his entire family, he became mentally deranged. Fannie tried to reason with Rawlins, but he was beyond listening. She was aided by the man’s sister, but neither of the women could penetrate his crazed state.

A bit later that evening, Fannie was sitting in the kitchen of the little house when she heard Rawlins scrambling around in the bedroom. When she went to check on him, she discovered he had located a handgun, and naked as he was on the day he was born, threatened both Fannie and his sister with death, as he blamed them for the loss of his family. Crying uncontrollably, and shaking considerably in his nakedness, he finally chased them out of the house onto Third Street, pointed the pistol in their general direction, and fired two shots at them. Luckily they were both untouched, but he continued to threaten them by waving the pistol in their direction.

Rawlins stood on one side of the street, while his sister and Fannie were on the other, trying to reason with him, yet simultaneously desperately attempting to conceal themselves behind a buggy. He shot again, and this time the lead came so close that Fannie heard the bullet whine past her ear. She tried harder to make herself small behind the buggy wheel.

Fortunately, John Johnson heard the gunshots from some four or five blocks down the street and came running. Hearing the man continue his curses and threats, Johnson was able to size up the situation from a half block away and began to sneak up behind Mr. Rawlins.

It would have been a simple thing to just shoot the fellow, but once again he was restricted by Chief Athey’s requirement that he could neither arrest nor kill a white man. He couldn’t help but believe that sooner or later, that damned rule was going to get somebody on the force hurt.

As he got closer, John realized the nurse who was in danger was none other than Fannie Lester. And so he hesitated. What if she were killed? If that happened, the only link to his crime of starting the epidemic would be no more. But what if the other woman saw him delay his responsibility to defend them? Worse, what if Fannie survived, yet realized he had failed to help her? It then struck him. Surely he was a better man than to allow someone else to be killed in order to save his own neck.

He had no choice. He snuck up behind Rawlins and smacked him in the head with his night stick. Fannie ran up to Rawlins, as he was still her patient—naked as a plucked chicken though he was—and pulled his face out of a puddle in the street, perhaps preventing his drowning in two inches of water. She looked up, recognizing her rescuer. "Thank you for saving us, Mister Johnson. This man completely lost his senses after his family died."

Embarrassed, Johnson took off his policeman's jacket, bent down, and covered the exposed man's nakedness before tipping his hat. "I reckon he's headed for the jail house tonight." He half-smiled. "And by the by, Nurse Fannie, yer gonna need yerself a new hat."

Fannie pulled her nurse's cap off, quickly noticing the bullet hole in the peak. "It's because he's out of his head with the fever and his grief." When Johnson turned back to check on his prisoner, Fannie was jolted to see the scar on his bare back. She took a step closer, and realized the mark was clearly in the form of the two letters "GF." She vaguely remembered this same mark from some time in the near past, but couldn't quite place the circumstances. "Mr. Johnson, would you mind if I asked you about the scar on your shoulder?"

The man turned around somewhat awkwardly, embarrassed by the question. "I got it when I was near-about eleven years old. Man name of George Fenton used a brandin' iron on somewheres around nine or ten of us after he heard 'bout thet 'Mancipation Proclamation. Said he was markin' his property in case somebody decided to run off and join up with Mister Lincoln. Used a rusty old iron he branded his horses and mules with."

"You mean," she was almost sick at the thought, "you mean he heated up a branding iron and marked people with it—even children?"

"I reckon so. But I try to bury them days—you know, leave it in the past. It sure ain't doin' me no good to think on it now." He paused. "Say, Nurse Fannie, would you mind tellin' me what you know 'bout that Doctor Josefson?"

"Why, I'm not sure what you mean."

"Do he know what he's about? You know, doctorin' folks with the fever?"

"Are you thinking about your wife, Mister Johnson?"

"I cain't stop thinkin' 'bout her, wonderin' if she'd be alive today, weren't for that doctor."

"Well, I've worked with quite a few doctors these last six weeks. I'd say Doctor Josefson is one of the best of them."

"Do he treat colored different than whites?"

"Not that I've seen. Remember, he's the same doctor who cured both your little girls."

Johnson nodded his head. "I know. But they say us Negroes ain't s'posed to die of the fever. Why was Marissa any different?"

"Mister Johnson, these doctors are doing everything they can to keep people alive. We've had almost 3,000 deaths just in Memphis. What would happen if all those families decided it was the doctor's fault their loved ones didn't survive? Every doctor is doing the best he can, just like all you policemen are doing the best you can.

"I'm really sorry about your wife, and I know you have every right to be upset, but what happened to her wasn't because Doctor Josefson treated her differently or did something wrong." She pointed toward the man lying limp at their feet. "This man here, Mr. Rawlins, just today lost his wife and all three of his children to the yellow fever. And it put him over the edge." She looked down at the still limp Rawlins. "In fact, considering what he's just been through, I can't say that I blame him for how he reacted. The fever is tearing this town apart, one family at a time."

"I reckon the judge is just gonna figger him fer a ravin' lunatic when he gets to court tomorrow mornin'. Prob'ly won't spend no tears on him nor his feelin's. But you right about the fever tearin' things apart. Losin' Marissa has ruined us—me and my girls. And I got no idea what to do about it."

"At least you've got each other. That's what you need to focus on. When this is over, no matter what, you'll have your girls. Thanks again for coming to our rescue tonight."

Fannie was a full three blocks away when it struck her. She remembered exactly the circumstances on the night when she had previously seen Johnson's scar.

September 30, 1878—Letter from Sisters of 3rd Order of St. Francis to Reverend Mother in St. Louis. "Do not advise anybody to come down here because it only takes three or four days before they are sick with yellow fever, and then they are a burden to others. Ten priests have died; four had only been here a few days. There is scarcely any white person in the city who has not had the fever."

Dr. Josefson had finally given in to his exhaustion and a piercing headache, as well as aching in his back and shoulders, and was slumped in a chair in the lobby. Fannie had seen these symptoms far too often in the last weeks and was fussing with the man, trying to talk him into going upstairs to the infirmary floor of the Peabody Hotel. "All right then, just let me take your temperature."

Josefson tried to look at her, but the sunlight was streaming through a window behind her and the brightness seemed to penetrate inside his skull. "I don't have a fever. I'm just worn out. I haven't slept more than two or three hours a night for what seems like a week. Let me go to my own room and get some sleep. I'll feel better in the morning."

"Doctor, if the problem is that you're just tired, then surely you won't object to this thermometer."

He couldn't come up with an excuse on the spur of the moment, and finally acquiesced to her request.

She looked at the thermometer and faced away from him so he wouldn't see her tears. "All right, Doctor, you're going to the top floor."

"What's my temp?"

"Just under 104 degrees."

He bowed his head for a second or two, then straightened himself, and finally came up with a lopsided grin. "I just hate it when the nurse is right and I'm not."

She got him settled in bed, gave him a dose of salts according to his order, as well as two large glasses of water, then went to fetch a bit of ice for a cold compress. Although his head was pounding, when she returned he was waiting for her. "Fannie, sit down here for a moment. There's something I want to talk to you about."

"Let me get this cool cloth on your neck first." She adjusted his pillow around the compress, then sat down beside him.

"Has anybody told you what a good nurse you are?"

She smiled self-consciously, "Why, no. Compared to all these others, I'm just a beginner."

"Several of the other doctors have talked about you. All of them have said complimentary things. So whatever happens with this epidemic, I think you can always have a job as a nurse—that is, if that's what you want."

"I always feel like I'm not able to do much for people. It seems like half of them die no matter what I do."

"All of us feel that way, Fannie, or at least we do if we're honest with ourselves. But curing people is just part of what's important. If we can make them feel like someone cares about them and about what happens to their family, then that's about all anybody can ask with a disease like yellow fever. You're able to perform that task just about as well as anybody I've seen. And have you heard any of the tales about what some of the Howard nurses have pulled?"

"I've seen a few stories in the paper. Some of it sounded pretty far-fetched to me."

"A few of the volunteer nurses are using this epidemic as an opportunity to steal from their patients when they're unconscious or delirious. One was caught the other day leaving town with a whole chest full of silver and china dishes. Another had a big box of fine dresses and jewelry. Many of them have deserted their patients, either when they became too difficult to deal with, or when they discovered the house had nothing left to steal. A couple of male nurses have been discovered in the bed with their sick female patients. Plenty of them have consumed all the liquor in the house, and even drank the whiskey that was supposed to have been used with ice compresses. There's no telling how many others stole the morphia their patients were supposed to receive. You can't get much lower than that."

She shook her head. "I did read about the man and woman who were hired to nurse a sick family, and after a couple of days the man reported the woman to the Howards. He told them she was nothing but a drunkard, and totally useless. So they fired her. Then they found out later the two were husband and wife!"

Josefson smiled through his headache at that, but then changed the tenor of his voice. "What I'm trying to say, and maybe not doing a good job of it, is that you are a real treasure. If I can come out all right the other side of this fever, I want to spend a lot of time with you—that is, if you'll permit it."

Fannie tried unsuccessfully to keep the blush from her face. "That's the nicest thing anybody has said to me in a long time, but you and I have got ourselves a bit of a problem. I'm Catholic, and you're Jewish."

"We believe in the same God, don't we?"

"Why, yes. I think so. But what would your parents say when they come back to Memphis?"

"You let me take care of that."

Fannie smiled, but couldn't help but think of her own father, now apparently deceased, who'd had a rabid reaction to anyone joining the family other than a Catholic—let alone an Israelite. Wisely, she chose not to disclose that bit of information. "All right."

"Then that's settled. There's just one more thing—I don't want you to be my nurse."

She began to tear up and tried to hide the catch in her voice. "But I thought you just said I was a good nurse."

"That's right, you are. But I fear I won't be a good patient."

"Oh, I'm not worried about that."

"No, listen to me. We've both seen how some people get with this fever—talking crazy, crying uncontrollably, taking all their clothes off, screaming all sorts of terrible things. Why, I hear you even had a man shoot at you the other day."

"He took all of his clothes off, too, but I know you won't be like that."

"That's just it, Fannie. Nobody knows what they'll end up doing when this yellow fever starts doing its evil work. It's not so hard to be strong when somebody else is sick, but it's a different matter when it's yourself who's perhaps at death's door. In fact after finding out I've got a fever, I'm already scared, and the really bad things haven't even started to happen yet. I don't want you to see me like that. I want you to see me as a good person. I want you to believe I'm a strong man, even though it's pretty obvious I'm not. I was hoping you would believe I'm a man you could count on."

"Doctor Josefson, I can't believe anything could change the opinion I've got. Not after all the unselfish things I've seen you do for people. Not after the long hours you've worked when you should have gone home to rest. Not after you stayed, even when you knew you hadn't had the fever before. Not after you decided to stay and help people, even though everybody in your family was trying to get you to leave."

"Just the same, I want you to pick the best nurse you can find for me, and I'll see you when I get well."

October 1, 1878—"From a correspondent in Collierville (25 miles southeast of Memphis)—*Since the yellow fever appeared in our quiet village, with a population of 125, we have buried 25 (23 white and 2 colored), and some 28 or 30 are currently sick. We pray to God that this scourge may soon be among the things that were."*

"From a correspondent in Bartlett (20 miles northeast of Memphis)—*Too much praise cannot be given to the four or five colored men who have watched and guarded Bartlett these past ten days while all our policemen lay ill. Not a house has been broken open, not a thing is missing. They are true men. Though their skins may be black, their hearts are pure and white."*

"From a correspondent in Brownsville (55 miles northeast of Memphis)—*54 deaths from the fever during September, and 54 more citizens who are currently sick."* Memphis Daily Appeal

Word had spread about the status of Dr. Josefson throughout the Howard physicians living in the Peabody Hotel. Most of those who knew him thought highly of his work. The exception was Dr. James Madison, whose opinion was colored by what he perceived as a threat: the special friendship between Josefson and Fannie Lester. However, his investigation had revealed that Josefson had specifically requested Nurse Nina Payne to take care of him. That was promising news indeed, as it could indicate the "friendship" was not as involved as what he had thought it to be.

When Dr. Madison walked into the infirmary to get a first-hand look, he noticed the nurse taking a catnap in a bedside chair, and was doubly surprised to find Josefson reading the newspaper. “Morning, Saul. It appears that rumors of your demise were somewhat exaggerated.”

“I figured I'd wait a couple days to keep everybody in suspense.”

Madison motioned toward the chair. “Looks like that nurse of yours has given up the ship.”

“She was up half the night, helping out with Doctor Purves next door. She might be small, but she's one strong woman, and a fine nurse.” Neither of them noticed Nina had opened her eyes just a slit, and had managed to suppress a grin.

“What's your status today?”

“I've got my intestinal tract cleaned out, and now we're trying to keep my fever down.”

“Are you still taking calomel?”

Josefson couldn't help himself. “I wouldn't give calomel to my dog. In fact, I wouldn't give calomel to your dog.”

“What! What do you mean by that?”

“Just what I said. I accomplished the same thing with magnesia.”

“Sounds like the fever is affecting your judgment. Maybe you need to stop treating yourself and get a doctor in here with some sense. What is it they say—a doctor who treats himself has a fool for a patient?”

“It certainly won't be some idiot who believes in using calomel. Does your medical college actually recommend giving mercury to people? Or maybe I should ask, did you attend a medical college?”

Madison couldn't keep the snarl out of his voice. “If you ever crawl out of your sick bed, I'll thrash you for that.”

“The first thing you should do is try and remember any patients you've actually saved by tearing up their intestinal tract with that damned calomel. Most of us who avoid that treatment entirely have saved well over sixty percent of our patients. I doubt your record is anywhere close to that.”

The sneer came to Madison's face too quickly not to have been employed previously on multiple occasions. In fact, it seemed to fit his face far better than any other look. “I'll have you know I've only lost eleven patients so far.” Josefson had already heard about the confrontation between Madison and Martin, but he kept that to himself. Madison took a step toward the door, then turned back. "I have to wonder what Doctor Mitchell would say about your treatment theory. Maybe I'll mention it to him. It would be interesting to hear his opinion about the quality of your own medical education."

As the door slammed behind Madison, Nurse Payne sat up. "Who was that nasty fellow, Doctor?"

"I've been waiting for the opportune time to say that to his face for weeks. Would you mind getting me a dose of sodium salicylate, Nina? All of a sudden I find myself with quite the headache."

October 3, 1878—"The journalists of the South reflect credit on their profession by the resolute and fearless manner in which they have discharged their duty in this time of peril. They have refused to run away, as so many others have done, and are determined to meet the danger. Scores of them have been down with the pestilence, many have died, but none have faltered or retreated."

"C.B. Rogan, of Sumner County, consigned his entire crop of tobacco to be sold, with all the proceeds going to the sufferers of yellow fever. The editor recalls this man is none other than Charley Rogan, that magnificent soldier of the late war, first a member of Company K, Bates Second Tennessee Regiment, later a member of Bates' staff. Like the true Irishman he is, he wears his heart upon his sleeve, and is never deaf to the call of country or humanity."

"The terrible number of deaths reported across Tennessee, Mississippi, and Louisiana is truly appalling, but does not include the thousands of sick and convalescing, the cost of their idleness, the prostration of commerce, the ruin of crops, the wreck of fortunes—large and small, the terrible situation of orphans, and the utter desolation spread over some of the fairest and richest portions of our nation." Memphis Daily Appeal

October 3, 1878—"From Vicksburg—The Howard Association received an earnest appeal for aid due to the destitute condition of the populace. Over 100 cases are under treatment in the northern section of the city, and the epidemic continues

its sway. The panic of the people is worse than that of a routed army. Two dying children were abandoned by their fleeing parents to strangers. When the children died, they were buried by the kindness of colored men." Chicago Daily Tribune

Chapter 26
Premeditated

Memphis

He had spent most of a sleepless night thinking about a final solution to his irksome problem. Despite his initial surge of emotion, it was not something which could be approached in a temper, let alone casually. It required a great deal of intelligent thought and planning. There were a number of options, but none of them were perfect, and some would dangerously cast suspicion in his direction. That was where his scientific expertise came into play. He went through his possible choices once more.

The leaves and berries of belladonna, also called deadly nightshade, had been used as a poison for a thousand years. In some quarters, belladonna was referred to as devil's berries. Oddly, the name *bella donna,* or 'beautiful woman' in Italian, was due to its being used cosmetically to dilate the eyes, hence making a lady appear to be innocent or seductive, depending on the mindset of the observer. However, the disastrous effects of belladonna could be very quick acting if the amount of drug administered was high enough. Also, the result could be accomplished with a single overdose. A commonly used drug, it was literally grown in every pharmacy's herb garden in the country—in fact, he had grown it successfully himself. In his current status, he knew it could easily be obtained without suspicion from a drugstore. However, a knowledgeable coroner might become suspicious that the cause of death was not yellow fever. While the pulse would be rapid, the skin flushed, and a rash perhaps present, accompanied by intense thirst and perhaps delirium at the hour of death, the main effect of the drug actually inhibited vomiting. Therefore, there would be no bloody vomitus. Worse, no presence of high fever.

Foxglove—another plant he'd had in his garden—was the source of digitalis. If given in sufficient dosage, it would significantly lower the pulse rate, cause uncoordinated contractions of the heart muscle, and result in physical weakness and cardiac failure. Additionally, in larger doses, it often caused nausea and vomiting. Foxglove was also easily obtained. However, there would be no high fever, no evidence of rash, and no bloody vomit. Also, an adequate toxic dose might be hard to achieve in a single attempt and could require more than one application, which might present a significantly greater risk to discovery.

Carbolic acid—or phenol—was currently being used by the barrel full in the streets and bayous as a disinfectant. It would be extremely easy to get, with no drugstore contact or suspicion necessary. When consumed by mouth, it caused a feeble pulse, faint breathing, muscle weakness, vertigo, vomiting, diarrhea, very dark urine, convulsions, and coma. However, it was very caustic, making it difficult to disguise when given to someone. In all likelihood, the victim would refuse to swallow more than the first sip of the substance, as their mouth would immediately burn with a fiery intensity. Additionally, they would undoubtedly raise quite a disturbance simply because of the immediate and intense pain caused by the acid. It would also leave evidence of a caustic burn on the lips and in the mouth.

Arsenic was the old standby. Unfortunately, it was extremely bitter, thus the amount given at any one time had to be equally small, while the drug gradually built up in the body over a long period before it finally finished off the victim. He didn't have that kind of time, let alone the opportunity to administer multiple doses.

Nux vomica—or strychnine—had been used as a poison for over a hundred years, and the drug's actions were very well known, often leading to charges of homicide rather than ruled as a death of unknown origin. Strychnine killed by asphyxiation, and usually within a very few hours. Its immediate effects were extreme soreness and muscle stiffness, particularly around the face, neck, and stomach, followed by muscle spasms and convulsions. Oddly, several physicians treating yellow fever and malaria sometimes prescribed miniscule doses of strychnine to try and stimulate their patients, so it would be possible to obtain the drug without suspicion. However, it would cause neither high fever nor bloody vomiting, and its very well-known effects would likely catch the attention of a knowledgeable physician.

He also knew he likely would have only one, or perhaps a maximum of two opportunities to administer the poison. Any option that required multiple doses was automatically cast aside. After considerable study, he had a solution, and only needed two items to complete his plan. He indulged himself with a smile. It was going to be simple.

October 4, 1878—"The fever has spread until it has embraced in its death fold every residence within a radius of twelve miles, and the end is not yet. It has branched off and followed the line of railroads running out of the city until it has extended for fully fifty miles, to the north, east, and south." Memphis Avalanche

October 4, 1878—"Yesterday, Memphis had 138 new cases of the fever and 27 deaths in the city. This should serve as a warning to any refugees anxious to return. It is not yet safe, and to return at this time is to court almost certain death."

"The mayor of Collierville (25 miles southeast of Memphis) *succumbed to yellow fever on September 25th. Mayor Davis was very well liked by the town. He was a man with a big heart as tender as a child's, and a truer man never lived than Harry Davis."* Memphis Daily Appeal

Dressed in civilian clothing and walking down Beale Street in late afternoon with an old flop hat pulled low, the black man was fairly sure his identity was safe. Uncharacteristically, he paid little attention to the jug band playing on the other side of the street. It was amazing to consider the sounds which could be coaxed from a pair of metal spoons, a washboard, a two and a half gallon clay jug, and a comb with a flimsy piece of paper. But when there was no money for traditional instruments, you had to settle for what could be assembled from nothing.

He spied the small sign he was seeking in the next block, on the south side of the street beyond Schwab's store, then nonchalantly paused to glance behind him to be sure no one who might recognize him was in the vicinity. Upon entering Mother Simone's Herb House, his olfactory senses were assaulted from every direction. Although there were a few live herbs and other plants on display, most of the shop was occupied by large glass jars, similar to what might be found on a grocer's counter, but in this case not containing peppermint sticks or horehound drops.

A very tiny Negro woman, wrapped head to toe in multiple layers of a flimsy indigo blue material and a brilliant red headdress, appeared from behind a curtain. "What troubles you today, sir?"

"Are you Mother Simone?"

He estimated the woman's age at somewhere north of Methuselah's. She was wrinkled as a raisin, and he couldn't help but observe that there was too much skin to properly fit her face. For some unknown reason, she had apparently plucked every hair in her eyebrows. "Indeed, sir."

"I'm lookin' for something my mama told me about. It's a weed with small white flowers what's sometimes eaten by cattle, and it poisons the milk. I recollect she called it snake plant or some such?"

"White snakeroot. Yes, most farmers try to get rid of snakeroot in their pastures. So it is becoming very difficult to find."

He started to speak, but his hand was trembling, so he decided to remain quiet.

"Of course, I always keep some in my shop. May I ask what you intend to use it for?"

"I want to get rid of some wild dogs around my house."

Mother Simone didn't seem convinced at that. "Wild dogs?"

He tried not to fumble his words. "Five or six of them runnin' near my place. Already chewed on my neighbor's boy. I got some little ones myself. Gotta git rid of 'em afore somebody really gets hurt bad."

"Sounds serious."

"How does this snakeroot work?"

"Snakeroot causes nausea, stomach pain, weakness, high acid in the blood, and death within eight to twelve hours. In people, it sometimes causes the tongue to turn blood red while it does its work." She hesitated, again giving her customer the once-over. "I'm not sure about dog tongues."

"Can I dissolve it in water?"

"No. It would simply float on water. You could sprinkle the powdered plant on meat, and the dogs might eat it. Of course, it's very bitter, so perhaps that wouldn't work. Let me see what I can do." The old woman shuffled over to one of the glass jars, opening it to reveal what appeared to be nothing more than dried leaves and stalks. She inserted a small wooden scoop no larger than a soup spoon, and placed two scoopfuls in a porcelain mortar. "First things first. I need to make this into a fine powder." She began to grind away vigorously with a matching pestle.

"How do you know thet's snakeroot?"

"I harvested it myself. Best time to collect this herb is in late spring, when all the juices are flowin'. Don't hardly trust nobody else to pick for me. Can't trust 'em to know exactly which plant is which, let alone the proper time to harvest. 'Bout the onliest thing I buy from somebody else is ginseng. I just cain't get around like I use to. Too much walkin' them hillsides to find thet 'sang." She finished her grinding, poured the contents of the mortar into a half-pint bottle, then added six ounces of vodka and vigorously shook the mixture for a couple of minutes. "Shake this up a couple more times when you get home, then let it sit overnight. When you go to use it, just pour the alcohol off what's left in the bottom of the bottle. All the poison will be dissolved in the alcohol. What's left in the bottom is just chaff."

Chapter 27
A Crime Scene

Memphis

One of the cruelest sights she had experienced during the epidemic lay before Emilie Christophe. Sister Frances, despite being the youngest of the Episcopal sisters at St. Mary's, had managed the Canfield orphanage for the church since its inception in early September. But on that morning, she lay before Emilie in the final throes of her life. No one had done more for the orphans of Memphis than Sister Frances.

She'd contracted the fever early in the epidemic, spent five or six days in her bed, and with a determination few could emulate, she rose and went back to work, ignoring all pleas to stay in bed to fully recuperate. Not a soul expected her to survive another week. And yet she had quadrupled that figure.

When the orphanage had opened, she had been there to receive twenty-four children the very first morning, and within four days, there had been over fifty. Within ten days, there had been close to one hundred children under her care.

When Emilie had arrived on September 26th, with Leisha and Ruthie Johnson in tow, she'd been impressed with how well the orphanage and the attached infirmary were being run. Even more remarkable was the quiet leadership exhibited by Sister Frances. It was obvious the nurses and the other two sisters were ready to do anything asked of them. On his arrival after Dr. Armstrong took sick, Dr. Sohm had simply said, "I wish every infirmary in the city was being run as efficiently as this one."

And so on the evening of the first of October—thirty days after her initial bout with the fever—when Sister Frances had approached Emilie, telling her it would be necessary for her to be put to bed once again, the effect had been crushing. A majority of the nurses and sisters frankly expected the orphanage to be shuttered without Sister Frances' leadership. All of them encouraged Frances to return to the infirmary at St. Mary's to be closer to a physician, but she would have none of it, insisting her place was at the orphanage, no matter what happened.

Emilie obviously had responsibilities far beyond Sister Frances' bedside. Because of her experience and temperament, she had been accepted by the other nurses as a knowledgeable resource, so some of the duties previously borne by Frances were shouldered by Emilie. She accepted that gladly, and would have willingly done more if necessary. She still spent a small amount of time each day with the children who were not sick, as they seemed to naturally gravitate to her. The Johnson girls were perhaps more dependent on her visits than any of the other children. Emilie recognized that, and realizing that she should pull away a bit, tried to divide her attentions more equally, but in truth, she was drawn to Leisha and Ruthie also.

She was also haunted by the memory of the anguish exhibited by the girls' father, who'd so obviously needed his wife's acceptance of the decision to place his daughters in the orphanage. Emilie had wondered more than once if she shouldn't try to contact Johnson's wife again in hopes of relieving the man's torment.

As Sister Frances worsened, Emilie also tried to spend more time with her. And yet the sister would not allow anything which she perceived as special treatment. Over a very few days, Emilie realized it would be unlikely if this time Frances would rise from her bed. Unlike many patients, whose initial fever generally subsided after a couple of days, then perhaps returned toward the last, Frances' temperature exceeded 104 degrees every day, with no reduction, despite all attempts to lower it.

Although she attempted to drink fluids, generally this was unsuccessful as well. With the resulting dehydration, her heart rate became rapid and often seemed to lose its normal rhythm. Her skin was dry as toast. Her eyes had been bloodshot, but now they almost seemed to be seeping blood. All urination stopped, and she began to move in and out of a delirium, her fate becoming obvious to all. Finally, late in the day on October 4th, just three days after taking to her bed, Sister Frances went home.

October 5, 1878—"The people of the South, whether under the provocations of war, pestilence, or famine, have shown remarkable pluck and endurance. But there is also much to be said for our brethren to the north, whose steadfastness and persistence in battle, and endurance in a prolonged contest that taxed all their energies and resources unequaled, have few parallels in history. Magnanimous on the field so contested, despite the hazards of political disputes, they have many times since April, 1865, extended us the hand of fellowship, flowing over with gifts. The same men who led the armies of the North, and the same noble women who sustained them during the battle, have been foremost in the heaven-sent work of our relief these past terrible weeks. Their gifts of intelligent help, touching sympathy, and money have come, saving thousands of lives, as well as the blessed assurance that we are indeed one people."

Letter to a Howard physician published in the paper—"Dear Doctor, How could you leave me here to starve? I am broken down for want of food and rest. Quinn will die, but he is so aggravating that he may live another two or three days. He has no friends, and no wonder, for a more cantankerous cuss I have never met with. The folks at the rum mill above his residence are only swine, and will not come near me. I am sick and starving, and in self-defense will have to leave or kill the patient, and I do not like to do either. Come at once." Memphis Daily Appeal

Just after midnight, the light emitted by the coal oil lamps in the hallway of the physicians' infirmary in the Peabody Hotel had been turned so low there was barely enough illumination to guide his footsteps. Despite the relatively

warm weather, he was wearing an outer jacket with the collar turned up, and a scarf wound around his neck concealed his face as much as possible. He quietly approached the identified room, just barely opening the door enough to allow him to confirm that the patient, as well as his nurse curled up on the bedside chair, were sleeping.

For the third time since leaving his room, a trembling hand sought out the tools of his trade in his left trouser pocket. He could feel the half-pint flask in which he had combined two ounces of belladonna tincture with six ounces of white wine. Beside the flask rested a jar filled with black vomit, which he had retrieved earlier from a severely ill patient's bedside. He'd had to return late in the day for the belladonna mixture, as the pharmacist had had to soak crushed belladonna leaves in alcohol for several hours in order to extract the alkaloid drugs from the plant. He'd justified his purchase of belladonna by simply saying he had a patient with colic and diarrhea.

Belladonna tincture was extremely potent. The normal adult dose for colic was ten drops before meals and at bedtime. But his eight-ounce bottle contained approximately one hundred times that amount. Even if only an ounce of the mixture was consumed in a short period of time, it should have rapid and disastrous results. Did he have any doubts about what he was about to do? If so, he hid them well with the sneering look of contempt on his face.

Suddenly he heard footsteps in the stairwell and quickly concealed himself in the maid's closet, leaving the door slightly cracked and peering out. He was surprised to see a Negro man stroll down the hallway, pause at Josefson's door, then enter. Who the devil was that? He thought he knew everybody who worked in the infirmary. Could they possibly have hired a new orderly? If so, what in the world was he doing up there in the middle of the night? Before he could fathom the reason for the man's presence, the orderly exited the door, glanced both directions, and walked rapidly back to the stairwell.

After waiting a full five minutes to be sure there would be no other interruption, the man departed the maid's closet and entered the sickroom himself. Both patient and nurse were lightly snoring—almost in an attempt at harmony. But he was agitated. His mouth felt like it was full of cotton, so he took a hefty drink from the patient's two-quart water pitcher using the dipper. He was surprised to taste the alcohol. Apparently the holier-than-thou Dr. Josefson was spiking his water pitcher! He refilled the dipper and drank as quietly as he could, smiling at the irony. One thing was for sure—Josefson wouldn't detect the alcohol and belladonna mixture he was about to add, since he apparently was already expecting the taste of spirits.

Finally he pulled the flask with the belladonna and gin mixture from his pocket and poured the entire amount as quietly as possible into the pitcher at the bedside. Next he stepped to the other side of the patient's bed and shook the vile contents of his jar on the floor, as well as a small amount on the bedding. If a parting smirk was any indication, there was no last-minute doubt, and certainly no twinge of guilt. He made his exit, unobserved.

Shortly after two o'clock in the morning, with the sensation of a dry, scratchy throat, a sleepy hand reached out, grasped the tin dipper, plunged it into the water pitcher, and took a long, refreshing drink. Was there a question about the unfamiliar taste of alcohol concealed in approximately fifty ounces of water? Possibly, but certainly not enough for an investigation in the middle of the night.

Around three-thirty, Nurse Nina reached out yet again for the relief of a drink of water. For some reason the room seemed to have gotten quite a bit warmer, and the sensation of a dry, parched mouth was much more noticeable than earlier. Perhaps two dippersful would be more appropriate.

At the same time, the man two floors below the infirmary awoke. He was nauseated, though not so much as to cause vomiting. His stomach was burning, and he reflected on what he might have eaten earlier that evening to cause his gastric distress. Not being able to sleep, he eventually got up, lit a coal oil lamp, fetched a mirror, and tried to examine the inside of his own mouth. Although he couldn't see any sign to justify a sore throat, he was surprised to see how bright red his tongue was. He gargled a glass of water from his own pitcher and returned to his bed. Surely he hadn't contracted something from Josefson's damned dipper!

As the black man walked the streets that evening, he thought about the ramifications of his deed. He was almost positive nobody had seen him in the hotel, but *almost* was not good enough to relieve his concern. Likewise, he had an almost overwhelming urge to run back to the hotel, enter the doctor's room, and accidentally knock the water pitcher to the floor, hopefully avoiding Josefson's death.

He turned back toward the Peabody, hurrying a bit. Then again, what if he'd already taken a deadly dose of the water? Wouldn't it be extremely suspicious if he entered the room now and broke the pitcher? He turned back in the direction he had come from. Perhaps the weight of what he had done slowed his pace.

An hour later, the thought entered Nurse Nina's mind that she might have a fever. It was highly unlikely, as she had previously been infected with yellow fever, but nevertheless, her skin was dry and hot, and her throat was raspy. She took two more long draughts from the dipper and decided to wake her patient, to try and encourage him to drink as well. Surely he was having just as much difficulty with the overheated room as she was.

She was careful to not allow him to drink from the dipper, as that seemed to be taking too great a chance for cross-contamination. So she transferred the water from the dipper to the patient's cup, then woke him and got him to drink about a half cupful. After all, she was very conscientious. She tried to wipe her eyes to clear her vision, but despite the effort, her vision seemed blurred.

When she lay her head back against the chair, she experienced just a bit of dizziness, and could feel her pulse pounding in her head. Not only was it inordinately loud, but it also seemed fast to her, and she realized she would have to speak to the doctor in the morning. She reached over and poured herself another drink to counteract the unusual warmth of the room. She suddenly thought she saw witches flying over her head! She closed her eyes as tightly as possible to block out the sight. At last, she was truly scared. She had to have a considerable fever.

The man downstairs had not slept since his original waking, and this time the nausea was bad enough that he was forced to use the thunder-pot. When he finally got his breath, he couldn't help but notice splotches of blood in the vomitus. What was happening?

In less than an hour, Nurse Nina's patient awoke with similar feelings of warmth, and got a drink himself from the pitcher. Uncharacteristically, his nurse didn't awaken when he stirred, but he acknowledged she was probably worn thin. His mouth was dry as sand. Surely his lips must be chapped as well. The water didn't taste quite right, probably because his mouth was so dry.

Just at dawn, he awoke again, seeking more water. Not wanting to wake his nurse, he tried to pour for himself, but the pitcher was empty. He waited until the morning light was visible through the drapes. "Nina—Nina, would you mind getting some more water?"

There was no response.

The man downstairs had vomited three times by daylight, and his stomach was cramping as though he had some sort of intestinal blockage. His mouth was on fire. Once he was able to escape the necessity of the thunder-pot, he resolved to seek out a doctor upstairs.

Lester Sellers and Israel Jackson arrived at the hotel kitchen's rear door with a wooden casket in hand. When the assistant manager spied what they were carrying, he almost shouted at them. "You can't bring a casket in here! For pity's sake, this is the Peabody! What will our guests think?" He almost pushed them back outside. "Take that back to your wagon. We've got a stretcher you're supposed to use."

As the two funeral wagon drivers entered the lobby of the hotel, they were agog at the elaborate furnishings, as neither of them had ever seen such extravagance. As a special favor to the Howards, their boss had sent them to the Peabody for the first stop in their day. It had already been determined that Nurse Nina Payne was a young woman of limited means, and neither she nor her extended family could afford something as extravagant as a funeral plot.

Hence, Lester and Israel were dispatched to deliver the nurse's corpse to potter's field at Elmwood Cemetery. It was bad enough to interact with the pompous assistant manager they had met in the kitchen. However, they certainly weren't prepared to also deal with a very upset, combative physician in the infirmary.

Josefson assessed the short, stout man standing before him. He had to have doused himself in toilet water in order to exude the concentrated aroma which completely filled the infirmary room within seconds of his entry. "Mr. Williams, as the manager of the Peabody, isn't it your responsibility to report a suspicious death on your property to the police?"

"Doctor Josefson, what makes you think this nurse's death is suspicious? We've had over twenty Howard physicians and perhaps a hundred nurses die on this very floor in the last six weeks. What makes this death any different?"

"Yesterday, Nina Payne was as healthy as you are. She had not a single symptom of yellow fever. In fact, she is immune to yellow fever because she had it previously. She woke me in the middle of the night and offered me a cup of water. Although it was dark, she didn't seem to be in any distress whatsoever. That was only about six hours ago." He gestured toward the nurse's body. "And now look at her. Dammit, man, yellow fever just doesn't work that way."

He paused for a moment, realizing he was still terribly dry, and poured himself another cup of water from the freshly refilled pitcher at his bedside. Even the drink did not seem to relieve his raw throat, let alone the stifling heat of the room. But he wasn't about to let his own discomfort interfere with what obviously had been foul play. "Good grief, man. I'm telling you this nurse did not die of yellow fever. Something else entirely has caused it, and I demand you contact the police."

The hotel manager found himself staring at the physician. "Doctor Josefson, excuse me for saying this, but what's wrong with your eyes?"

"Well, along with an awful thirst, I'm having trouble with blurred vision this morning. Why do you ask?"

"I've never seen pupils so large."

Josefson was surprised at this, and considered that development in silence before pointing to the windows. "Open the drapes. Let's see if my eyes constrict in the bright daylight."

Williams did as he was asked, then peered again at the physician. "No, they're still the same."

"Something's not right. The pupils should constrict in the light." Josefson pulled at his bedcovers before struggling to get out of bed. When he sat up facing away from the body, he recoiled at what he saw on the floor. "What on earth? Mr. Williams, look at this vomit at my feet."

Williams started to object, but came around to the other side of the bed, almost gagging at the sight. "It's the black vomit, Doctor Josefson. I'm afraid I've seen enough of it recently to recognize it anywhere."

The doctor experienced a sudden bout of dizziness and held his head with both hands to allay the spinning. "I know what it is, man. But I haven't vomited a single time while I've been in this bed. There was no vomit here yesterday. And I was not sick during the night. How did it get there?"

"Well, Doctor, if it wasn't you, it's pretty obvious it had to have been from your nurse."

"There's not a speck of vomit on Nurse Payne—neither on her clothes or her chair. Don't you see? Someone has put it there on purpose."

"Doctor Josefson, that makes no sense at all. Why would anybody put vomit at your bedside?"

"I don't know." He paused for a moment. "Mr. Williams, would you be willing to lift the eyelids on Miss Payne?"

"You mean, touch the corpse?"

"Of course, man. I want to be sure her eyes aren't dilated like mine."

"I—I can't do that, Doctor. I'm just a regular citizen. I'm not a medical man, you understand."

An unexpected voice spoke from the doorway. "I 'spect I'm used to it by now, Doctor. I'll do it for you."

"What's your name, sir?"

"I'd be Israel Jackson, Doctor."

"All right, Mr. Jackson. Please lift up the right eyelid, then the left, to see if the pupil, the center of her eyes, is bigger than normal." Josefson pointed to himself. "Like mine are."

Israel peered closely at Josefson's face before moving to the corpse and lifting her slightly before cradling the back of her head with a gentle touch. He then removed the pennies from her eyelids, and finally forced first the right eye, then the left one open. He pushed his face close to hers, squinting and calculating, before finally pronouncing, "Well, they ain't like yours. The blacks o' her eyes is big as my thumb."

"Thank you, Mr. Jackson. I really appreciate your help, and I want to thank you for the respect you show a corpse. I'm afraid we've all become far too accustomed to the dead to treat them with the respect they deserve. You've taught us all a lesson today." Josefson reached out from his sick bed to shake hands.

Israel started to turn away, then faced Josefson again. "I reckon I oughter tell you thet the nurse smells of liquor."

"Are you sure, Mr. Jackson?"

"I reckon I smelt it a thousand times on my brother. Ain't no doubt in my mind."

Josefson then turned to the hotel proprietor. "I never knew the woman to take a single drop. In fact, she told me she was part of the temperance movement. And no matter what, I won't believe she would drink while on duty. The woman was a saint, Mr. Williams. "

"Doctor, I didn't want to mention it, but now that it's been brought up, you've got the smell of alcohol on yourself. Have you and the nurse been drinking?"

"Now I know something is going on. The only alcohol I've been exposed to was a week ago when I first came here, and that was used with ice water to bathe my skin. This is all extremely suspicious, Mr. Williams. Until proven otherwise, you must consider this a crime scene. Please send someone to the police before the body is removed."

October 6, 1878—"There are some of our merchants desirous to open their stores and offices and get to business after the suspension of the last two months. The attempt would most likely prove disastrous. Lives now safe would be endangered, perhaps lost, and nothing gained. There is no trade in Memphis, and no likelihood of trade. The epidemic, which has played such havoc in our city, has now invaded the entire countryside, and planters, rich and poor, have all they can do to fight the fever. Cotton picking, and all harvesting, has been put off until a safer time. Trains are not running a regular schedule, and they have all they can do with their limited help to carry medicine and supplies to stricken communities. From Cairo, Illinois to New Orleans—a distance of almost 900 river miles, and from the river eastward for 100 miles, the yellow fever holds sovereign sway. It is idle, therefore, to talk of

trade. Our merchants can preserve their souls if they but wait. When the frost for which we are praying has cleared the atmosphere of the death-dealing poison, they can return with safety. There is great virtue in patience, and we recommend the cultivation of it to our too-eager businessmen."

"From a correspondent in Moscow, TN (50 miles east of Memphis)—*Out of a population of 80, only two families have escaped the sick list and death roll. There have been 65 cases of yellow fever and 34 deaths here since August."*

"From a correspondent in Water Valley, MS (90 miles south of Memphis)—*A few words on behalf of our Deputy Sheriff, L.M. Losher, who is now Acting Chief of Police, President of the Relief Committee, and Manager of the Howards Association. In short, he is filling about 6 jobs. Words are inadequate to express the value his untiring energies render to the people of Water Valley."* Memphis Daily Appeal

Chapter 28
A Suspect?

Memphis

Sister Clare and her visitor found Ruthie and Leisha Johnson out behind the orphanage. The girls were part of a group of six children who were moving a large pile of firewood to the covered back porch of the home, one armload at a time. The older children were carrying the larger sticks, while Ruthie and Leisha were in charge of transporting the kindling. The sight of their little arms full of sticks made John Johnson almost burst with pride in seeing his girls working alongside the others.

He'd had very little sleep the night before, having learned of Nurse Payne's death at the Peabody. It had never occurred to him that anyone other than Josefson might suffer from his deed. An innocent life gone, and all because of a determination to get even with the man who had allowed his Marissa to die. Here he was, a policeman, doing something like that. Were it not for the girls, it was the kind of thing a man couldn't tolerate—couldn't live with. He was no better than the worst of the men he had arrested. Thankfully, there didn't seem to be any recognition from the Department of Police that a murder had occurred.

He stood there for a few minutes, willing himself to come back to the present and focus on his girls. He watched the scene in front of him for a while, noticing that all of the workers seemed to be in a good humor, before Ruthie spied her father; and then the two girls ran to him, tears sparkling in their eyes.

"I see you girls are working real hard."

Little Leisha unwrapped her arms from around his neck, wiped her face with her sleeve, then puffed up her chest and pronounced, "This is our job for today. We all have 'sponsbilities."

"I'm proud of you girls. It's important for us all to do our part."

Ruthie eyed her father, trying to keep the tremor from her voice. "Papa, the last time, you said we could come home when the fever was gone. Is today the day, Papa?"

Johnson tried to smile reassuringly. "In a few more weeks, Ruthie, just as soon as the sickness leaves the city." He raised his head, looking around the yard. "Where's your nurse? I thought she was takin' care of you."

"You mean Nurse Emilie? Oh, she has to take care of all the sick children during the day. She comes to see us every night before bedtime to tuck us in and tell us a story."

Leisha added, "She knows lots of stories. Did you know there were so many stories, Papa? Do you know any stories about princesses? Are you going to eat lunch with us, Papa?"

Johnson smiled at all the questions, then looked back at Sister Clare. "Do you think it would be all right if I sat with the girls while they have lunch?"

"Why, I don't see why not. Most of the children don't have any parents, so they would all probably enjoy having you eat with them."

Cornbread, molasses, and milk was the entire lunch menu selection, but there seemed to be no complaints from the children. A bit of work in the morning was undoubtedly beneficial to their appetites. After observing the children's table manners, Johnson decided perhaps it wasn't a good idea to follow his usual custom of mixing his cornbread in the glass of milk and eating the resulting mush with a spoon.

As the meal concluded, there was a familiar voice behind them. "Good morning, girls. I heard you had a special visitor here today."

The girls responded in unison. "Good morning, Nurse Emilie."

John Johnson stood up, hurrying to wipe the lunch off his face. "Good mornin', ma'am."

Leisha giggled. "That's Nurse Emilie, Papa. You called her ma'am."

Emilie smiled at her. "He was just being polite, Leisha. Your papa is a gentleman. You girls always remember that every girl should have a gentleman for a husband, just like your mama did."

Johnson extricated himself from the small chair. "You girls finish your lunch. I want to talk to Nurse Emilie for a minute."

As they stepped away from the tables, there was a guilty edge to Johnson's voice when he asked, "How are they doing?"

"The first week or so was an adjustment for them. A new place, new people, new environment, new rules, plus they were still grieving their mother and wondering when you were coming back for them. But now, it seems like they've adjusted pretty well. Both girls have made some friends. They still ask me every night when you'll be back, but they don't cry any more. In my opinion, they're as happy as can be expected under the circumstances."

Johnson lowered his head, again seeming to argue with himself. "I still can't take them back home with me. We got a lot o' men out with the sickness, and those of us what can work are puttin' in some long hours. I feel terrible guilty about it. But I got no choice as long as the fever is in town."

"You needn't feel bad about them being here. You're doing the best you can. They're safe here, and happy by all appearances."

"I know my wife is rollin' over in her grave 'cause o' this." He looked at Emilie. "Don't take it wrong. I know they're better off here. But most ever' time I try to sleep, my wife haunts me to come get the girls."

"I'll bet she would understand if she could see how well they're doing."

"Wish I could be sure o' that."

Fannie Lester, still upset over the death of Nina, had paused for a few moments in the midst of her daily responsibilities and was leaning against the stairwell in the Peabody Hotel, reflecting on how in the world something like that had happened. Her thoughts were interrupted by the chambermaid, Leah Feathers.

"Fannie, I been lookin' for you, girl. I needs a favor."

"Sure, Leah. What can I do for you?"

"You know them two colored men what's always comin' to the hotel t' pick up the dead folk?"

"I'm afraid I see them almost every day. I suppose you mean Mr. Sellers and Mr. Jackson?"

"The young one—Israel, I think—he'd be the one I'm talkin' about."

Fannie looked appraisingly at her friend. "What's got you interested in Israel?"

"The other day, the two of 'em was here to pick up your nurse friend. And that Doctor Josefson talked about how fine a man Israel was because he treated the dead with such respect. The doctor said he was pleased to know him!"

"I did hear something about that."

"Why, Fannie, it's all over the hotel. All the coloreds—the cooks, the maids, busboys, even the fancy piano player—all of 'em are talkin' about Israel and how proud they all are of him. I'd sorta like to meet him myself. So I was hopin' you'd ask around and find out if Israel was married, or maybe spoke for."

Fannie couldn't hide the smile on her face. "I'd be happy to, Leah."

Dr. James Madison approached Fannie the next day. "I was sorry to hear about Nurse Payne. I understand she was a good friend of yours."

She took a moment before answering. "It's not that simple, I'm afraid. Some of the blame belongs to me. I'm the one who suggested Nina be assigned to Doctor Josefson."

"Surely there's no one who feels any of that is your fault."

"I don't know what anybody else thinks. I only know I can't help but feel some responsibility for what happened. The thing that really bothers me is that I don't see how this could have struck Nina so quickly. We had a conversation just the afternoon before she passed away, and if she was sick, I certainly saw no sign of it."

Madison didn't want that side of the story circulating throughout the Peabody. "I stopped in Josefson's room a couple of days before myself, and didn't notice anything obviously wrong either. Oh, she might have been tired, but no more than all the rest of us who work here."

"Doctor Josefson is convinced she didn't die of the fever. In fact, despite what the police say, I think he's convinced she was the victim of a poisoning. I can't imagine why anyone would want to harm Nina. She was good as gold to everybody she met."

Madison cocked his head to the side. "Apparently her eyes were extremely dilated. That makes me think of some kind of drug. You don't suppose she could have accidently taken someone's morphine? Or maybe she had a secret drug habit—perhaps with paregoric—that none of us knew about?"

"If that's true, I never saw any evidence of such a habit. And even if she did, she would have had to go to one of the other patients' rooms to get it. There was never any morphine or opium in Doctor Josefson's room. In fact, he would only take lavender tea to help him rest. He said he was against using narcotics except in extreme pain. That I'm sure of. Then there's the alcohol I heard about. There's no way Nina would ever take a drink, at least on purpose."

"I hesitate to mention this, but when I was visiting Josefson, I had a drink from his water pitcher, and I'd swear it had a strong taste of alcohol. In fact, I was sick myself that night and the following day. It's possible he was adding spirits to that water jug." Madison took Fannie's hand in his own. "You know, there is another theory making the rounds." He looked both ways down the hallway. "I didn't say anything, because I don't want to distress you. But some of the other doctors have been talking. They find it curious that Josefson would come up with the idea of a murder. In fact, a couple of them are saying if she was truly murdered, it might have been Josefson himself."

Fannie couldn't keep the startled look from her face. "Surely you don't believe that. It just makes no sense."

"They're saying that he might be talking about the symptoms he had in common with the nurse—the dilated eyes and alcohol on his breath—in an attempt to shift suspicion away from himself."

"I refuse to believe he's capable of such a thing."

"Another explanation might be that it's entirely plausible Josefson was under the fever's spell when he did it. You yourself had to deal with some fellow a few days ago who was at least temporarily insane when he chased you out into the street and shot at you. The same thing might have happened to Josefson. He might not even have any memory of doing such a vile deed. And now his claim of innocence is nothing more than his unconscious mind trying to make an excuse for what he did."

Fannie turned her head so Madison wouldn't see her reaction. "That's not possible, not Doctor Josefson. I—I have to help out in the infirmary." She fled down the hallway to hide her tears.

Chapter 29
The Relief Boat

on the Mississippi River

The National Relief Commission chartered an expedition from St. Louis, which was to head downstream on the Mississippi River for the relief of yellow fever sufferers in towns on the lower portion of the river, which had suffered from quarantine activity both north and south of them. The stern wheeler *John M. Chambers* had a capacity of 300 tons, and was packed with medical supplies, provisions, ice, and some medical professionals.

While awaiting the completion of loading, a telegram was received by the commanding officer, Lieutenant Hiram Benner, from Brigadier General Augur, alerting him there was good information that there could be an attack made on his vessel by lawless mobs downstream for the purpose of taking the ship's stores. The telegram directed Lieutenant Benner to take precautions, and so he obtained twenty carbines and 2,000 rounds of ammunition from the St. Louis arsenal. The *Chambers* started its journey downriver on October 4th just before noon.

On the morning of October 7th, the ship anchored in the current directly opposite the port of Memphis. One of the ship's crew was heard to remark, "*Memphis looks like a grave. The wharves are almost entirely deserted. Occasionally a small dray and a few Negroes are visible, but otherwise it looks like death itself. The city is mournful to the extreme, ap-*

pears gloomy and desolate, with a funeral pall overhanging it, and the dread disease hiding in the shadows."

The stop was not to deliver supplies to Memphis, as that particular city had been the beneficiary of rail shipments received on a regular basis, but the ship took on over ten tons of mail for delivery to points south, between Memphis and Vicksburg. The mail had been accumulating for some two months, and had been fumigated with sulfur every night. Yet when the mail bags arrived on board, Lieutenant Benner directed his men to disinfect them yet again with turpentine.

The ship arrived opposite Helena, Arkansas mid-morning on October 8th, but was not permitted to land. There were a half-dozen armed citizens with shotguns on the riverbank making unmistakably threatening gestures, with one firing a load of scattershot just in front of the ship in order to indelibly make his point. There was no reasoning with the fools. They even refused to receive their mail.

In fact, a succession of Arkansas river towns treated the vessel in much the same way, apparently fearful the contagion itself was hiding amongst the offered supplies and mail. No explanation served to penetrate their determination. Too many stories were circulating of towns which had broken their quarantine and paid dearly for it. The ship had no choice but to move on.

The small town of Greenville, Mississippi was located just a mile or so off the main river on an old river run, referred to as Ferguson Lake. The city had been completely destroyed during the Battle of Vicksburg in 1863, when the local militia had made the unfortunate mistake of firing on Union forces. In retaliation for this, Greenville had been reduced to rubble.

The steamboat met the mayor on a landing at the intersection of the Mississippi and Ferguson. He informed Lieutenant Benner that his town had been terribly affected, so far reporting some 200 deaths out of a population of less than 1,500. Although the city had been the beneficiary of supplies from Vicksburg a few weeks earlier, quite a large amount of stores and medicines were left on the dock by the ship, under the mayor's supervision. The *Chambers* left lesser amounts of supplies at three successive towns on the west bank of the river in Louisiana at Henderson, Goodrich's Landing, and Tallulah.

On October 11th, the ship arrived at the port of Vicksburg. After reading many news reports about the severity of the yellow fever's effect on that city, the crew was much surprised to hear the disease was finally subsiding there, and they had little need of the supplies on board. The small city and surrounding area would eventually estimate almost 1,500 deaths from the fever during the two and a half months they had been attacked.

The *Chambers* also received information that the small community of Beechland, Mississippi, twenty miles east of Vicksburg, had been completely eradicated, the fever leaving not a single survivor in that place. With that sobering news, the ship continued on downstream, but went no further than Grand Gulf, Louisiana, as it was discovered towns from that point downstream had been supplied fairly regularly via shipments from New Orleans.

On her return trip upstream, the ship picked up an older woman who had been in Louisiana, nursing one of her sons until his death, but now was trying to get to Greenville to care for a second child, who also had the fever. By the time the *Chambers* arrived in Port Gibson, Mississippi, the weather had taken a turn for the worse, and the ship put into the wharf so the crew and medical personnel could take refuge for the night in a local hotel. Unfortunately, when the town learned the woman had just finished nursing a yellow fever patient, they wouldn't allow her to disembark. This late-stage quarantine was certainly a case of closing the barn door too late, as Port Gibson had already experienced a horrific 101 deaths within its small population during the epidemic.

At any rate, in the absence of an available bed in town, Lieutenant Benner invited the lady to use his own berth until the Greenville packet boat arrived, so she could gain a decent night's sleep. She tried to refuse, but Benner was insistent in his invitation. He wakened her at five in the morning to catch the packet, and she departed for Greenville and the bedside of her sick child. Lieutenant Benner returned to his bunk to get what small amount of sleep he could before daybreak.

Two mornings later, Lieutenant Benner complained of feeling unwell and the ship's surgeon sent him to his quarters. By noon he had a fever and severe headache. The morning of the 14th, Benner was much worse. But the very next day he seemed to improve, and the crew breathed a collective sigh of relief. They were mistaken.

Benner died in his bunk early in the morning on October 17th. His bedding was burned, and the entire boat was fumigated with the burning of sulfur and alcohol. He was buried in the National Cemetery in Vicksburg. His death was widely mourned in the press, and his life was celebrated even in Washington City for the selfless mission which had taken him to his grave. Whether or not Benner was infected by the lady who shared his bunk would never be discovered.

October 8, 1878—"From Holly Springs, MS (50 miles SE of Memphis)*—Total deaths from yellow fever to date is 235. All the cases can no longer be accurately reported. As the Chairman of our Relief Committee, our situation is indescribable, and I am the only white citizen who has not had the fever. There is great destitution among the people."*

"Surgeon General Woodworth reports a telegram from Jackson, Mississippi, a town some 40 miles from the Mississippi River. That the yellow fever prevails there in epidemic form ought to convince the people of other interior towns the quarantine they have maintained is of but little avail. No city in the South was more rigidly quarantined than Jackson. Despite this jealous isolation, the dreaded disease has laid hold of its people."

"Surgeon General Woodworth has appointed a Yellow Fever Commission, composed of seven eminent scientists and medical men. They will endeavor to answer every possible question related to disease origin, contagion, spread, short and long-term effects, recommended treatment, prevention, and results."

(*Author's note:* Brother Maurelian at Christian Brothers College and Rabbi Samfield from B'nai Israel Synagogue in Memphis worked together to prepare a letter to the Surgeon General, wherein they requested he form a Yellow Fever Commission.)

"The colored people of Memphis have received aid without stint, and we have yet to hear of a case of discrimination on account of color by either the Howard Association or the Citizens Relief Committee. If any colored man knows of a case of

such discrimination, and will report it to us, we will have it promptly investigated and published." Memphis Daily Appeal

Memphis

At the Howards' infirmary in Memphis, Dr. John Sohm waited with some apprehension while Nurse Sara Davis untied the cords which restrained Mrs. Burke to her bed. She was supported by Nurse Margaret Reed on the opposite side of the bed, both nurses trying mightily to keep the poor woman from fleeing the room. Unfortunately, Lydia Burke's strength was more than a match for the two, and it took only seconds for them to realize the fact.

Mrs. Burke had been in a demented condition for over a month, ever since the deaths of her two-year-old daughter and husband on the same day. She herself had also been a yellow fever patient and was still seriously ill when she learned her little family had ceased to exist. As a result of this terrible news, as well as her feverish state, she had ripped off her nightgown, bolted through the door, and run stark naked for some six blocks down Union Street, screaming epithets the likes of which none of her friends would have believed she was capable. She had finally been cornered on the narrow bridge which spanned the Gayoso Bayou by an unlucky policeman.

Lydia had fought the poor man like a tiger, inflicting multiple bites and scratches, before being placed in irons with the aid of a helpful citizen. For most of the ensuing weeks, there had been no let-up in her ranting and raving. Only twice during that entire time had she been calm and cogent. Yet the respite had been brief, and she'd quickly resumed her out-of-control behavior.

It was Dr. Sohm's hope that she might be calmed after being removed from her restraints. But after witnessing fifteen minutes of fighting, screaming, cursing, spitting, and all kinds of bodily contortions, he was forced to acknowledge the failure of his treatment. He shook his head. "I'm sorry, Nurse Sara, Nurse Margaret. I hoped there might be a benefit in releasing her bonds. Here, let me help you get her under control again."

Nurse Sara panted after they had the poor woman back in restraints. “I’ve known Lydia for at least twenty years, way back when she was just a tot. She and I went to grammar school together. But I don’t think she’s recognized me at all during this whole time I’ve been nursing her. When do you suppose she’ll come to herself, Doctor Sohm?”

“There must be well over two hundred patients in the city who have recovered from the yellow fever but as yet still haven’t come back to their normal mental state. I’m afraid the question is not when she’ll come to herself, but if. And right now I don’t think we’re even close to knowing the answer of why some two percent of yellow fever patients experience this long-lasting deterioration. I hate to think what might become of these folks if their situation is permanent. I’ve seen quite a number who, like Mrs. Burke, are confined in the infirmaries, but also a significant population in cells down at the station house. Many of them can only be described as hopeless cases. I’d hate to think they may end up in the Central State Hospital for the Insane in Nashville.”

The death wagon stopped in the alleyway near the door to the kitchen. Israel Jackson started to hop off the wagon in anticipation of yet another stop at the Peabody Hotel when Lester grabbed his arm. “Hold on there, Israel. I need to tell you somethin’ afore we go in the hotel.”

“What’s up?”

“They’s a girl in there, name of Leah Feathers. She’s been askin’ ’bout you.”

“Is she one o’ the maids? I think I know who you’re talkin’ about. Purty girl, not bigger’n a minute?”

“I only know she’s one o’ the maids. She wanted t’ know if you was married, or if you had yourself another woman.”

Israel had a somewhat startled look on his face, which morphed to a hesitant grin. “What did she want?”

“I’m gonna leave that part up to you, Israel. Why don’t you ask in the kitchen—see if somebody knows where she is this morning.” Lester hesitated before adding, “And Israel—if’n I was you, I believe I’d say I wasn’t attached to nobody.”

While Israel headed tentatively to the kitchen, Lester found the assistant manager of the Peabody and asked if one of the porters could assist him in the infirmary. This was granted, and soon Lester, assisted by a rail-thin fellow introduced as Caleb, carried yet another victim of the fever downstairs to the wagon.

Lester gave Caleb a quarter for his trouble, then went to find Israel. He found his friend and Leah Feathers huddled up in a corner of the kitchen, drinking coffee. When Israel spied his friend, he flashed him a smile approximately twice as wide as his face.

October 9, 1878—"Our best physicians are all of the opinion that no relief from the fever may be expected until after a black frost, when ice appears in the gutters."

"The Citizens Relief Committee has established locations for the distribution of food in every area of the city. Distribution occurs beginning at 12 noon daily. 1st Ward—Market St, near Dr. Rennert's Drug Store, 2nd Ward—140 Main St., 3rd Ward—62 Jefferson St, 5th Ward—136 Beale St, 6th Ward—511 Main St, 8th Ward—Corner Poplar St and Carroll Ave, 9th Ward—142 Fifth St, 10th Ward—666 Main St, Visitors' Location—Corner Union and Cooper."

Letter to Citizens Relief Committee—"Sir, Yesterday I visited thirty-five families in the 4th Ward, and to my utter surprise, with three exceptions, I could not find a day's rations in any house. I am sure there are at least 150 families in this ward who require rations. Many of them recently ventured to the country to work on farms—to pick cotton, etc.—but were driven back to the city as if they were lepers. If their pantries are not re-supplied, most will assuredly starve to death."

"The steamer Joe Kinney *passed upriver yesterday with a light trip. A tugboat took the mail out to her, and received all which had accumulated from the south. She then steamed up river without touching our wharf. Twenty tons of mail material are at the post office awaiting sorting and delivery."* Memphis Daily Appeal

For the third time in as many days, Dr. Sohm arrived at the home of 'Poke' Green, who lived in a poorly kept two-room cabin just south of Raleigh Station. While Green had certainly been sick with the fever, he was also a nervous

wreck, having anticipated his own demise since the first hour he became ill. After observing his patient's improvement from the last visit, Sohm was not convinced of such a dire outcome, and decided to try a different treatment tactic.

"Doctor Sohm, I'm sure glad to see you. Fact is, you might be the last human I set eyes on. My brother took off to Arkansas when I got sick, and my friends and neighbors won't have nothin' to do with me."

"Why, Poke, I was just going to say how much better you looked today. In fact, it's a good thing you're well on your way to a recovery. I just heard this morning there's not a single coffin left in town. The undertakers claim another thousand have been ordered but won't arrive for several more days. It's a terrible thing to contemplate. I'd hate to see anyone just laid out in the yard, awaiting his coffin, let alone rolled up in a blanket and stuck in a bare hole in the ground."

Poke screwed up his face in horror. "You know, Doctor Sohm, I've always hated worms. Never could bring myself to touch the slimy things. Makes me shiver just to think about 'em. If I was to be laid out in the dirt, without no casket to protect me, don't you reckon the worms would be after me right quick?"

Sohm looked at his patient with what he hoped was a straight face. "It's an awful thing to contemplate, Poke, but I've witnessed the nauseating results of worms working on a corpse in less than twenty-four hours after death. However, without a casket in town, I'm afraid it just can't be helped. You'll just have to brace yourself for it."

Poke rose halfway from his bed, finally throwing his legs over the side and sitting up, while supporting his head with his hands. He reached over, poured himself a glass of water, and drank it all without much enthusiasm. Finally he looked toward Sohm, speaking in a resigned voice. "Well, I had concluded to die today, but under them circumstances, I reckon I can postpone it a few more days."

October 11, 1878—"The people of the North still continue to send us food, clothing, supplies, and money. They have not wearied of well-doing. Their committees are still at work and their dailies are still urging collections for our sick and desti-

tute people. Words will not tell the sense of gratitude we feel in good works surpassing anything the world has ever known before."

"Notice: All Israelites living in the suburbs of this city will send their address, and roads leading to same, to Rice, Stix, & Co. Signed J. Kohlberg, Acting President, Hebrew Hospital Association."

"From a correspondent in Hernando, Mississippi—Number of cases of fever to date—75, deaths—32, currently sick—31."

"From a correspondent in Water Valley, Mississippi—Our sorrow-stricken community, deprived of the consolations of religion through the cowardice of our preachers, proclaims the following facts: we had two Methodist ministers, a Baptist elder, an Episcopal reverend, a Presbyterian parson, and a Catholic priest on the 10th of August. Since that date, none has been seen in our midst except the Catholic priest, who has shown his face every day among us. Ever ready for any call, he has been with the Howards, reporting the sick and destitute, been a member of the Relief Committee, and sat at the bedside of many a non-Catholic these past two months." Memphis Daily Appeal

October 11, 1878—"From New Orleans, we learn that the report to the Howards over the last 24 hours is 213 new cases of fever, with a grand total to date of 13,356. They also report 48 deaths over the period, bringing that sad total to 3,351." Chicago Daily Tribune

Chapter 30
Calamity to the East

Memphis

Fannie faced the chief nurse, Letitia Smith, a wire-haired terrier of a woman. She was apprehensive about where the conversation might be headed. "Fannie, the Howards have asked for twenty nurses to travel on relief trains from Memphis to Humboldt and to Decatur, Alabama. Some of these towns haven't had any medical support whatsoever during the epidemic, so there's no telling what kind of problems you're going to find, but you're one of our best nurses and I want you to go."

"I thought I was needed here in the Peabody infirmary. We've still got twelve patients."

"We'll make do. Things aren't nearly as bad as they were just a few weeks ago. Besides, it'll be good for you to get away for a little while. Maybe a change of scenery and a new set of challenges will take your mind off that tragic situation with Nina Payne. Why don't you plan on leaving on the Charleston line on the thirteenth of the month?"

The first relief train on the Charleston and Memphis rail line departed the M & C Station on Lauderdale Street shortly after daybreak on October 12th. As the train began its journey, the roof of the station house glimmered as the first rays of the sun bounced off its tiles. The only thing that seemed to be missing from the scene was a crowd of people. Other than just a handful of porters, the platform—just like the city's streets—was deserted.

The train was headed toward Decatur, Alabama, as well as any towns in between which might be in need of supplies, nurses, and physicians. The plan was that the trains would run daily, carrying relief to the sick until a hard frost would hopefully put an end to the epidemic. This first relief train was comprised of two passenger cars, two box cars filled with ice, one crammed floor to roof with hundred-pound bags of lime, one with clean bedding, three with food, and another with medicine and medical supplies.

Although the train was traveling at a brisk twenty-five mile an hour clip, it could progress no further than Iuka, Mississippi, as every railcar was swept clean of supplies after stopping at only four towns in Tennessee and two in Mississippi. Their first stop had been twenty miles outside Memphis at Germantown. The little town was surrounded by large farms, perched astride a wide ridge between the Wolf River and Nonconnah Creek. Upon arrival, they were met by the sole surviving physician, who reported 65 cases and 29 deaths to date since the first of September. Supplies, ice, and two nurses were left on the depot platform as the train departed.

No more than five or six miles further down the track, they stopped at Collierville station. The report there was even gloomier—90 cases and 39 deaths, with 19 new cases occurring in just the last two days. It seemed to be the general opinion by the chief physician on board that the disease in Collierville was extremely virulent, spreading as fast there as it had in the early days in Grenada. Along with supplies, he agreed to leave behind three Howard nurses to help with the new cases. (*Author's note:* The final tally in Collierville would be 135 cases and 60 deaths.)

The small town of Moscow had endured much the same death rate as Collierville, and was desperate for food and supplies, as no trains had traveled the route for almost two months. Additionally, it was too far from Memphis to be resupplied by wagon, so the village had been forced to rely on its own resources, which had literally dwindled to nothing. A considerable portion of supplies and food were left on the station platform as the train proceeded further east. (*Author's note:* The final tally in Moscow would be 44 deaths.)

The train was met in Grand Junction, Tennessee by a nurse and a delegation of farmers. Nurse Shirley Broom, who lived in the little town, scarcely had strength to stand in the late morning heat, but she had a message to deliver. "We've already lost 35 people, including nine members of the Prewitt family. Our two doctors, both Prewitts themselves, are dead and gone. I'm the only one left in town who has any medical training at all, and I'm just gettin' over the fever myself. We've still got about twenty people who're sick, and at least three of them won't last through breakfast tomorrow. For God's sake, we need a doctor and some nurses—and all sorts of medical supplies." (*Author's note:* Grand Junction would experience 70 deaths.)

The three farmers' spokesperson was Jasper Lavinder. "See here, we need help on our farms. They's hardly anybody well enough to work 'round here. My two brothers is dead and gone. Cain't you send us at least fifty coloreds t' help us pick cotton? Most years the depot is stacked to the roof with bales o' cotton by now, but today it's empty. Our fields are 'bout to bust with the best crop we've had in years, but there ain't nobody around to pick."

One of the Howards on the train, Jacob West, was exasperated by this request. "Every time somebody asks for farm workers, and we get a bunch together, when they show up to work, a crowd of locals run 'em off at the town border—usually with double-barreled shotguns. They say to get on back to Memphis, and take your damn fever with you."

"Looka here, we're desperate for workers. Ain't nobody gonna run nobody off if they come to work."

"How much do you intend to pay, and do you provide food and shelter for the pickers?"

The three men put their heads together for a minute until Lavinder finally responded. "O' course, we'll feed 'em and house 'em. Pay will be twenty-five cents per hunert pounds."

"I doubt that'll get many takers. Even the gravediggers in Memphis are gettin' over a dollar a day."

"A good picker oughta make 500 pounds a day—that is, if he's a steady worker."

"Yeah, steady is right—mebbe pickin' daylight til dark and from can 'til cain't. I'll spread the word in Memphis, but don't get yer hopes up. A dollar an' a quarter a day draggin' a pick-sack don't hardly cut the mustard."

The train whistle interrupted the conversation, and the farmers had another quick discussion, with Lavinder finally throwing up his hands. "We'll go thirty-five cents a hunert, but that's all we can afford. You tell them gravediggers if they come here, at least they ain't got to put their hands on the dead, and our air don't stink with lime and sulfur."

West mounted the steps to the passenger car and nodded his head. "I'll see what I can do, but you might be watchin' them bolls rot in the field."

The first stop in Mississippi, at Corinth, was uneventful. Directly across the track from the Corinth depot was the Tishomingo Hotel—a decrepit two-story affair which possessed a decided lean. A good wind out of the south would surely turn the building into a large pile of kindling. But the sorry state of the architecture did not dissuade at least twenty families encamped at the hotel, all of them immigrating to what they assumed were safer quarters from infected areas both south and west.

As they had been advised of the train's mission via telegram the previous day, a small group of men from the town were gathered on the depot platform. Their assumption was they would be the beneficiaries of a large gift of food. But Corinth had been extremely fortunate, experiencing almost no yellow fever, so there was much fist shaking when they were told the train's supplies were only to be deployed to support victims of yellow fever. The train paused just long enough for the engineer to stretch his legs before they were off again, headed east.

It was well into the afternoon when the relief train reached the town of Iuka, Mississippi. After some inquiry, they learned Iuka had been just as lucky as Corinth, and so the Howard representatives met briefly before making a decision to return to Memphis for resupply, as they were down to less than ten percent of the supplies with which they had begun their journey. When they came back through Grand Junction just at sundown, they decided to leave all their remaining food, medical supplies, ice, and lime with that suffering city, as well as their remaining two nurses and a physician, to do what they could to assist the town.

October 12, 1878—"The Cheyenne have for some weeks been on the warpath, dealing death and destruction to the people of the western counties of Kansas. Women and girls have been outraged under circumstances of fiendish atrocity, and men have been butchered. We also learn that the Sioux, under Red Cloud, threaten to join the Cheyenne, and Spotted Tail is suspected to have had overtures made to him by the hostiles."

"Many of the convalescents are walking about, trying to smile and look healthy, but the smile 'looks like a silver plate on a coffin.' Unfortunately, we know how it is ourselves here at the newspaper."

"It is safe to say not less than $1.5 million has been sent by the people of the North to the yellow fever sufferers of Memphis, besides provisions, tents, ice, medical supplies, and clothing to amount to another $500,000. With these gifts, thousands of lives have been saved, and thousands more rescued from destitution." Memphis Daily Appeal

Memphis, Chattanooga, and points between

Fannie was at the Lauderdale Street station early the next morning, talking to the Howards personnel to see if she could determine what challenges awaited the train as they headed east. She was interrupted in her thoughts by two blasts on the whistle and the traditional call from the conductor, "All aboard!"

As she walked down the aisle, seeking a seat, she was shocked to see a familiar face grinning at her. "Doctor Madison, I didn't realize you were coming, too!"

"I figured I'd use this opportunity to go back to Charleston, at least for a little while. Maybe you should come with me. I think all of us need a little vacation after all we've been through." He failed to mention his primary objective.

For her part, Fannie made no comment.

There were no stops until they arrived just after noon at the first station in Alabama—the little town of Tuscumbia. There was some fever, but not enough to overly alarm the public. The relief train left some supplies and moved on. The next stop, Decatur, Alabama, was only five miles further down the track and had had similar experiences to those of its neighbor. So minimal supplies were provided, and the train continued eastward.

There was quite a gathering of people at Huntsville, the final stop in the state. At that city, Captain John Grant, Superintendent of the Memphis and Charleston Railroad, greeted the train from the station platform. Grant was a heroic figure at the moment, volunteering to provide the entire cost of the relief train service between Memphis and Huntsville out of his own pocket. When he came aboard, there was great cheering from the assembled crowd, recognizing his huge contribution to their welfare.

Having been the recipient of numerous telegrams in the previous two days, Grant lost no time in requesting the train travel further east, in particular to the city of Chattanooga, which was almost 400 rail miles from Memphis. The Howards agreed with his request. As darkness enveloped the train and visibility shrank to no more than an arm's length, the Negro porter entered each of the two passenger cars with a long stick. He lit a wick embedded in beeswax on one end, then reached toward the ceiling to light the eight coal oil lamps in each car, which provided at least some illumination for the racing east-bound train.

Finally arriving at Chattanooga near the ten o'clock hour, the medical personnel on board were immediately besieged with requests for assistance. While Chattanooga had previously only had comparatively few cases of sickness, just in the 72 hours prior to the train's arrival, there had been 205 new cases of fever and 15 deaths reported. The remaining resources of the relief train—supplies and personnel, including Superintendent Grant—disembarked in Chattanooga.

In the early days of the epidemic in New Orleans, Memphis, Vicksburg, and Grenada, the people of Chattanooga had held gatherings and yard parties to raise money for yellow fever relief and to care for refugees who had begun to arrive in their city. Two young girls had taken the initiative to contact Henry Wadsworth Longfellow and John Greenleaf Whittier, asking for their autographs. Both men submitted their signatures on cards and each were auctioned off in Chattanooga to raise more yellow fever funds. But now the epidemic had begun to attack in their own backyard, and it was they who needed help.

Dr. James Madison and a second Howard physician, along with all of the nurses on board, were immediately dispatched to a hospital which had been established in an old Masonic academy on College Hill. The same facility had been utilized during the Civil War as a hospital for Confederate casualties.

The very heart of the epidemic in Chattanooga was near the downtown area, close to the waterfront—the low-lying, swampy land composed of the Third and Fourth Wards. South of Eighth Street and west of Market Street was where a majority of poor white and black citizens lived, surrounded by sanitary neglect and foulness every bit as bad as that found in the most affected areas of Memphis, and that was exactly where the fever had focused with a cruel assault.

Chattanooga had actually suffered at least a dozen cases of yellow fever since September, when a few Memphis emigrants had arrived in the city. But the local physicians had continued to diagnose those patients as having "remittent fever," "pernicious fever," and "intermittent fever," which was understandable in that the medical men had seen little or no yellow fever in their entire careers, and depended entirely on seeing symptoms like jaundice and black vomit to confirm that diagnosis. But those symptoms generally did not occur in more than a third of cases, and hence the epidemic continued to build a base in the city, unknown to the populace until September 19th, when finally a firm diagnosis was made. At that point, the city was transformed.

The population of Chattanooga prior to that date had been composed of 7,500 white and 4,500 black citizens. But in a matter of days, between eight and ten thousand people fled the city—many of them locating to relative safety on the heights of the majestic Lookout Mountain, just to the south of the municipality.

As the cases began to build, the city received a small amount of medical supplies and personnel, mostly from Atlanta. Patients were initially ferried out of Chattanooga to a quarantined sick camp set up by the local relief committee. As citizens fled, so also did most members of the fire and police departments. As a result, chaos, burglaries, and assaults became rampant.

E.A. James, head of the local relief committee, made the announcement that henceforth, looters would be hanged. And to emphasize the point, a gallows was erected near the jail in preparation for new business. This seemed to get the attention of the miscreants, as law-breaking activities decreased dramatically.

Fannie's first patient was Miss Hattie Ackerman, who was in the last throes of the fever. Miss Ackerman, Fannie quickly learned, had come to Chattanooga from Detroit some nine years previously, to offer her services as a school teacher. In this she had succeeded so well that she had been selected as the assistant principal of the high school—certainly an unusual achievement for a woman. But that was not where she permanently endeared herself to the memory of the city.

When the outbreak of fever finally caused the closure of schools, Miss Ackerman volunteered to travel from house to house, nursing the sick, no matter how ill they might be. This duty she carried out just as she had her teaching career, giving it everything she had. The result of that dedication now lay prostrate before Fannie on a makeshift cot in the infirmary, struggling to take her next breath.

Fannie was determined to do her best for the woman. "Miss Hattie, just take these ice chips in your mouth and let them dissolve. We need to get your fever down." With this small task accomplished, Fannie began the almost continuous work of bathing her patient's arms, neck, and chest with the standard whisky and ice mixture. "Now, you just try to be still, Miss Hattie. This should help."

Fannie paid close attention to her patient's mental state, observing that she was frequently out of her head with the fever. Her eyes were flickering from side to side, probably lacking the capability to focus on any one thing. Likewise, she was unable to remain quiet in bed, constantly twitching, squirming, and jerking first one way and then another. Her struggles were hard to watch. Fannie bit her lip, knowing full well where this journey was going to end. "Miss Hattie, you be still now. I'm a nurse and I'm going to stay right here with you, no matter what. Don't you worry yourself about anything."

Hattie had taken nothing by mouth save ice chips and a little broth the entire time she had been ill. Her lips were dry as salt, cheeks sunken, and her normally curly auburn hair lay lank on her brow when she surprised Fannie and began to speak. “Tell Professor Fine I tried my very best.”

“I’m sure he knows that, Miss Hattie.”

Her eyes flicked around the room before finally fixing themselves on Fannie. “Be sure you tell him.” And she was gone.

Hattie Ackerman’s death struck a chord in the city, perhaps like no other. Everybody seemed to be asking the same question the next morning. “A Yankee—who had come to the South for no reason than to educate its children. A Yankee—who could have easily fled when the fever came, yet spent her blood on behalf of their sick. A Yankee—can you imagine that, brother?”

October 13, 1878—“On the other side of the planet, a deadly famine has been at work for over twenty months, over an area larger than six of our fever-stricken states, whose victims outnumber all who have perished of any pestilence in our country during the last century. The dense population of five provinces of the Chinese Empire, numbering many millions of inhabitants, are changed by famine into an immense graveyard. The people, having devoured every animal, every herb, and every living vegetable thing, having filled themselves with nothing but clay and rice chaff, have been driven to the last resource, and are now eating their own dead. A whole year has passed since they began to die of starvation, and now hundreds of thousands are dead—having received not one iota of relief.” New Orleans Picayune

Dr. P.A. Sims was a locally prominent physician who had been placed in charge of Chattanooga’s medical resources. But while he was respected in the city, he had not one whit of experience in treating yellow fever, nor did the other physicians in his employ. He had personally come to face that fact after a number of negative outcomes, so he was only too glad to immediately turn over the care of four sick physicians to Dr. James Madison when he learned of Madison’s self-described breadth of experience in Memphis.

The four affected doctors had never been exposed to yellow fever before, so it was almost a foregone conclusion that all of them would be struck down. It was obvious to Madison that Doctors Baird and Barr were beyond rescue. Both of them were enduring a return of fever over 105 degrees, as well as jaundice, while Barr was also suffering from recurring seizures. He ordered a nurse to bathe them in ice water and whiskey and give them each a quarter grain of morphine. With that, he turned his attention to Drs. Baxter and Freer.

These two physicians had come through the worst of the ordeal, and their high fevers of three days previous had not reoccurred. Madison felt fairly optimistic about their chances, and ordered their nurse to alternate every three hours feeding them chicken broth and herbal tea. He reported his divided sentiments regarding the four patients to Dr. Sims, trying his best to take at least some measure of credit for Baxter and Freer's optimistic outcomes, at the same time making sure Sims acknowledged that Baird and Barr had been beyond hope when he arrived.

While Dr. Sims was grateful for any positive news, his response was to hand over another difficult case to Madison, that of Father Patrick Ryan, a local Catholic priest. When Madison looked in on Ryan, he immediately put him into the same category as Baird and Barr, ordered similar nursing care for the reverend, and departed the infirmary, seeking out a bed in the Read House Hotel on Broad Street. He saw no point in sitting around, wasting his time for the benefit of Baird, Barr, and Ryan. All three of them would not survive. But Father Ryan would be faithfully visited at his bedside every day until his death by a Protestant minister, Dr. J.W. Bachman.

To his disgust, Madison was awakened before six the next morning with a request to take a look at the railroad superintendent, Captain Grant. After a quick examination, he confirmed that Grant was in the early stages of the yellow fever, ordered a dose of calomel for the next three days as well as extra fluids, and returned to his bed.

Against all advice, Captain Grant insisted that he be put on the west-bound morning train, which was headed back toward Huntsville and to the loving arms of his wife and family. He had been in Chattanooga less than twelve hours. Surely he had been infected before leaving Huntsville. Escaping the calomel may have been the best decision he ever made.

October 14, 1878—"An execution outside the walls of the city prison, and on a public street of Paris, was described by a correspondent. It took place in the gray of dawn, with a large crowd assembled, and at the precise hour indicated in the sentence. A squad of soldiers filed out of the gates, and in a twinkling put together the machinery of the guillotine, some of them sprinkling sawdust on the pavement while the blade was being pulled up. Before this was fairly finished, the gate swung open and the criminal, the executioner, and the spiritual advisor marched out. Whatever religious exercises were essential had been attended to within the prison. The criminal, with his hands bound behind him and a cap drawn down over his head, was led forth, his body bent forward over the carriage, which as he pressed upon it, shot forward on noiseless wheels, and the knife fell with a glitter of its keen, polished edge, the head dropping into a bucket awaiting it. The two body parts were placed in a coffin, the machinery taken down, the sawdust swept up, and the whole scene was over. Within ten minutes, by the watch of this witness, every trace of the execution had vanished. The soldiers, the executioner, and the priest had disappeared, and there was not even a single drop of blood upon the pavement to indicate that a tragedy had been there enacted." Los Angeles Herald

Dr. Madison had just finished examining Dr. Freer and exited his room, when he found a young nurse waiting on him in the hall of the makeshift hospital. The girl could not have been more than eighteen or nineteen years old, and by any account, she would be enthusiastically described as fetching. He issued his best smile in her direction.

"Excuse me—are you Doctor James Madison—the doctor I've heard so much about?"

His smile grew wider. "I am Doctor Madison."

"Are you the one who saved the lives of Doctor Freer and Doctor Baxter?"

"I'm the physician who is taking care of both of them, yes. Neither one is completely out of the woods as yet, but I'm doing everything humanly possible for them."

"I've also heard you were very successful in Memphis."

"My training at the Medical University of South Carolina has been a great benefit. I fear some of the doctors didn't receive the quality of education I had."

"Oh—you're from Charleston. I thought I recognized the accent of a Southern gentleman. I'm afraid I'm just a country girl by comparison."

"Nonsense. Have you been here in Chattanooga very long?"

"No, Doctor Madison. That's what I wanted to ask you. My old nursing instructor told me that the best way to learn as much as I could about yellow fever was to work directly with a very smart physician."

"That's probably good advice."

"So I was wondering if I could spend enough time with you to visit some of your patients, talk about your treatment strategy, and perhaps take notes for my own improvement."

"Have you had the fever yourself?"

"Oh, yes, some six or seven years ago—when I was just a girl."

He looked her over again, this time taking special notice of her more obvious attributes. "I don't know why that can't be arranged."

"Just ask for me by name at the Howards' desk downstairs—I'm Rebecca Monroe."

Chapter 31
Harry Savage

Chattanooga

After her night-long bedside vigil with Hattie Ackerman, Fannie found herself assigned to a newly admitted patient, Harry Savage. Mr. Savage was a local gambler of some renown, who had led quite a rakish life in the city. But with the coming of the epidemic, everybody who could afford to leave vacated the city. This included literally all of Harry's gambling cronies. Rather than flee for his life, Harry Savage did something that was totally out of character.

He opened his rather spacious rooms at the corner of Ninth and Market, which were located over Voigt's Drug Store, to all of the epidemic's freshly created orphans in the city. Of course, he spent his own funds to clothe them and feed them. Then, when some of his charges began to fall ill, he hired nurses to care for them. What had started out as simply a place for the orphans to stay had now developed into a full-service infirmary. What Harry failed to consider was that he might get sick himself.

Even in the infirmary, and although possessing a fever and a terrible headache, these temporary symptoms did not interfere with Harry's ability to quickly identify a very attractive female in his vicinity. Even though a cold sweat had popped out on his brow, a broad smile decorated his face and he even managed to put a twinkle in his eye. "And who might you be, lass?"

"I'm Fannie Lester, one of the Howard nurses from Memphis." She tried to muster her best withering look, even though she was somehow mysteriously attracted to the devil's green eyes and shock of red hair, before trying to put a damper on Harry's gab. "They tell me you're a sick man, and I'm supposed to take care of you, but I think perhaps they've made a mistake. You've far too big a grin on your puss for me to waste my time with the likes of you."

"Oh, no. You're jumpin' to one o' those conclusions, Nurse Fannie. It's awful sick I am. In fact, I may not survive the night. I'll be needin' a great deal of your personal care and sympathy, I will."

"'Tis true. I'll be feelin' very sympathetic, right after you take this two ounces of castor oil."

October 15, 1878—"We suggest to the Citizens Relief Committee the propriety of putting 1,000 or more men to work who are now drawing rations. The streets have not been swept in weeks, nor the gutters flushed. These men should be put to work without delay, and among other things, be put to covering all holes where there is stagnant water, or any offensive matter, with charcoal and lime. The city should be cleaned up at once, and every man who refuses to help should be cut off from any share in the relief supplies."

"From a correspondent in Garner, Mississippi—The situation of the people here is pitiful in the extreme, and unless supplies of food and money are sent, the suffering of both sick and well will be terrible. All business has been at a standstill for 2 months. The crops are un-gathered. The merchants have nothing to sell, and if they did, the people have no money to buy. The country people will not come near town, so we can get no food from that direction. Of 35 whites left in town, we've had 9 deaths and 16 are down sick."

"The fever figures in Memphis today are not encouraging—136 new cases and 55 deaths in the last twenty-four hours. The refugees are coming back so fast as to add ready fuel to the flame, and give new life to the epidemic. But they have been warned repeatedly. They have no one to blame but themselves, and are paying dearly for their temerity." Memphis Daily Appeal

Fannie couldn't help herself. Harry Savage certainly possessed the gift of the blarney stone. She couldn't remember laughing so much in—well, ever. "There was a nurse in Memphis who would be a perfect fit for you. His name was Harry Ring, and he could tell a joke that would raise a dead man."

"Sounds like me kind o' gent. If I happen to pass over to the other side, please be puttin' out an emergency telegram to Mr. Ring."

"Mr. Ring had the fever himself before he started nursing other people, and the story goes that he scared one of his patients completely out of his sick bed, just by his colorful tale of how terrible his experiences were when he had the fever himself." Fannie put one hand on her hip. "Methinks a good scare is exactly what you need, so you'll stop givin' me so much o' yer foolishness."

"Ooh, that truly wounds me, Nurse Fannie. Here I am in the depths of sickness and despair, and you accuse me of a lack o' sincerity when it comes to sufferin' and woe." He made a show of clutching his chest. "To think that you would doubt me need for your constant nursin' care. That truly wounds this weak heart o' mine. I feel a terrible outcome for meself due to yer heartless ways."

"Lie still and let me take your temperature."

"You won't be tryin' to kill me again with some more o' that evil castor oil you prepared just to make me miserable?"

"No more castor oil—that is, unless you get too aggravatin'. In that case I may double the dose on you."

"Ahh—ye'r a hard-hearted woman, Nurse Fannie. Do they not have nurses around here who aren't tryin' to make their poor, defenseless patients suffer?"

October 16, 1878—Advice received from Dr. Gourier in Holly Springs—"In no instance should anyone return to this city before a good freeze, and not then before each house has been fumigated with burning sulfur. Fires should be built in every hearth, and the houses aired for several days. The graveyard should be surrounded by a cordon of quick lime, and

each individual grave should have a bushel of lime spread upon it to neutralize the gases."

A telegram from Mr. C.S. Crofut in Chattanooga—"People are dying here like sheep."

"The weather, which is quite warm, promises another change, which may bring us, if not a heavy frost, a light one that may help to kill the lingering spores of fever. Frost, frost, frost! Our prayers are all for frost."

"The commissary of the Citizens Relief Committee issued 22,125 rations yesterday, making a grand total of 411,822 rations distributed in Memphis in the last two months."

(Ad) "After breakfasting on biscuits made with Dooley's yeast powder, what man would contemplate suicide, or grumble because his wife asked him for money?" Memphis Daily Appeal

W.T. Monger usually cut quite a figure on the streets of Chattanooga. He was always well dressed, neatly barbered, and a more physically fit man could not be found, at least until he was spied that morning by his good friend Charles George, who was a fellow member of the local relief committee. Monger was wearing a black suit, silk vest, black tie, and matching derby as he stood leaning against the side of a grocery at the corner of Eighth and Market Streets. He was perspiring heavily, and his unusually pale coloring was accentuated by a pair of extremely bloodshot gray eyes, which were filled with a bewildered look until he finally recognized his friend. "*Charley, I've got it.*"

George took one look at his buddy and retreated about three steps. "W.T., you need to get home and go to bed."

Monger lived only a few blocks down Eighth Street on the corner of Georgia. *"Everybody else with the fever goes to bed and then they die. I've decided if I'm going to go, I might as well die on my feet."*

"Look, W.T., you shouldn't be on the street. Go home and get to bed. I'll find a doctor."

In no more than thirty minutes, George had found one of the Howard physicians and they were on their way to Monger's house, but unexpectedly met up with him, still walking up and down Eighth Street, though at an erratic pace. His jacket was unbuttoned, his tie undone, and his derby was nowhere to be seen.

Despite the day's temperature being relatively cool, his shirt was soaked in sweat. Unfortunately, by the time they caught up with him, Monger was violently crazy, and, despite all attempts to the contrary by the doctor, kept repeating, *"I'm gonna walk 'til the very end, even if it kills me."* He refused to be guided by his friend or the physician, pushing them away from him when they tried to lead him to his home and his bed. Mr. George decided to shadow his friend rather than leave him to his own devices. So George was able to confirm later to his friends that Monger had continued his aimless walking, and in less than an hour, he realized his ambition and finally fell to the ground. By the time George located another doctor, his old friend was quite dead.

The sound of a man and woman laughing seemed completely out of place as it echoed down the hallway of Chattanooga's infirmary. Dr. James Madison retrieved a piece of paper from his pocket to confirm the room number of his newest patient, and was surprised that the number on the paper matched the number on the door beyond which all of the revelry seemed to be originating. He considered not even entering, as he certainly didn't want to waste time with his new nurse on frivolous behavior.

The first person he saw when he stuck his head in the door was Fannie Lester. She glanced in his direction and put a serious look on her face. "Doctor Madison, come in. This is Harry Savage. Mr. Savage was admitted two days ago."

"Fannie, I'd like you to meet a new nurse who is helping me with my patients—Fannie Lester, this is Rebecca Monroe."

"Thank goodness you and your nurse are here, yer honor. Nurse Fannie first tried to kill me with castor oil, and now she's feedin' me oxtail soup—or some such noxious potion. Might it be possible t' get a pork chop, an' mebbe a bite o' the fruit o' the gods?" He noticed the blank look on the doctor's face.

"Fruit of the gods?"

"Why, o'course, yer honor—Irish potatoes, that would be. Pure gastronomic perfection, particularly when you drown 'em in some lovely gravy."

"See here, Harry, you're at a precarious point in the disease process. Most people in your situation would not be turning this into frivolity."

"Oh, I got plenty o' time t' be serious, yer honor. But y' see, right this minute I'm kinda de-voted to talkin' Nurse Fannie into runnin' off with me to parts unknown. Mebbe I'll Shanghai us a buggy. I'm sorta de-termined to romance the young lady to a fare-thee-well. Fer sure, I got plenty o' time later t' be down in the mouth."

Fannie snorted. "Doctor Madison, you can see I've got my hands full with Mr. Savage." She smiled in spite of herself. "The man is incorrigible." Fannie noticed that Rebecca was trying very hard to conceal her own grin.

"Incorrigible, she says. That's no' right, yer honor. I might be determined t' be naughty, but I certainly ain't incorrigible."

Madison was getting thoroughly steamed at the way Savage was making smart-aleck jokes in the face of yellow fever. He turned his attention to Fannie. "Let me know when this patient wants to have a serious discussion about his illness."

"He means no disrespect, Doctor Madison. He's from Dublin. That might explain things."

Madison opened the door, gave Savage one last glare, then turned and spoke to Fannie again. "Let the clerk know when he's willing to be sensible. Until then, I haven't the time to waste." The door closed behind them with a bit of a slam.

Savage looked at Fannie. "Might you have noticed the look on the doctor's face, Nurse Fannie?" She turned expectantly to look at her patient. "The man looked like he was in a terrible strain—mebbe strugglin' to keep from passin' gas in public. I feel a special sympathy for that girl trailin' along behind him."

"Now, Mr. Savage..."

"Sort of a disagreeable fellow, ain't he now? Undoubtedly a Brit."

"I understand Doctor Madison is a good doctor."

"If I was a bettin' man, and o' course I ain't, I'd wager all you'd have to do t' confirm that suspicion would be t' ask the doctor himself. He appears t' have quite the opinion of his own self." Savage looked at Fannie. "I'd be figgerin' you t' be just as educated as he is."

She smiled without very much mirth. "I hope Doctor Madison made it a little farther than the sixth grade, Mr. Savage. If he didn't, your health may be in serious trouble." She was surprised at herself for sharing that kind of information. It certainly wasn't something she was proud of.

"Well, me myself spent three o' the happiest years o' my life in the sixth grade before I finally departed the halls of learnin'. And you know, that school had to close down completely the year after I left? Prob'ly couldn't survive without my advice to the teachers."

Madison was back the next morning, and after a cursory examination, managed to hide his satisfaction that Harry Savage had taken a considerable turn for the worse during the night. With the increase of his temperature to just north of 105 degrees, and both eyes shot full of blood, the man's devil-may-care sense of humor from the previous day had all but disappeared. Fannie, however, was still at his bedside. It was obvious to Madison that she was emotionally vested in this horse's ass, although he was unsure just how far that went. But her devotion to remaining with her patient all hours of the day and night certainly interfered with any plans Madison had for her.

The thought had already entered his mind that he might try a repeat of his activity in Memphis, with the hope of getting rid of Savage sooner rather than later. But then again, how could he be sure Fannie wouldn't be the one to fall victim to the water pitcher? The situation deserved more calculation. He decided to adjourn to his hotel for the night. He was looking forward to a nice dinner with Nurse Monroe. Hopefully it wouldn't all entail business.

For his part, Savage simply observed through chattering teeth, "This little rigor is just a temporary setback, Fannie. I'll be outa this bed and ready to take y' dancin' in no time atall."

It should not have been a surprise, but the long walk from the train station in Chattanooga to the infirmary, even after sundown, had left the doctor a bit dizzy. Given that he was only five days out of his own sickbed, any sensible person would say Dr. Saul Josefson should have been recuperating at his home in Memphis rather than volunteering for yet another assignment with the Howards.

Despite that, there he was, after a sixteen-hour train ride, and unsure of his own motive for coming. Was he really trying to comfort the sick in Chattanooga, or was the answer far simpler? Could it be he was simply trying to reconnect with Fannie Lester? He still had not completely answered that question to his own satisfaction. But what was he supposed to do? When he wasn't dreaming about her when he slept, he was fantasizing about her while he was awake.

Josefson introduced himself at the infirmary, asked an attendant for a towel and a bit of water to remove the grit of his train ride, then obtained directions to the location of Fannie's assignment. He paused for a few moments outside the room to collect himself, tapped on the door, and entered.

What he found was a very sick patient and an exhausted nurse who was slumped in a chair at the bedside. Josefson stood there watching for a few minutes before gently waking Fannie and literally pushing her out the door to an empty room across the hall. He laid her down on the cot, then bent down and unlaced her shoes before pulling them off her feet. "Get some sleep and we'll talk in the morning."

Fannie roused just enough to recognize her benefactor. "What in the world are you doin' here, Doctor Josefson?"

"I came to see if I could help. From the looks of things, it appears I got here just in time."

"But I can't be leavin' Mr. Savage."

"I'll stay with your patient tonight." He lifted her feet onto the bed and pulled the coverlet over her.

"But you're sick yourself."

"I'm as shiny as a new penny. I've slept the whole day on the train and I couldn't sleep now if I had to. I'll sit with Savage." He paused at the door. "Good night, Fannie." There was no response. The girl was out like a light. He stood there for a moment, then returned quietly to her bedside and looked down at her for at least five minutes. He finally bent low, kissed her forehead, and exited the room.

It was indeed a long night for Savage and the doctor. Savage was both in and out of his head multiple times. After twenty or thirty minutes of sponging his patient, thus bringing his temperature down, and seeing his rational thought return, Josefson would pause in his endeavors only to see, in the span of less than an hour, Savage's high fever return and his coherence depart. After spending most of the night engaged in this activity, Dr. Josefson developed a whole new level of respect for the tedious but necessary work performed by nurses.

Just at daylight, fatigue had finally gotten the best of Savage, and despite the resurgence of his fever, he fell into a restless sleep. After placing a cooling towel around his patient's neck, Josefson decided this was an opportune time for him to rest his eyes for a minute or two. Naturally, Fannie chose that moment to appear at the bedside.

She gave them both a critical look, checked Savage's pulse and temperature, and spoke softly to the doctor. "You're supposed to be recuperating. I thought for sure you being here was part of my dream. I don't even remember going to bed. Have you been here all the night long?"

"Just the dark part." He smiled at her. "I'm pleased to hear I'm part of your dreaming, by the way." He nodded toward Savage. "He's had a hard night. His fever keeps coming and going—pulse up to 130 a couple of times, then I'd manage to get his fever back down and he'd settle for a while."

"Is he going to get through this?"

Josefson shook his head. "I've been wrong on that question so many times, I've quit speculating."

"Have you managed to get any fluids down him?"

"Only a few ice chips. I expect he'll be more responsive if you're the one offering."

Fannie looked away before responding. "Yesterday I doubt he even knew who was sitting beside him."

"Well, he certainly asked for you several times through the night. I believe he said I wasn't his type."

She smiled in spite of herself. "I should hope not."

Josefson wearily pulled himself out of the chair. "Not the most comfortable place to spend the night. I'm beginning to sympathize with what you nurses are going through. I think I'll go find myself a bed for a few hours and come back later this evening to spell you for another nap of your own."

By mid-morning, Savage had indeed roused enough to carry on a cogent conversation with Fannie. "It was disappearin' you were last night. I feared you'd been kidnapped by that ugly man who was here."

"You mean Doctor Josefson? He was kind enough to take my place so I could get a bit of sleep. It might be difficult for you to realize, but you're not the easiest patient I ever took care of."

"Perhaps not the easiest, Fannie, but undoubtedly the most irresistible one you've ever had."

Their repartee was interrupted by a voice from the door. "Josefson? Since when did he get here?"

Fannie recovered from her surprise. "He arrived just last night, Doctor Madison. He stayed with Mr. Savage so I could catch up on some sleep."

Madison seemed to concentrate on the window when he spoke. "Remember what I told you about that fellow. I'd feel better if you avoided him completely. I don't know that you're safe around the man."

"Well, he took good care of Mr. Savage last night, and he promised to return tonight to relieve me. I know you're mistaken about him."

Madison had to turn away to avoid revealing his pleasure at this bit of news. "I hope you're right, Fannie." Of course, that would mean a change in plans. He had been looking forward to devoting more time that evening than what would be necessary to simply have dinner with Nurse Monroe.

He reminded himself that gratification delayed was often the sweetest fruit. Rebecca had already mentioned her desire to visit the old city of Savannah—and the unstated implication behind her lingering touch on his hand was that they should make plans to go together. The sooner the better, as far as he was concerned.

When Madison had departed, Savage turned to Fannie. "What's that unpleasant man got against Josefson? From where I sit, Madison hasn't given me more than a howdy-do. But not only did Doctor Josefson stay all night with me, he was doin' about all he could t' keep me from takin' the dirt nap. I'll have to say I'd choose to come down on Josefson's side if I was to be the chooser."

While Savage was certainly ill that evening when Josefson took over from Fannie, he was alert enough to respond to the doctor's question. "I've been wondering about something,

Harry. What possessed you to open your home to sick orphans?"

Harry shook his head. "Perhaps I didn't think very far ahead, Doctor. But the truth is, when I thought about it, I was ashamed to admit that I had never done any real good in all my life. So I just decided it was high time I did a little now."

"Harry, I've found it to be a rare man who is honest enough to be honest about himself."

"Being a poker player for the last fifteen years, I doubt that word has been used in the same sentence with Harry Savage in the past."

Josefson looked keenly at his patient. "I think you know what I mean. From what I hear around the hotel, there are quite a few people who're impressed with what you've done for the orphans. I'm proud to know you, Harry."

"I appreciate that, Doctor. Don't let anybody convince you that you're not a gentleman yourself."

Chapter 32
Karma

Chattanooga

Within a few minutes, and not long before eleven PM, Dr. James Madison quietly cracked open the door to Savage's room. Damn! Josefson was wide awake, apparently in the midst of giving his patient a sponge bath. Perhaps there was more than one way to skin this cat. Madison slipped the flask into his coat pocket and tapped on the door before entering. "Oh, sorry, Josefson. I was just stopping by to check on Savage."

Difficult as it was, Josefson managed to conceal his distaste. "His fever is spiking again. I'm not having much luck getting it down with ice packs."

Madison picked up the water pitcher at the bedside, giving it a bit of scrutiny. "Maybe you can get him to drink some cold water. Looks like you're low. Go ahead with what you're doing. I'll go down and fetch some from the orderly."

"Don't trouble yourself. I can get it later."

"No trouble. Be right back."

Having retrieved the ice water, Madison paused at the end of the dark hallway, pulled the flask from his pocket, and added four ounces of the contents to the two-quart pitcher. He then stepped to Savage's doorway, gave it a tap, and walked in. "Here you go. Plenty of ice in there. Looks like he needs a good drink. In fact, it appears you could use a little hydration yourself."

Josefson looked up from his patient and was a bit surprised Madison was already walking out the door. He called after him, "Say, thanks," but received no response. He poured a cupful for himself, drank it down, and then turned his attention to Savage. "Let's see if you can drink some ice water, Harry. We've got to get that fever down, and this is the surest way to accomplish it."

Resolutely, Savage attacked the water with a vigor not previously demonstrated. He had no sooner handed the empty cup to the doctor than Fannie appeared in the doorway. She was uncharacteristically excited. "Doctor Josefson, wait just a minute on that water. We might have a problem."

Savage wiped his lips with the edge of the bedsheet. "A problem, ye say? What about the water?"

Pausing in a doorway twenty feet away in the darkened hallway, a figure overheard almost the entire excited conversation from Savage's room. The conniving little witch had betrayed him. He back-pedaled quietly to the stairway, then began to hurry.

Fannie explained she had awakened to a strange sound in the hallway, and peeked out her door just in time to see Madison pour the contents of a whiskey flask into a water pitcher, which he then took into Savage's room. When he'd departed the room, the pitcher was left behind. She had only taken time to don a robe before coming to warn them.

"Both of us have already had a cupful of this." Josefson adjusted the mantle on the oil lamp, then held the pitcher up to the light. Seeing nothing out of the ordinary, he poured some of the ice water into a cup and smelled of the contents. He held it in outstretched arms toward Fannie. "Smell of this and tell me what you think."

"I can't smell anything."

Savage held out his hand. "Let me take a whiff." He glanced at Josefson. "I could swear the cup you gave me had the taste of spirits to it, and I just happen to be an expert in liquid refreshment." Taking a robust sniff, he observed, "It'd be alcohol, all right. Can you tell me why a doctor might spike our punch?"

"It struck me as odd that Madison offered to fetch water for us. I hate to say it, but this reminds me of an incident in Memphis. My nurse took sick and died at my bedside, and I had the same symptoms she had—dry mouth, eyes dilated to the extreme. Madison even had the gall to suggest I drink some of this water before he left."

He paused before turning to Fannie. "I just realized I'm the common denominator in both these events. Madison and

I have had strong words previously. Maybe it was me he was after, but Nina Payne and Harry just happened to get in the way. Fannie, I need a couple of favors. Would you mind going downstairs to ask the night attendant to fetch the police?" He dug into his pocket for some coins. "Also, would you go to a pharmacy and purchase two ounces of ipecac syrup?"

"Let me put my clothes on and I'll be right back."

When Fannie returned, both Josefson and Savage downed an ounce of the nasty tasting ipecac, plus a glass of water which did not come from the pitcher. Josefson stared at his empty glass. "I suppose we have to wait and see if we develop any symptoms. Whatever he put in there, we don't know how potent it might be. We'll just hope the ipecac gets rid of whatever might have been in the water before it gets into our system."

Chattanooga, Savannah, and points between

Madison went straight to Rebecca Monroe's room. Thankfully, she was still awake. "I've decided to go to Savannah on tonight's train. Would you like to go with me?"

"What about your patients?"

"I turned them over to one of the other doctors. I've been working seven days a week for two months, and have come to the conclusion that I need a vacation for a few days. Why don't you come with me?"

She smiled in such a way that he knew things promised to get very interesting. "I can be ready in ten minutes."

"I'll go check out. Meet me in room 237 in ten minutes. We'll need to hurry." Of course, he had no intention of checking out.

When she arrived at his room, the door was partially ajar and he was throwing things into his valise. She happened to notice the graduation certificate from medical school. "Your degree says James M. Madison. What's the M stand for?"

He stared at her with a blank look before responding. "I hate my middle name. I never tell anybody what it is. Come on, let's hurry."

The train ride would take thirteen hours, plus a delay of an hour in Atlanta, so Madison purchased tickets for a private sleeper cabin. They stowed their baggage in the cabin before making their way to the dining car.

Only a single waiter was on duty at that hour, and the solitary food option was a bacon sandwich, which the old man said he would prepare for them. But food wasn't the main objective of the night, and Madison ordered a bottle of champagne. Rebecca put her hand on his arm. "I don't like the bubbles. How about a bottle of bourbon?"

Far be it from him to deny the lady at such a time, and the bourbon was delivered along with a small bucket of ice. Madison excused himself briefly for a bathroom visit, and when he reappeared his glass was full. He took a healthy drink and pronounced it excellent. After a couple of sips, Rebecca leaned over and put her lips up to his ear. "I like to get a little tipsy before—well, you know."

He refilled his glass and looked at her. She replied, "This is already my second one. I don't want to pass out and miss anything."

"I guess I'd better catch up to you." Madison took another long drink, draining his glass. At about that moment, their sandwiches appeared. They each took a couple of bites. Rebecca continued to sip. Madison refilled his glass again in order to have something to drink with his meal.

By the time their sandwiches were almost gone, so was Madison's third glass of bourbon. "I think it's time we went to our cabin."

"I'm almost ready. Let me take just a couple more sips."

In five minutes, Madison decided the time was nigh, and stood up. She noticed he grabbed for the back of his chair to steady himself.

"Are you all right?"

"Just a little dizzy. That bourbon is stout stuff."

"Why don't we step out on the gangway at the back of the dining car? The cool wind will make you feel lots better. You're going to need your strength for what comes next."

He allowed himself to be led to the rear, leaning quite a bit on the girl for support. When she opened the door, they were standing on a metal platform, separated from the car immediately behind them by an open gap of a couple of feet. Within that gap was the steel coupling to the car behind. The rail-bed was not altogether smooth, the tracks having been torn apart by General Sherman's army some fourteen years earlier on his March to the Sea.

The irregularity in the ride was amplified by Madison's dizziness, and he held on to the rail for all he was worth. As he tightened his grip, Rebecca asked the oddest question. "Did you ever know any doctors who were addicted to opium?"

"Sure. I remember one old guy that was hooked on paregoric." He laughed out loud at the memory. "I b'lieve it ended up killin' him."

"Do you remember his name?"

His words were slurred enough that she had trouble understanding him. "Sure. What diffe'nce does it make?"

She held up a four-ounce bottle of Camphorated Opium Tincture with a label on it from Campbell's Pharmacy. "Did it look anything like this?" She held it in front of his face so he could focus, then slipped it into his coat pocket.

"Prob'ly. Don't remember."

As the train came out of the hills north of Atlanta, the tracks formed a long, looping curve. Madison chanced letting go of the railing. It was a relief when he remained upright.

But Rebecca's smile vanished. "Funny coincidence. You look just like the pharmacy clerk from Campbell's who delivered that bottle of opium. You're sure as hell no doctor!"

At this, Madison jerked his head around, and once more things began to spin. The curving path of the train added to his disorientation; his feet began to slip out from under him, and he reached out for the railing again. Instead, she grabbed his wrist in her left hand and pushed on his back with her right, giving the shove all the built-up hatred she possessed. He toppled forward over the rail, bounced on the large coupling, and as the great wheels spun, "Dr. Madison" disappeared with a discernible bump beneath the wheels of the following cars.

She spoke harshly into the darkness. "You didn't even know your middle name was Monroe—but you knew enough to quintuple the concentration of opium my father was used to taking for his diarrhea. You knew enough to steal his medical school graduation certificate, and you might have stolen his identity, but you could never steal who he was!"

Over and over, Rebecca Monroe Madison wiped the fabric of her dress, trying to remove any vestige of the man. She finally walked back through the dining car and paid for the meal and the bourbon—which she had heavily spiked with opium. The waiter looked around for her escort. “Oh, he went back to the cabin. He can’t seem to hold his liquor.”

Chattanooga

Some two hours had passed since Savage and Josefson had both vomited everything which remained in their stomach. Unfortunately, both of them had already begun to exhibit dilated eyes, as well as a thirst which was out of the ordinary. It was unknown whether the ipecac had gotten rid of enough of whatever had been in the water pitcher to avoid something drastic happening. When they passed this information to Officer Masters, he was perplexed about a next step. He turned to Josefson. “Any kind of test we can run on this here water to figure out what might be in it?”

“There are several things that could cause the symptoms we’ve got. But I don’t know how we could prove one versus the other without some extensive colorimetric laboratory analysis.”

“How long do y’ figger that metric stuff might take?”

“If we get lucky, maybe half a day. If we make several wrong guesses, it could take quite a bit longer. Right now we only know that something out of the ordinary caused our dry mouths and dilated pupils. Whether it’s poisonous or not, we don’t know that yet, but I’m guessing it might be the same poison that was used on Nurse Payne and me in Memphis. Savage and I are trying to dilute whatever we might have been exposed to from the pitcher by drinking as much good water as we can stand.”

“So in the meantime, this Doctor Madison is scot free.” A light went off in Officer Master’s skull. “I got myself an idea. But I’ll need to take some of this water for a little experiment o’ my own.”

“Just leave me about half of it to perform some experiments. I doubt we can find what’s needed here in Chattanooga. I’ll send a wire to Atlanta to get some laboratory equipment here. Perhaps we can get it late this evening.”

“First thing when I get back to the station house, I’ll put out a call for this Madison character to be picked up. I’ll get back to y’all as soon as I know somethin’.”

Officer Masters returned to the infirmary just before sundown. "Got some information for y'all. I gave some o' that water to a couple alley cats that live around the station house."

"Was that the 'experiment' you were talking about this morning?"

Fannie's reaction was not so wooden. "You mean you gave it to some poor cats on purpose?"

Masters didn't respond. "I never seen two cats drink so much water. The more they drank, the thirstier they got. The test ended just after four o'clock."

"Do you mean..."

"Yes, sir. Both of 'em, dead as a doornail." He looked first at Josefson, then at Savage lying prostrate in his bed. "How're you two fellers feelin'? Better'n them cats, I hope."

Josefson glanced toward Savage, then looked directly at Masters before shaking his head. Savage was less responsive, and his fever and pulse had accelerated yet again. Worse, he had no enthusiasm for drinking a large volume of fluid to flush out whatever had been in the water pitcher. "I hope neither one of us were exposed to enough to do any real damage, but Harry was already in a weakened condition. Have you found Madison yet?"

"We're still tryin' to locate him, Doctor. He's probably heard we're lookin' for him by now and may have already lit out."

Fannie remembered something. "Charleston—he said he was from Charleston."

"I'll send a telegram to the Charleston Police Department. Mebbe they can pick him up if he comes in on the Memphis and Charleston Line. Any results on your laboratory experiments?"

"The equipment is coming on the north-bound train this evening. I'll get the experiment set up and ready to go tonight. If we're lucky, maybe we'll have something figured out by tomorrow at mid-day."

Atlanta

Arriving in Atlanta, Rebecca Madison stuffed her own small bag inside the valise which her fellow passenger had left behind, departed the train with the larger bag, and purchased a ticket to Charleston. She would be home by the time they discovered what was left of an unknown opium addict strewn down the tracks.

Chapter 33
Neither Saint Nor Martyr

Chattanooga

Dr. Josefson placed an Erlenmeyer flask containing four ounces of liquid from the suspected pitcher over a flame in order to rapidly evaporate the water. Once accomplished, he added one ounce of pure grain alcohol to the flask, stirring it off and on with a glass rod until he was reasonably sure any material in the bottom of the flask was dissolved in the alcohol. Then he added four drops of a yellow-orange dye to the mixture.

He then clipped three identical pieces of porous paper above the work bench surface and placed one drop of his unknown mixture one inch from the top of each piece of paper. Next he placed four drops of the same yellow-orange dye in each of three products which he had obtained from Voigt's Drug Store, stirred them up, and finally used separate droppers to place single drops of each of those known substances at one-inch intervals at the top of the paper pieces. Then he settled back to wait.

In less than an hour, he was sure the mystery was solved. On each of the three paper experiments, all the drops of liquid had migrated down the sheets of paper, each absorbing more or less amounts of the dye, with those colors reflected differently by each product tested. On each sheet, two products were entirely different from the others, thus indicating no match. However, the first two sets of drops on the three sheets of paper were very similar. One set had come from the water pitcher, while the other he had purchased from the pharmacy.

Each of those two tests had three separate streaks of color migrating down the paper, with each streak's shade just a bit different. Although there was a very slight variance in the color on the two tests, Josefson knew that could be explained by the concentration of the product rather than the identity of the drug.

Just to be sure, he checked the label on the matching product which he had obtained from the pharmacy. As he'd expected all along, it was belladonna tincture. He knew the reason behind the three separate streaks of color. It was because of the three alkaloids contained in belladonna—atropine, hyoscine, and hyoscyamine. And each of them would cause dilated eyes, excessive thirst, inhibited urination, increased heart rate, and even death, depending on the dosage received. Of course, atropine was the most dangerous of the three, given the low dosage required to produce extreme effects.

Josefson walked upstairs with his evidence to show Harry Savage what he had discovered, but what he found was an empty bed and a weeping nurse. Now things were different. It was murder. While he was grateful he himself had been spared, he was furious that a fellow physician had done such a thing. He set out toward the police department to find Officer Masters.

Upon hearing the results of the test, the policeman nodded his head sadly. "I figgered it would come to that. I sent a telegram to the Charleston Medical Society. Their response came back just thirty minutes ago. They say the only Doctor James Madison they know of died five years ago in what they called suspicious circumstances."

October 18, 1878—"Yes, Harry Savage was a gambler, but he was also one of the best of the fighters against the fever. Harry was neither saint nor martyr, but he had some of the qualities out of which saints and martyrs are made—bravery of spirit and kindness of heart." Chattanooga Times

Thomas J. Carlile, the mayor of Chattanooga, was forty-five years old, a distinguished fellow with brown hair and eyes, a liberal mustache, and a sparse goatee. He was tall, thin, and well-liked by his constituents. Over the course of the epidemic, he had labored as hard as anyone to protect his city. And finally, in the latter half of October, Chattanooga was beginning to heal.

On the morning of the 19th, he and three friends were playing pool in the clubroom adjacent to the headquarters of the Citizens Relief Committee. Midway through their game, Carlile laid down his cue, squeezed his head between his hands, and said, "*Boys, I don't believe I ever felt so bad in all my life*." One of his friends volunteered to take him home, then fetch a doctor; but the mayor waved him off. "*We have a committee meeting at two o'clock, but if I go home I shall have to lie down, and if I lie down, I'm afraid I'll not get up again.*"

His friends, Jesse Hill, Robert Morrison, and A.J. Gahagan, looked at him with a mutual feeling of dread. "*Come, go with me, and let's have lunch so I won't go to bed before the meeting.*" They all went to lunch together, with his friends keeping an eye on the mayor, all trying their best not to risk unnecessary exposure to his illness. After the relief committee meeting was over, Carlile sought them out in front of the headquarters. "*Boys, I can't tell you how much I appreciate your friendship. Now I'm going home and get to bed.*"

The third day from this occurrence, his three friends met again, this time to escort the mayor's body to the cemetery. Thomas Carlile was among the last of his citizens to perish from the yellow fever in the city. Although there were some twenty people still listed as sick with the fever, the epidemic was essentially over in Chattanooga.

(*Author's note:* I found three completely different statistics for the number of those who died of yellow fever in Chattanooga—140, 193, and 366. Even the list of 193 deaths in Keating's *A History of the Yellow Fever* does not include the names of some people who should be on the list, such as Harry Savage. The *Chattanooga Times* reports the number should be 366, and it may be that some of the difference can be attributed to the local paper also including the deaths of patients who were affected early in the epidemic, but undoubtedly misdiagnosed or undiagnosed by local physicians. So I don't know what the true number is. Chattanooga's newspaper also stated that the city's population had been reduced to an estimated 1,800 citizens due to the panic and exodus after the first cases were finally announced. So 693 cases and 366 deaths are considerable numbers when compared to a remaining population of only 1,800.)

October 19, 1878—"The physicians of Cincinnati call attention to the poisoning of the Ohio River, especially at Pittsburg, Wheeling, Cincinnati, Evansville, and Louisville, with the contents of sewers, into which pours a steady stream of excreta from the privies and water closets of those places. So it is also along the Mississippi River, the upper part of which is thickly studded with cities and towns. We here in Memphis drink and bathe, and wash our clothes in this accumulated nastiness. The water of the Mississippi today stinks worse than some privies, and yet that is what tens of thousands use for drinking, washing, and cooking here in Memphis."

"Yesterday it was announced at the 6th Ward supply depot that a large number of colored men could get immediate employment at a cotton shed on Shelby Street. Three men agreed to go to work, but the others, numbering nearly a hundred, remained to draw rations in the usual style."

"Mr. Edison's reported invention of the electric light bulb, whereby he proposes to substitute electricity for gas, has created a panic among gas men. Those of New York are whistling to keep up their courage, and they try to pooh-pooh the promises of the great electrician. But those promises will be fulfilled, just as certain as day follows night." Memphis Daily Appeal

Chapter 34
Blood-letting

Chattanooga, Memphis, and points between

The morning of October 20th found Fannie Lester on the west-bound Memphis & Charleston Line. She felt her work in Chattanooga was essentially complete, and her next assignment, according to the Howards, should be back in Memphis, where the epidemic was still not under control. She had talked to Dr. Saul Josefson the evening before, telling him she wanted to travel back by herself "to do some thinking." Although obviously surprised, mixed with no small amount of disappointment, he had not pushed the issue. For that she was grateful.

Her thinking session was not going so well, as there were questions she could not begin to answer. She was forced to admit to herself she had been attracted to Harry Savage. How could she reconcile those feelings with what she also felt for Josefson? Did it mean she didn't care enough about Josefson? And if so, what had she felt for Savage? Was she so shallow that she could convince herself she cared for two men at the same time? Had she confused simple affection for a patient with something deeper? After all, wasn't it well known that Savage was a well-practiced ladies' man who could wrap a girl around his finger without too much effort?

Fannie acknowledged only to herself that she was attractive, so that very well could have been all that was required to ignite Harry's side of the so-called affection. He'd certainly possessed a lopsided grin that was very appealing, and maybe he'd reminded her more than a little of her devilish Uncle Sean. Or perhaps it had been because they came from similar backgrounds, and neither of them had any intention of pretending they were something they weren't. But was that all it took for her to be so easily swayed?

What would be the outcome of Josefson telling his family that he wanted to bring a Catholic into the family? She had no desire to come between Saul and his parents, but she could definitely understand the dynamics involved. If her own family had been part of the equation, things would have gotten ugly on her side, as well. Saul was a highly educated man. On the other hand, she had dropped out of the sixth grade. Besides the epidemic, what exactly did they have in common? Surely he would quickly get bored with her.

What would Saul think when it was eventually revealed that she was no longer virtuous? Surely a physician would know these things. Was there any resolution besides simply telling him the truth?

And then there was her newfound career. Although there was an overwhelming sense of helplessness where yellow fever was concerned, she actually liked being a nurse. In fact, she was proud to be a nurse. It made her feel good to help people who were in dire straits. But would nursing be as compelling during normal times, after the epidemic was past? Would she feel the same about the profession when the complaints were mundane problems like colic, poison ivy, rheumatism, and the grippe? However, it certainly couldn't be as mind-numbingly boring as being a chambermaid.

How would Saul feel about her continuing her vocation? Indeed, how would any man feel about that, unless he was the kind of fellow who was satisfied to sit idly by and feed off the work of others? Maybe she didn't want a husband who was happy to have her work. Then again, maybe she didn't want a husband who wouldn't let her work. Was the setting of an epidemic appropriate to even consider making a decision about what she wanted out of life, let alone who she might live with for the rest of that life?

At the end of her sixteen-hour train ride, she had not answered a single question on her list—her list had only gotten longer.

October 20, 1878—"From a Collierville correspondent—We had great hopes that the fever had exhausted itself in our town. The number of people remaining in our city after the first

alarm is estimated at 125 citizens. When 100 of them had fallen ill, we hoped the beast would have been stayed, but as our populace begins to return to the city, if we have no frost in the next few days, we fear none will escape the disease."

"From a Germantown correspondent—Of all the towns in West Tennessee, none have suffered in morbidity in proportion to population greater than this village. When the first case fell on September 12th, the town was almost depopulated by the 13th, not over 75 citizens, white and colored, remaining. Out of this number, some 60 have had the fever, 37 of which have proved fatal, and 12 to 15 are still sick." Memphis Daily Appeal

October 20, 1878—"Reports received by the Surgeon General of the Marine Hospital Service: New Orleans—89 cases and 36 deaths in last 24 hours, total 14,182 cases and 3,625 deaths. Vicksburg—32 deaths in city, 64 deaths in county in last week, total 1,074 deaths in city/county. Holly Springs—1,117 cases, 285 deaths to date, currently about 200 cases under treatment. Grenada—Total deaths to date 327 in city and county. Hernando, Mississippi—137 cases and 56 deaths total to date. Chattanooga—101 cases and 30 deaths this week, 268 deaths total. Brownsville, Tennessee—844 cases and 212 deaths. Baton Rouge—2,170 cases, 229 deaths to date. Memphis —3,892 total deaths to date." New Orleans Picayune

October 20, 1878—"The sheriffs of Sabine, Rice, and Hays counties in Kansas report attacking a rendezvous of a gang of train robbers with a strong posse about 200 miles west of Kansas City, early yesterday morning. They captured Mike Rourke, leader of the gang and a notorious desperado. They also wounded Dan Dement, who escaped along with three other gang members, but the posse started in pursuit at once, headed south toward Fort Dodge. It is believed Mike Rourke's capture will break up one of the strongest and most desperate bands of thieves and robbers ever organized." Chicago Daily Tribune

Memphis

When she spied John Johnson walking up the drive to the Canfield Orphanage, Emilie Christophe was surprised by the impulse she had to run out and give him a hug. Of course, she resisted such a foolish thing, but still, she wondered where that unexplainable feeling had come from.

As a more acceptable alternative, she met him at the front door. The second surprise was that he seemed to have just as big a smile on his face as she did when he saw her. They walked together to the rear of the building, where Ruthie and Leisha were playing with half a dozen other children. Once again, there were tears and squeals of delight accompanying the reunion.

Johnson spent a couple of hours with his girls. Although he was still unable to take them back home, at least he made the promise that the day would come someday soon. There was no doubt the worst of the epidemic was past, but it still was not at an end. Likewise, he wasn't sure if the Negro police would be retained once the epidemic was over. If he had to guess, he imagined that the whites would be reinstated as soon as they were well enough to go back to work. Hell, they'd probably rehire the ones who'd run away when the epidemic first started. Despite his hopes for equal recognition, he worried that maybe the Negro police were nothing more than a desperate experiment.

Before beginning the long walk back to the city, he sought out Emilie. "My girls 'pear to be gettin' along real fine. I cain't tell you how much that means to me."

"I don't get to spend as much time with them as I'd like, but we manage to see each other at least once a day, usually at bedtime."

"They told me you was quite a storyteller."

She laughed. "I'm just telling them the same stories my mother told me when I was a girl."

"Looks to me like you'd be a real good mama yourself."

She smiled. "I'm really going to miss those two when they're gone."

"What do you intend on doin' when this here epidemic is done?"

"I made some promises to people who died with the fever, to give messages to their families. So I'll need to go back south again, at least for a little while. I've got a grandmother in New Orleans. But I haven't decided whether to go back there or not." She paused. "She's not the easiest person to live with."

Johnson cleared his throat, fidgeting with a stick. "What would you think about bein' a full-time nurse and teacher for my girls?"

Emilie frowned at him. "Why would they need a full-time nurse?"

Johnson fumbled around, doing his best to concentrate on making it come out right. "They know you, and like you a lot. I know they'd be comfortable with you." He paused to try and adjust his approach. "They need a woman's touch. It's for sure that I can't do the things you can do. Shoot, I don't even know no stories."

"Aren't you just looking for a full-time housekeeper to look after the girls while you're at work?" Johnson turned his hat around several times, unable to come up with a response. Emilie pressed her lips together. "Mr. Johnson, let's be honest with one another. You just lost your wife a month ago. From what I could tell, you loved her very much." She noticed a large tear on Johnson's cheek, but she kept going because it needed to be said. "I know you want your girls to come back home, and you're trying to figure out a way for that to happen. But I don't believe you're ready for a full-time nurse, or housekeeper, or whatever you might call it. Nobody could take Marissa's place right now. Maybe you should let the girls stay here at Canfield for a little longer. That might give you time to figure out not only what Ruthie and Leisha need, but what you want yourself."

"I wish I could talk to Marissa—mebbe see what she thinks about this whole thing."

Emilie nodded her head, though not without a tinge of regret. "I think you've just confirmed my point. Marissa is still too much a part of your life to try and start something else right now."

Fannie's first assignment when she returned to Memphis was within two blocks of her flat in the Pinch. When she arrived at the residence, she was met at the door by a man of fifty-odd years who was as wrinkled as someone who might have reached the century mark. He was obviously blind in his left eye, as it was opaque as a quart of milk. As a result, he held his head about thirty degrees to the left so he could concentrate on her with his good eye.

She had never seen a man wear an earring before, but this old codger possessed one made of an old Spanish piece of eight which hung from his left ear by a copper wire. The coin was composed of a full ounce of silver, and over the years the additional weight had stretched his earlobe so that it hung at least an inch lower than the other. This simply added to his angled appearance. He looked her over with an expression as though he had just bit into an unripe persimmon. "What might ye want, missy?"

Fannie tore her eyes away from the earring. "The Howards sent me here to nurse a Minnie Fitzpatrick."

"'Tis a slight misunderstandin', missy. I tole the young doctor we had no need of a nurse here."

"Are you Mr. Fitzpatrick?"

"'Tis I himself, Finn Fitzpatrick. I'd be the father of Minnie. Reckon I can do all the nursin' she might require."

"Mr. Fitzpatrick, I know it probably doesn't matter to you, but you don't have to pay for my services. The Howards pay my salary."

His eyes lit up a bit, but then he thought more about it. "I s'pose you'll be eatin' our vittles whilst yer in this house?"

"You can obtain rations for all three of us at the commissary for this ward, Mr. Fitzpatrick. It won't cost you a penny."

The eyes glowed a bit brighter. "Where might ye expect to sleep? We ain't got but the two beds in the house."

"I'll make a pallet beside Minnie's bed."

"Well, as long as ye'll not be eatin' all the vittles nor expect a bed, I 'spect you kin stay—at least fer a day er so."

Fannie made a quick survey of what passed for a kitchen, then stepped into the bedroom to take a look at her patient, who had a filthy sheet drawn up to her chin. Minnie was probably no more than a year or two younger than Fannie herself. In truth, the two of them resembled one another enough to have been confused as sisters. Minnie, however, was very pale, had a bit of fever, and her face was covered with a pimply rash, which she had obviously been vigorously scratching. Several places appeared to be infected. "I'm your new nurse, Minnie. My name is Fannie Lester. Tell me, how long have you been ill, and what kind of medication have you taken?"

"I took sick four days ago with a headache. I ached all over, particularly my neck and shoulders. It felt like I had a fever. Papa gave me some castor oil."

"Have you been drinking anything?"

"Not too much."

When Fannie pulled back the covers to see if the rash was also present on her arms and legs, she spied a very dirty bandage wrapped around her wrist. When she unwound the wrapping on the girl's arm, she found the remains of two nasty cuts on the inside of her wrist. "What happened here, Minnie?"

It took a moment for the girl to respond. Her voice trembled when she finally spoke. "Papa bled me."

Fannie did not comment to the girl on the advisability of this old-time practice, but reserved the question for her father when she emerged from the bedroom. "Mr. Fitzpatrick, I'll need you to get a few things from the Howards' infirmary. We'll need ten pounds of ice, a pint of whiskey..."

He interrupted her. "Whiskey? I don't truck with whiskey no more. Seen it do too many bad things."

"The whiskey is not to drink. We'll mix it with the ice to sponge her off and help lower her fever."

"You ain't a drunkard yerself, is you?"

She laughed. "No, Mr. Fitzpatrick. Let me finish the list. I need the makings for some beef or chicken broth, some iodine tincture, a bottle of Beef, Iron, and Wine Elixir, some clean bandages, two blankets, and a sheet."

"Is some o' that fer her arm?"

"Yes, Mr. Fitzpatrick. That cut on her arm is hot to the touch and I'm sure it's infected. I'm going to clean up the cut and saturate it with iodine. There will be no more bloodletting while I'm in this house. She needs all the blood she can get to gain her strength back."

"Why, I seen many a man get bled on board ship runnin' twixt Charleston and Portsmouth. Warn't no doctor fer over three thousand miles o' ocean. Sometimes it worked, sometimes it didn't. Either way, 'tis better'n the medicine these so-called doctors is usin' fer this here fever."

"We'll not be using any more medicine except for the Beef, Iron, and Wine, which is to help rebuild her blood. We're going to concentrate on getting her stronger. Right now she's very weak, and some of that is due to her blood loss."

October 22, 1878—"Surgeon General John Woodworth, of the Marine Hospital Service, has appointed Colonel Harder, sanitary engineer, of New Orleans, on the national commission to inquire into the cause and spread of yellow fever. The commission of seven nationally prestigious men will visit New Orleans, Vicksburg, Grenada, Memphis, and perhaps other places afflicted with the disease, with Colonel Harder inquiring especially as to the sanitary condition and drainage of those cities."

"Policeman J. Johnson, colored, is the right man in the right place. He proved his efficiency on Sunday by silencing a couple of loud-mouth profaners, who were making the atmosphere in a street car hideous with their blasphemies. Johnson has a reverence for the Sabbath, as well as respect for 'polite company'." Memphis Daily Appeal

There was a farewell dinner that evening for the surviving members of the Howard Association. During the address by R.W. Mitchell, Medical Director of the Howards, he called out the names of those members who had so nobly given their lives for the people of Memphis. *"I am sadly daily reminded of those who fell by our sides in the darkest moments of our dreadful and deadly strife. They have passed beyond the reach of temporal praise or gratitude. They have gone to their reward, higher, more priceless and imperishable than any man can bestow; and yet they have not gone beyond the reach of our recollection and love."*

"Twenty-nine Howard physicians passed away here, and seven more are now extremely ill. Beyond a shadow of a doubt, we know none of you volunteers did this to draw attention to yourselves. Perhaps you recall Doctor W.L. Coleman, who came to Memphis in early September from his home in San Antonio. He labored on behalf of the sick here for six weeks, and when he returned to his home last week, a public reception was planned to honor him. But Coleman would have none of it. I received a copy of the letter he sent to the organizers of that reception. It bears reading. *'I did not go to Memphis to gain honor or glory or reputation—but simply for humanity's sake. I deserve no honor for simply doing my duty. There were braver men and women in Memphis than I am.'"*

The audience was completely quiet for a full thirty seconds before the applause started, and when it began, it built quickly until it was deafening. Dr. Mitchell was finally able to continue. "Before your very eyes, you have seen entire families pass away, one by one, in quick procession to the grave. What you have witnessed can scarcely be described, but what you have done and endured will need no language to be perpetuated in the hearts of this people. Despite Doctor Coleman's humble letter, I here acknowledge that I am in the presence of heroes."

Within two days, Minnie Fitzpatrick was recovering well, and Fannie had every intention of leaving her with her father and checking in with the Howards for another assignment. However, her plans were put on hold that morning with the sudden decline of Finn Fitzpatrick. His symptoms identified him in the early fever stage of the disease, and so Fannie decided to prolong her stay. She made herself a short list, then said to Minnie, "I'll be gone an hour or so to pick up some medicine and ice for your father, and some provisions for you. He should be fine until I return."

When Fannie re-entered the Fitzpatrick home, the girl was hollering at the top of her lungs. "Don't you leave me, Papa! Don't you leave me!"

Fannie found the two of them on the floor, the old man lying on his back, and Minnie, in a panic, trying to hold a bandage to his neck. Both of them were covered in blood, and it was still spurting from a wound in his neck, although with much less enthusiasm than it must have shown a few minutes previous. Finn Fitzpatrick was still as he could be and gray as dirty dishwater.

Fannie took the bandage from Minnie and tried to put enough pressure on his neck to stop the bleeding, but did not have any more success. She spoke to Fitzpatrick, but got no response. His milky eye stared back at her. "What happened, Minnie?"

"He decided to bleed himself. He wanted to do it before you got back, as he knew you wouldn't allow it. Instead of cutting his wrist, he said that would take too long, and you would surely catch him at it, so he thought he should cut a bigger blood vessel. I think he just intended to nick himself with his razor, but I guess he cut too deep."

"Does your mother live here in town, Minnie?"

The girl looked away, realization of just how dire the situation was beginning to dawn on her. "She died about ten years ago, tryin' to have another baby. Pa and I are all the kinfolks we got, except some I never met in Ireland, and truth be told, I don't have any idea where to find them."

The blood had stopped running through her fingers. There was no more pulse. "I'm so sorry, Minnie. He has bled himself to death. We'll need to talk to the Howards about finding you a place to live." Fannie closed both good and bad eyes with her fingertips.

Chapter 35
Three Conversations

Memphis

Emilie asked for a day off, catching a ride back to the city with a wagon sent out by the Citizens Relief Committee to resupply the orphan home. It was her first trip back to Memphis in a month, and she was surprised to see several businesses open which had previously been shuttered. Although there had been a couple of cold nights, she had seen no evidence of a hard frost, and had her doubts that people coming back into the city were out of danger. Despite the influx of people, Emilie couldn't help but notice the prevalence of widows' weeds among the pedestrians. All the black clothing served as a sobering reminder of the power and widespread impact of the epidemic.

Emilie had converted to her civilian clothing. Again a first for the last month, but she did not want to get sidetracked by the Howards before she reached her destination. The walk from Court Square to Fort Pickering took the best part of a half hour, and she arrived around noon.

As she stood in front of that part of the barracks which had been home to the Johnson family, she removed the locket from her pocket and placed it around her neck. Although she would never be accustomed to the result of that action, she concentrated very hard on hearing only the voice she sought from among the multitude that cried out to her.

"Why hasn't my husband brought our daughters home?"

"He promises to do that soon, Marissa, but the epidemic is not over yet."

“Why does he need to wait on the end of the epidemic?”

“I believe he intends to keep working as a policeman. And he can’t figure out how to care for the girls while he’s at work.”

“For the life o’ me, I cain’t understand why he’s so dead set on bein’ a policeman for those white folks. If he’s not gonna be at home with the girls, why don’t he just hire someone to stay with them?”

“He’s thought of that, but he wants the girls to be happy with whoever stays with them. Not only that, Ruthie is going to be starting school in a few months, so Leisha will be home by herself during the day. He wants to know what you think about the whole situation. He still is dependent on you to help him make decisions, and he’s almost lost without you. What kind of advice can you give him?”

“What makes you think he gonna believe you talked to me?”

“Maybe if you told me something that only the two of you know about?”

“Well, we argued over leavin’ his home-place north o’ here in Drummonds. He wanted to stay, and I wanted to come to Memphis.” There was a pause. “You kin tell him I’m dreadful sorry ’bout that.”

“That sounds convincing. What do you want me to tell him?”

“Maybe he needs to put away that foolishness of being a policeman. Maybe he needs to go back to fishing for a living. At least he’d be home nights.”

“I think he wants to continue with the police. He feels like he’s making a contribution to the city. Besides, if he’s fishing all day long, that really doesn’t change his problem of leaving the girls alone.”

“Thet city ain’t never done nothin’ fer us. He needs to ’member that.”

“Marissa, what would you say if John was to get married again?”

“Married? Dammit, I’m just barely in the ground. Ain’t even cold yet.” The voice paused for a few moments. “I always figgered he had deeper feelin’s than that. Least he could do would be wait long enough to be decent ’bout it. Let the girls get used to it, too. Maybe you could make sure he don’t just pick some floozy thet wants what little money he got, and not care nothin' 'bout my girls."

Dr. Josefson found Fannie Lester in the Peabody Hotel, assigned to two sick physicians and three nurses. "You're hard to catch up to, Fannie. I got back just yesterday. The Howards said you were working in the Pinch, but when I got there this morning, nobody answered the door."

"I finished there just yesterday. It was another sad situation. The Howards are sending the surviving daughter out to the Canfield orphanage. She's really too old to be treated like an orphan, but all her family is dead. Hopefully they'll put her to work out there and give her a place to stay."

Josefson cleared his throat. "Did you have an opportunity to think about whatever was troubling you?"

"Yes, but I can't say I made much progress."

"Can I help?"

"Actually, I suppose you're a big part of the problem."

He grinned, then, seeing her face, he got serious. "Well, then, will you talk to me about it?"

"A few weeks ago, you said you wanted to spend more time with me when the epidemic was over."

"Nothing about that has changed since then."

"While this epidemic has been going on, the two of us have had plenty to talk about. But what happens later? You have degrees from two colleges. I didn't finish grammar school. How could you possibly find me interesting?"

"Actually, we've got a great deal to talk about. I know very little about you, about what you think, about what things interest you, how you feel about children, what makes you mad, what makes you sad, what makes you glad. What do you want from life? We could talk for twenty years and not catch up."

"The main concern I have—and I've tried to think about it from two directions. What if we start seeing a lot of each other, and I decide I can't get along without you. Theoretically speaking, of course. So then you go to your parents to seek their permission, and they say no. All of a sudden, I'm in a bad spot. I've developed all these feelings for you, but then your parents step in and forbid the whole thing."

Josefson tried to speak up, but she wouldn't be sidetracked. "On the other hand, what if you go to your parents first to ask permission, and they say no? Then you've gotten your family upset over a situation that might not even exist. I just don't see a good outcome for us."

"You're assuming two things. First, that their answer is going to be no, and second, that I'm just going to do what they say, no matter what my feelings—our feelings, are for each other. You're too important to me to allow anybody else, including my mother and father, to make that decision."

"I would never want to come between you and your family."

"I'm thankful you feel that way. But the relationship between a husband and wife is more important than that between a man and his parents. Besides, I'm twenty-seven years old, and I don't need a parent telling me how to feel, or what I can feel, let alone who I can have feelings for."

"It will probably be easier for you if we just go our separate ways."

"My parents and my sister are supposed to be arriving Wednesday afternoon on the train. They've spent the last two months in Baltimore, staying with old friends. Why don't the two of us go by to see them the next evening?"

"Maybe you should give them time to get used to the idea first?"

"Fine. I'll tell them about you day after tomorrow when their train comes in. They can get used to the idea before we go to their house the next night."

"That's not what I meant."

"If you look me in the eye right now and tell me you don't care about me, I'll leave you alone. Otherwise, we've got a date Thursday evening."

October 23, 1878—"A meeting was held at Avery Chapel yesterday to consider the interests of the colored orphans of Memphis and vicinity."

"Of the old Memphis police force of 41 men, there are presently only 9 on duty. Thank God for the colored policemen who have stepped forward to protect our city."

"From a correspondent in Springdale, Mississippi—If this plague is directed by Divine Providence as a scourge upon his

people for their rebellion and wickedness, there is no telling when it will end. In the past 100 years, never before has such panic, death, and destruction been known on this continent. This scourge must be a parasite like smallpox, measles, typhoid, and whooping cough. It has a germ and we may call it a parasite; the atmosphere is its best propagator in miasma districts. If not, how can the germs be carried in articles of merchandise and into an area that previously was clear of miasma?—Dr. F.G. Shipp" Memphis Daily Appeal

Early Wednesday morning, Fannie was making her trek to the Peabody Hotel when she saw John Johnson on the corner of Third and Union Streets. He spied her as well and doffed his policeman's cap when she got closer.

"I believe I saw your name in the paper a couple of days ago, Mr. Johnson. Congratulations."

"Thank you, Nurse Fannie. Wasn't much to it."

"They don't generally put things in the paper if there wasn't much to it. By the way, something has been bothering me ever since seeing you the first time at your home in Fort Pickering. I knew I had seen you somewhere before, but for the life of me couldn't remember. Then a few weeks ago, when you came to my rescue when that poor, tortured soul ran out in the street shooting at me without a stitch of clothes on, I finally realized where we had seen each other."

The smile on Johnson's face disappeared, displaced by dismay—shock—fear? He couldn't have accurately described it.

Fannie continued. "I didn't make the connection until I saw that terrible scar on your back. And then I remembered." She paused, waiting for him to speak.

He prayed she wouldn't remember the exact details. "I don't rightly remember when that was myself, Nurse Fannie."

"It was early in August, late one evening down on the waterfront. You were in a rowboat, and you had a passenger."

"I don't recollect."

"Your passenger was a white man. He appeared to be pretty sick. You helped him out of your boat, and that's when I saw the scar on your back."

Johnson shook his head. "I don't remember none o' that."

"I'm betting you picked him up out at the quarantine station. Are you sure you don't remember?"

He made no attempt to deny anything else. "Have you told anybody else 'bout what you seen?"

She suddenly realized the potential threat behind the question and decided to lie. "Yes, I have."

"What do you figger on doin' about it?"

"I don't know yet. What would have happened this summer if you hadn't brought that man into the city?"

He shook his head. "He just tole me he needed to see a doctor. I didn't have no idea what was wrong with him."

"Why wouldn't you have had an idea? After all, he was at the quarantine station."

"I never took time t' figger that, Nurse Fannie." That time, he knew what showed in his eyes was sadness.

October 24, 1878—"Tomorrow the Citizens Relief Committee will issue its last ration and close its good work. The food sent to us by every state in the union has been dispensed without favor or affection. Many of the Committee have died of the scourge, and yet another has always stepped forward to take their place. Coolness and courage were manifested by those men every single day for the benefit of the poor and destitute."

"We hear from the planter who advertised for workers to pick cotton or pull corn on the island above Memphis that he had two workers step forward. As rations will no longer be distributed after tomorrow, we recommend the slackers go back to work."

"Notice to the policyholders of Connecticut Mutual Life Insurance: As soon as it is safe for us to return to the city, we will give our personal attention to getting up Proofs of Death of those policyholders who died, and forward the same to our home office for payment to the beneficiaries." Memphis Daily Appeal

John Johnson returned from his work shift on Thursday morning and was surprised to find a letter stuck in his door. He couldn't remember the last time he'd received any mail.

He opened it, but after a half hour of studying it, could not figure out what the missive said. He had always depended on Marissa for whatever needed reading, so he finally decided to ask Officer McNair to decipher it for him. He found his partner early that evening, before his shift started.

Dear Mr. Johnson,

I have decided to depart Memphis this Sunday. I'll be leaving on the morning train on the Mississippi and Tennessee Line, headed back to New Orleans. I made several promises to people along the way which I swore to keep. Hard as it will be, I'll be saying my goodbyes to Ruthie and Leisha on Saturday morning. If you're in the neighborhood of the Memphis depot, perhaps you'll have time to stop by Sunday morning before I go, as I would like to see you again. As a matter of fact, I have an important message for you.

Sincerely,
Emilie Christophe

McNair looked expectantly at Johnson. "So have you got yourself a new girl, or what?"

"No, no—she's the nurse who's been lookin' after my girls." He looked perplexed. Did she really want to see him again, or was it something to do with a message? "Say, McNair, did that letter say what kinda important message she's talkin' about?"

As if the letter wasn't enough to worry about, Johnson had been stymied over what to do about his recent conversation with Fannie Lester. She obviously remembered the entire scenario from that night on the first of August. If she had a mind to, all that was necessary would be a short discussion with Chief Athey. Not only would his police career be over, he could very well be charged with a crime. Far worse than that, what would happen to him if word got out that he was the one responsible for the whole epidemic in Memphis? The entire population of the city might be ready to string him up. Then where would his girls be? They might end up without a mama *and* a papa. He definitely had to ponder it.

Chapter 36
I Haven't Forgotten Who I Am

Memphis

October 25, 1878—"The Nashville American *offers good advice when it says, 'This is no time, and Tennessee is no place, for a third party. Let those who have been beguiled and deluded by any such political nonsense, stop, reflect, and come back to the Democratic Party. There will be but two parties in the contest in 1880. Let all those who do not expect to act within the Republicans, come into full fellowship with the Democrats.'"*

"As a precaution against students bringing yellow fever here from infected districts, the Board of Trustees have postponed the opening of the fall semester at the University of Mississippi until November 21, 1878." Memphis Daily Appeal

Fannie and Josefson were on the way to meet with his parents when she stopped under a hazy street lamp. "I need to tell you about something. I was a little bit scared yesterday when I talked to John Johnson, the colored policeman, on the street." She told him about seeing his tattoo, finally remembering their first meeting, and then the confrontation of the day before and the unease she'd felt.

"Maybe we need to go to the police."

"Not right now. I think he just did something extremely foolish. There was no way he could have known what would happen as a result. If we reported it, people might rise up and lynch the man. I know they'd like to have someone to blame for all that's happened. For sure, quite a few folks in this city would prefer the guilty party be colored!" She paused, looking at Saul to see his reaction to what came next. "And while we're talking about this, I have to admit I'm ashamed of my part in the whole thing."

"Whatever do you mean?"

"I've been asking myself, why didn't I step forward and report what happened to the police? I can't imagine why I simply watched the arrival of that rowboat—realizing that the passenger was sick—and still did nothing about it. Am I not just as guilty as Johnson?"

"You couldn't have known where the boat was coming from, let alone what was going to happen to the city. The thing I'm most concerned about is the underlying threat it sounds like he made. Please let me know if he says anything else to you. He may feel like you've got him cornered, and his only solution is to get rid of the witness. I don't think I could stand it if anything happened to you."

She patted his arm. "I'm not worried about that, and you shouldn't either."

He shook his head. "Easier said than done!"

They paused on the doorstep of his parents' home. "Don't be nervous in there, Fannie. Just be yourself."

"I wouldn't know any other way to be." She looked at his apprehensive expression and sniffed. "Maybe you should take your own advice."

Four rooms on the south side of the Josefsons' home had been set aside as waiting rooms and examination rooms for the doctor's practice. The remainder of the large house on Fourth Street was occupied by the family. While not as ornate as some of the homes in Victorian Village where Fannie had worked, the living quarters in the Josefson home were certainly impressive.

Fannie and Josefson were met at the door by his father, Samuel, who escorted them into the parlor to his wife, Ruth. Saul Josefson's parents were almost exactly the same height. Samuel was certainly not short for a man; however, Ruth would be considered quite tall for a woman. Samuel was sparely built; his wife was not. Samuel wore a full mustache and well-trimmed beard. His wife's hair was very long and piled high on her head, thus making her appear even taller. Fannie studied them both, trying to detect what their thoughts might be related to her presence within their household. Neither of them were giving any obvious hints in their expressions or body language to indicate their opinion.

Just about the time they got settled and glasses of wine were being poured, Josefson's sister, Sarah, entered the room. She was definitely an amalgam of her two parents—tall like her mother, thin like her father, with curly dark hair and a smile which seemed to reach out and embrace Fannie.

Fannie returned the smile. "It's nice to see you again, Sarah. You probably don't remember me, but I was a patient here at the very beginning of the epidemic. I remember being impressed with the way you managed the patients in the clinic. The morning I was here, there must have been fifty or sixty people waiting to be seen. Most of them were convinced they had the fever, and you were trying to weed out the ones who might from the ones who didn't."

"Thanks for noticing, Fannie. I wish my big brother paid attention to those things as well as you did." She smiled again. "Saul tells us you're a nurse, too."

Fannie shook her head slightly. "There's no use me pretending, Sarah." Saul started to interrupt but Fannie waved him off. "No, the truth is I volunteered to be a nurse after the epidemic really caught fire, for two reasons. First, I had already been infected with the fever, so I knew I could be around sick people and not worry about my own safety; second, the pay was better. I never had a stitch of formal training. Anything I learned was because several good nurses and doctors helped me, including your brother."

Sarah's smile got bigger. "From what I heard in the newspapers, there were lots of nurses who volunteered to come here who should have been run out of town. I would imagine your patients were lucky to have you."

Dismissing the current conversation, Ruth Josefson cleared her throat for attention. "Tell us, Fannie, what of your parents?"

"Ma'am, my mother was a laundress and my father was a drayman on the docks. He used to say he came from a family of Irish peat cutters. My mam died four years ago of the cancer, and I haven't see my da since the day of the funeral. I've been told he got drunk and fell into the Mississippi that very afternoon, but whether that's true or not, I couldn't say. His body was never recovered. I've been on my own since that day. Until I turned into a nurse, I was just a chambermaid at the Peabody."

"But what of your father's family—your mother's family?"

"Ma'am, I only know they both had one—back in Ireland. For sure they each had a mam and a pap, but I couldn't tell you who they were. My da was sent over to America during the famine when he was just a boy. He met my mam on the docks in New York City when she arrived about ten years later with her younger brother Sean. The fact is, poor people usually don't know much about family—maybe just one or two generations, but nobody from way back." Fannie paused and looked from Ruth to Samuel Josefson. One thing was for sure—they were paying attention. Ruth's mouth was standing open, while Samuel's wineglass was poised in mid-air as though he was modeling for a sculpture.

Saul examined his shocked parents. "When is the last time you heard someone tell you the whole truth and nothing but the truth?"

Ruth was the first to find her voice. "What about your schooling, Fannie? Of course, you know that Saul had a wonderful education back east."

"Indeed, ma'am. And you should be proud to know he is regarded as one of the very best doctors working for the Howards during the epidemic, even though they came from all over the United States." She shrugged as though the rest of her response meant very little. "As for me, I dropped out of school during the sixth grade to help my mam with her laundry business. You already know I have no formal nurse schooling."

"Tell us about your religious training, Fannie. How firmly are you tied to the Catholic faith?"

"When my mam was alive, she took me to Mass at least once a week. She was very devoted to the church. My da didn't have much use for religion of any sort. But that didn't stop my mam."

"What do you know about the Jewish faith, Fannie?"

"Not very much at all. I know we worship the same God. But I also know I couldn't stop believin' in Jesus and his Holy Mother. I've been prayin' to them my whole life—far too long to quit now."

Ruth looked accusingly at Saul. "Did you know all this?"

Saul shrugged. "Some of it, yes. Some of it, no. But what I heard loud and clear was a young woman who tells the truth, no matter how it might affect her relationship with her potential in-laws. Who you heard was a girl who survived a very hard time and came out of it just fine. I can't help but wonder if I would have done as well if faced with the loss of two parents as a teenager, no money, no chance to continue in school, and no social standing. I seriously doubt it." He looked hard at his parents. "Where do you think you might be if the same thing had happened to you?"

Samuel Josefson looked first at Fannie. "Saul is right about one thing. You've certainly got gumption. And please believe me when I say I truly admire you for it." He then turned to Saul. "You'll get no argument out of me that Fannie is a determined young woman, and I'd wager honest to a fault. But the differences between the two of you are great. In fact, I can't fathom how you two can find enough common ground to hold a marriage together. And that doesn't even begin to include deciding what religion my grandchildren might observe." He glanced back and forth between them, pointedly at his son. "This is a matter that should be taken up at another time, Saul."

Fannie couldn't miss the smug smile on Ruth's face. She stood up, placed her untouched wineglass on the sideboard, and looked straight at Saul while she spoke. "Unfortunately, those were my concerns as well, Mr. Josefson. I can assure you, I haven't forgotten who I am or where I come from. I can't see myself ever forgetting those things. The last thing I'd want would be to come between Saul and his family."

Saul jumped to his feet, quickly positioning himself at her side. "This is definitely not the end of the discussion, Fannie."

Fannie waved Saul aside and took a couple of steps toward the door before turning. "No, Saul, I'll see myself home."

Before she got any further, Saul's sister rushed to her side. Sarah hugged her before whispering in her ear, "Don't let this be the last of it. You're just exactly the person my brother wants and needs."

Fannie smiled at her newfound friend before looking again at the Josefsons. She motioned toward the north to drive her point home. "I just live a few blocks from here, up in the Pinch." She decided to add one more descriptor to emphasize the divide. "Just on the south bank of the Gayoso Bayou."

October 26, 1878—"From a correspondent in Brownsville, Tennessee—Our town is as yet in a bad condition. A great many of our citizens are returning, thinking things are all right, but watch out. Our town has been well taken care of by colored policemen, and our citizens say they shall be paid for their service." (*Author's note:* In the small town of Brownsville, 212 people died of the fever. Included in that number was Mr. Cog Grove, who was deserted by his nurse when he was in a delirium. He unfortunately turned a coal oil lamp over, set the house on fire, and burned to death.)

"All volunteer physicians with the Howard Association on duty within the city limits are relieved of duty after today."

"The Citizens Relief Committee closed their commissary yesterday, and will not make further distributions. The total rations they supplied during the epidemic being 681,982."

"Preaching at the Central Baptist Church will begin once more on Sunday morning at eleven AM by the pastor, Dr. Landrum."

"From a correspondent in Water Valley, Mississippi—In our small town, we have experienced 49 deaths from the yellow fever, among them 19 railroad men." Memphis Daily Appeal

J.M. Keating gazed from one face to another in the newspaper office. "I saw something this morning that sort of illustrates what we've all been through. Maybe some of you are familiar with the two little bootblacks who had their stands on either side of Court Square before the epidemic. Neither one of them could be over nine or ten years old. Well, back in August, one of them took the fever, and the other one decided he would stay by his side and help to nurse him. This he did until he got sick himself and was removed to another infirmary.

"One of the boys was told that his friend had passed away. In fact, neither one of them thought their friend was still alive until this morning, when they both showed up at their usual places around the Square. Well, the two little fellows ran to each other and embraced on the street—right in the middle of all the commerce going on around them. With their arms encircling one another, the boys cried their eyes out. I don't have to tell you that quite a few tears were shed by passersby as well.

"Our whole city has had a hard go of it. In walking up and down Main Street over the last couple of days, several times I've seen grown men come up to one another, who obviously hadn't seen each other in quite a while. It looked as though they were having a difficult time meeting the other's gaze, oftentimes being unable to even speak, and even breaking into tears themselves when they became overcome by emotion.

"Indeed, I had to fight against my own tears when I entered this room just now and saw each of you. Moode, I don't know what I would have done without you. The two of us never missed a day's work these last ten weeks. Those of you who were here through the most of it—Helms, Broom, Holomon, Bartel—I owe you a great debt as well. The only reason you weren't here every single day was because you were caring for yourselves or your families." He looked at the faces of the other six men who had returned to work. "I hope the rest of you, and your families, have recuperated enough that you are able to come back without fear of a relapse.

"We've been through a terrible ordeal. Nineteen of our employees, and almost as many family members, have gone to rest beyond Jordan's stream. Several are still sick, and we don't know whether some of them will be lost in the days ahead. No matter what we do, this newspaper will never be the same. What's more, our city will never be the same.

"For eight weeks, we've been forced to print only a two-page newspaper, simply because we didn't have the staff here to do more. We're still extremely short-staffed. But let's face facts. The population of our city is much reduced. We will only be able to increase our staff as the city grows. However, in the meantime," he paused for effect, "starting tomorrow, we're going to publish a four-page newspaper again."

There was some foot-stamping, back clapping, and a few huzzahs. They looked at one another with something akin to amazement. The newspaper had survived, and so had they.

October 27, 1878—"Of the 25 employees of the Western Union telegraph office, 11 have died, 9 are convalescing, with only 5 escaping the fever. And of these 5, only Mr. Putnam has been on station throughout the epidemic."

"The news from Bulgaria is alarming. The notables are encouraging extermination of the Mohammedans, and Russia supports special commissions in procuring arms to accomplish same. A great struggle is likely to take place this winter."

"The Supreme Court will next month hear arguments involving the constitutionality of all laws heretofore bearing on the question of polygamy in Utah." Memphis Daily Appeal

Chapter 37
Heading South

Memphis, Grenada, and points south

Emilie had arrived early at the station, thinking that perhaps John Johnson would drop by in time for them to talk for a half hour or so before the train departed. After an unbelievably delayed autumn, they finally were experiencing a very chilly, breezy morning. It was uncomfortably chilly standing on the platform, and she prayed it had gotten cold enough overnight to finally eradicate the fever.

With less than ten minutes before her scheduled departure, she had about given up hope. Perhaps he had not received her letter. Then again, he may have been unhappy at her rather abrupt decision to leave Memphis.

She saw the engineer mounting his engine, then the conductor entered the first passenger car, and finally the brakeman walked down the platform and stepped onto the caboose, signaling in the direction of the engineer. Resignedly, she picked up her two bags, deciding to go ahead and find a seat, then get settled on board. But just at that moment she saw a buggy careening down the street, headed toward the station. Unless she was mistaken, she recognized the passenger.

Surprise, however, did not begin to describe what happened next. Not only did John Johnson alight from the buggy, but he was accompanied by Ruthie and Leisha. If that wasn't enough, Johnson's arms were quickly filled with baggage. The three of them spied her at the same time and rushed to greet her.

The whistle sounded twice, and there was only time for quick hellos before the four of them had to hustle on board. They were still looking for seats when the train jolted forward and began its journey.

Johnson finally let out a whoosh of breath. "I was afraid we weren't gonna make it."

Emilie looked from one to the other of her new travel-mates. "Is somebody going to tell me what's going on?" She looked in Johnson's direction, but he was studiously focusing his entire attention toward the few occupants of the train platform as it disappeared behind them.

Ruthie could always be counted on to render her two cents' worth. "Papa says we're going with you."

Raising her eyebrows in Johnson's direction, Emilie only commented, "Well, it will be nice to travel with my favorite girls."

As they began to exit the city, all three of the Johnsons had their faces glued to the windows, watching the view of the passing countryside. None of them had ever traveled on a train before, and conversation mostly consisted of each one pointing out items of interest along the way. Johnson leaned over and whispered, "We'll talk when the girls take a nap."

Emilie shot him another look, but didn't respond.

The train made brief stops on its way south, until finally at Senatobia, they exited briefly to see if they could obtain a bite to eat. The girls had missed their breakfast in the hurry to depart that morning, so they were happy to locate a nearby grocery. Emilie selected a bottle of milk, a small round of cheese wrapped in cloth, a tin of crackers, four apples, and a pound of roasted peanuts, then stepped to the counter to pay. She was surprised to be greeted by an old friend. "Good morning, missy."

"Mr. Szen, I'm so glad to see you again."

He smiled broadly. "You remember."

"Of course, Mr. Szen. Did the fever miss your town?"

He shook his head. "No, missy. Nine peoples die here. My wife still sick. I think she make it, though."

"I'm sorry to hear that. I hope she gets well soon."

He motioned toward Johnson and the girls. "This your family?"

"No, no." Emilie bent and hugged the two little girls at her side. "But they're really good friends."

"You go back home now?"

"I'm not sure. I have some promises to keep first."

He nodded knowingly. "Only for good, missy, only for good."

Before the train reached Batesville, the girls had dropped off to sleep. Emilie leaned closer to John and whispered, "Do you mind telling me what you're doing on this train?"

Johnson visibly gathered his thoughts before speaking. "I guess you could say two things happened. The main reason was I—we—didn't want to lose you." He looked at her for reaction, but only got a smile in return. "The other thing is, I might be in quite a bit of trouble."

"What does that mean?"

He described the street corner conversation he'd had with Fannie, his particular role in surreptitiously bringing the first fever victim to Memphis, and her veiled threat to report him to the police. He wasn't about to verbalize his crime involving the poisoning of Nurse Nina Payne. He realized speaking about that could never be allowed, no matter how close he might feel to someone.

"Did you resign at the police department?"

"No. I didn't tell a soul what I was going to do. I told the sisters at the orphanage that I'd decided to take the girls back home with me. I didn't even tell my own partner goodbye. So as far as everybody is concerned, I'm still in Memphis."

"Did you consider going to the police chief and telling him what you did?"

"Much as I respect Chief Athey, I couldn't trust him not to arrest me, or even worse, tell folks it was me that started the epidemic." He looked at his hands folded in his lap. "The truth is, I'm guilty. That epidemic was the last thing on my mind when I picked the sick fellah up on the quarantine island. He begged me to take him to town so he could see a doctor. All I could think about was the money he offered to pay me. I know that ain't no excuse, but I don't want to go to jail for it, let alone get my neck stretched."

Emilie looked at him for a full minute before she responded. The signs were definitely there. He was holding something back, not telling her the full story. Perhaps he wasn't ready yet. However, she had no tolerance for half-truths or subterfuge. She decided to give him a little time before a confrontation. But sooner or later, there would have to be a reckoning.

Johnson was uneasy when he saw the way she was looking at him, and found himself staring at her eyes. Had he not noticed before that they were green? Worse, it felt like she was looking inside him. Did she sense he wasn't telling her everything?

He didn't feel like this was the time to mention that when he and the girls were departing their residence in Fort Pickering that morning, he had spied two men in police uniforms not less than fifty yards away from his front door. If he'd had to guess, they'd seemed to be heading in the direction of his address. Like a thunderbolt, it had struck him that they were likely coming for him. He was hopeful they had not seen him and his family departing in the hack, but certainly could not be sure they had not been pursued to the train station. It would be a simple matter to ask the ticket agent where they were headed.

He couldn't help but wonder what the next steps might be if they were indeed after him. Johnson knew he hadn't discussed anything with his neighbors, but he tried to think back over every conversation he'd had with Officer McNair. Surely he'd given no clue that would lead the police to New Orleans.

He forced himself back to the present. "So what is this message you've got for me?"

She considered him again. "It would probably be easier for me to show you rather than explain it to you. We should be arriving in the little city of Grenada in the next little while. I'll need to switch trains there anyway in order to go on to New Orleans." She looked at the sleeping girls. "They should be all right for a couple of minutes. Wait until the other passengers step off this car, then perhaps you'll understand why I had to come back."

As the train slowed to pull off on the Grenada siding, Emilie reached into her pocket, withdrew the locket, and began to affix it around her neck. She looked over at Johnson to be sure he was paying attention. He was.

The two of them made sure the girls were still sleeping, then stepped to the far end of the railcar. As she expected, the voices assaulted her from every direction as soon as the necklace clasp was closed, but she was seeking one in particular. When Colonel Butler P. Anderson finally spoke to her, his question was straightforward. "Nurse, were you able to speak to my wife?"

Emilie glanced toward Johnson before answering. "Yes, Colonel Anderson. I spoke to your wife seven weeks ago in Hernando. I gave her your message just as you requested."

"I can't begin to thank you enough. I was afraid you had forgotten, or maybe you had not been able to find her."

"Actually, I didn't find her. She found me, just like you did. She had her own message for you, Colonel. You see, she died from the fever just two days after you did. Neither of you had any idea that the other had passed away. She wanted me to tell you that she's waiting on you as we speak, in paradise."

"Do you mean to say—?"

"Yes, Colonel. She's there now."

"Then I mustn't keep her waiting any longer. Thank you always."

Emilie turned to Johnson. His eyes were glued to hers.

"Miss Emilie, what do this mean?"

Emilie removed the locket to quiet the voices. "I don't understand it myself. All I know is when I wear the locket, the people who died nearby all try to talk to me. Most of them beg me to help them with some task or some communication they weren't able to complete before they passed on. They just want an opportunity to set things right." She paused for a moment, looking at Johnson. "Sometimes I can actually help them."

"Was you just talkin' to Colonel Anderson, the man who came down here from Memphis and died helpin' these people?"

"Yes. When I left Grenada in September, he had been dead just two days. When I was about to leave Grenada, I placed the locket around my neck. He spoke to me then, and asked me to tell his wife he loved her when I arrived in Hernando. But he didn't know his wife was already dead. I spoke to her in Hernando, and she asked me to come back and put his mind at ease. That's one of the reasons why I'm here today."

"My Lord. I had no idee such a thing could happen. Do y'all tell fortunes and cast spells and the like?"

"No, not me. That would be my grandmother. I have no desire to be any part of those activities."

"Do this have anythin' to do with the message you talked about in your letter?"

"Several times in the past, I have heard you say that you wish you could talk to your wife, particularly when you were tormented with whether or not to keep the girls at the Canfield orphanage. So a few days ago, I went down to Fort Pickering." Johnson was completely focused on what she was saying. "I put on the locket and spoke to Marissa, told her you needed her advice, and she responded."

Johnson's hands suddenly had a tremor which he tried to hide, and his voice shook. "You spoke to her? What did she say?"

"She said you should quit the police force and go back to fishing. She thought that would allow you to bring the girls back home. When I mentioned you felt like you were making a positive impact, she made it clear that Memphis wasn't worth your trouble."

"I've sure heard that before."

"She said you ought not be in a big hurry to get married again—that her body wasn't even cold yet. And she made me promise to warn you not to marry some floozy that just wanted your money—somebody who didn't care about your daughters."

Johnson had a pained look on his face. "I want to believe what you're sayin'. I really do. But is they a chance you've just imagined all this?"

Emilie willed herself to remain calm. "You have every right to be doubtful. Three months ago, I wouldn't have believed this myself. But Marissa did tell me something that might convince you. She told me the two of you had argued about leaving your home in Drummonds and moving to Memphis. She said she wanted to apologize for pushing you to come to Memphis. Apparently she believed neither she nor the girls would have gotten sick if it hadn't been for her begging you to move to the city."

Tears began to run down Johnson's face. He wiped them off as best he could. "I'm sorry fer doubtin' you. I promise you I won't never do that again."

"There's something else you need to consider. You and I both know you're still in love with your wife. Don't do anything until you can make peace with that. If you move too quickly, it's bound to fail." She looked intently at him. "Now then, you've got a decision to make in the next hour and thirty minutes. This train is about to return to Memphis, so if you want to go back, now would be a good time. On the other hand, if you and the girls want to continue heading south, you need to get them and your baggage off this train so you can get tickets for the New Orleans train. While you make up your mind, I've got to hurry over to the post office, and then one more stop."

The little postal facility was deserted save for a single surviving clerk. In the last couple of weeks, as the trains had begun to run again, the town had received several tons of accumulated mail. But with only one employee left standing, a mere fourth of that accumulation had been sorted to date. And with nobody around to make deliveries, the sorted mail simply sat in its piles.

That was only part of the story. An estimated three hundred and fifty of Grenada's citizens had perished. So for those individuals, the mail either needed to be redirected to their surviving family—if such existed—or returned to the sender. With only one employee well enough to work, this would not be resolved quickly.

Emilie approached the harried man behind the counter. "I hope you can help me, sir. I'm looking for the surviving mother of little Mamie Peacock."

"They was only one family o' Peacocks in Grenada. I know the father and the little girl died within a couple days o' one another. Josephine Peacock—that'd be the little girl's mama—moved over to Water Valley to live with her in-laws right after all that."

"I'd like to send a letter to Josephine. The daughter made me promise I'd tell her mother where she was buried. She wanted her mama to come and see her in the cemetery. And I've also got a message for her from her husband."

"I don't know whether she'll ever come back here or not. Lots o' people are gone fer good, I'm afraid. I got no address for Josephine. Just put her name and Water Valley, Mississippi on the envelope, then write 'General Delivery' underneath. She'll be gettin' it one way or t'other."

Emilie's final stop was the orphanage. She wanted to be absolutely sure that Joshua Butler had returned to Grenada to get his son, Exodus. Her inquiry at the front desk was met with a shake of the head. "We haven't heard a word from Mr. Butler—not a single word. That little boy of his asks me almost every day."

"Can I see Exodus?"

"Of course. He hasn't had any visitors since he's been here."

She was back in five minutes, Exodus running ahead of her. Emilie was afraid he'd be terribly disappointed when he realized his visitor was not his father, but just his nurse. Whether he was or not, she'd never know, as he ran up to her and buried his face in her dress, trying to hide his tears. "I knew you'd come back, missus. I knew you wouldn't forget about me."

She hugged him, trying not to cry herself. "I don't think I could ever forget about you, Exodus."

His pleading eyes said it all. "Have you come to take me, missus?" That thought had not entered Emilie's mind when she'd entered the orphanage, and he must have sensed her hesitation. "I can work real hard. I wouldn't never be a bit o' trouble. And I don't eat much."

Tears began to roll down his cheeks again, and then she could feel her own eyes beginning to overflow. Emilie was not ready for his emotion, but was certainly totally unprepared for her own response. She took his hand in hers. "Let's go talk to the lady in charge."

The two of them stood in front of the desk, not really knowing what to expect. Emilie turned to Exodus. "Would you sit down over there so I can talk to this nice lady?

"I wrote to his father in Tupelo about six weeks ago, letting him know that Exodus' mother had passed away, and telling him that his son was here at the orphanage." She lowered her voice further. "His mother told me that Joshua was not much of a father, so I can't say I'm terribly surprised."

"Oh, my. This is just a temporary orphanage. We'll have to find homes for these children one way or another as soon as possible, but there's hardly anybody left in the town to take them."

Emilie was surprised at her own response, but straightened her shoulders resolutely. "Exodus has already found his home."

"He hasn't said a word to any of us. Where is he going?"

"He's going with me. In fact, we're leaving today on the afternoon train."

Emilie returned to the station, doing a fair job of hiding her pleasure that Johnson had gathered the girls and their luggage on the platform, waiting for the arrival of the Chicago, St. Louis, and New Orleans train. At the sight of Exodus, the three of them gathered around, full of questions.

"Is he going with us?"

"Yes. All the way to New Orleans."

"Is this your son?"

"No. But we've known each other a long time, and we're very good friends—isn't that right, Exodus?"

The boy looked at Emilie with eyes still wet with grateful tears, and could only respond by tightly hugging her.

"How'd you get a name like Exodus?"

He wiped his eyes with a ragged sleeve. "My momma told me that I is named after the book in the Bible where all the slaves was set free."

"Is that true, Daddy?"

"I believe it is, Ruthie." Johnson smiled in the boy's direction. "My momma would say that Exodus is a blessed boy."

It was early afternoon before they began the next leg of their journey. Like the girls when they departed Memphis, Exodus sat at the window, transfixed by all that passed by. It wasn't long before the three children were holding animated conversations.

Although the countryside was mostly flat, the rail line's bed and tracks were not exactly level, having been vandalized by local people who had purposely torn up the track bed to prevent access of the fever to their towns in the worst days of the epidemic. In a duplication of what had occurred during the war, some local men had pried loose the rails, set a large fire underneath them, then once they were heated, twisted them around trees. The railroad companies had been forced to spend considerable funds to replace the tracks, but the ride remained quite bumpy, and as a result, the train's speed was slowed considerably.

It was past sundown when Emilie spoke to John again about her further obligations on the trip. "Annandale is the last stop before we get into Jackson. I've got to leave the train there. You and Exodus and the girls should stay on board and go on to New Orleans. As I remember, Annandale is a very small village. There won't be any accommodations there for you."

"Well, don't you reckon we all oughta stay together? Besides, I don't know New Orleans from sic-em. I wouldn't know where to go when we got there."

"All they've got in Annandale is a station platform. There's not even a building at the stop, and it's going to be cold again tonight. These children can't just sleep out in the weather. The four of you should stay on the train. You'll get into New Orleans right after daybreak in the morning. The Vieux Carrè Hotel is owned and occupied by Creoles. It's just a short walk from the train station. I know they take Negro guests. Get yourselves something to eat, then get a room."

"You know people in this Annandale?"

"No. I'll have to find a ride out to the Britton Plantation just north of the little town. I've got a message from one of the Episcopal preachers, Reverend Parsons, who died in Memphis. He asked me to talk to his wife and two sons. They're supposed to be at the plantation."

"When you gonna get to New Orleans?"

"The New Orleans train runs once a day through Annandale. I'll get there twenty-four hours after you do."

Chapter 38
The Power of Peppermint

October 30, 1878—"A Tennessee Democrat has declared that the great generosity showered upon the South by the people of the North obliterates the last trace of bitterness, and binds together North and South more firmly than ever. We are willing to believe these utterances reflect the sentiment that predominates now among southern people. Even Jefferson Davis himself has said as much."

"We are competing successfully with Russia, next to ours the greatest agricultural country in the world. Over the last three years, our exports of bread stuffs into Great Britain were four times that of Russia, even though they have more acres in cultivation."

"The old men who turned gray so suddenly during the absence of their barbers, can now 'fix up,' as the shops are opening again. But the old ones had better hurry, or the town will be full of people before their hair turns black again."

"D. Canale, of No. 8 Madison Street, has returned. While absent he purchased an excellent stock of fruits, wines, liquors, macaroni, mushrooms, and olive oil." Memphis Daily Appeal

Memphis

Saul Josefson finally spied her on the top floor of the Peabody. Obviously, given her choice of clothing, she was still engaged in nursing. Considering the reception she had endured from his parents, Saul was unsure of how he himself might be received, but he was absolutely convinced he was doing the right thing. “Hello, Fannie. I came by yesterday but couldn’t find you. I was hoping you were still here.”

She pushed her hair back. “Oh, I’m still here, but I doubt this infirmary will be open more than a couple more days. It looks like I’ll be a chambermaid again in no time.”

“Actually, that’s one of the things I want to talk about.”

“After the conversation the other night, I thought I might not see you again.”

“Well, I’d be a sorry excuse for a friend if that happened. I want to apologize for you having to sit through that interrogation with my folks.”

“It was pretty much what I expected.”

“You didn’t deserve it, that’s for sure.” He paused for a moment, getting his thoughts back on track. “I realized that night I had become too dependent on my parents, not only by using their home as my clinic, but also feeling like I needed their approval for everything I did.”

“They both appear to be strong-willed.”

“Maybe they were surprised after you left to find out that I am, too. Anyway, I’m moving my clinic out of their house, and have found a location on Court Street, just three blocks from here. Do you suppose you could go over there with me and give me your suggestions about how things should be arranged?”

“What about Sarah? Won’t she help you with that?”

“I guess maybe she could, but I was hoping you would be willing to take a look.”

She started to decline, but something about his eyes changed her mind. “Give me about fifteen minutes. Let me make sure everything is under control in the infirmary.”

It was spitting a cold rain when they exited the hotel, and Fannie almost reversed her decision, at least until Saul pointed at his buggy. “It’s too miserable to walk. Let’s ride over.” It had rained just enough to turn the city streets into a sticky mush, and Fannie was thrilled not to have to walk through it.

She was surprised when Saul stopped his horse in front of the almost new Gaston’s European Hotel and Restaurant. The four-story structure had just been completed in the last year. It was located three blocks north of the Memphis depot, and its restaurant had been well attended by local residents before the epidemic had forced both the hotel and restaurant to temporarily close down. She eyed him suspiciously. "Why are we stopping at a hotel?"

Saul said, "We're only about eight blocks from my parents' home. So my patients won't have much further to travel to reach me here. The hotel is trying to re-open soon, and I've got an opportunity to rent three adjacent rooms on the second floor for a decent price. Come on up and let's take a look. All the rooms have got gas lighting, running water, and porcelain water closets, to boot."

Upstairs, he unlocked the door. "The space is still set up as hotel rooms, so you're going to have to use your imagination, but now is the time to set things just the way we want."

Fannie walked through the rooms, keeping her comments to herself until she had seen it all, then she asked for writing materials. Josefson looked over her shoulder as she sketched out the space, then redrew the whole thing, removing several interior walls and adding others. She finally looked up from her work. "It might be a little cramped, compared to the area you've been using." She pointed to her drawing. "You've got space for a waiting room, a reception desk that would include the records you keep, and three small examination rooms. However, I think you'll probably get quite a few complaints, having only one waiting room."

He nodded. "I see what you mean. I don't think there's a white doctor in the city who just has one waiting room." He pointed at her drawing. "I suppose we could rent a fourth room on this end and turn it into a second waiting room. They've offered me this space for thirty-five dollars a month. Maybe an additional room won't break the bank."

"I'm afraid you'll lose quite a few patients with only one waiting room. I doubt the city is ready for it."

"So when can you start work?"

"You've already got a nurse, and I've already got a job. Besides, we both heard what your mother and father had to say the other night."

"I've already talked to Sarah. I think she's going back to work in my father's garment factory. She agrees with me, by the way, that you should come to work with me, and yes, I heard what they said. I just don't happen to agree with it."

"We've only been around each other for less than three months, and all of that was during an extreme period of stress. An epidemic is not exactly a good time to make a decision about someone you've only known a short time, let alone a decision to last the rest of your life."

"Well, I heard an argument to counter that just yesterday from a friend of mine, Doctor Besancny, who came to Memphis to volunteer with the Howards from a little town in Mississippi. The first day he arrived, Doctor Mitchell assigned him to a sick family, the Rutters, on Adams Street. One of the most seriously ill of the five people in the house was a young lady who had just reached her twentieth birthday.

"Besancny apparently did a wonderful job, as the whole family began to convalesce in a few days. But before the doctor could leave the household, he himself took the fever. Miss Rutter apparently felt a great deal of gratitude for what Besancny had done for her family, and so when the Howards came to pick up the doctor and take him to their infirmary, she made it clear that she intended to nurse him back to health there in her home.

"Miss Rutter faithfully stayed at his bedside night and day until Besancny was past his crisis and finally well enough to declare himself cured. He went back to the Howards and they put him to work."

Fannie looked at Josefson. "I don't see what that's got to do with our situation."

"That's because you didn't let me finish. Two days ago, Besancny and Esquire Quigley rode over to the Rutters' home with a few friends, and within less than two hours, Doctor Besancny departed with the new Mrs. Besancny, headed back to Mississippi. I'd say they have every intention of spending the rest of their lives together."

"You left out the part about whether or not their parents stood against the marriage."

"Today, Fannie, I'm just asking you to come to work with me. No strings attached."

She had to admit, he was persistent. "I'm still not sure it's such a good idea."

"Why don't you give it a chance? Try it for just two months, and let's see what happens. If you want to leave after that, then maybe it wasn't meant to be. But it would be a complete waste of your talents if you went back to being a chambermaid. I'll help you find another nursing job anywhere else in the city if you're not happy with me."

October 31, 1878—"The southern Democrats could not perpetrate a more serious blunder than to commit acts against the colored race which would negatively impact public opinion in the North in favor of equal political rights in the South. A fresh crop of outrages is precisely what the Republican Party needs to reinstate it in public confidence and enable it to elect the next president by appealing to that sense of justice toward the colored race. We warn our fellow southern citizens that the old fires are merely smothered, but not extinct. Not only must the great body of the South treat the freedmen with fairness, but its political leaders must use their influence to restrain abuses and outrages in rough and turbulent localities."

"At a camp meeting, when penitents were called up to be prayed for, an old reprobate by the name of White asked the minister to say a special prayer just on his behalf, as he needed it in the worst way. The minister complied, and asked the Almighty to have mercy on Mr. White, for he knew what a torn-down sinner he was, that he would get drunk, and swear, and in fact, break most of the Ten Commandments, but as he was penitent, to please forgive him. The old sinner returned to his seat and happened to sit beside an attorney, who observed to him that the preacher had just defamed his character, and that he should be sued. The case was carried to court and the preacher was fined $100."

"Resolved: that the thermometer having fallen three degrees below freezing, it is entirely safe for refugees to return, provided their residences have been thoroughly ventilated and fumigated. R.F. Brown, Secretary, Board of Health." Memphis Daily Appeal

New Orleans

Despite the early morning hour, Emilie's first stop when she arrived in New Orleans was to go straight to the Hotel Dieu. It wasn't necessary for her to enter the building, as she was of the opinion that she could conduct her necessary business on the street in front of the hospital. Although this particular stop did not involve promises she had made, there were things which had been bothering her since she'd first heard about the problems. Perhaps she could accomplish something positive for other families. Her first step was to once again place the locket around her neck. She visibly flinched at the thunderous appeals for help. Thankfully, within a few moments, she heard Musa Monroe call out to her from among hundreds and hundreds of pleas for her attention.

"Mr. Monroe, your sons are trying to find the paperwork you have which gave you your freedom as well as title to your property. Apparently the Osborne family is trying to take the land away from your family. Can you tell me where you've put it?"

"I knew them Osborne boys was gonna be trouble. They ain't got near the good heart Colonel Osborne had. Tell Amos and Abednego to look in the chicken house—the northwest corner. They's a big flat rock there. Underneath is a metal box. The paper they lookin' for is in that box."

"I'll send your sons a message to Jefferson Parish, Mr. Monroe."

"Bless you, Nurse. I'll be thankin' you."

The next voice Emilie looked for belonged to Lucienne St. Pierre.

"Lucienne, your son Jules is trying to find his little sister, Emma. You sent her to safety in Texas to be with some friends, but he has no idea how to contact her so they can be reunited. Where is your six-year-old daughter?"

"I sent her with old family friends, Jean and Francine Beaudenais, who fled New Orleans in late July to travel to their home in Corpus Christi, Texas. They live on Tenth Street in that city."

Emilie made a quick note, then reached in her small leather coin purse and retrieved another piece of paper. "I have your son's address. He's at the Battle House Hotel in Mobile. I'll write to him today. I'm sure he'll be contacting the Beaudenais family so your surviving family can be together again."

"May you find love and peace in your own life, madamoiselle."

November 1, 1878—"An undertaker was recently called to prepare the body of a woman for burial. From some cause, the

lower limbs had been seized just before death, and were drawn up out of shape. In the attempt to straighten them, the undertaker finally sat down upon them and was pressing them into proper position in the coffin when something struck him from behind, and turning his head to see what it was, he was confronted with the face of the corpse close to his own. The pressure on the legs had tilted the body upright, but the poor undertaker ran from the house in mortal terror."

"For the first time in the history of Memphis, during the recent pestilence when the white police force was reduced but to a few members due to sickness, resignation, and death, colored men were employed on the force. While at the time it was a necessity, it was also an experiment, which resulted so satisfactorily that Chief Athey resolved to recommend that the colored citizens be represented on the regular force in proportion to population. This has been done, and we hope the results will be as satisfactory in the future as they were in the terrible past."

"Grand re-opening of the Globe Saloon, 155 Main Street, at 10 o'clock today. Johnnie Rourke's smiling countenance will once more be seen behind the bar, dealing out the fine liquors, wines, and cigars. Boys, don't come all at once." Memphis Daily Appeal

Although it was terrifically embarrassing, Emilie had warned John Johnson, and to some extent the children, about her grandmother's prejudices and potential rudeness. She attempted to make the woman sound less fearful than she was, as she didn't want to scare Exodus and the girls. "She will probably tell you the story of how she is a princess of Haiti. In fact, she preferred to be called *Princesse* by her customers."

So as they awaited an answer to their knock on her front door, Emilie was praying the old woman would be uncharacteristically polite when they met her. There was no immediate response, and Emilie knocked somewhat more forcefully. Finally she heard a faint response from within. "*Entrer.*" With a final admonition from their father to behave, the girls entered the house, followed by Emilie, Exodus, and John.

Emilie didn't immediately see Vivienne, but eventually found her sitting in the parlor, almost lost in an upholstered green velvet chair. Emilie went to her, giving her a hug. "Good afternoon, Grandmère. I'm so glad to see you." She was surprised to see the food stains on her grandmother's dress. If anyone was meticulous, it was Vivienne.

The old woman looked at Emilie with a puzzled expression. "I don't think I know you."

Emilie was taken aback by this and started to respond with a gentle reminder, but before she could manage an explanation, her grandmother looked beyond her and saw Ruthie, dressed in her best clothes. Vivienne held out her arms to the child. "Emilie, *ma chérie,* I've missed you so much. Come give your grandmère a kiss."

Ruthie looked first at her father, then at Emilie, and made a quick decision all on her own. She walked tentatively over to the old woman, who quickly embraced her, and in turn she bravely gave Vivienne a quick peck on her cheek. The old woman then held her at arm's length. "Let me look at you. You've grown so much, and you're so pretty." She glanced toward Emilie. "Your mother doesn't bring you to see me very often."

Ruthie looked up at Vivienne with her big brown eyes. "Would you tell me the story of when you became a princess?"

The old woman smiled broadly. "Why, of course, *ma chérie.*" But before she could go further, she spied Leisha peering at her from behind her father's legs, and Exodus studying the situation. "And who are these children?"

Ruthie said, "That's my sister, Leisha."

"Leisha—what a pretty name you have." She turned, eyebrow arched, to Emilie. "I wonder why someone didn't tell me you had a sister. And is this good-looking boy your brother?"

"This is Exodus."

"Exodus! My, that is a fine biblical name." She lowered her voice, nodded across the room toward John Johnson, and spoke again to Emilie. "Is this some other liaison I didn't know about?" Her voice then changed again. "Eugenie, would you go into the kitchen and see if we don't have some peppermint sticks for these children in the cupboard?"

Emilie beckoned to John Johnson from the kitchen door, and seeing the children involved with the old woman, he followed her signal.

"Something is wrong with my grandmother. She's got me confused with my mother, Eugenie."

"Is that who she was talkin' about?"

"Yes, and apparently she thinks Ruthie is me when I was a little girl."

"What was she saying when she looked over in my direction?"

"I'm not sure. Either she thinks you're my father, or else she thinks Eugenie has got a new boyfriend or husband, and we have a daughter—Leisha—together."

"What do you figger on doin'?"

Emilie found the peppermint, then turned to John. "I don't know. I guess tell her the truth."

"Well, let me ask you this. What harm is there in lettin' her think she's right? See, I think she's got that old folks' problem. She might not even believe you when you try and set her straight. Might get more upset if you confuse her any more than she already is."

"An old doctor in Memphis, Doctor Sohm, told me there were several diseases which caused people's minds to play tricks on them. We were talking about it because yellow fever is one of them. But he mentioned things like syphilis, sugar in the urine, melancholia, and apoplexy that could do the same thing. Maybe that's what's happened. Let's get back in there before she gets more confused with Exodus and the girls."

Emilie approached Vivienne with four peppermint sticks in her hand. She remembered very well that the old woman loved the candy every bit as much as she had when she was a girl. She made a quick decision to follow Johnson's advice. "Here you are, *Maman.*"

Vivienne was obviously pleased that she was included in the treat, and she and the two little girls immediately began to lick the sticks. Vivienne looked at Exodus, who was still stand-offish. "Don't you like peppermint, Exodus?"

He smiled and wandered over—still unsure of his status. "Yessum."

Vivienne reached out and gave the boy a hug and a peppermint. "You sure are a handsome boy." He grinned—perhaps for the compliment, or more likely for the piece of candy.

Leisha looked up at the old woman and tugged at her sleeve, both of them with the pink and white candy stuck in their cheeks. "What should we call you?"

"You should call me *Grandmère, mon cher.*"

Emilie took this opportunity to bring Johnson to her. "*Maman*, this is John Johnson."

The old lady still did not surrender her peppermint, but looked him up and down. "Are you still a gambling man?"

"No, *Princesse.* I work too hard for my money to be throwin' it away on cards and dice."

"Hmmm." She gave him a dubious look, but being called by her proper title put her in a generous mood, and she said nothing else on the subject.

Emilie sat down in front of Vivienne, hoping to understand what was going on with her. "*Maman*, do you have help in the household? I haven't seen anyone yet."

"I had to get rid of that girl—you know the one. She was stealing my silver."

"Is someone working in your garden?"

"No." She looked around the room, seeing Johnson again. "What about him?"

"I'll be glad to get your garden goin' again, Miss Vivienne."

Emilie smiled at that development, but had more on her mind. "Does someone go to the store for you?"

"Mr. Bertucci was coming by, but I think he caught the fever. I haven't seen him in a while."

"Your pantry is almost bare. Would you like me to go to the store for you?"

"Why, yes, Eugenie." She looked at the two little girls at her feet and Exodus at the side of her chair. "Don't forget, now that Exodus and Emilie and Leisha are here, we're going to need a lot more peppermint."

November 3, 1878—"Southern Democrats declare with joy that there will not be a single Republican Congressman chosen from the South. They say it is because southern Republicans have been converted. The daily dispatches from every district in the South prove that there has been no conversion, but a brutal, cruel, systematic defiance of the Constitution. At each election, new localities are chosen for subjugation by

massacre and terror. The story sent from the South always is that bad Negroes, instigated by worse white men, 'threatened to burn a town, or do some other mischief,' and the spotless white Democrats killed a few leaders in sheer self-defense. But the thing never happens unless there is a Republican majority to overcome. Peace—of the Democratic sort—follows the bulldozer; peace, and no votes for Republican candidates." New York Tribune

Memphis

Late in the day on November 4th, Fannie looked around the medical office to make sure no patient had been forgotten or misplaced. It was not only Saul's first day in his new location, it was his first day back in private practice after his many assignments with the Howards. They had posted notices at various places near the Pinch and in the downtown area, advising people that his office had moved. Fannie hoped he was pleased with the first day's results. They had seen thirty-one patients, only two of whom believed, beyond a shadow of a doubt, they had the yellow fever.

Thankfully, their suspicions had been unfounded. Perhaps the epidemic was indeed past. Apparently many people believed that was so, as the city was flooded with returning refugees. Of course, thousands of others would probably never return. Over the past three months, many had found employment in far safer locations—cities which had never experienced cases of yellow-jack, and probably never would.

However, businesses were re-opening every day. The store owners' main concern now was relocating old employees or hiring new ones. The labor force was much reduced, but then again, the population of the city was still less than half what it had been in early August.

Saul had finally decided to rent five adjacent hotel rooms, keeping one as his own living quarters, as he was determined to relocate his own residence. Fannie was still making the trip from her flat in the Pinch to the office and back, but now she rode rather than walked, as Saul had offered to pick her up in his buggy in the morning and deliver her to her home each evening. As far as she was concerned, that was an employment benefit which trumped almost everything else.

Fannie sought out Saul as he finished writing a note in his records. He saw her standing in the doorway, stood up, and walked over to her. She put her hand on his shoulder. "Well, you did it."

"No, Fannie. We did it." Rather than force something she wasn't prepared for, he bent and kissed her on the forehead. "If you'll stay with me, we'll do a lot of great things together."

She smiled at him, her voice revealing a slight catch of emotion. "It's possible that I just might get used to you, Saul Josefson."

November 5, 1878—"We must have our streets paved with stone, and we must have a perfect system of sewage. Without these prerequisites to good health, we might as well give up the race and abandon the city."

"The Commission appointed by Surgeon General Woodworth to investigate the causes and effects of the epidemic arrived in our city yesterday, and all are staying at the Peabody. While here, they will pursue their investigation, interview many in our city, and create maps and charts which portray the cases and spread of the epidemic. Their investigation will form the framework, perhaps, of national legislation which may secure us from future epidemics."

"The women of New York held a mass meeting and expressed their dissatisfaction with all political parties. The Republican Party has promised 'respectful consideration,' but for voting a straight Republican ticket, Miss Susan B. Anthony was fined $100. The Democratic Party claimed to be for universal suffrage, but so far has only given women the right to vote in Wyoming Territory. The Labor-Workingmen's Party killed the women suffrage plank offered at their convention. The National Party's convention only found that the Constitution guaranteed every male citizen the vote—when every schoolboy knows that it guarantees that right to every citizen."
Memphis Daily Appeal

The surviving members of the Citizens Relief Committee, all of the physicians of the city who were well enough to attend, the mayor, the chief of police, the editors of the *Memphis Daily Appeal* and the *Memphis Ledger,* as well as everybody who was anybody in the vicinity of Memphis, Tennessee, assembled that evening to hear a public discussion led by the seven members of the National Yellow Fever Commission. In truth, everybody in the hall wanted to see and hear the country's surgeon general, John M. Woodworth.

Woodworth was not a striking physical specimen. He couldn't have been more than five feet, six inches in height, although his voice managed to reach every corner of the room. He wore a long black coat, a knotted tie, a huge handlebar mustache, and a full head of hair. He had an impressive medical and scientific resumé, augmented by sterling service in the Union Army during the war.

In the evening's discussion, there was a great deal of emphasis on not only what they had discovered in their investigation, but also an admittance by the committee members that the deeper they delved into the subject of yellow fever, the more they found they did not understand. In fact, they now had more unanswered questions than when they began their work.

They spoke of the horrific experiences of the cities they had visited, and of individual stories, not only of suffering but great heroism. And that heroism they had discovered in every city and town they visited. The room was silent for several seconds, as every attendee quietly acknowledged the heroes and heroines each of them had seen, and often grieved over, during the past three months.

The committee admitted what almost every medical man worth his salt had come to realize, that no one treatment currently known was superior to another. In fact, as the Surgeon General himself said, "*Everything depends upon nursing. A good attendant and a pail of clean water will accomplish more than all the medicines in the land.*"

In the back of the room stood a group who had been invited more or less as an afterthought—a handful of nurses from among the almost 3,000 who had worked for the Howards, among them one Fannie Lester, who was accompanied by Dr. Saul Josefson. Upon hearing Woodworth's comment, Saul placed his arm around Fannie and bent down close, whispering, "I believe he's talking about you." She glanced at Josefson, her eyes shining. She thought for a moment her chest would burst with pride at what she had just heard from the most eminent physician in the land.

November 6, 1878—"As of 4 AM this morning, election results reveal that states have elected enough Democratic Congressmen to secure a good working majority in the next Congress."

"After election hours yesterday, many of the boys got their usual quantities. Quinine and gin, or sulfur and whiskey, have all been thrown to the winds since the epidemic, and the straight stuff is again all the go." Memphis Daily Appeal

November 23, 1878—"Whether justly or unjustly, New Orleans is held responsible for the yellow fever epidemic which has recently desolated so many towns, villages, and cities of the South. New Orleans is accused of having transmitted to the country a terrible and fatal disease, against which she might have guarded by rigorous quarantine or proper sanitary measures within our city. These affected communities demand that New Orleans shall prevent the recurrence of such a calamity, on penalty of total severance of relations with her, which, if repeated from year to year, would cause her certain ruin." New Orleans Picayune

Chapter 39
The Aftermath

The yellow fever epidemic of 1878 was by far the worst of any which had struck the Western Hemisphere, the first of which occurred in 1596. The yellow fever appeared in what would become the United States of America 37 times in the eighteenth century, and then occurred every single year from 1800 to 1879 at least somewhere within these states.

The first yellow fever epidemic in Memphis occurred in 1828, with 650 cases and 150 deaths. The numbers sound small, but it must be remembered that in 1828 the population in Memphis was only 1,000 souls. There followed four more epidemics in Memphis prior to 1878.

It might be revealing to review the comparative analysis of Dr. H.M. Walthal, who had come to Memphis during the epidemic in 1873, as well as on August 26, 1878, in order to establish leadership of the yellow fever infirmaries:

"Entering Memphis at night, as at a similar stage of the great epidemic of 1873, the contrast was startling. On the former occasion there were no external signs or tokens of pestilence in the principal streets. Shops and saloons were open, people passing to and fro, groups gathered, as usual, about the hotels and bar-rooms, billiard tables in activity, and life presenting its ordinary aspects, except in the 'infected district,' to which it was then fondly hoped that the fever would be confined. Such was the case, in some degree, during the whole prevalence of the epidemic of that year.

"Now, on the contrary, the streets are dark, deserted, and silent. At the Peabody Hotel—the only hostelry open to the public—there are no loungers to relieve the solitude of the single clerk. A solitary light shone from the door of a saloon on

Monroe Street, and a few others twinkled from drugstores here and there. The only place that presents a scene of activity is the office of the Howard Association, where I was greeted by a dozen true and tried comrades of the former campaign, now girded with full armor for another. As I write, five of them lay ill of the fever, brought on, most probably, by overwork and exhaustion. It is a singular fact that only three or four members of this Association have ever had the yellow fever, although nearly all passed through it unscathed in 1873. With the exception of the nurses, a few sisters of religious orders, and some Negroes, no female figure is now seen in the streets. The scarcity of physicians is a great evil, but that of skilled nurses is greater. One of the most distressing things in daily experience is the necessity of turning a deaf ear to the piteous appeals for a doctor, a nurse, or other help.

"The striking and most remarkable distinction between the phenomena of the two epidemics is the confinement of the pestilence in 1873 within a limited area, beyond which there was scarcely anything more than a sporadic extension during the whole duration, while in 1878 it has spread through the whole city as a fire spreads through a dry prairie."

Because individuals who had once been infected with yellow fever were considered to be immune, one would think that everybody would eventually have immunity. But the disease had never occurred in Europe, and so the large number of immigrants who continued to arrive in America every year provided a new pool of potential victims. As verification of this, approximately fifty percent of those infected with yellow fever in Memphis in 1878 were Irish immigrants.

Over the course of five months, the epidemic in 1878 spread from what started out as two or three infected boatmen in New Orleans, to eventually create over 120,000 cases in fourteen states and Nova Scotia. However, most of those states claimed that their only cases involved visitors from the infected zone who simply died within their borders, rather than any patients from among their own population. So the great majority of cases were concentrated in three states.

Total yellow fever deaths in the U.S. during the summer and fall of 1878 were over 20,000, and were reported in 154 American towns and cities. The states to report the highest number of municipalities involved were Tennessee with 33, Louisiana with 37, and Mississippi with 46. According to the Howards, Vicksburg experienced between 1,300 and 1,500 deaths, but acknowledged that perhaps hundreds more were buried in unreported graves in the countryside and never officially recorded. This under-reporting was a common story in every town which was stricken. New Orleans had over 4,000 deaths, but the city's health commissioner admitted in September that the numbers of yellow fever cases and deaths were no longer able to be accurately reported. Memphis recorded 5,150 people who died from yellow fever.

Perhaps better than other large cities, Memphis recorded the names, ages, and dates of their death, as well as their addresses. However, many addresses were recorded as being at the corners of such and such streets. Likewise, a few of the dead were recorded as 'adult male' or 'small child'—simply because sometimes all of their relatives and friends had either fled or were dead.

In most previous outbreaks, the death rate had hovered around ten percent. When the epidemic started in 1878, this typically was what was expected among the cities of the South which had previous experience with yellow-jack. But this particular outbreak was unbelievably virulent, with the average death rate including both whites and blacks at about 33 percent.

In Memphis, a town with a population of approximately 47,000 people in July 1878, when the first cases were diagnosed in August, around 22,000 people left the city in a panic within the first week of the outbreak. Quickly, nearby towns established a quarantine against all those coming from Memphis, so in the next week, some 5,000 additional citizens from Memphis moved into temporary camps which had been established several miles from the infected city. According to the Howard Association's count, this left a citizenry of 19,600—composed of those who were either too poor to afford to leave, or those who had decided to stay in order to save their city. By November 1878, 17,600 people had been infected with yellow fever, and 5,150 had died. Of the total population of 19,600, just under 14,000 were black, and some 6,000 were white. Among the 14,000 blacks, 946 died; of the 6,000 whites, 4,204 died. So the average death rate of 33 percent quoted above was dramatically skewed according to race.

Also in 1878, the fever spread far beyond the municipalities along the Mississippi River, which had been previously the only sites affected. This unexpected geographic expansion was often blamed on the railroads as the entity which had carried the infection far into the interior of the country. And when the fever arrived in towns which had never been previously affected, and thus might not have any citizens who had ever been exposed before, it spread rapidly, killing with unbelievable vengeance. Many of the physicians in these towns had never seen yellow fever in their practices, and hence an accurate diagnosis was often delayed for days or even weeks, with the result that many of the townspeople were exposed before being alerted to their risk. In the city of Grenada, Mississippi, all nine of the local physicians died, none having ever been exposed to yellow fever previously. Similarly, four of the local pastors died and all three telegraph operators passed away. At the close of the epidemic, the Howard Association's General W.J. Smith indicated that only four white people who had remained in Grenada had not been struck down.

Among the physicians who came to Memphis from other cities, 88 of them were un-acclimated (never had the fever before). Of that number, 33 died, 54 others became ill but survived, and only one of those 88 did not get sick. Eleven Catholic priests and "almost a score" of sisters perished in Memphis, while at least sixteen more priests and approximately fifty sisters died in all other epidemic-affected areas. A high percentage of other religious leaders met similar fates.

Nurses from across the nation arrived in Memphis, with 529 of them volunteering to work for the Howard Association. Another 2,466 from the immediate area volunteered. Many, many of them, despite claiming otherwise when they were hired, were un-acclimated. An accurate number of nurse deaths is not available, as they apparently weren't recorded as a separate group, but the *Memphis Daily Appeal* reported that "many hundreds" of them died. One unofficial estimate was that over 500 nurses died in Memphis. There is no accounting for the actual number of nurses and physicians who died across the breadth of the Lower Mississippi Valley.

The Memphis Fire Department suffered 24 deaths among their membership, with only 13 men remaining available for work. The police were similarly affected—of an original total force of 41 men, only 7 were able to report for duty. The local telegraphers reported 31 sick, including 12 deaths, and only one employee escaped the fever. Among the three newspapers in town, a total of 84 men were employed. Of that number, 76 employees were taken ill, 36 of that number died, and only eight of the total were not infected. A report from one of the railroad companies stated that 145 of its employees had become sick and 71 had died, with the majority of those deaths occurring on a single rail line between Memphis and Paris, Tennessee (a distance of some 140 miles).

There had been 26 original members of the Memphis Citizens Relief Committee. As the epidemic progressed, many of them had to be replaced by other volunteers. Of their membership, 36 became sick and 16 died. The author's distant ancestor and member of the Committee, Benjamin Babb, came through unscathed, although he may have been immune due to an unknown previous yellow fever infection.

Among the Jewish community, 78 people were buried in the B'nai Israel Cemetery as a result of the 1878 epidemic. There was a dramatic decrease in the Jewish population from 2,100 to 300 from mid-summer to year's end during 1878, thus significantly decreasing the financial wellbeing of Temple Israel. Much was made during the epidemic of the Jews' ability to take care of their own people; however, this population decrease made it extremely difficult for the congregation to continue to provide sustenance for their membership.

Rabbi Max Samfield was cited in a resolution by his congregation at the end of the epidemic thusly: "*Throughout the long days he labored. Throughout the long nights he watched. No call upon his services unheeded; no demand upon his time ignored. He ministered to the sick; brought consolation to the stricken; gave sympathy to the orphan; and by torchlight buried his dead. In his services for good, he made no distinction, either in race or condition, but the Gentile as well as the Jew were the beneficiaries.*"

The undertaker John Walsh was only one of several men engaged in the funerary trade in Memphis, but because he obtained the city contract to bury all paupers, his funeral wagon drivers, casket builders, and gravediggers were responsible for putting 2,000 "paupers" in the ground, plus some 500 others who had sufficient means to have purchased an individual or family plot in one of the cemeteries. In the neighborhoods where corpses were discovered, there quickly arose a demand for immediate removal and burial. In many cases, people who actually owned a cemetery plot were sent to potter's field simply for lack of a family member or friend to advise Walsh's workers that such an arrangement existed. And so, rather than resting in their own private plot with a stone of identification, they still sleep in unknown graves.

The cities and towns of the South were showered with gifts of money, as well as boxcar loads of medical supplies, clothing, bedding, food, and ice. A majority of the donations were funneled through the various Howard Associations or the citizens relief committees. Although most donations originated in those states which had previously composed the North during the Civil War, donations came from 32 states as well as the Dakota, Montana, Utah, Wyoming, and Indian Territories. Money and supplies also came from as far away as England, France, Germany, Australia, India, Cuba, several countries in South America, and three Canadian provinces.

Additionally, all shipping costs incurred by railroads and express companies were entirely donated. Likewise, Western Union donated the costs related to all telegrams to and from yellow fever-infected communities. Without these generous gifts, the numbers of those dying, starving, and suffering would have been far greater. In fact, the Citizens Relief Committee in Memphis distributed 681,982 rations to the poor and sick during the epidemic. Almost every bit of those rations were donated. (A listing of donations, by state or foreign nation, and the amount of money and/or value of donated goods, can be found at the end of the last chapter.)

Five years after the 1878 yellow fever epidemic, Mark Twain published his memoir *Life on the Mississippi.* In that classic, he made the following observation related to the many benevolent acts visited upon the city of Memphis. *"Memphis is experienced, above all other cities on the river, in the generous office of the Good Samaritan." (Life on the Mississippi, 1883.)*

Jefferson Davis, former president of the Confederate States of America, lost his only surviving son to the yellow fever epidemic in Memphis. Due to the risk of exposure to the fever, most burials were not attended by even a single friend or family member. Davis' son's funeral had fifteen attendees, which was apparently a record during the epidemic. Jeff Davis himself issued a statement of appreciation to the people of the North for their support of the people of the South during the epidemic.

The entire federal budget of the United States in 1878 was $238 million, yet the negative financial impact of the yellow fever on the nation that year was estimated at $200 million. This figure included lost income, decreased productivity, trade restrictions (related to quarantine), un-gathered crops, costs incurred in fighting the disease, and burying the dead. $200 million translated to 2019 dollars is approximately $13 billion, making the 1878 yellow fever epidemic one of the most expensive disasters in American history.

Assistance provided to the affected cities and towns was mostly from private sources, including medical caregivers and supplies from the Howard Associations, the Can't Get Away Club of Mobile, the Masons, the Odd-Fellows, the Knights of Honor, the United Order of Workingmen, the Knights of Pythias, the YMCA, and many lesser known fraternal and religious organizations. By comparison, there was a small amount of federal assistance related to establishing camps outside cities, as well as providing rations for the sick and the poor. Otherwise, communities were expected to fend for themselves. The several state governments basically looked the other way, recommended reliance on prayer, and spent almost no funds nor sent any state resources to assist the many towns and cities which were most often unable to muster anything beyond minimal financial support themselves. While there was plenty of talk in state capitols about states' rights, it was hard to find a governor and legislature who acknowledged states' responsibilities.

November 20, 1878—"Administrator's Sale: I will sell, at the following site, within the next ten days, the property belonging to the estate of William Meyer, now deceased, the debt secured by deed of trust not having been paid, a tract of land

situated seven miles from Memphis, in sections 2 and 3, range 7, on the New Raleigh Road, 275 acres, once being part of the Kerr tract, where the Meyer family did reside, along with 2 horses, 3 mules, 2 cows, 15 hogs, 4 geese, 3 sprinkling wagons, 3 farm wagons, 1 spring wagon, 1 buggy, 2 carts, 3 double sets of harness, 2 sets single buggy harness, 2 sets dray harness, 1 saddle, 1 plow, and household and kitchen furniture. Terms cash. Henry Luehrman, Trustee." Memphis Daily Appeal

It seemed as though half of the city of Memphis was for sale. In fact, hundreds, if not thousands, of properties were on the market. Every day for months, an entire page of the *Memphis Daily Appeal* was filled with ads similar to the above, attempting to settle the debts of families and businesses. Widows and orphans were hopeful that not only would debts be settled, but that there might be some money left to prevent them from becoming destitute. Unfortunately, because so many properties and accoutrements were for sale, prices were artificially low. Opportunists with cash paid pennies on the dollar. Many survivors walked away from their sale, possessing nothing, yet still in debt.

Memphis historian Gerald M. Capers wrote, "It can be suggested with some justification that Atlanta owes its present position as the New York City of the South to the work of the *Aedes aegypti* mosquito in Memphis in 1878."

December 15, 1878—Russell Dorr letter—"My Dearest Mother—I have just arrived in St. Louis after a long trip up the Mississippi River selling marble for Ripley and Sons, as well as caskets for the company. I regret that I could not yet stop in Vicksburg, for I am satisfied I could have sold considerable there; but I felt to be at risk for the fever. I left Memphis at midnight the day I wrote you previously, and had a mean time of it, but was glad enough to get out of town at all without sleeping in any of their infected beds, for I am afraid of them. Ever yours aff, Russell"

January 30, 1879—"Despite all the handwringing and recent campaign rhetoric over City Hall's financial problems—and they're significant—they are nothing compared to our financial crisis of last fall. Memphis was hollowed out—thousands fled, thousands more died, businesses shut their

doors—leaving too few taxpayers to meet the city's obligations. And so the legislature has revoked our charter and established a 'Taxing District' to manage the city's affairs. The editorial staff is grateful for the legislature that freed the city from its creditors, but incensed they waived taxation of our residents for seven months. This was the city's only means of cleaning up massive health problems on our streets—and this raises the prospect of yet another epidemic. Is there not a patriotism in Memphis which will rise superior to a clap-trap demagoguery that is absolutely criminal in view of its horrible past? Are the destinies of this city and its health—nay, the lives of its citizens—forever to be the sport of ignorance or selfishness?" Memphis Daily Appeal

In Dr. R.W. Mitchell's final communication with the Howard Association, he made several suggestions to better organize the association, so that it could be ready to respond promptly and efficiently. *"1) The calling of a convention of representatives from every Howard organization in the country, 2) Organization of a permanent medical corps of physicians who have had yellow fever, 3) Enrollment of a permanent corps of nurses possessing the proper mental and moral qualifications, 4) Local Howard organizations will have their nurses enrolled with them, and 5) Whenever a call for help is heard from any city in the country, each organization will be required to supply a certain number of trained physicians and nurses, and to increase this number if necessity demands it."*

"Yellow fever should be dealt with as an enemy which imperils life and cripples commerce and industry. To no other great nation of the earth is yellow fever so calamitous as to the United States of America." Surgeon General John M. Woodworth, Report to Congress, 1879

Chapter 40
Long Term Effects

The leaders of Memphis got their wish. The state revoked their charter and instead created a Taxing District. Their onerous debt was forgiven, which would allow the new entity to use the funds they collected to pay for urgently needed infrastructure. Unfortunately, the state's revocation of their ability to tax the citizenry for the first seven months as a taxing district removed the opportunity to pay any new bills, let alone begin any new projects. Most likely, this step was taken to not only give the former city a breather, but also to allow their residents a short period of recovery by not paying any of the usual municipal taxes for a few months.

Unfortunately, the city was visited yet again by a yellow fever epidemic during the summer of 1879, this time infecting 2,000 people, and resulting in 600 deaths. In all likelihood, this much smaller number of cases was directly related to the huge number of citizens who had been infected during the previous year's epidemic and thus were immune.

As the Taxing District started to climb out of its hole, they finally began an aggressive campaign to clean up their city. They took the important step of creating a Board of Health possessing real authority. They pushed for stringent sanitation laws which made it illegal to own open privies, outlawed the "*throwing of filth or noxious substances onto public streets and property,*" required the removal of horse, mule, ox, and cattle dung from the city twice weekly, regulated the sale of unwholesome foods, and began the long process of constructing an underground sewer system and a separate wastewater system. The Taxing District began regular trash collection. They removed the "Nicholson pavement" from city streets and replaced the road surfaces with a combination of limestone and gravel. Of course, these changes were begun first in the more well-to-do areas of the city, and only gradually were completed in less affluent neighborhoods; but progress was certainly being made.

In 1879, the Forty-Fifth Congress passed an act establishing a National Board of Health which was led by representatives from the Department of Justice, the U.S. Navy, and the Marine Hospital Service, and assisted by the Academy of Science. The Board would be responsible for further defining rules of national and international quarantine; establishing requirements for the inspection, disinfection, and sanitation of vessels of commerce at American ports; continuing to investigate contagious and infectious diseases; evaluating the health of animals imported into or exported from the United States; and advising the states as to their findings and recommendations. This National Board of Health had been a dream of the country's first Surgeon General. Alas, Dr. John Woodworth would not see this come to fruition. He died working at his desk in Washington in March 1879.

Perhaps the most enduring achievement locally was the discovery of an artesian aquifer in the late 1880s, which provided Memphis' citizens with some of the best drinking water in the nation. That water source is still utilized today, although concerned voices are now being heard related to groundwater threats to the aquifer.

In 1889, the Marine Hospital Service, mentioned several times in the text, was transformed into the U.S. Public Health Service Commissioned Corps, which continues to be led by the U.S. Surgeon General. That organization is utilized even today to respond in force to public health emergencies—hurricanes, floods, forest fires, earthquakes, tsunamis, mass shootings, terrorist attacks, and epidemics such as influenza, ebola, and zika.

By 1893, the Taxing District's population had increased from the less than 14,000 survivors of the 1878 yellow fever epidemic, to approximately 70,000 people. Remarkable improvements had been made related to sanitation and clean water, fiscal health had been restored, and thus the state of Tennessee acted to reinstate the Charter for the City of Memphis after a fourteen-year hiatus.

As a way of expressing its gratitude for their many heroic contributions and sacrifices during the yellow fever epidemics, Memphis did not charge a fare for riding its horse trolleys, streetcars, and city buses to Catholic and Episcopal priests, sisters, and brothers from about 1880 until about 1970. This finally was discontinued when many of the religious orders either stopped wearing identifiable religious garb or reduced their bus ridership. Nevertheless, the city's ninety years of appreciation should be acknowledged.

The Black policemen and firemen who stepped in to rescue the city of Memphis in 1878 were retained in those positions until 1895, when this "experiment" was entirely dismantled—probably due to the demands of segregationists, as well as pressure from other cities in the South, who perhaps felt threatened by any neighboring city which could display successfully integrated police and fire departments.

Also short-lived was the collective memory of the South related to the generosity exhibited by their brethren to the North during the great yellow fever epidemic of 1878. All too soon, previously held biases again held sway.

In 1881, Cuban physician Dr. Carlos Finlay proposed that yellow fever was transmitted via the bite of a mosquito, and recommended that yellow fever could only be controlled via mosquito control. Most American physicians and scientists of the day placed no faith in his theory.

Major Walter Reed, U.S. Army pathologist and bacteriologist, was sent to Cuba along with a team of physicians and researchers by Surgeon General G.M. Sternberg in 1900 to investigate several tropical diseases. They worked at Camp Lazear, named for Dr. Reed's assistant who had died from yellow fever a few months previously. Dr. Reed would be credited with finally proving, via controlled field experiments using Army volunteers in 1901, that yellow fever was caused, not by an infected patient's bedding or clothing, and certainly not by miasma, but by the bite of a female *Aedes aegypti* mosquito (or other varieties of *Aedes*) which was carrying the disease by virtue of previously biting an already infected person or monkey. Dr. Reed himself, however, in all his speeches and papers, always credited Dr. Carlos Finlay for the discovery in view of his previous work.

Aedes mosquitoes are not only responsible for the spread of yellow fever, but also dengue fever, chikungunya, and the zika virus. These mosquitoes continue to populate the lakes, bayous, creeks, and other bodies of water across the southern United States, although the presence of yellow fever in the United States has disappeared. Along with the *Anopheles* mosquito, which is responsible for the spread of malaria, these two insect varieties still account for over a half-million deaths worldwide annually.

The discovery of the mosquito as the vector in yellow fever finally allowed work to be completed on the much-delayed Panama Canal.

In 1927, yellow fever became the first virus to be isolated and identified.

In 1937, a successful yellow fever vaccine was developed by Max Theiler, who won the Nobel Prize in Medicine for his work.

Today, there are approximately one billion people in the world who live in areas where yellow fever is common. The World Health Organization (WHO) recommends routine vaccination of babies between the 9th and 12th month of life in those areas at risk. The WHO reports that the vaccination rate is unfortunately less than 50 percent in at least half of the countries in Africa, South America, and a few locations in Asia where yellow fever is found. There was recently a significant outbreak of yellow fever in Brazil, which had a negative impact on the availability of vaccine. In the United States, yellow fever vaccine is not used except to vaccinate travelers headed to foreign areas identified by the WHO as being at risk.

Because of a recent increase in the presence of yellow fever among monkeys, a less than optimal vaccination program in some countries at risk, and enhancement of the mosquito-friendly environment by a warming climate in some tropical areas, the disease is again on the upswing. Before 2000, some five million vaccine doses were used annually. The vaccine demand is now some seven or eight times this number.

In addition to the use of DEET, treated bed-nets, getting rid of standing water, and avoiding being outside in the evening and early morning, the WHO recommends that potential travelers to specific areas of the world be vaccinated for yellow fever. It takes approximately 10 days for the vaccine to become effective, and its efficacy should last for 10 years.

There is currently no known cure for yellow fever. Management of patient symptoms remains the only treatment.

Although Memphis was widely acknowledged as the filthiest city in the country in 1878, it was an eventual five-time winner of "The Nation's Cleanest City" designation—from 1948 to 1952, and again in 1983. It's truly miraculous what can be accomplished when science and public determination come together. Think about it.

Total Donations to the South in 1878—Money and Goods—by State or Country

Arkansas	$37,446
Arizona Terr.	4,750
Alabama	68,920
Connecticut	40,275
California	132,118
Colorado	21,186
Delaware	28,938
Florida	25,615
Georgia	113,684
Illinois	192,845
Indiana	117,826
Iowa	48,120
Indian Terr.	918
Kansas	22,535
Kentucky	169,052
Louisiana	189,639
Maryland	86,022
Maine	19,621
Massachusetts	149,256
Minnesota	40,671
Missouri	199,353
Mississippi	119,675
New Hampshire	6,920
New Mexico Terr.	1,175
Nevada	9,681

Idaho	1,050
Nevada	9,681
Nebraska	15,981
New Jersey	36,988
New York	679,340
North Carolina	33,727
Ohio	196,298
Oregon	11,041
Pennsylvania	248,090
Rhode Island	11,041
South Carolina	60,242
Tennessee	145,882
Texas	139,529
Utah Terr.	5,522
Virginia	89,145
Vermont	11,125
Washington D.C.	39,981
West Virginia	13,912
Wisconsin	46,163
Wyoming Terr.	2,859
Dakota Terr.	663
Alaska Terr.	375
U.S. Government	100,000
Railroad Transp. (free)	285,000
Express Companies (free)	255,000
Western Union Tel. (free)	44,000

Total Donations to all Affected States—$4,548,703

Resources and Acknowledgements

My editor, Gunnar Grey, at *Dingbat Publishing*, for her expert advice, as well as her steadfast belief in me and this story.

April Jones, for her professional editorial recommendations, many corrective actions, and friendship.

A History of the Yellow Fever, J.M. Keating, The Howard Association of Memphis, Wright and Company, Printers and Binders, Memphis, TN, 1879

Memphis Daily Appeal, available online at https://chroniclingamerica.loc.gov/, 1878

Memphis Avalanche, available online at https://chroniclingamerica.loc.gov/, 1878

Memphis Public Ledger, available online at https://chroniclingamerica.loc.gov/, 1878

Chicago Daily Tribune, available online

Los Angeles Herald, available online

New Orleans Picayune, available at New Orleans Public Library, Historical Collection, (microfilm), 1878

https://chroniclingamerica.loc.gov/ (accessed June 2017)

The Sisters of St. Mary at Memphis: with the Acts and Sufferings of the Priests and Others Who Were There with Them during the Yellow Fever Season of 1878, Project Canterbury, New York, NY (printed but not published), 1879

Outposts of Zion: A History of Mississippi Presbyterians in the Nineteenth Century, Robert Milton Winter, Alphagraphies, Memphis, TN, 2014 (with special thanks to Reverend Milton Winter for his great knowledge related to the Presbyterian struggles during the 1878 yellow fever epidemic, as well as his thoughtful review of the text)

Heroes and Heroines of Memphis, Reverend D.A. Quinn, E.L. Freeman & Son, State Printers, Providence, RI, 1887

Between the Rivers: The Catholic Heritage of West Tennessee, McGraw, Guthrie, & King, Catholic Diocese of Memphis, Starr Toof, Inc., Memphis, TN, 1996 (with special thanks to Brother Joel McGraw for access to his library, his insight into the many Catholic contributions and sacrifices during the 1878 yellow fever epidemic, and his superb review of the text)

The Book of Common Prayer, The Protestant Episcopal Church in the United States of America, New York, 1790

The Mississippi Valley's Great Yellow Fever Epidemic of 1878, Khaled J. Bloom, LSU Press, Baton Rouge, 1993

Children of Israel—The Story of Temple Israel, Judy G. Ringel, Temple Israel Books, Memphis, TN, 2004

A Biblical People in the Bible Belt, Selma S. Lewis, Mercer Univ. Press, Macon, GA, 1998

Daughters of Charity Provincial Archives, from the Provincial Annals of 1878, Daughters of Charity Archives, 1878

Angels of Mercy, Sister Mary Paulinus Oaks, R.S.M., Cathedral Foundation Press, Baltimore, MD, 1998

Report of the Expedition for the Relief of Yellow Fever Sufferers of the Lower Mississippi, Executive Committee of the Yellow Fever Commission, War Department, Washington City, Nov. 30, 1878

The Yellow Fever Epidemic in Mississippi, Deanne Love Stephens Nuwer, Dissertation for University of Southern Mississippi for Doctor of Philosophy, UMI Company, Ann Arbor, MI, 1996

The Chamber over the Gate, William Wadsworth Longfellow, 1879

Dr. William Armstrong Letters to Louisa Hanna Armstrong, copies available at Memphis, TN Central Library Historical Collection, 1878

Russell Dorr Letter to his Mother, New Orleans Public Library, City Archives, 1878

Belle Wade Diary, copies available at Memphis, TN Central Library Historical Collection, 1878

Yellow Fever Strikes Collierville, Memphis, TN Central Library Historical Collection, 1878

Yellow Fever as it Existed in Chattanooga, Tennessee—Origin, Progress, and the Possible Remedy For its Abatement in the Future, J.H. Vandeman, Read at Annual Meeting, Richmond, Virginia, Nov 21, 1878

The Tennessee Genealogical Magazine, Vol 45, No. 2, Summer, 1998

Brian Hicks, Museum Director of the Desoto County Museum, Hernando, MS

Brooke Mundy, Museum Director of the Morton Museum of Collierville History, Collierville, TN

Memphis Central Library, Historical Collection, Memphis, TN

Warren County/Vicksburg Public Library, Vicksburg, MS

Grenada Historical Museum, Grenada, MS

Hill Country History Tour, Holly Springs, MS

Laura Plantation Tour, Vasherie, LA

Elmwood Cemetery Yellow Fever Tour, Memphis, TN

Christina Bryant, New Orleans Central Library, City Archives, New Orleans, LA, for her help in discovering the effects of the epidemic in Louisiana

Elisabeth Scott, Mississippi Library Commission, Reference Department, Jackson, MS, for her help in discovering the effects of the epidemic in Mississippi

Jennifer Welch, University of Tennessee Medical Library, Historical Collection, Memphis, TN

Chattanooga Public Library, Local History Collection, Chattanooga, TN

Mark Estes, Asst. Director, Haywood County Public Library, Brownsville, TN for his assistance in researching the effects of the epidemic in Brownsville, TN

Patrick Posey, Director, Catholic Cemeteries, Diocese of Memphis

Reverend Andy Andrews, Dean of St. Mary's Cathedral in Memphis, for his advice related to the many Episcopal heroes and heroines of the epidemic.

Rabbi Feivel Strauss, Senior Educator at Temple Israel, for his advice related to the activities of B'nai Israel Temple and Rabbi Max Samfield during the epidemic.

Jennifer Kollath, Archivist at Temple Israel, Memphis, for allowing me to have access to their library as well as her review of the manuscript related to the many Jewish contributions during the epidemic.

The *Memphis Writers* for their kind and constructive comments and review of a portion of the manuscript.

Burial Registry, 1878, Calvary Cemetery, Diocese of Memphis

Jimmy Ogle, Shelby County Historian, Elmwood Cemetery Guide, and Peabody Hotel Duckmaster, for sharing his extensive knowledge of the history of Memphis.

Dr. Eugene McKenzie, long-time Memphis internal medicine physician, for his review of the historical accuracy of the medical components of the story.

RADM Robert Williams, USPHS (ret), as an environmental engineer, for his review of the sanitary conditions of American cities in 1878.

To my old friend and mentor, Dr. J.J. Sohm, for the use of his grandfather's name in the story, and thanks as well to Sarah Sohm Strong, for her review and advice.

To my grandson, Nicholas Helms. I hope you enjoy your character in the story.

To my friend and Memphis Police Officer, Lucas McNair, for the use of your name in the story. I hope you recognize something of yourself in your character.

To my friend Nina Payne, for the use of her name. I hope the poisoning death of your character was not too upsetting.

To my long-time friends, Chester Hollomon, Steven Broom, and Mark Bartel for the use of their names as members of the staff of the beleaguered *Memphis Daily Appeal.*

To my old friend Garry Rose, for the use of his name as a telegrapher in Memphis.

And finally, to literally thousands of heroes and heroines, long dead now, named and unnamed, black and white, pious and not so pious, Northerner and Southerner, who, through unbelievable courage, service, and generosity, helped to save, care for, and bury the people of the Lower Mississippi Valley.

John Babb

If you thoroughly enjoyed this novel, please leave a review on the book's page at www.amazon.com or on www.goodreads.com

If you'd like advance information about my NEXT novel, please sign in at www.johnbabbauthor.com or connect with me on Facebook.

About the Author

John Babb is a former U.S. Assistant Surgeon General as well as a retired rear admiral in the U.S. Public Health Service. His background in pharmacy and public health has allowed him to accurately portray some of the diseases, treatments, and primitive medical remedies, as well as curative folklore, as practiced by our ancestors. He makes a significant effort to be historically accurate in his writing. He lives in Tennessee with his wife Victoria and wonder dog Rooster.

Coming Soon!

A new novel by John Babb and Victoria Babb

Emilie Christophe began her day like any other, walking the short distance from her grandmother Vivienne's home in the Faubourg Marigny neighborhood of New Orleans to the corner of Rue Rampart and Esplanade, where she boarded the new streetcar just before six-thirty AM. After a short ride, she transferred to the horse trolley on Common Street, before finally arriving at her place of employment at Charity Hospital. It was necessary to arrive a few minutes before seven o'clock in order to exchange information with her nurse counterpart, the one who had just completed the night shift.

The crotchety chief nurse, Rebecca Chaney, had gradually come to realize how valuable her new employee was—particularly because of her broad experience in both private nursing and hospital settings, caring for all sorts of critically ill patients. In fact, Emilie had recently been entrusted with assisting the city's medical examiner, whose responsibility it was to investigate all suspicious deaths and homicides within the city of New Orleans.

At least half of her time now was spent poking, prodding, and opening dead bodies on a concrete slab, checking livers for signs of poisoning, searching for pieces of lead embedded in gunshot victims, and uncovering signs of emboli or hemorrhage in people who simply "fell dead," in the parlance of family members. She tried very hard not to bring any of this baggage home with her. It was upsetting enough to her—seeing, touching, and smelling all of these foul, disgusting things. She certainly didn't want the children to discover this was often her daily responsibility.

On this morning, she was called from her ward duties to the morgue, which was located in the basement of the hospital. Impatiently awaiting her was Dr. Henri Lamont. The young physician had received his education at the *Faculté de Mêdecine* within the *Université de Paris*. As a result, he was forever using French terminology for various bodily organs and functions, while Emilie was attempting to translate his verbiage into an understandable report in English for the benefit of local law enforcement.

Emilie was willing to overlook this shortcoming, as Dr. Lamont was extremely pleasant to her, and unlike almost every other physician in the hospital, he never acted as though she were subservient to him. It also didn't hurt that his almost-black eyes sometimes had a twinkle in them which she found appealing.

He would be considered very handsome by most casual observers, at least until one spied his imperfections. He possessed two white patches of skin at least as large as a silver dollar—one on his left cheek and the other on the left side of his neck. He was obviously self-conscious of his *Pityriasis alba*, always attempting to seat himself so that he could speak to someone with his right side facing toward them. He also had a habit of holding his hand on his left cheek to conceal his affliction. Admittedly, it was more noticeable on the doctor, simply because the remainder of his complexion was a perfect shade of caramel. Emilie was determined to pay it no mind whatsoever, but did wonder if there were other patches hidden elsewhere on his body.

On the slab in front of them lay a young woman with coarse auburn hair. Her features were very fine, yet her once porcelain skin was now quite grey. She had been discovered in a hotel room bed in the Quarter that very morning. Although that establishment had a certain reputation for sponsoring prostitution, no one had any recollection of a second party during the time the girl had checked in the evening before. The examining inspector had found no evidence of a struggle, or even a drop of blood in the room.

The doctor's cursory exam revealed not a single mark on her body, save a missing little finger on her right hand. From appearances, it had only recently been severed, as a piece of string was still tightly tied directly above the wound.

Despite the lack of visible external wounds, when Dr. Lamont opened the body cavity, it was awash in blood. A quick check of critical organs revealed a heart muscle with multiple punctures in the right ventricle, and slash marks on several blood vessels. Looking over his shoulder, Emilie asked, "How did these injuries occur, Doctor?"

He examined the body's exterior again, this time lifting the left breast enough to reveal a tiny spot of dried blood on the chest wall. "Look here. I overlooked this before. Here is the entry wound, but it's far too tiny to be caused by a knife or a small-caliber bullet. I think it's even too small for a stiletto."

"Could something like an ice pick have created such damage to the heart?"

He considered the suggestion. "I believe you may have it. That might also explain the lack of blood on the outside of her body. Once the killer penetrated her chest, he apparently moved the pick back and forth, thus creating these slicing injuries to the heart and vasculature."

"Doctor Lamont, have you seen any other bodies recently with these kinds of injuries?"

Shaking his head gravely, he said, "After a year in this job, I've discovered there really is a first time for everything!"

After her return to New Orleans at the close of the 1878 yellow fever epidemic, Emilie had sworn she would no longer penetrate the world of the dead. Their cries for help had been overwhelming, and there were too many requests—thousands, in fact—which she simply could not fulfill. Too many times, the only result had been a fall into depression.

The key to contacting those anguished souls who had passed—her grandmother's locket—was now safely wrapped in cloth and hidden in a hat box. However, the sight of this poor girl on the slab seemed to reach Emilie in a way which suddenly provided the justification she needed to intervene.

Thinking it might be helpful to speak to the young woman via her locket, Emilie glanced hesitantly at the physician. "Will you keep the body here in the morgue overnight, Doctor?"

"We're very short on ice. I'm sure Oscar and Thomas will pick her up this afternoon and she'll be on her way to potter's field. Nobody seems to know who she is or where she comes from."

"Would it be possible for me to accompany her to the cemetery?"

"Whatever for?"

"It's a tragic situation. The girl died with no family. I thought I'd at least say a prayer over her."

He nodded in acknowledgement. "Sometimes I find myself taking these poor souls for granted, forgetting they once were just as human as the two of us. As long as we have no pressing cases at the time, go right ahead."

Having identified the site of the girl's grave, Emilie departed her house a half-hour early the next morning, heading directly to the cemetery located on the grounds of the hospital, just north of all the buildings. Standing at the fresh grave, Emilie fastened the locket around her neck. Suddenly, all the normal sounds of nature and civilization disappeared. Chattering birds quieted, the loud voices of men in the distance, and even the whinnying of horses ceased to exist, as instantly, many voices reached out to her. Her focus, however, was on the plea from the murder victim of the day before.

"If you please, miss, might you say a proper Catholic prayer for me? I wasn't given a decent Christian burial when I was placed in this pit with these other poor wretches."

"Of course I will."

"I have another favor to ask. Would you contact me mum and da?"

"First tell me your name, little one."

"Mary McCarthy. 'Tis only a week I've been in this city. I told me family not to worry—and now I'm guessin' I'm dead."

"What are your parent's names, and where do they live?"

"Sean and Margaret McCarthy. They stay at 110½ Girardi Street in Baltimore."

"I'll send them a letter for you. Now tell me what happened to you."

"It's sleepin' I was at that Rampart Hotel. A nasty place—people comin' an' goin' all hours o' the night. I finally get to sleep, an' first thing I knows, somebody comes in my room and sticks a wad o' cloth in my mouth so's I couldn't cry out. It's fightin' I was, but he was terrible strong. Then the divil tied me hands to the sides of the bed and..." the voice trembled, "...and he had his way with me."

"Did you recognize him?"

"'Twas dark as pitch. I could na' even tell if he was black or white."

"Could you tell if you'd heard his voice before?"

"Nary a word he said. Just went about doin' his dirty deed. But I do remember he smelled like the candy me brother and I used to steal at Mr. Flanagan's grocery."

"Have you had a boyfriend who's gotten angry with you?"

"I ain't been here long enough fer that."

"Have you noticed anyone following you?"

"Oh, there's divils at ever' street corner what tried to get me attention. But none was any different than another, as far as I could tell."

"If you couldn't recognize him, why would he kill you?"

"'Twas my finger. I s'pose he was after my finger."

"Did he use an ice pick on your chest?"

"'Tis only a terrible pressure I felt. I figgered he was tryin' to squish the life outa me, but the way he had me trussed up, I could na' fight back. Then all of a sudden, he got up, wiped what little blood there was off my chest, and the last thing I recomember was the door openin' and closin'."

The Girl With No Shadow

Also from Dingbat Publishing

Prologue

28 May 1940
seven kilometers east of the Aa Canal, France

Fear squeezed the prisoners in an iron and icy grip. Clarke could smell it, more pungent than stale uniforms and fresh sweat, taste it in the dust caking his face and lips. The other British officers, sitting in a huddle around him, stared at the dry turf between their knees or off into some unknowable vacuum. None would meet his gaze.

"How many of us are there?"

Beside him, Brownell shrugged and swiped at his brow with one sleeve. With his hands bound, it looked as if he shielded his face from a blow. It grated on Clarke's nerves, revved his rumbling temper.

"Does it matter?" Brownell asked.

"It does to me."

Brownell shot him a look, not so much baffled as vexed. Good; a fight was better than collapse. They'd argued often in the last weeks, as their steady school-age friendship underwent some sort of relational twist while the British Expeditionary Force retreated across France. But for now Brownell held his peace. He half-rose, dark eyes scanning the small crowd and lips moving. Clarke's temper twisted, bitterness rising at the sight: Brownell had a well-deserved Oxford first in mathematics, but he still counted like a five-year-old.

He didn't deserve to be murdered.

Not far from Brownell, in the midst of a small emptiness left by the lower ranks, a light colonel with tired eyes slumped over his lap, epaulettes drooping to match his mustaches. He was the senior officer in the group. He should take command, organize a fight. All they had to do was get one man outside the guards' field of fire, and they'd have a chance. A suicidal chance, but better than being murdered without a struggle.

But he just sat there, staring into space. Around him, none of the many second lieutenants lifted their chins. One young subaltern wept. All huddled together, as if needing warmth even in the direct sunlight.

Beyond their circle, two grey-clad soldiers lounged on ammunition crates behind a tripod-mounted machine gun. They weren't typical German Army soldiers, although the uniforms and weapons were the same. These were something new the Germans had invented, something called the Waffen SS, whatever that meant.

Clarke lit his last cigarette, the binding cord cutting into his wrists. They weren't soldiers. They were criminals—murderers dressed up and playing soldier, like a bunch of teenaged hoodlums wearing Dad's collar and tie whilst robbing the corner sweet shop. It was ludicrous. Obscene.

"Do you want to use my fingers, too?"

Brownell's cautious settling back ended with a thump and one savage word. "There's twenty-two of us."

Clarke's swearing was whole-hearted and much lengthier. "Wonder who's going to dig our graves. Think the bastards will make us dig them ourselves?"

"Shut up, Clarke. We don't know anything for certain." Brownell crossed his legs again. His shoulders and bound hands drooped, as if the knowledge he denied was heavier than he could support.

"The hell we don't." Clarke took a long drag, yanking the smoke into his lungs until he choked. "Wonder how our kids have grown."

Brownell peered up at him without turning his head.

Clarke flicked ash. "The last photo Cezanne sent, Bobby looked as if he's almost too big for her lap. I tried to figure out how tall that would make him. But it wouldn't matter if she'd taken his photograph against a yardstick. I have to measure my son against my leg or it means nothing."

"You should have taken the leave."

In February, with the invasion season in cold storage, the 48th (South Midland) Division had offered its staff and line officers a brief visit home. None of them had seen their families since the previous September. Brownell had gone and now his wife was expecting their second baby. Clarke had made a point of staying with the troops, who hadn't been offered the option.

Now Cezanne would never have his second child, never have the daughter she wanted so terribly—unless she remarried. And that thought, more than his impending death, made Clarke squeeze his eyes shut and swallow the tightness in his throat.

"I know." He glanced from his cigarette to the turf. Maybe starting a grass fire would help them escape. More likely the Germans would let them burn.

"Clarke, you've always been a bloody fool."

"I know that, too."

Angry voices rose, climbing over each other, not close but loud. Clarke stared past the machine-gun emplacement to the command tent, camouflaged beneath wispy trees. The Germans inside had to be shouting toe to toe.

"What do you think the row's about?" Brownell asked.

"I hope it's about us, and I hope that German Army chap wins."

Brownell lifted his head. "You think so?"

Clarke shrugged. "Don't recall much German from school, and I can't make out their words even if I did. They could be arguing about us, their orders, or a skirt, for all I know."

Brownell's head sank again.

The voices fell silent. The tent flap whipped aside and two German officers emerged. The Army officer, a non-com's sidecap replacing the usual peaked cap, stalked toward the huddled prisoners, his riding boots raising puffs of dust. The Waffen SS officer, Greis, followed more slowly, a little smile curving the corners of his narrow lips.

Clarke's heart sank. It was only too obvious who had won.

Near the edge of their huddle, the Army officer stopped, legs spraddled, hands on hips, staring in a slow sweep as if he wanted to impress every man on his memory. His face was pale, with scorching blotches of color in his tanned cheeks. He breathed as if he'd been running.

"What do you think?" Clarke glanced at Brownell. He froze.

Brownell's staring eyes were huge. His mouth hung open for a long moment. Then he snapped his jaw shut and wet his lips. "Clarke, that's—"

But the Army officer was issuing orders, German words stuttering in a staccato rhythm like a machine gun, and Brownell swallowed the rest of his sentence. Automatically, Clarke turned to see what the fuss was about—and smashed into the German officer's smoking glare, aimed right at him.

"You," he said in English. "Come on, I don't have all day."

Two of the Waffen SS soldiers waded into the sitting Englishmen, grabbed Clarke by the arms, and heaved him to his feet. So this was it; he'd go first. His legs were asleep, but damned if he'd take any help from these murderers. He shook off their arms, dropped his cigarette butt, and forced his tingling legs to carry his weight as they escorted him, one on either side, to the German officer.

Halfway there, he glanced back at Brownell. Brownell's mouth was open again and he was half on his feet, legs beneath him as if for a sudden push. Clarke shook his head—Brownell needed to save his major effort for his own life, not waste it on a fool's attempt at gallantry—and mouthed *goodbye.* Without waiting for a response, he turned away.

It was a ruddy awful way to part.

When Clarke turned, he was eye to eye with the German officer. Although they weren't close and sunshine blazed between them, there seemed barely room between their bodies to breathe. The heat of the German's anger smoldered still, like a flare not quite burned out. But his brown eyes were clear and even a trifle desperate as he gazed into Clarke's, as if he awaited some response and they were all running out of time.

Clarke sniffed in his face.

The German turned away. Was it Clarke's imagination, or was the tinge of color in those cheeks even darker? He could only hope.

"Right," the German said over his shoulder, "come on." He led the way to his open staff car, on the far side of the tent.

The SS guards crowded Clarke on either side, forcing him along. He passed close enough to Greis—the murderer—to punch him. He nearly did.

The guards put Clarke into the front passenger seat of the staff car. A layer of dust coated the faded interior. The officer slid behind the steering wheel. Greis sauntered to the driver's side and leaned one gloved hand against the door panel as the officer started the engine.

"Are you certain you can handle the prisoner alone?" A mocking half-smile still adorned Greis's lips, the smile of the winner. He adjusted his black leather gloves, never glancing at Clarke. Despite the smile, there was no humor in his narrow hatchet face, only contempt. "Perhaps I should have one of my soldiers accompany you."

Clarke seethed. He should have chanced that punch.

The officer shifted gears. "He's welcome to run along behind."

The smile slipped by a hair, then resumed. Only now it seemed fixed.

The officer released the clutch and gunned the engine. A spurt of dust slewed over Greis' polished boots and up to his squenched eyes.

Clarke stared back at Brownell's strangely hopeful face until the encampment was cut off by rising ground. Then he swung about. The dusty road rolled toward the staff car then vanished beneath it. Strong sunlight baked the interior, and he smelled fresh sweat along with the mechanical blend of oil and petrol. The engine vibrated up his spine, tapped against his eardrums.

One man. One pistol. No rifle, no tommy gun. No guard.

After that wisecrack at Greis, he'd regret killing this man. But he'd do it. A single pistol wasn't much firepower, but with it he could take this one, then return to the encampment for the prisoners. They didn't have to die today.

The Wehrmacht officer took the road over the crest of a small ridge and down into a grove of trees. To their left, the land dipped into a shallow valley, matted with brush and low trees that swarmed up the slope to the road. To their right, the trees thickened into a forest toward the ridge's crest.

Under the midday twilight of that canopy, the Wehrmacht officer steered the staff car onto the verge and killed the engine. In the silence, Clarke listened to his heart beating and knew, with cold certainty, that he didn't want to die for the hopeless defense of France. He twisted his wrists, trying to break the cords, but they only cut more sharply. The silence was so deep he thought he could hear the German's heart, too; then Clarke wondered if the man even had one.

He turned to face the German as he, too, slewed in his seat. Again they stared at each other, and Clarke took stock of his new captor. This was the man he had to defeat if he and the others were to live.

They seemed the same height, an inch or so beneath six feet. But while Clarke was solid, the German was more slender, shoulders tapering to hips that needed suspenders. His face echoed that line in a wedge shape, broad at the forehead and narrowing through well-defined cheekbones to a pointed chin. His brown hair was dark, the color of cocoa, and combed back from his high forehead in the Continental fashion. A formidable reserve of energy fired his eyes from within; even sitting motionless behind the wheel of the car, he seemed to vibrate like a tuning fork, and Clarke wondered how he kept his hands still.

Like most modern German officers, he was clean-shaven, his uniform tailored although not of the highest quality. The Iron Cross ribbon, red and white and black, decorated his left breast pocket; the knotted silver cords on his shoulders were bare of insignia, in the manner of a major. His earlier anger had drained, leaving his brown eyes clear, and Clarke knew he wasn't imagining the touch of derision now in their depths.

For one crazy moment, Clarke believed he had known this man at some point in their past, that he had only to sweep away the agitation to remember a more innocent age. But of course that was impossible. His subconscious thoughts were returning—to Sandhurst, University College, Eton, or even his father's estate, this German officer symbolizing someone haunting his memory. One thing for certain: this man didn't have the polish of rank. There was an earthy edge beneath his combat-hardened sophistication.

Clarke pushed the thought aside and cleared his throat. "Is this it, then? Shot while attempting to escape?"

The German produced a pack of cigarettes and shook one halfway out. "Do you use these things?"

Clarke fought his pride—he didn't want to accept anything from a German—but his sudden nicotine craving was stronger. He took the fag and the light that followed, and cradled it in his bound hands for a drag. "A last cigarette?"

"Every condemned man deserves one." But the German's tone was light.

"It's not a joking matter."

This time the German's stare was considering. "You're right," he finally said. "It's not."

"I know what happened at Guise."

"So do I." The German seemed to reach a decision and opened his door. "Step out. I want to show you something."

Clarke hesitated. The German shrugged, drew his pistol, snapped the magazine from its butt and pocketed it, and tossed the gun itself onto the dashboard. "We don't have much time. Come on." He closed the driver's door softly and stepped to the opposite verge of the road.

For a moment Clarke stared, flabbergasted. But he wasn't hallucinating. His only guard truly had unloaded his only weapon and turned his back. The shelter of the trees was on his side of the road and temptingly near. But his curiosity won the brief struggle. There had to be a reason for this otherwise senseless behavior, and Clarke wanted to know what it was. He followed the German to the opposite side of the road and stood beside his enemy.

The German cupped his cigarette in his left hand, glowing edge toward his palm, and gestured to the shallow valley at their feet. Neither hand left the deepest shadows spread by the trees overhead.

"See them?"

It took a moment. Then a motion caught Clarke's eye. The valley was alive with almost-hidden yet shifting forms. He peered closer and made out camouflage netting, a half-track, machine-gun nests, hammocks.

"On the left," the German continued, "those are Greis's Waffen SS troops, from the *Leibstandarte Adolf Hitler*." He paused for a drag. "Undoubtedly some of the best soldiers I've ever seen."

"Murdering bastards."

"That, too." He pointed with his chin. "On the right, those are elements of my own division, the First Panzer." He peered sideways at Clarke through the gloom, smoke drifting from his mouth. "A Wehrmacht unit."

Clarke peered back, blankly.

The German sighed. His gaze dropped openly to Clarke's upper-sleeve regimental insignia for the Royal Warwickshires. He straightened and grunted. "Infantry: oh, frag. I'll try using small words."

Heat climbed Clarke's neck. "Was that an insult?"

He got another sideways stare. "If you're in any doubt—" The German took another drag, eyes slitted against the smoke. "We're all tired, you know. The campaign hasn't been long—"

"Six frigging weeks."

"About right—but we haven't stopped until today. Are you catching on?"

"No," Clarke snapped, "I am not catching on. What are you getting at?"

The German closed his eyes. "The two units haven't joined up all that well, have they? You could march a brass band through there at full volume and nobody would notice." Again the sideways glance. "Especially if the brass band in question kept to the Wehrmacht side."

Clarke got it. "Did you have any particular brass band in mind?"

"Progress." The German nodded once. He ground the butt of his cigarette underfoot without ever showing the fire edge to the valley. "Three days ago, Greis—that pig back there—"

"I know who he is."

"—murdered thirty British officers at Guise. He didn't have facilities to hold them; he didn't want to spare the troops to guard them. He claimed he had orders, that it was in retaliation for the officers he'd lost in combat. So he ordered them shot."

"I know." An admission of knowledge seemed to be the only intelligent thing he'd said all day. He dropped his own cigarette and asked the question that mattered most to him. "Did he make them dig their own graves?"

"French privates," the German said, his tone cool but not as cool as it sounded. "The mass grave was multinational. I heard him give the order, I saw the massacre, and I saw the grave filled. Well, the situation hasn't changed. He's amassed British officer prisoners, whom he particularly hates because you didn't flock en masse to the Anglo-Saxon banner Hitler waved. He doesn't have facilities prepared for you, and he doesn't want to spare the troops to guard you or move you to the rear. He still claims he's under orders, although I let him know I couldn't find any reference to them at headquarters. And nothing else I said made any difference, either."

Clarke fought his mulishness. His decency won. "Thank you for trying."

The German spared him a puzzled glance, then pulled a penknife from his pocket and sliced through the cord binding Clarke's wrists. As he folded the blade away, he nodded toward the distant glint of water. "That's the Aa Canal."

"I know what it is."

"Just checking. We have orders to stop there."

Clarke stared. "Can't imagine why."

"Neither can I." The German shrugged. "It's a mistake, of course. If we truly wanted to destroy you, we should keep going all the way to the beach and drive you into the water." His sideways glance this time was a curious mixture of pride, shame, and defiance. "You and I both know the B.E.F. doesn't have the firepower left to stop us."

Just another German bastard after all. "That's your opinion and not any sort of fact."

The German grinned. In the shadows and gloom beneath the trees, his face lightened as if by magic. They had to be close in age. A vague tremor of unease made Clarke's fingers tingle; he refused to call it envy. While he had frittered away his—and his wife's—youth in an all-out assault upon law-court silks, this German had learned how to live. While he had developed a career, this man had developed his character.

"I expected no less from you," the German said. "Our orders come from the highest. They say stop at the Aa Canal—so no matter what we think, we'll stop at the Aa Canal. And that means—"

"—that means," Clarke interrupted, "anyone down on the beach will be out of range of your artillery."

The German nodded. "So long as that brass band reaches the canal before, oh, five o'clock tomorrow morning. That's about how long it will take us."

So there it was. This German major offered life and freedom—for him. Not for Brownell, nor the colonel with the drooping shoulders, nor the weeping subaltern or anonymous lieutenants squatting on the scuffed turf. Clarke tried to harden his heart. He couldn't.

He cleared his throat. "Why are you doing this?"

This time, the German's sideways stare was compounded of equal parts derision and hilarity. He shook out two more cigarettes, passed one to Clarke, and lit both behind the cover of his turned shoulder. As an afterthought he handed over the remainder of the pack and the matches.

"Do you remember the cricket match against Cambridge?" he asked.

Clarke forgot the landscape and even the doomed prisoners. He stared at the German officer and it was as if a spotlight slowly illuminated the man within his memory.

"Of course," the German continued, "I couldn't follow cricket in those days. For that matter, I still can't. But even I knew we were in deep trouble. We were so far behind we could barely see daylight."

The face in Clarke's memory wasn't sophisticated or battle-hardened. It was a younger face, uncertain, wide-eyed, softer about the edges, but nevertheless the same. The body was more slender, bulked out by a cheap, rusty-black academical robe, the thinner arms juggling an armload of used poetry textbooks. Even the memory made Clarke sneer. And in a heartbeat he was ashamed of the sneer and of himself.

"But then the coach sent you in to bat," the German rambled on, oblivious, "and it was as if the whole field came alive, the spectators, the team, everyone. You strode onto the pitch with your head in the air, the bat in your hand, a swagger in your step, and for one shining moment there was no doubt within the entire of Oxfordshire that you could do it." He shrugged and flicked ash. "We still lost the match, of course, but I have to admit you looked magnificent just walking onto the field." No sideways stare this time; the German turned to face him squarely. "Do you recognize me yet?"

"You're—"

"—yes, that grubby foreign exchange student, the one who was too poor to buy a sweater for the winter." He dropped his half-smoked cigarette onto the verge and stepped on it. "I never forgot you, Clarke. Of course, there's a world of difference between the upper classes laughing, and the lower- and middle-class sources of their amusement."

"Look—"

"Don't bother." The German strode back to his car.

Clarke thrashed his memory and dredged up a name. "Faust—your name's Faust."

"Really." Major Faust retrieved his pistol from the dashboard of the staff car and handed it butt-first to Clarke, his left hand hurling the loaded magazine into the deepest grass within the forest shadows. "I don't have anything heavier with me, so that's the best I can do for you. The evacuating British troops are massing on the beach outside Dunkirk. I suggest you get down there as soon as it's dark. There should be enough soldiers who haven't lost their Lee Enfields to make up a raiding party to rescue the encampment. Who knows, they might even have some ammunition."

Clarke ignored the pistol in his hand and stared at Faust. It was an insane risk, the sort taken by the legendary Dr. Faustus—a practitioner of dark, mysterious metaphysical arts, someone who commanded the sun and the moon, the winds and tides, the forces of Mars, with utter disregard for his own future safety.

Clarke shuddered.

Still oblivious, Faust opened the car door and paused, one foot on the running board. "At Guise, Greis waited until dawn before opening fire. But there's no guarantee he'll be so patient this time. He thinks I'm taking you to headquarters for interrogation, so they won't expect you back and they won't wait. Wear something over your face, and I might get away with this." He stepped into the staff car. "Good luck, Clarke. My regards to Brownell after you rescue him."

"Wait." Clarke didn't recognize his own throttled voice. "Why are you doing this?" Even as he said it, he knew that wasn't the best way of asking his question, it wasn't even the proper question and in his current agitation he didn't know how to rephrase it. But Faust was pressing the starter and his moment was over.

Faust rolled his eyes. "You don't have time for this. Oh, and if you get a chance, put a bullet through Greis for me, will you?" He shifted gears and the car rolled forward. "Pigs like him give all us Germans a bad name."

The staff car disappeared around the next bend, leaving Clarke standing in the middle of the shadowy road. He desperately wanted the answer to his question. He'd never hear it now, and that bothered him most of all.

He fell to his knees in the long grass, scrabbling for the loaded magazine.

Thanks for reading! Dingbat Publishing strives to bring you quality entertainment that doesn't take itself too seriously. I mean honestly, with a name like that, our books have to be good or we're going to be laughed at. Or maybe both.

If you enjoyed this book, the best thing you can do is buy a million more copies and give them to all your friends... erm, leave a review on the readers' website of your preference. All authors love feedback and we take reviews from readers like you seriously.

Oh, and c'mon over to our website:
www.DingbatPublishing.ninja

Who knows what other books you'll find there?

Cheers,

Gunnar Grey,
publisher, author, and Chief Dingbat

δ

Made in the USA
Middletown, DE
14 August 2019